Baby Trouble

CINDY DEES
BETH CORNELISON
CARLA CASSIDY

All rights reserved including the right of reproduction in whole or in part in any form. This edition is published by arrangement with Harlequin Books S.A.

This is a work of fiction. Names, characters, places, locations and incidents are purely fictional and bear no relationship to any real life individuals, living or dead, or to any actual places, business establishments, locations, events or incidents. Any resemblance is entirely coincidental.

This book is sold subject to the condition that it shall not, by way of trade or otherwise, be lent, resold, hired out or otherwise circulated without the prior consent of the publisher in any form of binding or cover other than that in which it is published and without a similar condition including this condition being imposed on the subsequent purchaser.

® and ™ are trademarks owned and used by the trademark owner and/or its licensee. Trademarks marked with ® are registered with the United Kingdom Patent Office and/or the Office for Harmonisation in the Internal Market and in other countries.

Published in Great Britain 2015
by Mills & Boon, an imprint of Harlequin (UK) Limited,
Eton House, 18-24 Paradise Road, Richmond, Surrey, TW9 1SR

BABY TROUBLE © 2015 Harlequin Books S.A.

The Spy's Secret Family, Operation Baby Rescue and *Cowboy's Triplet Trouble* were first published in Great Britain by Harlequin (UK) Limited.

The Spy's Secret Family © 2011 Cindy Dees
Operation Baby Rescue © 2011 Beth Cornelison
Cowboy's Triplet Trouble © 2011 Carla Bracale

ISBN: 978-0-263-25226-2
eBook ISBN: 978-1-474-00405-3

05-0815

Harlequin (UK) Limited's policy is to use papers that are natural, renewable and recyclable products and made from wood grown in sustainable forests. The logging and manufacturing processes conform to the legal environmental regulations of the country of origin.

Printed and bound in Spain
by CPI, Barcelona

THE SPY'S SECRET FAMILY

BY
CINDY DEES

Cindy Dees started flying airplanes while sitting in her dad's lap at the age of three and got a pilot's license before she got a driver's license. At age fifteen, she dropped out of high school and left the horse farm in Michigan where she grew up to attend the University of Michigan. After earning a degree in Russian and East European Studies, she joined the US Air Force and became the youngest female pilot in its history. She flew supersonic jets, VIP airlift and the C-5 Galaxy, the world's largest airplane. During her military career, she traveled to forty countries on five continents, was detained by the KGB and East German secret police, got shot at, flew in the first Gulf War and amassed a lifetime's worth of war stories. Her hobbies include medieval re-enacting, professional Middle Eastern dancing and Japanese gardening.

This RITA® Award-winning author's first book was published in 2002 and since then she has published more than twenty-five bestselling and award-winning novels. She loves to hear from readers and can be contacted at www.cindydees.com.

This book is for Shana Smith because it absolutely, positively couldn't have happened without her. Truly. You're the best!

Chapter 1

Why wasn't he dead?

Nick stared up at the featureless white ceiling of his hospital room as the beeping of a heart monitor punctuated the panic flowing through his veins. Why hadn't they killed him? Why five years of captivity instead—in a shipping container, on a cargo ship, floating around in international waters?

And why couldn't he remember what came just before his kidnapping? The doctors told him he'd sustained a serious head injury at some point during his incarceration. Whether a captor had hit him during an interrogation or he'd fallen during one of the massive open-sea storms that had tossed him like a cork inside his steel prison, he had no recollection.

He coughed thickly. Supposedly, his pneumonia was mostly under control now. It had been touch and go there for a while. But the worry lurking in his nurses' eyes had eased in the past day or so. He gathered he was out of the woods, which was good news.

They were still working on clearing his body of various other infections and trying to restore normal function to his digestive tract. The only way he was putting on weight was via the massive calorie infusions running through his IV.

They'd cut his dark hair and shaved off his matted beard, revealing the unnatural paleness of his usually olive complexion. The psychiatrists said he might never remember the lost time, a memory gap spanning approximately two years prior to his capture and the first three years or so of his imprisonment. Funny how the shrinks were trying so hard to retrieve those memories and he was trying equally hard *not* to retrieve them. Absolute certainty vibrated ominously in his gut, warning him that whatever lurked in that black hole of lost time was best left there.

Was whatever he'd forgotten the reason he was still alive? Had his captors been waiting for him to remember something? Or was there some other, more sinister reason that someone had been hell-bent on imprisoning him?

Maybe he was just being paranoid. Although it wasn't paranoia if someone was really after him. Even now, he expected his keepers to burst into his hospital room and haul him back to his box. The idea actually made a certain sick sense. If his captors had orders to keep him alive and he'd gotten too sick to treat on the ship, they could've cooked up this whole rescue ruse to fatten him up and get him healthy enough to toss back in Hell.

Laura Delaney—the woman who'd rescued him from his metal prison and one of the only faces he remembered from the lost years—claimed the two of them had been lovers before he'd disappeared. She'd introduced him to a little boy who looked so much like him it was hard to discount her story that he was the child's father. He desperately hoped it was true.

She was an extremely attractive woman. It wasn't difficult to imagine dating someone like her. But was she for real? Or was she part of his captors' evil head games? Was she here to trick him into revealing whatever secrets his subconscious was guarding so fiercely?

If only there was someone he could trust, really *trust*, to tell him what was real and what was not.

And then there was the troubling fact that he knew for certain his name wasn't Nick Cass. Nor had he grown up entirely in Rhode Island. But Laura apparently believed both to be true. He must've told the lies himself. But why? If he and Laura were lovers like she claimed, why hadn't he told her his real name or the most basic facts about his past? Why the deception?

Everywhere he turned, there were only questions and more questions. Frustration sang through his blood as sharply as his secret hope that his freedom, at least, was real. But he dared not share that hope with anyone. Not until he knew if anyone at all was telling him the truth.

Laura paused outside the hospital room, steeling herself not to react to Nick's emaciated state. It wasn't his fault he looked fresh out of a Nazi concentration camp, and he didn't deserve to see her cringe at the sight of his skeletal frame, hollow face or his shadowed blue eyes. God, his eyes. The haunted look in them was terrifying. Would he carry it with him forever?

The shrinks doubted he would recover the years stripped from his memory. But they felt he should recover enough to be a functional member of society once more with time and counseling. He *should* recover. Not he would.

At this point, she didn't care if his memory ever came

back. She just wanted *him* back. The man who'd swept her off her feet in a whirlwind romance in Paris. The man who'd captured her heart and taught her what true love could be. If even part of that amazing man came back to her, it would be better than the hollow shell of a man on the other side of the door. She vowed to be grateful for whatever piece of him survived his ordeal. It was surely better than having no part of him at all. The past five years of waiting and wondering had been pure hell.

She knew he wasn't convinced yet that his rescue was real in spite of that first night of freedom they'd shared. They'd gone to her estate, where he'd bathed and eaten. Then she'd made love to him with all the pent-up passion and relief in her soul.

They'd both cried that night. She'd interpreted his tears as a cathartic release, but she'd been wrong. The shrinks told her he believed that night to have been some sort of elaborate torture by his captors to taunt him with what freedom would be like. Apparently, he'd been crying because the idea of going back into his box after what the two of them had shared had finally broken him. *She'd* broken him.

The man hadn't even known who she was, and she'd been so caught up in her euphoria at finding him that she'd never slowed down enough to realize how lost he'd been. Guilt at her thoughtlessness rolled through her. She'd always been a take-charge, full-speed-ahead kind of person. But that tendency had hurt the man she loved. Part of his paranoid state now was her fault. When would she learn to rein herself in? Had her impulsiveness cost her his trust forever?

She took a deep breath and pushed open the door. "Hey, handsome. How are you feeling today?"

"You're back." The abject relief in his voice broke her

heart a little. What he clearly meant was, "So I get to live another day in this beautiful illusion? Thank God."

"The doctors say you can go home soon. You'll still need around-the-clock medical care, but I can hire nurses to look after you."

Terror flashed in his eyes at the mention of leaving the hospital.

She pretended not to see it and asked lightly, "Do you think when you actually come home to live with me and Adam you'll believe all of this is real? That you're free and you have a family?"

He answered slowly, "I don't know. I hope so."

Hey, progress! He'd spoken of his feelings. Maybe he'd finally accepted that he was not living in a dream or a terrible trick. She picked up his bony hand and cradled it in hers. It had been so strong once, so capable of giving her pleasure, so confident in its gestures. She murmured, "I love you, Nick. If you believe nothing else, please believe that."

"Even if you're lying, the notion makes me happy."

She smiled down at him. "Give it some time. Give *me* some time to prove this is real."

He shrugged. "It isn't like I have any choice. I'm along for the ride, here. So far, it's a great dream."

She smiled bravely while the knife twisted in her gut. "You'll be on your feet and kicking up your heels in no time. You'll be able to do whatever you want."

And please God, let that include staying with her and Adam. Their son desperately needed a father, and she desperately needed the man she loved. Yes, she hadn't seen him in five years. And yes, he might be an entirely different person than the one she fell in love with way back then. But surely, at least part of the intelligent, passionate, confident man who'd swept her off her feet was still in there, somewhere.

"How can you possibly be real?" he asked reflectively. "You're too perfect."

She laughed lightly, praying her panic at his declaration wasn't audible. "I'm far from perfect. Trust me."

"Trust. That is the thing, isn't it? Who will trust whom first in this little chess game?"

"This isn't a game, Nick. You're free, you're going home soon and I love you. That's the God's honest truth."

He made a noncommittal sound, and his cobalt gaze slid away from hers.

He really did have to give his captors credit for playing out this farce to the hilt. Six weeks since his "rescue" and still no hint of tossing him back in his box. He gazed around the plush bedroom suite, decorated in dark woods and deep, comforting colors. It was a far cry from his former prison. Hard to believe he actually caught himself missing the container's bare metal walls now and then. After a while, its confines had felt safe. Comforting. A steel embrace that kept out worse horrors.

He supposed if he had to trade one cage for another, this one wasn't bad. It was warmer and softer, and definitely had better food. The hallway door opened and Laura slipped into the room, wearing a slim wool skirt and a silk blouse that clung to her elegant curves in all the right places. Her cheeks were pink and her eyes bright. He added better-looking captors to his list.

In all fairness to her, she'd been nothing but kind and loving to him since she'd opened his box and let him out. She really was a delightful woman, witty and warm, with a quick smile that made her impossible to resist. And she was a devoted mother.

She moved to his side, and he closed his laptop. Yet again, his unreasoning fear at what lurked in his past had prevented him from typing in his real name to an internet search engine. Just a few simple keystrokes, and he'd finally know what monsters lurked in the recesses of his mind. But his terror was just too great. He'd sat there for an hour with the damned computer in his lap and never managed to type a single letter.

Leaning over the chair, Laura kissed him warmly. He didn't find it hard to believe that he'd loved her once. The only thing keeping him from giving in to serious attraction to the woman was the prospect of losing her. He figured as soon as he fell for her, that would be when the rug got yanked out from under him.

"How're you feeling today?" she asked eagerly, almost impatiently.

"Fine. You look about ready to burst. Do you have a surprise for me?" His gut clenched. He hated surprises. He was still waiting for the big, nasty one where his captors swept him out of this paradise and whisked him back to Hell Central.

"I do have a surprise for you, Nick. A good one, I hope. Are you strong enough for a bit of a shock?"

Every cell in his being froze. This was it. Sick heat and then icy cold washed through him, leaving him so nauseous he could hardly breathe. His heart pounded and his breathing accelerated so hard that, in seconds, he was light-headed.

His gaze darted about, seeking escape. Seeking a weapon. Anything to defend himself from the attack to come. His gaze lighted on the window. He could make a dash for it. Fling himself through the glass. It was three stories to the ground. If he went head first, the fall ought to kill him. If nothing else, maybe he'd be hurt so bad they couldn't throw him back in his box. Maybe they'd have to hospitalize him for a few more months.

"I'm pregnant, Nick. We're going to have a baby."

His mind went blank. Ever so slowly, his brain managed to form a thought. Not a particularly coherent one, but a thought. *What new game was this?*

"Did you hear me?" Laura asked excitedly. "You're going to be a father again."

His brain simply refused to absorb the information. He couldn't find a context to put the words in. Couldn't comprehend the purpose of this new torture.

Laura was laughing. "…too fertile for our own good… first time we made love we got Adam, and now, after that first night you were free, we're going to have another baby…should really be more careful about birth control in the future…"

She was making words and sentences and probably was even stringing them together in some sort of logical order. But he didn't understand a thing she was saying.

He did understand, though, that the hallway door was not bursting open. No thugs had come for him yet. The next few minutes passed with him murmuring inane nothings at proper intervals in response to Laura's babbling joy. And still no one had come.

Could it be? Was this real? Was Laura really pregnant and expecting his child?

Something cracked in his chest. It hurt, but it was a good kind of pain. Was he truly free? Was a life, a future with Laura and his children a possibility? Did he dare hope?

Hope. Now there was a concept.

A baby, huh? His and Laura's. A little brother or sister for Adam. How he'd love to experience all of it—the morning sickness and messy delivery and midnight feedings. Another child to crawl inside his heart and hold it in his or her tiny, precious hands. Lord knew, Adam had already completely wrapped him around his little finger in the short time he'd spent with the boy. Nick said a fervent prayer every night that, even if all the rest of this was a horrible, cruel lie, God would please let Adam be real. He loved the little boy with all his heart.

And now there might be another child for him to love?

Something exploded in his gut with all the bright fury of a fireworks display, burning away everything that had gone before, cauterizing old wounds, and leaving him empty. New. Reborn.

And then he gave that something a name. Joy.

He was free. Really, truly free. The nightmare was over. He surged up out of the chair and wrapped Laura in a crushing embrace. And then, for the first time, he cried for the right reasons.

Laura didn't know what clicked for Nick, but after she told him she was pregnant, he changed. He took new interest in food and exercise and spending time with Adam and generally engaged in life more. He got stronger, and gradually, as her belly grew, the haunted look faded from his eyes. He quit eyeing closed doors suspiciously, and the nightmares seemed to fade.

For a while there, she'd wondered if he was too far gone, if she'd be able to pull him out of the emotional abyss into which he'd fallen. But this baby seemed to have done the trick. She rubbed her rounded tummy affectionately. Things were working out better than she could ever have dreamed. Life was darned near perfect.

Nick stared at the laptop on his desk for the hundredth time. He'd been avoiding the thing for months, ever since Laura had told him she was pregnant, afraid to rock the boat of this new life. Everything was so good for him—for all of them—that he had no desire to do anything to threaten the perfection of it all.

But his curiosity had been building. Maybe it was a sign of his recovery that he was starting to feel the tug of waiting answers. What had happened during those lost years? Why the lies about his identity? Who'd had him kidnapped and thrown into a box? And why hadn't that person or persons just killed him outright?

Certainty that he did not want to know the answers, no matter how tantalizing they might be, still raged in his gut. Whatever his former life had been, he had no pressing need to resume it. Laura was wealthy enough for them and their children to live in the lap of luxury for several lifetimes. Whoever else he'd left behind in his old life had no doubt made peace long ago with his disappearance and gotten on with their own lives. His return now could only cause disruption and chaos.

But what if his old life, his old identity, came looking for him?

Nah. Surely that had been the whole point of his kidnapping. To turn him into a ghost. Make him disappear for good. As long as he stayed a ghost, made no effort to resume his former life, there was no reason for his past to come looking for him. Right?

The key was to keep a low profile. He closed the laptop with a solid thunk. Nope. Curiosity or no curiosity, he was not going anywhere near his old life.

Chapter 2

Laura sighed. Her perfectly orchestrated schedule for the day had been blown to heck by her obstetrician running nearly two hours late. Not that she begrudged some other patient an emergency C-section. But today, of all days, she'd really needed her doctor to be on time. Because of the delay, she hadn't had time to swing by home and drop off the baby with the nanny before this important meeting with Nick's lawyers.

She winced at the sliding noise of her minivan's side door. Baby Ellie, six weeks old today, was asleep inside, and Laura desperately needed her to stay that way for the next hour. She detached the baby carrier from the car seat base, threw the baby bag over her shoulder and hurried across the parking lot toward the glass and chrome high-rise housing Tatum and Associates, the law firm that would be representing Nick in the upcoming AbaCo trial.

Nick was the star witness for the prosecution. As such,

Carter Tatum expected him to come under withering cross-examination by the defense lawyers representing the company's chief of security, Hans Kurtis Schroder. He'd been accused of masterminding a kidnapping and human-trafficking ring using AbaCo ships without the company's knowledge. Personally, Laura doubted Schroder was the top dog in the scheme. He was the sacrificial lamb to protect his bosses.

Today was a coaching session for Nick in how to act on the witness stand. It was guaranteed to be stressful. A part of her that she was trying darned hard to ignore worried that Nick wouldn't be able to handle it. But he'd endured worse. He'd be fine, right?

She stepped out of the elevator and a receptionist ushered her to a plush conference room. Nick smiled and came over to relieve her of baby and bag. Her heart still swelled when he looked at her like that, so tall and dark and handsome. He'd filled out in the past year, lost the gaunt pallor, rebuilt the athletic physique that had first caught her attention in Paris. A shorter haircut than he'd worn then gave him a polished air that felt more Wall Street than European Bohemian. He cut a smashingly gorgeous figure. Her hands itched to get inside his shirt.

As observant as ever, his gaze went dark and smoky. "You are quite a temptation, yourself," he murmured. "Shall we cancel this meeting and go somewhere private?"

She smiled regretfully even as she leaned toward him, pulled in by his magnetic appeal and completely uninterested in resisting it. He stepped forward and his head lowered toward hers. Her breath hitched and she was abruptly hot from head to toe.

A door burst open behind her and several people walked into the room. Nick's gaze shifted briefly to the intruders and then, ignoring them, he completed the kiss. It was a relatively chaste thing, but her toes still curled into tight little knots of pleasure in her Jimmy Choos heels.

"Ahh. You're here, Ms. Delaney. Good. We can get started."

"Sorry I'm late," she murmured. "The doctor was backed up, and I had no time to get home and back here."

Nick cupped her elbow, escorting her to the table and holding her chair for her. "And how's our little angel?" he asked, gazing down at his daughter fondly.

Laura's heart swelled at the adoration in his voice. "Mother and daughter both received clean bills of health." More precisely, daughter was over her mild jaundice, and mother was finally cleared to have sex again. The past six weeks of abstinence had been murder on her. Nick had just laughed, saying that five years locked up had taught him a great deal of patience.

"Can I get you something to drink, darling?" Nick asked. She shook her head, and his fingers brushed lightly across the back of her neck as he made his way to his own seat. She shivered from head to toe in anticipation of tonight.

Carter Tatum spoke from the end of the table. "This afternoon we're going to try to approximate how AbaCo's lawyers will question Nick. As unpleasant as it may be, I would remind you we're on your side."

Laura, a former CIA operative, had been through training at their infamous Farm, and she highly doubted a bunch of lawyers could throw anything at Nick that she hadn't seen before.

Carter gestured and in short order a trio of lawyers was taking turns rapid-firing questions at Nick. They started with his kidnapping. The Paris police believed he'd been drugged at the Paris Opera and taken to the shipping container in which he spent the next five years. Nick denied remembering any of it. If only she'd gone to the opera with Nick that night, but her CIA partner—and ex-lover, truth be told—had been missing, and she'd been following up a lead.

The lawyers pressed Nick about any enemies who might have paid people to ghost him, and she listened with interest. This was a subject he'd flatly refused to discuss with her. It worried her mightily that whoever'd had him kidnapped was waiting to pounce again. Again, he denied knowing anything.

The next lawyer pushed harder and Nick's shoulders climbed defensively. When the third lawyer pressed even more aggressively for information about Nick's past, he crossed his arms stubbornly and quit speaking altogether. Darn it. That was the same thing he did to her whenever she brought up the subject.

"Water break," Carter announced abruptly.

Laura released the breath she'd been holding. Nick slumped in his chair, his head down. She put a supportive hand on his arm. "Are you okay?"

"Yes," he answered roughly. But his arm trembled beneath her palm, and his jaw clenched so hard he looked about ready to crack a molar.

She suggested gently, "Let's call this for today. We'll come back another time when you're feeling better—"

"We finish it now," he snapped uncharacteristically.

She drew back, startled. Nothing ever flustered Nick. He was always the soul of gentlemanly composure.

"I'm sorry." He sighed. "I have no past. It's over and gone. My life started anew when you rescued me. This is who I am now. You are my life. You and the kids."

She appreciated the sentiment, but he was going to have to face his past eventually. The psychiatrists had told her repeatedly not to push him, to let him investigate his previous life at his own speed. But it had about killed her to contain her curious nature for so long.

The lawyers' badgering resumed, continuing until Nick finally declared, "Gentlemen, this line of questioning is over. My past is not relevant to the fact that I spent five years in an AbaCo box on an AbaCo ship at the hands of kidnappers in the employ of AbaCo."

Laura stared. It was the first time he'd shown even a flash of the decisive streak he'd had in abundance in Paris.

Carter replied mildly, "AbaCo's lawyers will, without question, go on a fishing expedition into your past in hopes of finding something they can make seem relevant."

Nick scowled. "As far as I know, I never had anything to do with AbaCo before I wound up on that damned ship."

The lawyer sighed. "President Nixon's lawyers had the eighteen-minute gap to explain. We've got your five-year blackout to overcome. Have your doctors said anything more about the chances of you regaining some portion of your memory?"

Nick shrugged. "They think everything's gone for good. I remember Laura's face, and that's it."

"Can't you remember something from *before* your memory loss to give you a clue about who you are and what you do?"

"I know who I am and what I do. I'm Nick Cass, and I spend every waking moment enjoying my family."

The lawyer looked regretful, but said firmly, "You're going to be under oath at the trial, and I guarantee they'll ask you for explicit details of your past. If you won't talk, they'll have investigators dig up everything they can find."

Laura observed closely as Nick's gaze went hard. Closed. He'd never talked with her about his past in Paris before he disappeared, either. What *was* the big secret? She'd lay odds he wasn't a criminal. She'd worked with plenty of them over the years, and he just didn't have the right personality for it. He was too honorable, too concerned about doing the right thing.

The lawyers started up again, asking about Nick's connection to AbaCo. He stuck firmly to his story that he'd never had any dealings with AbaCo that he was aware of, and knew of nothing that would've provoked the shipping giant to kidnap him of its own volition. Nick maintained steadfastly that his had to have been strictly a kidnapping for hire.

Frankly, she agreed with him. Laura tapped a pencil idly on the pad of paper before her. With first his long months of physical and emotional recovery and then the new baby coming, she'd been distracted enough this past year to abide by his wishes to leave his past alone. But she felt an investigation coming on.

Somebody'd messed with the father of her children, and that meant they'd messed with her. Furthermore, that person or persons might still pose a threat to her man. She smiled wryly. Her mama bear within was in full force these days. Must be the baby hormones raging.

She listened with a mixture of anger and sadness as Nick tonelessly described his incarceration. The psychologists said he had completely disassociated himself from his imprisonment and would have to make peace with it in his own time. For now, though, he held the emotions at arm's length.

The lawyers moved on to the night of Nick's rescue. He didn't have a lot to say about it other than his door opened and a man named Jagger Holtz let him out, and Holtz and Laura led him to safety.

The lawyers left alone the events to follow Nick's rescue—his weeks in a hospital recovering from various illnesses and malnutrition, his paranoia, the long silences, his difficulties with crowds and open spaces. None of that would help AbaCo's case, apparently.

Then the lawyers attacked the veracity of Nick's whole story, claiming it was entirely too far-fetched to be true, doing their damnedest to trip him up or get him to contradict himself. The only evidence he had of this supposed capture of his was a grainy video that could just as easily have been faked, and they demanded to know why he had it in for AbaCo.

She was ready to explode herself by the time Nick surged up out of his chair. "Why do I have to withstand this sort of character assassination? I'm the victim here! And now you make me a victim a second time!"

Carter nodded soberly. "You are correct. It's the nature of our legal system that the victim often endures outright assault in the courtroom. *That's* what we're here to prepare you to face."

Nick shoved a hand through his hair. "Why exactly do I have to testify?"

"Because AbaCo will try to convince the jury that the video is faked. The government has to have your direct testimony that the events on the tape are real."

"Other people were there that night. Why not put my rescuers on the stand?" He sent Laura a quick, apologetic look, no doubt at the notion of dumping this mess into her lap. Not that she minded. She'd love to say a thing or two about AbaCo to a jury.

Carter grinned. "AbaCo won't touch Laura with a ten-foot pole. She's a former government agent, which gives her credibility, and they bloody well don't want to give her a chance to vent her righteous fury in front of a jury.... The mother of your child alone and frantic for years? Oh, no. Way too damaging a story for AbaCo."

He omitted the part where the government prosecutors

wouldn't put her on the stand because she'd illegally obtained most of the information that led to Nick's rescue. They'd rather not open up that can of worms for AbaCo to pry into.

After his outburst, Nick settled into stoic silence, refusing to respond to any of the leading and obnoxious questions the lawyers threw at him. No matter what they tried, they couldn't shake him. Laura was proud of him, but she didn't like the way he was hunching into his chair, physically withdrawing into himself. He was approaching overload but too macho to admit it.

Thankfully, Ellie woke up and gave Nick the excuse he clearly needed to call a halt for the day. Laura gathered up their fussing daughter apologetically and adjourned to the minivan to nurse and change her.

Nick came outside a few minutes later and stopped by the van to tell her to drive carefully. With troubled eyes, she watched him guide his sporty BMW out of the parking lot. A worrisome, brittle quality clung to him.

Ahh, well. She would make that all go away tonight. The nanny had instructions to entertain the kids for the evening, leaving her and Nick to enjoy a romantic dinner by themselves in the master suite. Smiling, she turned out of the parking lot and pointed the minivan south toward the rolling hills of Virginia's horse country and home.

Nick drove like a man possessed. Heck, maybe he was possessed. What madness was this to subject himself to cross-examination under oath with as many secrets as he clearly had to hide?

If Laura ever found out he wasn't who he said he was…

She couldn't find out. Period. He had too good a thing going, *they* had too good a thing going, to let anyone mess it up. As appealing as revenge against the bastards who'd held him captive might be, it was a no-brainer that his family came first. He'd made that choice months ago, and he'd had no reason to regret it since.

Someone honked at him. He jerked his attention back to the highway and the traffic streaming along it. He could do this. He could hold himself and his life together. One day at time. One hour or one minute at a time if that's what it took. The only honest and good things in his life were Laura and the kids. He wasn't about to lose them.

As the city turned into suburbs and the suburbs into open countryside, his jumpiness increased. After all that time in a shipping container, he'd have thought he would love nothing more than big, blue skies and broad horizons stretching away into infinity. But it turned out the exact opposite was the case. He'd become so used to living in a tiny, mostly dark space that anything else seemed strange and scary.

The panic attack started with sweaty palms and clenching the steering wheel until his knuckles hurt. Then his forehead broke out in a sweat, and an urge to crawl under a blanket in the backseat nearly overcame him.

As Laura's estate came into view, he stopped the car and parked by the side of the road. He had to pull himself together before he got home and scared her or the kids. He hyperventilated until he saw spots before he managed to slow his breathing. He concentrated on Adam's laughter, on Ellie's tiny perfection, on Laura's warm brown eyes looking at him with such love it made his heart hurt.

Gradually, his pulse slowed. He mopped his forehead dry. There wasn't anything he could do about his sweat-soaked shirt, but hopefully Laura would put it down to the grilling earlier from the lawyers. Relishing the car's smooth purr, he put it into gear.

After keying in his security code he drove through the

tall iron gates, as always enjoying the bucolic sight of Laura's prized horses grazing in manicured pastures behind freshly painted oak fences. As he pulled into the six-car garage, he was relieved to see that Laura's van wasn't inside yet.

Mumbling a greeting to Marta, the housekeeper, he hurried upstairs to take a shower. The enclosed shower stall with its rain-heads and steam jets soothed away the last remnants of his panic attack. When he emerged from his dressing room/walk-in closet, he heard Laura cooing to Ellie in the nursery. She was a great mom. It added a whole new dimension to the courageous woman who'd rescued him and spent the past year saving his soul.

He poked his head into the nursery. "Anything I can do to help?"

Laura smiled up at him. "I'm afraid you lack the proper anatomical equipment to provide what Ellie wants at the moment." He gazed at his daughter's silky, dark head nestled against the pale globe of Laura's breast. He might have missed Adam's babyhood—another outrage to lay at his kidnappers' feet—but he was savoring every minute of Ellie's.

"Dinner will be ready in a half hour," Laura murmured. "I've asked Marta to serve it in our rooms."

He nodded and retreated to the other end of the hall to play with Adam. It wasn't that he didn't want to sleep with Laura. Far from it. She was as generous and adventurous in bed as she was in life. It was just that he was still rattled from the interrogation, panicked that his past was about to rear its ugly head and ruin all of this perfection. What had happened during those lost years to make him hide his identity, even from the woman he loved?

"Daddeeeeeee!"

Grinning, he braced himself as Adam launched into the

air and splatted against Nick's chest. He caught his son's small, wriggly form against his, savoring the smell of soap that clung to the boy's still-damp hair.

"Did you do anything fun today?" he asked as Adam dragged him over to the corner to play with the toy du jour—Hot Wheels race cars.

Adam described his day in charming detail while the two of them built an elaborate racetrack. With dark hair and blue-on-blue eyes so like his own, Adam bent over the task with concentration far beyond his years. He was a frighteningly intelligent child and would go far in life if he used his talents to their maximum potential. They laughed together as too tight a turn sent cars shooting off the track and across the room in spectacular crashes.

Lisbet, the English and shockingly Mary Poppins-like nanny, interrupted the crash fest to announce that Adam's dinner, and Mummy and Daddy's, were served. Nick gave his son a bear hug and tickled him until Adam was squealing with laughter before turning him over to Lisbet.

Nick stepped into the private sitting room in their suite and stopped in surprise. The space was lit by hundreds of candles and a white-linen-covered table sat alone in the middle. A red rose in a crystal bud vase sat between the two place settings, and a sumptuous meal was laid out. Marta had really outdone herself. It was some sort of exotic fowl served *en croute*—grouse, maybe. Among other things, the German woman was a Cordon Bleu-trained chef. A real treasure. But then Laura didn't settle for less than the best in any aspect of her life. She'd be as intimidating as hell if she weren't such a genuinely warm and kind person. No doubt about it. He didn't deserve her.

Laura stepped out of her dressing room and his breath caught. She was wearing a little black dress that highlighted her newly slender body, which had already mostly regained its pre-pregnancy shape partly due to long hours with a personal trainer over the past month. Frankly, the additional curves added to her appeal.

"You look ravishing," he announced.

"And you are as handsome as always," she replied as he held her chair for her.

Something within her called to him at a fundamental level, a pull at his soul to protect her and make her happy. It went so far beyond mere attraction he didn't know how to give it a name. Even calling it love didn't seem adequate to encompass his need for her or the bond he felt with her. Maybe it was sharing parenthood of two amazing children.

Or maybe it was the fact that he owed his life to her. He would never forget the sight of her the night he was freed. His own private angel. And then the long months of patiently nursing him back to health, gradually convincing him his ordeal was actually over. Putting up with his unwillingness to face his past. And through it all, her love had been steadfast.

He wondered sometimes if there was anything that could shake her loyalty to him. What was it that lurked so dark and frightening in his past? Was it bad enough to drive her away? It really wasn't something he wanted to find out.

"How are you holding up after being raked over the coals by those lawyers?" Laura asked.

He shrugged. "Today wasn't fun. But I expect the trial will be worse."

She sighed. "It'll all be over in a few weeks, and then we can get on with our lives."

His gaze dropped involuntarily to her naked left hand. She never once hinted at it, but she had to be thinking about marriage and wondering why he never brought it up. The truth was, he didn't know if he was married or not, and the only way to find out would be to investigate those ominous, lost years.

He picked up his water glass—since Laura couldn't drink wine while nursing, he wasn't drinking either—and said, "A toast. To a long and happy future for us and our family."

She sipped her water and then asked reflectively, "Why don't you ever talk about the past?"

He frowned. "I've told you why." *Repeatedly, in fact.*

"I'm concerned that, with all the publicity this trial's going to receive, whoever had you kidnapped five years ago will see you and come after you again."

He swore mentally. He hadn't thought about the publicity. Was there some way to declare a moratorium on filming or photographing him during the trial?

"Talk to me, Nick. Between the two of us, we can beat any threat that comes our way."

A naïve notion at best. "My previous life happened a long time ago in a galaxy far, far away. Let it be."

"The psychiatrists keep telling me to let you deal with your imprisonment and the memory loss in your own time. But I have a gut feeling that your time is running out."

So did he.

Thankfully, she let the subject drop. For now. He had no doubt she would bring it up again, though. And one of these days, she wasn't going to back off. She'd insist they find answers. His throat tightened until he could hardly swallow the delicious food. What the hell was he going to do? His entire being shied away from thinking about the past. What could have freaked him out at such a soul-deep level? He put the problem in a mental drawer and slammed it shut. *Later. He'd think about it later.*

They finished eating, and he changed the music. "Dance with me?" he asked her.

"I thought you'd never ask, Mr. Cass."

Nick held a hand out to her and she took it, rising gracefully to her feet. She wasn't particularly tall, but she made up for it by being impossibly elegant in build. He might not remember meeting her, but he had no trouble understanding why he'd fallen for her the first time around. Or the second time around. He figured falling in love with the same woman twice was proof positive he'd chosen the right one.

She came into his arms, soft and willing and smelling of Chanel No. 5, his favorite. "Have I told you today that I love you?" he murmured as they swayed to the slow jazz tune.

"I do believe you've been remiss in that department."

"My sincere apologies. Perhaps I can show you how much I love you instead?"

She laughed. "I *really* never thought you'd ask that. I was beginning to think you didn't miss making love with me."

"Ahh, sweet Laura. I was only trying to think of your health. I will want to make love to you until the day I die."

"Here's hoping that's a very long time from now."

He smiled down at her. "I don't know about you, but I'm planning to live to be one hundred and fifty years old."

"That sounds like a plan."

They danced in silence after that, letting anticipation build between them. Finally, he turned her in his arms toward the bedroom. Her dress had a long zipper, which he drew down by slow degrees as they went, his fingers dipping inside to relish her satin skin and the inward curve of her back. Gratitude swelled in his heart for whatever fate had brought them together.

For her part, Laura tugged his shirt clear of his trousers and made a slow production of unbuttoning it, kissing her way down his chest button by button. His stomach muscles contracted hard as she approached his belt buckle. Her clever fingers did away with that barrier, and then he was sucking in his breath hard, falling back onto the bed when she pushed him gently. She'd obviously given tonight a great deal of thought, and he was happy to go along with her plans for them. For now, at least.

She took her time, teasing him until his entire body thrummed with terrible tension. Finally he rolled over to return the favor. He kissed every inch of her body, reacquainting himself with it, enjoying the new firmness across her flat stomach, loving the extra fullness in her breasts—and the added sensitivity that came with it. Her soft gasps of pleasure were just as he remembered, the way she arched up into his hands, the fire in her eyes as he stroked her body until it sang for him.

A shadow of fear crossed his mind, but he shoved it away. Nothing must hurt her. Hurt them. He ordered himself to stay in the moment. Focus on the now. "You drive me out of my mind," he muttered against her skin. "I'll never get enough of you."

Moaning as his fingers made magic upon her body, she pulled him down to her impatiently. "Nick," she gasped, "Please. I've waited so long for you. I want you now."

Ahh, always direct, his Laura. "I could never deny you what you want, my love."

Taking into consideration her long abstinence, he entered her gently, stunned at how tight and slick she was. She surged up against him immediately, crying out in pleasure. Her eyes glazed the way they always did when they made love, and he relished the way she bit her lower lip. As if she'd actually be able to hold back the cries of pleasure about to claim her. He withdrew slightly and then filled her again in a single slow stroke. She cried out against his shoulder, shuddering from head to foot.

He smiled down at her. "Let us see just how much pleasure you can stand, shall we?"

He paced himself carefully, driving her farther and farther over the edge. With each climax, her smile became more brilliant, her eyes more limpid, his own pleasure more intense. And the happier he became, the more afraid he became. He drove himself mercilessly, forcing himself not to think of the darkness creeping up on him, holding it back from Laura by sheer force of will.

Finally, when his mental strength was at an end, the battle lost, he gave in to the dark tide sweeping over him, surging into her, driving her over the edge one last time. As they climaxed together, it was so magnificent and terrible that, as tears of joy ran down her face, he wasn't far from tears himself. Tears of sheer terror. The better things were between them, the more certain he was that all of it could end at any moment.

He was losing it. Happiness made him unhappy. Joy terrified him. It was all coming apart before his eyes, his life unraveling because he was too screwed up just to enjoy what they had. But he couldn't shake the sense of something bad approaching, something stealthy and evil. And it was coming for him.

"I love you, Nick." Her gaze was clear, untroubled. She sensed nothing, and she had the finely honed instincts of a CIA agent. Desperate, he ordered himself to hold on. Keep it together. He mustn't lose what little sanity he had.

He rolled to his side, propping himself up on one elbow to gaze down at her. "I love you, too, darling." *Must concentrate on that.* Laura. Love. The darkness retreated a little from his mind. His left hand idly stroked down her rosy body. "Better?" he murmured.

"Spectacular. I feel like a woman again."

He leaned down to kiss her. "You were always a woman. A beautiful one. You're an amazing mother, and it only makes you sexier."

"You're just saying that to be polite."

"No, I'm not." He frowned. "Never doubt your attractiveness. The more sides of you I see, the more attracted to you I am."

"Never change, Nick."

If only. He felt as if he'd been living in a state of suspended animation for the past year. As if time was passing, but he wasn't really living. As Laura drifted to sleep beside him, the darkness pushed forward again, nearly choking him with certainty that this sweet interlude was about to end, and life was about to come looking for him with payback in mind.

Chapter 3

The bedside clock had passed 2 a.m. when Nick gave up on sleep. He slid out from under the covers and dressed quietly, tiptoeing downstairs in anticipation of Ellie's imminent feeding. He pulled a bottle of pumped breast milk out of the refrigerator, warmed it in the microwave and went back upstairs.

Turning off the baby monitor, he sat down in the rocking chair to wait. Sure enough, in about ten minutes, the baby started to stir. He picked her up, inhaling the sweet scent of her. "Good evening, little angel. What say we let Mommy sleep tonight?"

Ellie, a happy and cooperative baby, readily took the bottle from him, snuggling close against his chest with a trust that took his breath away. He loved Laura with all his being, but the feelings that swelled in his heart as he gazed down at his daughter pushed his capacity for love to new heights he'd heretofore had no idea existed. Adoration mixed with protectiveness, hope for her future, and wonder at the miracle of her existence expanded in his heart to make room for his tiny daughter.

He changed her as she grew sleepy and rocked her for just a minute or two before her eyes closed. He laid her down gently in her crib and watched her sleep until it dawned on him that he was standing there grinning like a blessed fool.

Restless, he wandered downstairs. Predictably, his feet carried him to his office. Or more accurately to his laptop computer. He sat down at his desk in the dark and cranked it up. He didn't stop to question what he was doing. It was time.

He typed in the name, Nikolas Spiros, and hit the search button. Skipping the tabloids, he read story after story from the business pages chronicling the tragic mental breakdown of Greece's richest shipping magnate. There were even pictures of him, bearded and wild looking. Abrupt memory flashed of his captors hanging a white sheet in his box and taking pictures of him standing in front of it. Bastards.

According to the articles, he'd been institutionalized at a private facility. Later stories talked about his withdrawal from public life. His wish to live quietly and not involve himself with business affairs. How in the hell could anyone who'd known him have believed that drivel? He'd loved running Spiros Shipping. Had thrived on it. The company had been his life, dammit!

He checked his anger. Nikolas Spiros was dead—or at least resting comfortably in an asylum and happy to stay there.

His shipping company had been sold quietly about a year after his "breakdown." Such a pleasant word for such an unpleasant thing as kidnapping. An entirely new management group had taken over the company. A bunch of Germans. They'd renamed it—

His heart nearly stopped right then and there. Spiros Shipping had been renamed AbaCo. The betrayal of it was breathtaking. He'd been kidnapped and held by his own employees! Had they known who he was? Had he been that bad a boss? Surely not. Morale had been great at Spiros before his memory went black. A sense of family had pervaded the firm. Sure, the work had been hard and times were tough, but he'd prided himself in never laying off an employee and paying as much as he could afford to every single worker. Surely so much hadn't changed after his memories stopped that his employees would have turned on him so violently and completely.

In shock, he researched the financials of his renamed company. Profits were down, but AbaCo was still in the black. He shrugged. It would have been darned hard not to make money given how financially sound the company had been when he last remembered it. He studied the quarterly earnings reports for the past few years and cracks were definitely starting to show. But nothing that couldn't be corrected with wise and careful management for a few years—

Not his company any more.

At least not in any way that mattered. He had Laura and the kids. And at all costs, this other part of his life had to be kept away from them. The new owners could have Spiros Shipping.

Best to just stay hidden. A ghost.

But how in the hell was he supposed to do that with this trial coming up?

What had happened to Nikolas Spiros? Had he gone mad for real? Had something horrible happened at the shipping company that had driven him over the edge? What would leave such a residue of terror within him?

The walls of his office started to close in on him unpleasantly—which was a first—and he actually felt a driving need to get out of there. He erased his browsing history and shut down the computer before heading for the kitchen.

Pulling on a jacket, he turned off the elaborate security system and headed out the back door toward the woods behind the house. Tonight he didn't feel up to trekking across one of the pastures and challenging his agoraphobia. He'd been taking secret hikes for several months now, trying to desensitize himself to open spaces. It was getting better, but by maddeningly slow degrees.

He'd been walking for a few minutes when the panic attack hit. It slammed into him like a freight train, sudden and overwhelming. He stopped, breathing as if he'd been sprinting, and glanced around in terror. And then something odd dawned on him. This panic attack was different. It was accompanied by a strange certainty that he was being watched. Great. Was he slipping back into the paranoia of the early days, too?

He couldn't help himself. He slid into the darkest shadow he could find and crouched, pressing his back against the trunk of a huge sycamore. He let his gaze roam, his peripheral vision taking in a wide angle view of the woods. The night sounds had gone dead silent. Maybe he wasn't so paranoid, after all. The crickets never lied.

Who else was out here? And why?

The motion sensors at the house would warn of any human-sized intruders…if he hadn't turned the alarm system off before he came out here. He swore at himself. Laura and the kids were unprotected. He had to get back to the house. Get the alarms back on. Protect his family.

He stood up and was stunned to discover his feet

wouldn't move. Literally. By sheer force of will, he overcame his panic, ignoring the hyperventilation, ignoring the wild imaginings of being kidnapped again, crammed in another box. His family came first, dammit. He'd die for them!

His stumbling walk turned into a jog, and finally into a full-out run. Whether he was running toward Laura or away from the bogeyman in the woods, he couldn't say. But either way, his long legs devoured the distance with powerful strides and his lungs burned with exertion by the time the mansion came into sight. Its Georgian grandeur was dark. Quiet. Undisturbed.

The silliness of his terror struck him forcefully. His mind was playing tricks on him. It was only his past pursuing him. A figment of his imagination. With a last look over his shoulder into the shadows of the night, he let himself into the house and turned on the security system.

Shaken to his core, he climbed the stairs quietly. No sense waking everyone because he'd had a panic attack. He put his hand on the doorknob to let himself into the master suite, but he couldn't bring himself to enter. He was still too wired to lie down beside Laura as if everything was perfectly normal.

Instead, he headed for another door farther down the hall. A small, walk-in linen closet. About six feet by eight feet inside, its tight quarters felt like a comforting embrace. He slid down the wall and sat on the floor, his elbows on his knees and his head on his arms. He had to get over this. Get a grip on himself. But how? If anything, he was getting worse, not better.

As understanding as Laura tried to be, she couldn't begin to comprehend what he'd been through, what the past few years had been like. It was his own private hell, and no one could climb into it with him and lead him out. He was lost, and getting more lost by the day. Oh, the shrinks said all the right things, but they had no more clue what he'd been through, really, than Laura did. They had a little more book learning about it, had a list of suggestions to offer out of some counseling text, but their psychobabble was mostly crap.

How could everything be so perfect and yet so screwed up? He ought to be insanely happy. But instead, he was marching at a brisk pace toward the mental meltdown he'd been falsely accused of having six years ago.

There hadn't been anyone in the woods. A deer or some other creature had moved, and the crickets had gone quiet for a minute. He'd flipped out over nothing. So why was his fight-or-flight response still in full readiness? He took several deep, calming breaths, the way the yoga instructor had taught him, breathing out the fear and stress.

It accomplished exactly nothing, dammit.

He sat there, panting in terror for who knew how long when, without warning, the door swung open. He started to surge to his feet when a little voice whispered, "Daddy?"

Nick sank back down to the floor, his heart about pounding through his rib cage. "Hey, buddy. What are you doing up at this hour?"

"I dreamed a bad man was coming for me."

He held out an arm to Adam, who wasted no time climbing into his lap. "No bad man will ever get you. Mommy and I will always protect you and keep you safe."

"Promise?"

"I promise."

"Cross your heart and hope to die?" Adam added.

"Cross my heart and hope to die," he repeated. "Need a pinkie swear on it, too?"

Adam held out his right pinkie finger, and Nick hooked

his much larger finger in his son's. They shook on it soberly.

"Why are you in the closet, Daddy? Are you hiding from the bad man, too?"

"I didn't want to wake up you and Ellie and Mommy, and I needed some time to think."

Adam's little palms rested on his cheeks. "Is your heart hurting again?"

Since when were five-year-olds so damned perceptive? "I guess it is, a little. I'm so happy it hurts. I think about all the ways it could go wrong…"

Adam nodded wisely. "And then you're not so happy anymore."

He stared down at his son, but it was too dark to make out his face. "Nothing's going to go wrong, Adam. Not if I can help it."

"Don't be scared, Daddy."

"I won't if you won't. We can be brave for each other. Okay?"

Adam nodded against his chest. They cuddled in the dark for several more minutes, and predictably, the boy drifted back to sleep, his nightmare long gone. Nick stood awkwardly, careful not to wake his son, and carried him back to his rocket-ship bed. He tucked the little boy in and kissed his forehead, memorizing Adam's face in that peaceful moment.

He was going to defeat his own demons if it killed him. No way was he about to let his paranoia bleed over to his children and damage them. And furthermore, his past wasn't going to hurt them, either. He knew what he had to do. And he had to do it alone. Leaving no note that Laura could use to track him down, he treaded quietly back down the stairs, this time being sure to reactivate the alarm from the panel in the garage, and headed out into the night.

* * *

Laura woke up to Ellie's fussing amplified through the baby monitor, disoriented at how well rested she felt and that the first light of dawn was peeking in around the curtains. She looked at the clock. Six o'clock? Nick must've taken the 2:00 a.m. feeding, bless him. She rolled over to thank him and was startled to see his side of the bed empty. He hadn't struggled with insomnia for months, now.

Shrugging, she got up, threw on a bathrobe and headed for her daughter. Ellie was hungry, and nursed for longer than usual. Laura carried her into the bathroom and laid her on a big soft bath towel on the heated floor while Mommy jumped into the shower. She dressed herself and Ellie and headed downstairs in search of Nick.

He wasn't in the kitchen watching the financial news and drinking coffee, as was his habit. She strolled through the entire downstairs and didn't find him. Had he crawled into bed with Adam sometime last night? He did that now and then when Adam had a particularly scary nightmare. The boy had had periodic bouts with them ever since a team of killers had broken into the house after Nick's rescue in search of her and Nick. Thankfully, the babysitter had gotten them into the mansion's panic room and locked it down before Adam was hurt or worse. But the incident had left its mark on the little boy.

She headed upstairs and peeked into Adam's room. He was sleeping alone. A low-level hum of alarm started in Laura's gut. She checked the linen closet and Nick's walk-in closet. No sign of him.

She pulled out her cell phone and dialed his. Not in service? What was going on? She ran down to the garage to check the cars—they were all in their places. The alarm system was still on, too. Where had he gone? He hated being outdoors. It wasn't like he'd have gone for a morning stroll.

Starting at one end of the house, she searched it methodically, checking every place a grown man could possibly hide. Something was wrong. Very, very wrong.

Memories of Paris flashed through her head with horrifying clarity. How he'd just disappeared. No trace. No evidence. No ransom call. Nothing. He'd just been gone. *Please, God. Not again.* She couldn't live through losing him again. Not like that.

An hour later, she was on the phone to the police and local hospitals. Nada. And then she started calling their friends and associates, the early hour of the morning be damned. No one had seen or heard from him overnight. Panic hovered, vulture-like, waiting to close in on her.

Adam came downstairs and didn't help matters one bit by immediately picking up on her stress. The child was far too observant for his own good sometimes. "What's wrong, Mommy? Where's Daddy?"

"I don't know, honey. But there's nothing to worry about."

Adam frowned. "His heart is hurting again."

She turned on the child quickly. "Why do you say that, sweetie?"

"He was in the towel closet again last night."

"When last night?"

Adam shrugged. "It was dark. I had a bad dream and was coming to sleep with you. I heard him breathing funny in there."

"What did he say?" She tried not to sound hysterical but suspected she'd failed when Adam frowned worriedly.

"He promised he'd keep me safe from the bad man. He pinkie swore." The little boy started to cry. "The bad man got him, didn't he?"

She gathered him into her arms. "Daddy? Are you kidding? He's big and strong and smart. No bad man has a chance against your daddy."

But the bad man had gotten Nick once before. Had history sickeningly repeated itself? Had he been ghosted out of their lives yet again?

Chapter 4

"May I help you, sir?" The receptionist at the swanky Boston law firm was predictably beautiful and efficient.

Nick replied, "I'm here to see William Ward."

"Do you have an appointment?"

"No, and please don't tell him I'm here. It's a surprise." He flashed his most charming smile at her. He wasn't vain about his looks, but very few women could resist him when he turned the charm all the way up.

She simpered something about being delighted to help. He waved off her offer to show him the way and strode down the familiar hallways. A feeling akin to déjà vu passed over him. This place was from another existence, another life, familiar and yet entirely strange to him.

He stepped into Ward's office and the man glanced up. *"Sweet Jesus!"* he gasped, falling back in his chair heavily. "Is that really you?"

Nick closed the door and stepped up to the desk. "You look like you've seen a ghost, William."

"My God. Where have you been? The things they said about you—"

Nick propped his hip on a corner of William's expansive desk. "What *did* my kidnappers say to explain my absence, anyway?"

"Kidnappers?" The lawyer stared, aghast. "The reports said you had a mental breakdown. Had to be institutionalized. There were doctor's statements. Psychological evaluations. Pictures. You looked like hell."

"Lies. All of it," Nick said shortly.

William's shocked pallor was giving way to a sickly shade of green. "Was our power of attorney over your estate illegal, then? What about your signatures on all those sales documents?"

"What documents?"

"The ones signing over your company to the new management group? Were those real?"

"I never signed anything, to my knowledge." *He hoped.* Surely he never would have signed away Spiros Shipping under any circumstances.

It took William a few seconds to quit spluttering and form words. "Please forgive me for asking, I mean no disrespect. But have you been in a sufficiently…alert…mental condition for all of the past six years to know for certain that you never signed any legal documents?"

Nick swore under his breath. God only knew what he'd done during the blackout years. "I'm actually not here to talk about my company. And to answer your question, I was kidnapped and imprisoned for five years. It has taken me most of the past year to recover physically from the ordeal."

The lawyer devolved into a shockingly uncharacteristic bout of mumbling to himself. Poor guy must really be shaken up. Eventually, William collected himself enough to go into attorney mode. "I'm going to need an affidavit from you describing exactly what happened to you in detail. I don't have any idea how we're going to contest the sale of your company. It's going to cause a massive uproar to try to get it back—"

Nick interrupted the man sharply. "I don't want it back. That's not why I'm here."

William stared blankly. "Why are you here, then?"

"I need you to tell me about the last two years before I…disappeared."

"I beg your pardon?"

Nick sighed. "It's a long story, but I've experienced a memory loss as a result of a blow to the head. I need your help to fill in the gap."

"Are you serious?"

"As a heart attack."

William nodded dubiously. "I'll do what I can."

The lawyer started talking and Nick listened grimly. He'd thought if he heard about the lost time it would jog his memory, but none of the names or places or dates rang any bells. His memory wasn't just buried. It was truly gone. The danger of the black hole loomed even larger as the true depth of it became clear to him.

"I can get all these facts off the internet, William. Tell me what I was like. How I was acting."

The lawyer spoke of Nikolas growing bored with running a company that functioned like a well-oiled machine pretty much on its own. Of his forays into ever more dangerous hobbies—skydiving, extreme skiing, boat racing, Formula One car racing. He'd apparently blown through a string of beautiful and ever wilder women as well. He'd become a regular on the pages of the European tabloids. And there'd been the partying. Ward didn't say if he'd dabbled in drinking or drugs, just that the lawyer had been very worried about his longtime client.

Finally, he fell silent.

Nick didn't even know where to begin processing the information dump he'd just received. It was odd to hear about his own life and feel so completely disconnected from it. Nothing the man had described would account for the pervasive terror that was the only thing he'd carried forward from that time. Nick asked grimly, "Was I—Did I…get married?"

William looked surprised. "There were rumors of a quickie wedding just before you disappeared. But I hadn't seen you for a few weeks prior to that. I couldn't say."

Rumors of a wedding? Nick swore under his breath. "Do you know how I came by the Nick Cass identity?"

The attorney cleared his throat. "During that time, you occasionally preferred to travel under an alias to avoid the publicity and scandal you were generating."

He had no memory of being assaulted by paparazzi. "Where did the fake ID come from?"

William visibly squirmed at that one. "For the record, I arranged no such thing. I put you in touch with a gentleman who was expert at facilitating replacement of lost identity documents. Perhaps he was the source of your… alter ego."

Nick dismissed the lawyer's double-talk with a flick of his wrist. If he was going to keep up the charade of being Nick Cass and no one but Nick Cass, he had to know everything there was to know about the man. Had someone of that name really existed at some point, or was Nick Cass an entirely made-up entity? "I need to get in touch with the fellow who made those documents. I need to know more about the identity he provided for me."

William frowned. "It's my understanding he's no longer

in the business. He ran into some legal troubles. Last I heard, he left the country in a hurry. I would have no idea how to get in touch with him."

Damn. Frustrated, Nick moved over to the floor-to-ceiling glass window to stare down at Boston Harbor. His kidnapper surely knew who he really was. But did the people who'd held him captive? Did the powers-that-be at AbaCo? Had it been an inside job, or had his kidnappers merely had a sick sense of humor to have imprisoned him on one of his own ships?

If AbaCo's lawyers penetrated the Cass identity, they would come after him with both barrels, and the sum total of what he knew about his last years before his capture he'd just heard from the man behind him. He turned to William. "Can you recommend a top-flight private investigator to me? Someone thorough and discreet."

"Of course." William looked close to puking in relief that Nick didn't pursue the fake ID thing any further. As Nick recalled, William had been paid plenty well enough back then that he could darn well suffer a little for the cause now.

"Oh, and one more thing, William."

The lawyer looked up sharply from the sticky note on which he was copying a name and phone number.

"Don't tell anyone you've seen me. Consider this little visit a privileged interaction between the two of us. As far as you know, I'm still sitting in a padded cell somewhere, staring at my toes and drooling down my chin. Got it?"

The attorney frowned. "I understand. Actually, I don't understand, but I will abide by your wishes."

"Thanks, William."

"Will you tell me the whole story someday?"

"If things go well, you'll never see or hear from me again." As the finality of that struck Nick he made brief eye contact with the attorney who'd been a friend and confidante for many years. "Thanks for everything. You're a good man."

"You, too. If you ever need anything, just let me know. And good luck."

Nick turned and left the office. Good luck, indeed. He'd probably need a bona fide miracle before it was all said and done to avoid the clutches of his past.

He waited until he was back in Washington D.C., leaving Reagan International Airport to drive home, before he called Laura. She had too many scary resources with which to track him down for him to risk calling her any sooner. She would be completely freaked out by now, but he'd had no choice. He had to deal with his past on his own. And after hearing what William Ward had to say about his last years leading up to his capture, it had turned out to be a damned good call to keep Laura and the kids far away from the mess he'd apparently made of his life.

Laura answered her cell phone on the first ring with a terse hello.

"Hello, darling. It's me."

"Thank God, Nick. Are you all right? Are you hurt? Where are you?"

He felt terrible hearing her panic and relief. Good Lord willing, he'd never scare her like this again. "I'm fine. I'll be home in about an hour. There was something I had to take care of."

A pause. "Can you talk to me about it?"

"I'm afraid I can't. But it's handled. No worries." At least he hoped there was nothing to worry about. The P.I. he'd spoken to in Boston had been confident he could find everything that had ever existed on one Nick Cass prior to six years ago. If the man had ever actually existed, Nick would know all about him in a few days.

The cab delivered him to the mansion's front door in closer to two hours than one—there'd been an accident and traffic was hellish. As he stepped inside, Adam shouted a greeting that warmed Nick all the way to his soul. Laura held herself to a walk as she came to greet him, but she squeezed him so tightly it hurt and he thought he felt a sob shake her momentarily.

"I'm sorry, darling. I knew you'd want to go with me, but I had to take care of a piece of old business on my own."

Her muffled voice rose from his chest. "Did you kill anyone?"

"No," he laughed.

"Are we okay?"

His arms tightened convulsively around her. "That's the whole idea. I love you and the children more than life." They stood locked together like they'd never let go of each other for a long time. Finally, he murmured, "Am I forgiven?"

"Of course. I could never stay mad at you. If you say you had to do something, then you had to do it. If you can't talk about it with me, there's a good reason for that, too. And if you say you love me, I believe you."

He tilted her chin up to kiss her. "I am, without question, the luckiest man on Earth to have you."

She stood on tiptoe to kiss him back. "And don't you ever forget it," she murmured.

"Never." Their lips met, and the passion that always simmered between them boiled over immediately. His mouth slanted across hers, and she clung to him eagerly.

"Eeyew! Gross!" Adam exclaimed from the steps above them.

Nick lifted his mouth away from Laura's and smiled up at his son. "For now, you hold on to that thought, young man. But trust me. In a few years, girls won't be nearly so disgusting."

"But Mommy's not a girl. She's a…mommy."

Laura laughed in Nick's arms. "Gee, thanks, kid." She scooped up Adam and swung him around until they were all laughing.

And just like that, life was back to the way it was supposed to be. As Nick followed his family toward the kitchen, he experienced an overwhelming sensation of having dodged a bullet.

The sensation lasted exactly one hour. That was when Carter Tatum called to inform him that he was to appear at a pre-trial hearing in three days' time. Three days for the private investigator to give him enough ammunition to hold off a pack of sharks out to tear him to pieces. It was almost enough to make him reconsider enlisting Laura's prodigious skill with computers to help him research his Nick Cass identity.

Almost. But not quite.

Laura understood Nick's nervousness as his first encounter with AbaCo's lawyers loomed only a few hours away. But there was something else going on with him. He kept checking his cell phone like he was expecting a message, and the longer it didn't come, the more tense he was quietly becoming. It took knowing him exceedingly well to see the signs of his stress—the tightness around his eyes, the absent quality to some of his comments, the very occasional twitch of a thumb. She had to give Nick credit. He had amazing self-discipline to give away so little as a limousine whisked the two of them toward Washington, D.C.

His self-control held through the hearing, but he wasn't put on the witness stand and grilled, either. The legal proceeding mostly consisted of motions and technical arguments between the lawyers. As far as she could tell, they were wrangling over the rules of engagement for the trial to come. All in all, it was rather anticlimactic.

The hearing was adjourned, and Nick joined her in the aisle, looping an arm over her shoulder as they stepped outside…

…into a barrage of lights and microphones and shouted questions.

Nick reared back hard beside her, going board stiff. The Tatum team of attorneys leaped forward to intercept the phalanx of reporters, but it was too late. The press had spotted Nick. The story of his kidnapping and rescue had made a brief sensation last year, but thanks to his inability at the time to give interviews and put a poster-boy face to the story, it had faded quickly.

Unfortunately, the media had put two and two together, and they wanted the scoop on the miracle man now. Laura was half-blinded by flashing lights exploding at them from all directions. Good thing she was completely out of her old line of work. One media assault like this would've blown her cover permanently.

Nick swore quietly beside her. To the lawyers, he said tersely, "Get us out of here. Now."

The Tatum support team hustled her and Nick down the front steps and into the waiting limousine. He collapsed on the plush upholstery, swearing steadily under his breath in what sounded like Greek. What was up with that?

The car door closed, and silence descended around them.

He yanked out his cell phone and punched in a number. She caught only the first few digits—617 area code. Boston?

"It's Nick Cass," said into the device tersely. "What have you got for me?"

He listened in silence for a long time, his jaw clenching tighter with each passing minute. And then he finally ordered, "Keep looking."

"Who was that?" Laura asked as he put away his phone.

He looked up at her grimly. It was like staring into the eyes of a total stranger. Cold shock washed over her. Who was this man sitting beside her? She couldn't ever recall seeing that expression of irritation or determination in his gaze before.

He answered tightly, "That was my past."

She waited for him to elaborate but was immensely frustrated when he didn't. It was all she could do not to demand answers right this second. But she'd vowed when she found him to just be grateful that he was alive and accept whatever part of him he chose to share with her, no questions asked. But, darn, that was hard to stick to now!

The ride home was silent, with him lost in his thoughts, and her convincing herself to respecting his privacy. She would *not* turn her investigative skills on the father of her children, the man she loved with all her heart. She would trust him and take him at his word and support him. But her fingers literally itched to start typing, to dig into the internet and tap her network of resources built up over years of hunting down disappeared and deadbeat dads.

At dinner that night, she and Nick let Adam dominate the conversation with an eager description of his outing with Nanny Lisbet to Colonial Williamsburg that afternoon. Afterwards, Adam went upstairs with Lisbet to take a bath, and Laura and Nick adjourned to the family room. Nick flipped on the news.

Laura started violently as his face flashed up on the

flat-screen TV at several times larger than life size. He froze on the sofa beside her.

The reporter narrated over footage from the courthouse this afternoon, recapping the story of Nick's rescue from a container ship a year before and moving on to report in detail how federal prosecutors were going after several high-ranking AbaCo executives for their roles in Nick's kidnapping. The reporter devolved into speculating on how high in the company the complicity reached.

Nick turned off the TV, scowling ferociously.

Laura commented soothingly, "It was an essentially accurate report. You came off completely sympathetically. You're an innocent victim of a heinous crime. And I have to say, you're incredibly photogenic. The public is going to love you." She smiled. "Particularly women."

His scowl deepened and he leaped up off the sofa to pace. He kept mumbling something under his breath that sounded like, "Not good. They'll see me."

"Who'll see you?" she asked carefully.

When he turned to stare at her, it was like looking into the eyes of a wild creature, hunted and cornered. "Everything will be ruined," he bit out. And with that, he stormed out of the room.

Laura eyed her laptop computer. Just a quick search. Nothing in depth. A brief check to see if something about his past would pop up. No, darn it! She headed for the gym in the basement to drown her temptation in some good old-fashioned sweat.

Nick was restless that night. To her vast disappointment, he didn't come to bed when she did, and the clock was turning toward 4:00 a.m. when he finally slipped in beside her. His arms went around her and she snuggled into his embrace, pretending to sleep.

But as she lay there in the dark, listening to his quiet

breathing, she couldn't help but wonder who exactly she was in bed with. What in his past had him so frantic? Was he a criminal after all? Who were his enemies? What baggage clung to him? What kind of trouble was he so afraid of bringing to her doorstep? She was a former CIA field agent, for goodness' sake. What was so bad that he didn't think she could handle it?

She finally gave up on getting any more rest at around 6 a.m. and eased out of bed quietly so as not to wake Nick. She went to the nursery and scooped up Ellie who, orderly child that she was, was beginning to rouse exactly on time for her 6 a.m. feeding.

"Such a good baby," Laura crooned as she sat down in the rocking chair in the family room to feed Ellie. As the baby latched on and began sucking hungrily, Laura picked up the remote control and flipped on the TV. Was Nick still the star attraction of the all news channels, or had some real story come along overnight to bump him off the airwaves?

"…reclusive billionaire Nikolas Spiros may have surfaced yesterday in a Washington, D.C. courtroom… appears to be living under a new name…rumors of kidnapping and conspiracy surround his disappearance six years ago after a mental breakdown…unable to contact his people to confirm or deny his identity…you judge for yourself."

Laura lurched up out of the chair as a photograph of a dashing man in his early thirties was flashed up beside a still picture of Nick yesterday on the courthouse steps.

She knew that younger man very well, indeed. He'd been her lover in Paris six years ago. He was the father of her son. And the man in the other, more recent, picture was the man she lived with now, the father of her daughter. Ellie squawked as she lost her grip on breakfast, and Laura was momentarily distracted resettling the baby.

"I'm sorry, honey," she murmured. "Mommy was just surprised."

Although surprised hardly described the sick nausea rumbling through her gut. Nick was a Greek shipping tycoon named Nikolas Spiros? A billionaire? Why had he turned his back on all that? Why did he continue to live under this Nick Cass identity?

Her mind flashed back to Paris. To meeting Nick Cass there. *He'd lied to her.* He hadn't told her who he was back then, and he was perpetuating the lie now. No wonder neither she nor her attorney had been able to learn anything about him back then. Nick Cass didn't exist. The first stirrings of anger started low in her belly, building by steady degrees. Only Ellie's tiny body nestled against her breast, sucking sleepily, kept her from storming up the stairs and bursting in on Nick—Nikolas—this very second and demanding the full truth and nothing but the truth.

Who in the world was he?

Chapter 5

Laura reached her desk just as the phone rang. Who on earth would be calling her at this time of morning? Alarmed, she picked up the receiver.

"Good morning, this is Shelley Hacker from *The Morning News Hour*. I'm calling to speak to Nikolas Spiros."

"I'm afraid you have a wrong number." Laura hung up fast, not giving the reporter time to ask any follow-up questions.

The phone rang again. Oh, Lord. She glanced at the caller ID: *unknown caller*. She picked the receiver up an inch and set it back down. The feeding frenzy had begun.

"What's going on?"

Laura whirled to face Nick. "You tell me. The phone's ringing off the hook with reporters wanting to speak with Nikolas Spiros."

Beneath his olive complexion, Nick went a sickly shade of gray. He gritted out, "I'm Nick Cass."

"You are now. I get that. But were you this Spiros guy at some point in your past?"

"My past is dead."

She gritted her teeth. This was about her and the children as much as it was about him, darn it. She had a family to protect. "I understand your desire to move on. To start a new life. I really do. I support you all the way. But if you were Nikolas Spiros before, you're going to have to deal with him sometime. What are you going to tell the media?"

"I'll tell them nothing. It's none of their business."

A new hardness, or maybe an old hardness for all she knew, clung to Nick. This was not the gentle, laid-back man she'd spent the past year with. This man resembled much more a savvy, tough businessman who might run a billion-dollar shipping empire. Did she know him *at all*?

The phone rang again. She glanced at the caller ID and stopped herself at the last second from hanging it up. "It's Tatum Carter. Your lawyer wants to talk to you…Nikolas."

Nick sighed and held a hand out for the receiver.

"What the hell's going on, Nick?"

"Tatum. Good morning. I gather you've seen the news?" Nick asked evenly.

"What's this about you being some Greek billionaire? Hell, you owned AbaCo Shipping until a few years ago. What have you gotten me into?"

Ahh, the ass-covering had commenced. Nick sighed. "If you want to remove yourself from this case, I won't stop you."

"No, no," Tatum quickly replied. "I just want to know what's going on."

Nick rolled his eyes. Greed won out, then. He took a certain comfort in knowing what made the attorney tick. And then he jolted as he realized his old, sharklike business instincts were roaring back to the fore. He didn't want to return to this part of his life, this part of himself.

He glanced up and caught Laura staring at him in equal parts dismay and horror. He was losing her. As sure as he was standing here, she was pulling away from him—from the stranger he'd become. "I'll call you later, Tatum."

He hung up on the man without any further ado and sat down beside Laura on the sofa. "I lied to you in Paris."

"I already figured that out," she replied dryly. "Why?"

No way was he going to tell her all the things William Ward had revealed to him. There was still a chance he could keep her and the kids out of his past, and he was going to do his darnedest to make that happen. The private investigator had found nothing on any Nick Cass. So far it appeared such a man had never existed. If that held true, his new family was in the clear.

He shrugged. "I apparently created an alter ego for myself. An identity under which I could travel anonymously and unobtrusively. Nick Cass could go into a coffee shop or sit at a café and no one paid any attention to him."

"Who were you hiding from?" Laura asked shrewdly.

"The media, I imagine. My employees, maybe. Hell, maybe an ex-lover." He added candidly, "And myself, if I had to guess."

"Why didn't you tell me who you were?"

"I expect you fell for Nick Cass, the regular guy, not some Greek billionaire. Knowing you and loving you the way I do now, I'll bet I wasn't about to risk what I had with you."

"So you *lied* to me? You trusted me so little? Didn't you think I would understand? Am I that judgmental or just that stupid?"

She didn't raise her voice, but the anger in it was unmistakable.

"I'm sorry, Laura. I don't remember any of it. I have no answers for you. Undoubtedly, I was wrong and should have told you everything from the start."

She threw up her hands. "Do you have any idea how hard it is to be this furious with you and not be able to be mad at you because you can't remember doing any of it?"

He smiled sadly. "I really am sorry."

"What are you going to do now?"

"Deal with the fallout as best as I can, and when the excitement blows over, go back to being plain old Nick Cass, the man who loves you and our kids."

"What fallout should I expect from this revelation?"

He grimaced but forced himself to look her squarely in the eye. "I honestly don't know. But I can tell you this. I plan to do everything in my power to keep you and the kids out of this."

"This *what?*"

She was too smart for her own good, sometimes. She'd heard the evasion in his voice and put her finger exactly on the source of his discomfort. "I've had a gut feeling since the moment you fished me out of that box that I should let sleeping dogs lie. I feel that way more strongly than ever. It's nothing concrete. Just a feeling."

He reached out and took her icy hands in his. "I don't know what's hidden in those lost five years, I swear. But I think it's bad, and I think it could put you and the children in danger. You've got to let me deal with this alone. Stay away from it, Laura."

She stared at him, her dark gaze brimming with frustration. "No way—"

He cut her off gently. "I have to know the children are safe. You have to take care of them for me—for us—while I put my past to rest."

Ellie must've sensed her mother's tension for the infant

started to fuss. He was a cad to be so relieved at being saved by a baby's distress. Ellie, uncharacteristically, wanted no part of being soothed. Her fussing escalated to crying outright and soon to screaming. Not appreciating mommy's stress, apparently.

Laura spared him a look that promised this conversation was not over as she left to find Lisbet.

The phone rang again. He glanced at the caller ID and jolted. William Ward. How had his former attorney found this phone number, and furthermore, why on earth was he calling it? Nick picked up the receiver quickly lest Laura take the call.

"Good morning, William."

"Nikolas. We need to talk."

"Then speak."

"This is confidential. Needs to be face-to-face."

Nick sighed. "In case you haven't seen the news this morning, I'm a little busy at the moment." Not to mention he had serious damage control to do with Laura. He knew her well enough to know that she wasn't about to let him deal with this mess on his own.

The lawyer huffed and then said heavily, "I've been doing some digging about you. I've found something. It's bad."

Nick froze. "What is it?"

"I'm at my beach house on the Cape. Get here as fast as you can."

"I can't just drop everything here and come see you!" Nick exploded. "The AbaCo trial is about to begin. And furthermore, my old life is *over*. Finished. I'm not that person anymore."

"Based on what's sitting on my desk in front of me, your old life is about to come after you whether you like it or not."

"I won't let my past *touch* my new life," Nick bit out sharply. He turned to pace and stopped in his tracks. Laura. She was standing in the doorway, the color draining from her face as he watched.

"I've got to go," Nick snapped.

William said forcefully, "I'm not kidding. You need to come up here—"

He hung up on the lawyer.

"What's up?" Laura asked. Her cool voice sounded brittle, like she was barely hanging on to self-control.

"My past," he bit out. "I don't know." He shoved a frustrated hand through his hair. "I don't remember any of it."

"You knew your real name. It would've taken you two minutes on the internet to find out all about yourself, and maybe even what's got you all freaked out."

How was he supposed to explain his dead certainty that he had to leave his past alone? To stay far, far away from anything having to do with Nikolas Spiros? It would sound like a lame excuse to her. Hell, maybe it was a lame excuse.

Laura's voice fell, dropping into a hurt hush that was a hundred times more painful than if she'd yelled at him. "I thought you loved me."

He didn't try to stop her as she whirled and ran from the room. He'd been worse than a fool to avoid his past, and she was right to be furious with him. Every accusation she'd thrown at him was less awful than the ones he was flinging at himself right now. It didn't even make things better that he was dying inside. She was everything to him, and he'd hurt her terribly. He'd rather endure torture than cause her an ounce of pain. But he'd pretty well blown that. He'd blown *everything.*

Now what was he supposed to do? How was he ever going to make this better?

Swearing long and hard at himself, he headed upstairs to Adam's room. The child was still asleep, which was just as well. He didn't think he'd have the strength to say goodbye to his son if Adam were awake. Stroking the dark, silky hair so like his own gently, he murmured, "I love you more than life. Never doubt that. Take care of your mother for me. And be brave."

He turned and left quickly before he could weaken. He had to protect them all. No matter the cost to himself. Feeling every bit of the past six years in his bones, an ache that had never quite gone away, he headed downstairs. Laura and the kids had kept it at bay with their love and laughter, but all of a sudden, the withheld agony was back.

"Are you going out, Mr. Cass?" Marta asked in surprise. "Breakfast will be ready soon."

He rasped, "I won't be taking breakfast today. And you'd better send Laura's up to her office. I suspect she's going to be busy in there for a while."

By noon, with her connections she'd probably know more about Nick Cass than he did. And she would definitely know everything there was to know about Nikolas Spiros. Every last ugly, selfish, tawdry detail.

He'd lost her. The lies had finally caught up with him. *But, Lord, the cost of it.* His eyes hot and his throat painfully tight, he stepped out of the house and drove away from the best things that had ever happened to him. He'd ruined it all. Everything that was good and right about his life retreated in the rearview mirror as he pulled out of the estate. If it was the last thing he ever did, he'd make this mess right. Put his family back together.

He thought he'd known hell before in a box. Hah! That had been a walk in a park compared to the hell embracing him now. A hell of his own making.

* * *

Laura was hanging on by a thread. The phone wouldn't quit ringing, and she was developing a horrendous headache. How on earth had she never connected Nick to Nikolas Spiros? She should have recognized him in Paris, and sometime in the past year she definitely should have searched for disappearances of men matching Nick's description six years ago. But no. He hadn't wanted to know, and she'd gone along with his plan to bury their heads in the sand and avoid facing whatever demons lurked in his past. She'd willfully ignored the signs that Nick was not what he appeared to be, had been so caught up in her own selfish bliss that she hadn't asked any of the obvious questions.

Why didn't he have any other family or friends he wanted to let know he was alive and free? Why was he so at ease living in the luxurious world she inhabited? Why did he flatly refuse to talk about his past prior to his memory loss? And the granddaddy of them all—why was he kidnapped and thrown into a box for five years? Who were his enemies, and why did they bear him so much malice that they chose to make him suffer rather than simply kill him?

At lunchtime, Lisbet apologetically poked her head into Laura's office. "I'm sorry, ma'am, but Adam is hysterical and really needs to be with you. I've tried everything I know to calm him, but he's panicked that something bad has happened to you and his father. Nothing will do but for him to see you."

Laura stood up quickly. The needs of her children would always come first over her work…even if that work was investigating their father. She hurried to the playroom, where Adam was curled up in a sobbing ball in the corner, hugging the stuffed elephant that had been his special toy forever.

Laura stroked his back gently. "Hey, kiddo. What's the matter?"

The child flung himself at her, wrapping his arms around her neck and squeezing her tightly enough that it was a little hard to breathe. Not that she complained. She hugged his shaking body. "Everything's okay," she soothed him, rocking back and forth.

"Daddy's gone, and the bad man got him!"

"Daddy's not gone. And the bad man definitely didn't get him," Laura declared.

Lisbet cleared her throat. "Begging your pardon, but Mr. Cass left the house before breakfast."

Laura's entire being clenched in shock. He'd left? Where had he gone? And for how long? She shoved back her panic, focusing for the moment on her son. "Adam, Daddy has some business to take care of. It's all right."

"No, it's not. He told me to take care of you for him. And to be brave. He wouldn't say that if he was coming back. He went to fight the bad man."

"Well, honey, even if he did, Daddy will win. It'll be okay."

"No, it won't!" Adam wailed.

"Do you need me to go help Daddy?"

Adam lifted his red, wet gaze to hers. "Can you do that?"

"Sure. I'm pretty ferocious, you know."

"Daddy says you're like a mama bear with cubs," Adam replied dryly, his humor already so much like his father's.

A burning knife twisted in her gut. She replied stoutly, "He's right. Grrrr."

Adam smiled reluctantly. But he wasn't about to be diverted so easily. "You won't let the bad man get you, too?"

"Never."

"Promise?"

"I promise. Cross my heart, hope to die, alligator in my eye."

"Alligator in your—" Adam giggled. "That's silly."

"Made you laugh, didn't it?"

"Yes." He waxed thoughtful once more. Impossible to distract, he was. Just like both of his parents on that score. "Where do you think the bad man is?"

"Hmm. I don't know. But I'm really, really good at finding people. I found Daddy before, didn't I? I'll find the bad man, and I'll find Daddy, again. I'd never let anything happen to anyone in our family. I'm a mama bear, and you and Ellie are my cubs. Don't you ever forget that, okay?"

Adam nodded against her neck.

She closed her eyes and prayed for strength. She had to find Nick. Figure out what had gone so wrong so fast. And somehow, some way, put it right. Her children needed their father.

Chapter 6

Laura was startled when Marta announced that Tatum Carter was at the house and waiting in the library to speak with her. Since when did lawyers make house calls? He must be panicked over Nick's abrupt disappearance yesterday. *Join the club.*

She left her computer, which had been giving up a treasure trove of information on one Nikolas Spiros, and walked down the hall to the library. "Tatum. This is a pleasant surprise. What can I do for you today?"

"Tell me where Nick is. The feds are going to have my head on a platter if I lose their star witness for them. The trial starts next week."

She replied quietly, "If I knew where he was, do you think I'd be standing here talking to you?"

"What the hell's going on with him, Laura?"

She sighed. "I think we all underestimated the trauma he's suffering from. And I think we all ignored the possible problems his memory loss could be concealing."

"What's your gut feel about him? Is he stable enough to put on a witness stand? If AbaCo skates on this kidnapping charge, it'll be like letting Al Capone get off on the tax evasion charges that finally landed him in jail where he belonged."

She wasn't concerned about Nick's stability as much as she was about the state of his heart. Had he already abandoned her and the kids and returned to his old life? Goodness knew, Nikolas Spiros had lived a life of glamorous excess that went well beyond even her wealth to provide.

She spoke with a conviction she was far from feeling. "If Nick goes on the witness stand, he'll do what he has to do to put away his captors." *Even if it messes up his personal life? Costs him the Spiros fortune?* She'd like to think he was that honorable, but at this point, she had no way of knowing.

"Where is he, Laura? What's your best guess?"

"My best guess—" her best hope "—is that he's gone away to deal with the fallout of his past and that he'll be back when it's resolved."

"How long is that going to take? He's got about a week to get his ducks in line."

She shrugged. If only Nick had confided in her. Had let her help him. She had enormous resources, official and unofficial, at her fingertips with which to help him. She understood his impulse to protect her and the kids, to keep his new life far away from his old one. But she was still as frustrated as all get out at her current helplessness. If only she knew where he was!

"Tatum, if you were a wealthy man who's been out of touch with his life for a while, where would you go to pick up the threads?"

"Easy. My stock broker and my lawyer."

She nodded. "How do I go about finding out who Nick's—Nikolas's—personal attorney was six years ago?"

Tatum frowned. "Client lists are confidential. But I could make a few phone calls. Maybe find out something off the record. Where was Nick living prior to his kidnapping?"

"His shipping empire was headquartered in Athens and had offices all around the world." *Including Paris.* "His North American headquarters was in Boston."

Tatum called an attorney buddy of his from law school who practiced in Boston. That guy didn't know anything, but referred Tatum to someone else. As the lawyer placed a second call, she reflected on the enormous power of good-old-boy networks.

The second lawyer knew something. She could tell by the way Tatum's face lit up as he listened intently.

"Ward, MacIntosh and Howe," Tatum announced as he disconnected the call. "Want me to contact them and see if Nick's been in their offices recently?"

"Sure."

If Nick had been to visit his lawyer, he might still be in the Boston area. During his incarceration, his shipping company had been sold out from under him, and he might very well be trying to reverse that sale. If not that, Nick was probably getting funds released into his hands to finance whatever he planned to do next. She had an alert set on their joint bank accounts to notify her the second Nick accessed any of them, but so far, he hadn't. He was welcome to whatever he needed or wanted from her accounts.

Funny how love and family made something like money seem so trivial. Not that she'd ever been that hung up on wealth. She just wanted to have enough to do what she wanted to without having to worry about it. Case in point:

It had been handy over the past five years to finance her own investigations as she helped women find the fathers of their children. Most of her clients had been in desperate financial straits and couldn't have paid her a dime even if they'd known who she was.

Tatum was on hold with Nick's law firm and muttering to himself as he waited. "…fly up to Boston and try to contact him before the federal prosecutors get wind of the fact that he's fled."

"I don't think he's fled," she responded. "I think he's taking care of personal business."

"Yeah, well, he'd better take care of it fast—" He broke off and spoke into the phone. "This is Tatum Carter of Carter and Associates in Fairfax, Virginia. I represent Nick Cass—Nikolas Spiros—in an upcoming trial against the people who allegedly kidnapped him. I need to speak with Nick's attorney at your firm."

Laura frowned as Carter visibly paled.

"I'm so sorry," he stammered. "I'll be in touch in a few days. Of course. My sympathies."

Alarmed, Laura blurted the second he hung up, "What happened? What's wrong?"

"Nick's lawyer is dead. Someone broke into the guy's house last night. The police think William Ward startled the intruder and was murdered."

Warning bells clanged wildly in Laura's head. Home robbery, her foot. What were the odds that someone randomly broke into the lawyer's house the day after his kidnapped billionaire client surfaced? *Ohmigosh. Nick.* How much danger was he in? Her gut yelled that he was the prime target on the hit list.

"I have to go, Carter. I'll be in touch." She raced out of the room and upstairs to pack. Somewhere in the next ten frantic minutes, she ordered up an emergency corporate jet to fly her to Boston ASAP.

Ellie squawked over the baby monitor, startling Laura out of her panicked packing. The baby. What was she going to do about her daughter? The infant nursed exclusively, and after her recent bout of jaundice, Laura was loathe to shift Ellie over to formula. She didn't have enough pumped milk in the freezer to be gone for several days.

Laura closed her eyes in frustration. Mother or frantic lover? How was she supposed to choose between the two? With a sigh, she headed for the nursery to feed the baby. Afterward, she quickly packed a bag for Ellie as well.

She popped into the playroom to say goodbye to Adam. "Hey, kiddo."

He flung himself at her and she laughed as he planted a sticky kiss on her cheek. "I'm off to go rescue Daddy. Call me whenever you want to, okay?"

Adam nodded against her neck. "Promise you'll save Daddy from the bad man."

"You've got it. I promise. Daddy and I will be home in no time. You and Lisbet have fun while I'm gone and don't eat anything healthy, okay?"

Adam laughed. They both knew his health-freak nanny would never dream of letting Adam exist on junk food.

"I love you, Adam."

"Love you, too, Mommy."

Her heart ached at having to leave her precious son for even a few days. She nodded at Lisbet over Adam's dark head, and the nanny smiled and nodded back. Lisbet knew full well how deeply Laura treasured her children and would take care of Adam like her own son in Laura's absence.

"I'll be back as soon as I can. No more than, say, three days."

"Yes, ma'am. Have a safe trip."

Before she could dissolve into completely un-superhero-like tears in front of her son, Laura spun and left the playroom, giving a theatric leap as she passed through the doorway. "Super Mommy away!" she called out.

The last sound she heard as she scooped up Ellie and headed out was Adam shouting, "Go, Super Mommy!"

The drive to the airport and subsequent flight to Boston took several hours. It was late afternoon when Laura and Ellie arrived at Logan Airport. The baby traveled like a champ. She must take after her mother when it came to enjoying adventure and new experiences.

A newspaper purchased in the airport terminal told Laura that William Ward had been at his home on Cape Cod when he was killed. She plugged the town into her rental car's GPS and in a few minutes was crawling down I-93 in the remnants of the day's rush-hour traffic. Big Dig or no Big Dig, traffic in Boston was horrendous.

It was nearly 10:00 p.m. when she finally found Ward's house just outside Hyannisport. In full spy mode, she turned off her headlights and drove past. It was impossible to miss with yellow crime scene tape stretched all around it. She turned down the first side road and parked parallel to Ward's house. Time to go cross-country. Although how Super Mommy was supposed to pull that off with a baby in tow, she wasn't sure.

She donned a baby backpack and settled Ellie into a nest of blankets within it. The baby had just dined and was ready for a nice warm nap. Thankfully, as Laura set out hiking toward the Ward house, the motion seemed to soothe her daughter.

Ward was not a criminal lawyer, which eliminated some disgruntled client or victim of one of his clients being the killer. It had to be Nick who triggered the attack. What information could Ward have on Nikolas Spiros that was worth killing for? Laura had no idea what it could be, but she'd bet Nick had a good idea what it was. Or if Nick didn't know what it was, he'd darn well be dying of curiosity to know. And in either case, she figured Nick planned to find out what information Ward had been murdered over.

A clearing came into sight ahead. Assuming she hadn't lost all of her CIA field skills, that would be the backyard of the Ward house. Hopefully, Nick would be paying this place a visit soon. And if she was lucky, she just might spot him and hook up with him. At least that was the plan. It was admittedly a sketchy plan, but better than having no plan at all. Given that Nick hadn't used any of his credit cards and still had not withdrawn any funds from their checking accounts, she could only assume he was using cash and an assumed name. It was what she'd do in the same situation. And Nick was nothing if not highly intelligent.

She cursed under her breath as a branch whapped her in the face, showering her with wet, cold dew. She hadn't snuck around in the woods for years, and she abruptly remembered why she'd never liked this sort of work. She'd always been more at ease in urban environments and had gravitated to assignments in major metropolitan areas. Like Paris.

Ellie made an unhappy noise as some of the cold dew sprinkled her. Laura reached awkwardly to pat her. "Hush, sweetie. Mommy's trying to be sneaky."

Although how on God's green earth she was going to pull that off with an infant in tow, she had no idea. It was pure insanity to try it. But for now, Ellie was stuck in the woods playing spy with Mommy.

Laura pushed forward a few more yards and the baby bag caught on a bush. Of course, it spilled. Swearing under her breath, she crouched and picked up miscellaneous baby gear and stuffed it all back in the bag.

She rose to her feet and continued forward.

If William Ward's killers had broken into his house to kill him instead of in a simple mugging or drive-by shooting, that meant his killers also had orders to search for something. Something in this house.

She stopped in the shadow of a huge tree as Ward's "cottage" came into view. The house had to have at least five bedrooms, if not more. If that was a cottage, then it was a cottage on serious steroids. The sound and smell of the ocean were unmistakable as Laura reached the edge of the woods crowding the rear of the structure. No wonder the killers had gotten away last night. This forest made for a perfect escape route.

She hunkered down to wait for someone to show up and prayed it would be Nick and not the killers coming back to finish their search. Time passed, and Ellie snoozed happily at her back. The baby was like having her own personal heater snuggled up against her. Laura's legs got stiff, and she moved through the trees until she could see the front of the house. The front porch was brick with tall white pillars and looked strangely out of place on the otherwise Craftsman-style home.

"How tacky," she muttered to Ellie.

Ellie stirred long enough to burble her disapproval of the architectural faux pas as headlights came into view on the road in front of the house. Laura plastered herself against a tree trunk as a sedan pulled up in front of the house. A tall form unfolded from the driver's seat and Laura gasped in spite of herself. He might be wearing a gray wig and be hunching over as if he were decades older, but there was no mistaking Nick.

His head came up sharply, almost as if he'd heard her. But surely that wasn't possible over the roar of the ocean behind him. She didn't put it past him to sense her presence, however. In her experience, people often became incredibly intuitive in high-threat situations. And there was no denying that the connection between them had always been electric.

She watched tensely as Nick approached the house. He had the good sense to walk around the house and approach it from the back, out of sight of the road. She drifted along beside him, maintaining her cover in the trees. How was he going to get in? As far as she knew, he had no particular skills in breaking and entering. She was startled when he merely stepped up to the alarm pad by the back door and entered a series of numbers. He reached for the back door and slipped inside.

Her spy within was indignant at how easily he'd gained entrance. She'd have been forced to go through a lengthy and difficult process to bypass the security system and pick the door lock. But the woman within who worried about Nick was incredibly relieved that he was safely inside.

She was just stepping clear of the woods when a quiet sound in the dark threw Laura onto full battle alert. It was a car. Coming down the road with its headlights off. Nobody with honest intentions drove around on a cloudy night on an isolated road like this with no lights. Crud. She had to let Nick know he was about to have company. She eyed the open expanse of lawn between her and the house warily.

If she was going to go, it had to be right now before the darkened car turned into the drive. She took off running as fast as she could. God bless her personal trainer for the misery he'd put her through this past month. She wasn't in the best shape of her entire life, but at least she wasn't a complete marshmallow.

She darted onto the back porch as Ellie roused, complaining about being jostled around so hard in the baby carrier.

"It's okay, sweetie. Go back to sleep," Laura soothed as she pushed open the already partially ajar door. She closed it behind her and somewhere nearby, the house's security system beeped, reactivating.

She slipped into the deep shadows of a coat room and then into a kitchen. She had to hurry. The bad guys would be here in a minute or so. "Nick!" she called out. She moved into a long hallway that led toward the front of the house. "Nick!"

He emerged from what looked like an office, looking thunderstruck. "Laura? What are you doing here?"

"Later," she bit out. "We're about to have company. The kind with guns."

Nick darted to a window to look outside. "I don't see anyone."

"They've pulled around back, then. Can we open the front door without setting off the alarm system?" she asked urgently.

"Who cares? Let's set it off. The police will be here in a few minutes and it'll chase off these bastards in the meantime."

She nodded and they stepped forward. That was when he spotted Ellie.

"You brought the baby with you?" he exclaimed incredulously.

"I'm a nursing mother, and I wasn't exactly expecting armed men to threaten us," she snapped. "Let's go. They'll be inside any second."

Nick nodded.

She nodded back and he opened the front door. A piercing alarm screeched deafeningly as they raced across the front porch. Ellie lurched against Laura's back and immediately commenced screaming at the top of her lungs. It was that special, baby-in-mortal-danger wail that absolutely demanded an instant response, and it was all Laura could do to keep running across the front yard toward Nick's car and not stop to comfort her.

A bang behind her and a simultaneous metallic ping in front of her did get an immediate reaction out of Laura, however. Someone was *shooting* at them! Ducking instinctively, she looked over her shoulder. A dark figure was coming around the corner of the house.

Out of her peripheral vision, she caught sight of a second figure coming around the other side of the house. Plus a third man entering the house…she swore mentally. She and Nick were outnumbered, which meant they were also outgunned.

The two men advanced cautiously, not shooting any more after that first volley of shots aimed at Nick's car. Then it hit her. The shooters must have disabled the vehicle so she and Nick couldn't escape. *Which meant they wanted to capture Nick.*

No! Not again! He couldn't disappear again. This time it would undoubtedly be for good. They'd capture him over her dead body. Super Mommy roared to the fore, and Laura fumbled frantically in the baby bag banging around at her side as she ran after Nick.

"Your car's dead," she panted. "Mine's that way."

He veered in the direction she pointed and sprinted for the woods with her on his heels.

Her fingers frantically identified objects inside the baby bag. Bottle. Diaper ointment. Pacifier. Dammit, where was her gun? Finally, she felt its cold weight and yanked it clear of the fabric bag. She and Nick gained the edge of the woods and slowed down to navigate the heavy underbrush. Thankfully, Ellie had fallen mostly silent. Nick held back a jumble of vines for her and she slipped past him. She turned to face their pursuers. The pair of men were advancing slowly, now, weapons held out in front of them in grips that looked entirely too competent for Laura's comfort.

"My car's through the woods," she whispered urgently. "That way."

Nick whispered back, "You go first. I'll go behind you. That way if they shoot at us they'll hit me and not Ellie."

"Take my pistol."

He reached under his coat. "I have one. Keep yours."

Where in the heck had he gotten a hold of a gun? Did he even know how to use the thing? She eyed him in dismay but was relieved to see him holding it in a reasonable grip. They might just get out of this alive, after all. If they could keep Ellie quiet so she wouldn't give their position away.

Nick moved close as they crept forward cautiously. He crooned to Ellie, "Hush, sweetheart. Be an angel for Daddy."

How he could be so cool with armed men chasing them, she had no idea. Shockingly, his calm tone seemed to mollify the baby and she quieted completely.

"That's my brave girl," Nick continued to murmur.

Laura looked back over her shoulder. The pair of men had been joined by a third and they were moving cautiously in this direction. She and Nick needed a diversion. Something dramatic. She dug around in the baby bag until she felt the steel cylinder of a silencer. She screwed it onto her weapon, assumed a shooter's stance, took careful aim and fired at the gaudy chandelier on the front porch. It exploded spectacularly, glass shattering in all directions, and the three men ducked at the abrupt noise behind them.

Laura sprinted like a madwoman through the woods with Nick panting right on her heels as they dodged left and right around trees. Shots rang out behind them. Thankfully, in the real world, most people couldn't hit the broad side of the barn when they were running themselves and aiming at another fast-moving target.

Bark flew nearby. Uh-oh. It didn't look like their pursuers were shooting to take out tires anymore. That looked like a shot aimed to kill.

Waaaaaah! Ellie let out a renewed scream.

Laura fumbled through the contents of the bag desperately, as she ran, seeking the familiar shape of the pacifier. Ammo clip. Bottle. Diapers. No pacifier!

Bingo. A soft rubber nipple. Laura yanked it out as she ducked under a low branch. She stumbled as her foot slid off a half-rotted log buried in the leaves, staggered left and barely managed to right herself. But she'd dropped the all-important pacifier. She paused a precious second to look around. Thank God. White plastic caught her eye. Laura pounced on it and took off running once more.

The men behind them were close enough for her to hear their heavy breathing. At this range, they might actually hit a moving target. She put on a terrified burst of speed, zigzagging like a rabbit fleeing for its life.

Ellie's screaming took on a rhythmic quality as the baby was jostled by Laura's steps. No way were they going to escape their pursuers until the child quit giving away their position like this. They needed to turn this into a stealth exercise.

More gunshots rang out behind them. Nick swore behind Laura. "Hurry," he grunted. "That was close."

Desperate, she wiped the pacifier on her shirt and

stabbed backward over her shoulder. She was so going to mommy hell already for putting her child in the line of fire, she supposed giving her a dirty pacifier wouldn't make matters much worse. But what choice did she have? It was that or die.

Miraculously, she hit Ellie's mouth, and even more miraculously, the infant took the pacifier, sucking it angrily. Laura slowed, ducking into an area of thick brush. Nick followed closely, helping her lift brambles aside as they crept forward. Male voices called back and forth behind them. Apparently, their pursuers had lost sight of them. Hallelujah.

She pointed off to their left in the direction she thought the car was, assuming she wasn't completely disoriented out here in the pitch-black night and bewildering tangle of trees and undergrowth, and Nick veered that direction.

They burst out of the trees as a dirt road opened up before them. "This way," she gasped. The car's blessed bulk came into sight and she nearly sobbed in relief. Nick hung back a little, still protecting Ellie with his body as Laura used the last of her strength to tear toward the vehicle.

"I'll drive," Nick called out low behind her.

Like any good field operative, she'd left the doors unlocked and the key fob inside the vehicle. She dived for the passenger door and flung herself inside awkwardly, half-lying across the front seat so she wouldn't crush Ellie, while Nick leaped into the driver's seat and punched the ignition button. He wasted no time throwing the vehicle into gear and stomping on the gas. The car jumped forward.

Shots behind them announced that the bad guys had reached the road. The car squealed around a curve and the shooting behind them stopped.

"They'll follow us," Nick announced.

"Then drive like a bat out of hell," she panted back.

While he commenced doing just that, she wriggled out of the backpack and half-climbed over the backseat to strap Ellie, red-faced and furious, into her car seat. Laura wiped the pacifier off as best she could, and offered it to the baby once more. Yup. Mommy hell for her. But sometimes a mommy had to do what a mommy had to do. And given that they were careening along a twisting dirt road at something like seventy miles per hour, she wasn't about to unstrap the infant and try to nurse her.

Nick muttered, white knuckled, "Mother of God, Laura, what are you doing here with Ellie?"

"Saving your life, apparently. Where did you learn to drive like this?"

"I'm told I did some Formula One racing in my previous life."

"Had a death wish, did you?"

"Something like that."

"Have you got more ammunition?" he asked.

Right. Because every prepared mommy hauled around extra ammunition along with spare diapers and a change of clothes for baby. She dug into the bottom of the baby bag for spare clips. She came up with two full fourteen-shot clips and counted back fast to the firefight in her head. "I've got nine shots in my weapon now and twenty-eight more here."

He nodded tersely. "I've got five shots left. I don't have spare clips. It was all I could do to buy an unregistered gun without getting arrested, let alone acquiring extra clips for it."

Ellie was finally subsiding. Laura smiled at the vigorous sucking noises coming from the car seat. It was good to know her daughter had spunk when provoked.

"Where does this road go?" Nick asked.

"I have no idea. There's not a straight road on the entire Cape. My suggestion is we keep driving until we get to some road the GPS recognizes."

He nodded tersely. "How did you find me?"

"Carter Tatum found out William Ward was your attorney. When we discovered he'd been killed, I figured it couldn't be a coincidence. Clearly, he had something the people out to get you want. Which meant you were bound to come looking for it, too. So, I staked out Ward's house and waited for you to show up."

"You know me too well."

She shrugged. "Lucky guess."

Nick smiled wryly. "Luck had nothing to do with it. I always knew you were brilliant."

"Are you going to let me use that brilliance to help you, now?"

He sighed. "I wanted to keep you out of this. I knew it could get dangerous, and I didn't want you or the kids to get hurt."

She winced at the faint note of reproach in his voice. He was right. She'd been an idiot to put Ellie in danger. But she'd only expected a nice, quiet stake-out. As soon as they were safe, she'd make other arrangements for the baby.

"I appreciate the sentiment, Nick, but it's time to let me help you. I'm good at this sort of thing, and I want my children's father alive." She carefully avoided adding that she wanted her lover alive, too. She had no idea whether or not he planned to remain with her now that his true identity was out in the open.

The dirt road abruptly intersected a paved road. Nick turned west and in a moment the GPS popped up a road map. They followed the residential street for a mile or so and turned onto a larger road. As Nick accelerated into the desultory traffic, she watched carefully in the rearview mirror for any sign of followers. No lights or cars were hanging behind them acting like tails.

They'd made it.

Her hands started to shake, and then her whole body got into the act. Nick glanced over at her in concern. "Are you okay?" he asked.

"No, I'm *not* okay. Would you care to tell me why those men just tried to kidnap you again?"

Nick frowned. "It looked to me like they were trying to kill us."

She shook her head in the negative. "They didn't shoot at you when you were running across the lawn. They only fired at your car. They didn't want you to leave, but they didn't want you dead. In the woods, only a few of the shots came anywhere near us, and I think those were mistakes. They were trying to scare us into surrendering but definitely weren't trying to kill you. Which means someone wants you alive. I can only infer that means someone wants something from you."

Her declaration put a heavy frown on Nick's handsome features.

She continued, "Why weren't you killed six years ago? Why the elaborate kidnapping instead? I'll bet that's the same reason those men weren't trying to kill you tonight." Lord, it felt good to finally ask the question. "What's going *on,* Nick?"

Chapter 7

Nick sighed. Laura, of all people, deserved answers. Answers he was far from having, however. "I truly don't remember anything of those five years. I swear," he stated.

Laura nodded and crossed her arms expectantly, announcing silently that she wasn't going to back off this time. Her child had just been put in mortal danger, and she was at the end of her prodigious patience. Not that he blamed her. He just hoped she'd forgive him when she heard the entire, sordid tale. Although, it wasn't like he forgave himself.

He picked up the story reluctantly. "That trip I took a few days ago was to Boston to pay a visit to my old attorney, William Ward. It turned out he was able to fill in some pertinent details of the two years prior to my kidnapping."

When Laura opened her mouth to ask about it, he raised a hand gently for her to let him continue. She nodded and subsided.

"I'll fill you in on that in a minute. The morning after my face got splashed all over the news, William called me. He said he had important information to show me. He insisted I come up to his house on the Cape immediately."

"What was it?" Laura blurted.

"I don't know."

Her hopeful expression fell.

"But when we get somewhere safe, I have a flash drive in my pocket that I took from the secret drawer in William's desk. I'm hoping it'll give us some answers."

"How did you know about his house's security code, not to mention this secret drawer?"

He made a face. "William was practically a second father to me. I spent a lot of time with him and his wife on the cape. He represented me when I turned eighteen and took over Spiros Shipping. He's been my attorney ever since."

"Who do you think killed him?"

"I have no idea."

Laura mulled things over, and Nick let her. In his experience, she was eminently reasonable when left to her own devices to figure a thing out. He only prayed that reason led her to accept his words as truth.

They were off the Cape and approaching Boston proper before she finally asked soberly, "Why do you think someone killed your lawyer?"

"I can think of about a billion reasons," he answered grimly.

She nodded in agreement. "I've been reading on the internet about the sale of Spiros Shipping after you dropped out of sight. I'm assuming someone faked your permission and sold it out from under you?"

"I don't know if they coerced me into signing something

or just forged my signature. I can't imagine ever giving anyone permission to sell the family business."

"Who hated you enough to steal your business?"

He briefly considered pulling off the road to address her question but decided she'd be less likely to attack him if he were at the wheel of a moving car with her and Ellie in it. He answered carefully, "When you arrived at William Ward's house, I was browsing through the most recent documents on his computer."

"And?" she prompted cautiously.

"And it turns out that shortly before I met you in Paris, I took a secret trip to Las Vegas." Laura went still. She must see it coming. He continued grimly, "I wasn't alone on that trip. It turns out I was secretly married there to a woman named Meredith Black." The name felt strange on his tongue. Vaguely unpleasant, like the remembered taste of bitter medicine.

If Laura had been still before, she went statuelike now. Alarmed, he alternated between glancing over at her and keeping an eye on the highway.

Finally, he couldn't stand the suspense of her complete nonreaction any longer. "Talk to me," he urged.

"What do you want me to say?" Laura's voice was hollow. Hoarse. Unlike how he'd ever heard it before. Guilt and self-loathing consumed him. He'd caused the woman he loved this pain.

He spoke in a rush. "I swear. I have no recollection of her whatsoever. I don't know why I married her, and I surely don't know why I got involved with you in Paris so soon afterward. I can only assume the marriage was an impulsive thing and didn't work out. Maybe I was drunk and it was all a big joke."

"A joke?" Laura choked out.

"A really, really bad one?" he offered. Based on the

thunderous frown settling on her brow, Laura clearly failed to see the humor. He didn't blame her.

He drove in silence while guilt and misery ate at his gut from the inside out. It was his worst nightmare come true. Something—someone—out of his past had the power to destroy everything he and Laura had built between them, including their happy little family. He'd contact this Meredith Black woman and get a divorce. The woman could have whatever financial resources had been left to Nikolas Spiros. He'd make it all better.

But then Laura asked, "Why hasn't she come forward or contacted you now that your face is being splashed all over the news?"

"Maybe she hasn't heard about me."

Laura snorted. "You're an international sensation. The playboy billionaire back from a mysterious, six-year absence. She'd have to be living in a cave not to have heard about you."

He frowned. Laura was right. Why hadn't this Meredith person contacted him? Or had she? Was she the urgent reason William Ward had insisted on him coming to the Cape to discuss?

"Did she have control of your financial assets while you were gone?" Laura asked.

"I don't know. Possibly."

"Then your return would throw a serious monkey wrench into her life. You'd be a massive problem for her."

He laughed with scant humor. "Gee. Thanks."

"Sorry. Just trying to think like my enemy."

Warmth burst in his gut. If Laura considered Meredith her enemy, he almost felt sorry for the woman. But not quite.

Laura made an angry sound under her breath. He'd bet

she wasn't even aware of having made it. Her unconscious loyalty warmed him all the way down to his soul.

"You truly have no recollection of her whatsoever?"

"None."

"Convenient," Laura muttered.

Alarmed, he glanced over at her. "I'm telling you the truth. I have no idea why I married her."

"She must be hell on wheels in the sack," Laura commented sourly.

Nick laughed. "I'll take you any day of the week and twice on Sunday over any other woman on the planet in that department."

Laura threw him a vaguely skeptical look. "The thirty-year-old mother of two with a body under attack by gravity and who needs a slave driver of a personal trainer to keep her even remotely non-jiggly these days?"

"Yes. Exactly," he replied firmly.

She didn't look convinced.

He swore mentally. Just how much damage control did he have ahead of him to convince Laura that, in spite of this wife, *she* was the love of his life?

"Could your wife be behind tonight's kidnapping attempt?"

The idea shocked him into silence.

Laura continued, "But why?"

"She wants to renew our vows?" he quipped.

"Not funny," Laura retorted.

He sighed. "I imagine she wants to aggressively renegotiate control of my estate."

"With a gun pointed at your head?"

"Precisely."

"Bitch," Laura breathed under her breath.

Nick laughed quietly. "My sentiments exactly."

"What are you going to do?"

"Give her whatever she wants to divorce me."

"She has probably taken almost everything you own already."

He shrugged. "I'm not concerned about the money. I can always make more. I just want to get away with my life and my soul intact. I refuse to live always looking over my shoulder, worried that she might come after you and the kids someday."

Laura's expression snapped closed. Unreadable. Stubborn enough to give him a severe and unpleasant jolt. "Are we okay?" he blurted.

"No, Nick. We're not okay. You're married to another woman. You knew who you were and didn't tell me. And now your past has put not only you, but me and Ellie, in danger."

He nodded slowly. He couldn't blame her for feeling any of that. But there was also no way he was giving up on them. He'd fight to the death to keep her and the kids.

They drove in heavy silence to his hotel and he led her up to his room. He'd just fished William's flash drive out of his pocket to plug into his laptop when Laura's cell phone rang. He frowned. It was nearly 2 a.m. Who'd call her at this time of night? Was it Adam, waking up from a nightmare and needing his mother's voice to comfort him? Guilt at tearing Laura away from their son speared through him.

But then he heard a shrill female voice babbling through the line and Laura's face drained of all color. Panic unlike anything he'd ever experienced before, including the moments after he first woke up in his box, ripped through him. Adam. Oh, God. What had happened to his son?

Laura was going to throw up. "What have you done?" she gasped in a horrible, unrecognizable voice at Nick.

She shoved past him and ran for the toilet in the tiny connected bathroom.

"What happened? What's going on?" Nick demanded right on her heels. "Whatever I've done, I'll fix it. I swear."

"They've kidnapped him," she sobbed. "Adam and Lisbet are gone. Marta was drugged and just woke up. The police are at the house and the FBI's been called." Her stomach rebelled then, and she emptied what little she'd had for dinner into the toilet.

Ice-cold terror washed over Nick's face. "Is there a ransom note?"

"No." Laura splashed cold water on her face. It didn't do a thing to drive back the nausea washing through her. She rinsed her mouth and headed into the bedroom.

"What else did Marta say?" Nick demanded.

"That's it. Adam and his nanny are gone. There are signs of a struggle in the playroom. Lisbet must have put up a fight. The kidnappers have a six-hour head start and could be anywhere by now."

She couldn't stand still and moved around the room searching it frantically for she knew not what. Nick finally caught her in his arms and held her board-stiff body tightly against his until the worst of her panic passed.

"They've got my baby," she wailed. "He must be so scared. If they hurt him—" she broke off on a sob "—oh, God."

"I'll kill Meredith if she's behind this," Nick gritted out.

Laura was swinging back and forth between terror and rage so fast she could hardly keep up with it. She gazed up at Nick with tears streaming down her cheeks. "What do we do?"

He gripped her shoulders tightly and stared into her stricken gaze, clearly willing her to hold it together. "We fight. We do whatever it takes to find him and get him back safe and sound."

Under his hands, she squared her shoulders. "You're right. Nobody's messing with my baby and getting away with it." Death dripped in her voice. Super Mommy had just gone over to the dark side. Whoever'd kidnapped Adam was going to pay in blood. She *would* find her son and get him back.

Perceptive as ever, Ellie started to fuss in the crib in the corner.

Nick suggested, "You take care of Ellie. I'll make the arrangements to get back home."

Laura nodded and stumbled to the crib the hotel had sent up while Nick called the airport and hired a private jet to take them back to Washington with all possible haste.

Nick joined her in the bedroom. "A plane will be ready in an hour. We've got about twenty minutes before we have to leave for the airport. The concierge will have a taxi waiting for us downstairs."

Ellie's tiny body snuggling tightly against hers calmed Laura enough that she could begin to think rationally. When the baby had fallen asleep in her arms, she said quietly, "I'm not entirely sure your wife is behind this. At least not directly."

"Why's that?" Nick asked in surprise over his shoulder as he threw his things into his suitcase.

"If she was involved in your original kidnapping, surely she was told when you were rescued. Which means she's had a year to react to your escape. Why this, why now?"

"If she was involved with my kidnapping, then she'd have known I suffered a memory loss. If I didn't come forward for a year, she might have figured I was never going to identify myself as Nikolas Spiros."

"Either way," Laura reasoned aloud, "she had no reason

to believe you were ever coming back. Why would she have planned an elaborate kidnapping of your son? Because believe me—nobody got through my house's security without some serious planning."

Nick made a rueful face. "Maybe she found out I'd visited my old attorney and figured I was going to make a run at getting my company back."

Laura thought aloud. "Okay. She had a motive to grab Adam. But still. Just a few days to hire a kidnapper, get him in place, find your son, figure out how to get past my estate's formidable security, and execute a kidnapping? That's just not plausible."

"Who else could it be?"

She answered grimly, "It's not like you and I don't have other enemies. What about AbaCo? Could they be trying to blackmail you into not testifying against them?"

Fury glittered in Nick's gaze. "They most certainly have experience with kidnapping and the personnel to pull one off on short notice. And they know you and the children are my life. But going after a child? Those bastards…" His voice trailed off as he choked on his fury.

She knew the feeling. "The trial starts next week. If they have Adam, we're going to have to find him fast."

"I know just the person to ask if AbaCo has Adam."

"Who?"

"AbaCo's CEO."

"Werner Kloffman?" Laura echoed. "Where on earth would we find him? High-profile people like him tend to move around the globe and don't exactly advertise their whereabouts."

"What do you want to bet he's in Washington pulling strings and trying to get the government to drop its case against his company?"

"Good point. If you'll step aside and give me access to

your laptop, MysteryMom needs to contact a few strategically placed people within the government."

"MysteryMom?" Nick asked.

"That's my email handle when I'm doing work for DaddyFinders, Inc. I built up a pretty decent informant network over my years of searching for you."

He looked at her soberly. "I am eternally grateful you never gave up on me. You and I won't give up on Adam, either. We'll find him."

A sob threatened to erupt from her chest, but she shoved it down. Her baby boy needed Super Mommy firing on all cylinders right now.

Nick must have sensed her momentary weakness because he said encouragingly, "Lisbet's with him. She'll protect him as fiercely as you would."

She nodded gamely, refraining from suggesting that Lisbet might very well be dead and out of the picture by now. She knew all too well how important it was not to dwell on the negative, but instead to focus on hope and determination and keep moving forward.

Nick's arms came around her. She clung to him tightly. Despite the unresolved problems between them, they were united in purpose when it came to retrieving their son. And that was all that mattered for now.

She disentangled herself from his arms and headed for Nick's laptop computer.

Nick woke up as gray dawn crept around the jet's window blinds, surprised that he'd managed to catch a nap. Fear for Adam slammed into him moments after his eyes blinked open, so heavy on his chest that he could hardly breathe. He tossed and turned in the uncomfortable airplane seat, tearing himself apart with guilt over having brought this danger to his son. Thankfully, Laura was asleep stretched out across several seats and Ellie was crashed in a playpen. He slipped out of his seat and tiptoed over to check on Ellie. The poor baby'd had a rough night last night and was sleeping deeply.

This aircraft was equipped with Wi-Fi, and he used it to connect his laptop to the internet and check the morning news. The gossip sites were having a field day over his return to the public eye. Even serious news outlets were commenting freely on the status of the Spiros fortune now that Nikolas Spiros was back. Analysts were speculating gleefully on whether he would attempt to seize control of his company from the German firm that had owned it for the past half-dozen years.

A limousine met them at the airport when they landed and whisked them south to Laura's estate in Virginia. The mansion was crawling with police and FBI investigators who had frustratingly little information to share about Adam and Lisbet's disappearance. The FBI kidnapping expert on scene seemed alarmed by the lack of a ransom note.

When Laura pushed the fellow to speculate on who'd taken her son, the FBI man hinted that perhaps whoever'd taken Adam didn't feel a need to leave a note but felt the message was loud and clear enough without one.

Nick's jaw tightened grimly. Which was a fancy way of the guy saying he thought AbaCo had Adam and that the kidnapper's intent was clear—stop the child's father from testifying against the company.

It didn't help matters that, by midafternoon, the estate's front gate was crowded with luridly curious reporters. The FBI had felt it would be best to go public with the story, plastering the news with pictures of Adam and putting the public on notice to look out for the little boy. It was a close call to say who hated the media attention more—him or

Laura. Both of them were stretched to the breaking point by the lack of progress and the feeling of being trapped in their own home.

Finally, as they picked at the sandwiches a red-eyed Marta put in front of them, Laura's laptop beeped to indicate an incoming message. She leaped from her seat to check it.

"It's for MysteryMom," she said tersely as she opened the message. Instinct had warned her not to reveal all her sources to the FBI team that had invaded their home. She'd kept her MysteryMom identity and email account to herself since the FBI was monitoring all her phones and other email accounts. Nick moved to her side quickly. The message, short and to the point, popped up. Kloffman is borrowing a home from friends at the following address. A posh street in the Washington, D.C. suburb, Old Town Alexandria, was named. The message was not signed. Not that he cared who had sent it, other than to want to thank the person someday…after Adam was safe.

Laura murmured under her breath, "We'll have to sneak out past the FBI and the police."

He nodded slightly. "I'll engage them in conversation while you make arrangements for Ellie."

He went downstairs and didn't engage in conversation as much as he threw a tantrum, demanding that the law enforcement agencies *do* something. Personally, he understood that they had no leads to go on and their hands were tied until the kidnapper made the next move. But he kept that opinion to himself as he ranted and generally forced everyone's attention onto him while Laura had a quiet word with Marta about watching Ellie for the night and milk in the freezer.

Laura slipped into the living room and made eye contact with him. He allowed her to talk him down off his fake ledge and the police were more than happy to let the two of them retire upstairs to the privacy of their suite.

"Are we good to go?" he asked Laura when the door shut behind her.

"Yes."

He eyed the black turtleneck and slacks she'd laid out on the bed. "I gather you're planning to break into the guy's house?" he asked doubtfully.

"Do you have a better idea?" she demanded.

"Actually, yes." He headed for her closet and pulled out an elegant linen sheath dress, silk stockings, fashionable stilettos, and an expensive pearl necklace. "Put these on. And do up your makeup and hair to the hilt."

"What do you have in mind?"

"Let's knock on his front door. Or more precisely, you knock on the front door. He won't think twice about opening the door for a woman who looks like you. Once he's got the door open, I'll join you. If we have to force our way in after that, so be it. But I bet he doesn't put up a fight. He's a businessman, not a thug."

"You're probably right. I'm not thinking all that clearly right now." She glanced at him gratefully, and the spark of warmth in her eyes shot through him like a lightning bolt. Even in the midst of this crisis, she attracted him like no other woman.

She was authorized to be off her A-game. It was no surprise she'd fall back on her old CIA habits in a situation like this. But he knew life as a CEO. And if a beautiful, elegant woman showed up at his front door, he'd have let her in.

Laura dressed quickly and came back into the sitting room looking like a million bucks. Her flesh impact hit him like a physical blow. "You're a hell of a woman," he murmured.

"I'm a freaked-out mommy."

"Stay strong, sweetheart. For Adam."

She nodded and stepped close, leaning against him. They stood together quietly for a moment.

"Ready?" he murmured.

"Let's do it."

It was ridiculously easy to sneak out of their house. Laura knew every detail of the security system and made easy work of slipping past it. They pushed his BMW out of the garage in neutral and let it roll down the slight hill behind the house until it was out of sight of the mansion. Only then did Nick start the engine and guide the vehicle toward the back gate.

The trip to the Virginia suburbs of D.C. went quickly. Laura was grim and silent beside him. She definitely had her Super Mommy game face on.

The GPS efficiently led them to an elegantly restored row house in the heart of Old Town. Nick pulled into a driveway a few houses down and turned off the engine. He murmured, "You go first and I'll lurk in the bushes until Kloffman has opened the door."

Laura nodded coldly. Super Mommy was in full grizzly-bear mode. Satisfaction coursed through him. AbaCo's senior leadership had coming whatever Laura could dish out and then some.

He followed her to the front porch and crouched beside the lush rhododendrons flanking the front steps. She rang the bell and stepped back so she'd be in plain sight through the door's peephole.

The door opened.

Laura pitched her voice in a sexy contralto. "Mr. Kloffman? I work for the United States government. Do you have a few minutes to speak with me?"

"Of course. Please come in."

Bingo. Show time.

Chapter 8

Laura was surprised at how easily it all came back to her—the technical skill, intense focus, the cold calm. Her mindset also included absolute willingness to do whatever violence was necessary to find and rescue her son.

As she passed through the front door, she placed her shoe strategically in front of the wood panel. Nick materialized behind her and had slipped inside before Kloffman was even aware of the man behind her.

"Who in the hell are you?" Kloffman growled as he caught sight of Nick.

"My name's Nikolas Spiros, Herr Kloffman."

The German spluttered, looking back and forth between the two of them. "You! I thought I recognized you. You're that Delaney woman."

"That's correct," Laura answered grimly. "We need to chat, sir."

"How dare you? How did you find me? I want my lawyer."

"This isn't that kind of chat, Werner," Nick said in an entirely too pleasant tone of voice. "Shall we step into the living room?"

The German must have sensed the threat underlying Nick's words and moved without comment into an antique-filled parlor. A thrill coursed through her at the danger in Nick's voice. She remembered sharply why she'd been attracted to him in the first place. It had been this sense of sexy risk that had clung to him.

Kloffman sank down in a wingback chair and stared defiantly at the two of them.

"So here's the deal, Werner," Laura said reasonably. "We're going to ask you a series of questions. If you give us the right answers, we'll leave and not bother you again. If you give us the wrong answers, you are going to have a very long night. We'd like to keep this civilized, but we are under no obligation to do so. Understood?"

Kloffman swore under his breath in German. "I know who you are. I'll see you both in jail for this."

Nick shrugged. "Panicked parents politely question the man most likely to have kidnapped their son, and you think any jury in the world is going to do more than slap our wrists?"

"I didn't kidnap your son!"

"Of course you didn't," she replied smoothly. "The same way you didn't kidnap Nick. Your flunkies did it for you. Plausible deniability is important for a man in your position, is it not?"

He shrugged, obviously aware that answering the question couldn't help his cause.

"Surely you knew about Nick's kidnapping and the kidnappings of dozens of other people who were held aboard your ships. It must have been a profitable little side business. What were you getting for your special guest service? A million dollars a year per prisoner? More?"

Nick stiffened beside her. His rage was palpable at being in the presence of the man who very likely was the kingpin behind his kidnapping.

"Care to comment on who paid to have Nick kidnapped?" she asked without warning.

Kloffman's gaze darted back and forth between them. He definitely knew something he wasn't sharing with them.

"His loving wife, perhaps?" Laura snapped.

"I have no idea." Kloffman's eyes slid down and to the left, a sure tell that he was lying.

Laura leaned in close. "Was it her? Yes or no."

"No." Another glance at the floor and a jump of the pulse pounding in his temple.

She looked up at Nick grimly. "At least that mystery's solved. It was your bitch of a wife." She looked back down at Kloffman. "Where's our son?"

"Why would I kidnap some child?" Kloffman demanded angrily. "I'm not a monster."

"Five years in a box on one of your ships says that's not true," Nick snarled.

Kloffman subsided, glaring belligerently.

Laura spoke grimly. "The fact remains that no one but you has both the means and the motive to kidnap our son and pressure Nick not to testify against your firm. AbaCo's going down in flames next week and Nick is the spark that's going to ignite the firestorm."

Kloffman smiled coldly. "AbaCo is by no means going down in flames. Quite the contrary."

A chill passed down her spine. The German was entirely too sure of himself for her comfort. He should be sweating bullets if he was involved in Adam's kidnapping. But instead, he was sitting here as smug as could be, actually smirking at her.

She pulled out her pistol, and it had the desired effect on Kloffman. He paled. She spoke grimly. "Convince me why I should believe that you and AbaCo had nothing to do with our son's disappearance."

Kloffman's lips pressed tightly shut and she leaned forward, caressing his cheek with the barrel of the weapon. Her voice was velvet. "You see, Herr Kloffman. I'm a mother. And if something bad happens to my baby boy, I'm not going to give a damn whether or not I live or die. It won't matter to me one bit if I rot in jail for the rest of my life. So I have nothing to lose by putting a bullet through your knee—or through your head."

Kloffman began to tremble and a fat bead of sweat ran down the side of his face. Now he was getting into the proper spirit of things.

"I swear. I had nothing to do with your son's kidnapping."

Nick replied tersely, "Convince us you and your goons didn't do it."

Kloffman stammered, "I'm sure nobody in the firm would do such a thing without my approval."

Nick leaped all over that. "So you're admitting that no major black ops happen at AbaCo without your knowledge?"

"Are you kidding?"

Kloffman looked like he'd blurted that out without thinking. He fell silent and a thoughtful look entered his eyes. She gave him as long as he wanted to work through whatever was on his mind. Nick also looked inclined to let the man stew in his thoughts for the time being.

Eventually, Kloffman said heavily, "Many things happen

without my knowledge at AbaCo. I'm purely a figurehead around there."

Laura stared. The statement had a definite ring of truth to it. The guy was a figurehead? "Who's the real power at AbaCo, then?"

Kloffman glared at Nick. "As Ms. Delaney put it so succinctly, a cabal of criminals put in place by your bitch of a wife."

"Can you prove that?" Laura demanded.

"Why should I?" Kloffman shot back.

She considered him carefully. "Because I'll hold you responsible for kidnapping my son and kill you if you don't?"

He let out an exasperated sigh. "Look. They pay me a small fortune to be the public face of AbaCo. But I'm not about to go down in flames, as you say, for all the activities they're into."

Nick leaped on that right away. "What else is AbaCo up to besides human trafficking?"

Kloffman snorted. "That's the tip of the iceberg."

Laura had no trouble believing that. "Again, I ask if you have any proof."

"Why should I hand any of it over to you?"

Nick asked reasonably, "Who else would you give it to? If you were going to hand it over to the U.S. government, you'd have done it before now—when it became clear the feds are going to come after AbaCo with everything they've got in the upcoming trial. But you saw what Meredith's goons did to me. I think you're afraid to cross her. And rightly so, by the way."

Nick was doing an excellent job of playing good cop. Which left her to play bad cop.

She leaned forward. "Don't be stupid, Werner. I have the gun, and I won't hesitate to use it."

The German looked back and forth between them. "Let me make a phone call to inquire about your boy."

She considered briefly. Why not? What could it hurt? She nodded and allowed the man to pull out a cell phone. He put it on speaker and laid it on the coffee table in front of him before hitting a speed dial number.

Nick commented as a man's voice came on the line, "I speak fluent German."

She threw him a grateful look. That could prove immensely helpful.

Kloffman nodded irritably at them. "Klaus. It's Kloffman. Did you hear that Nick Cass's boy was kidnapped?"

"It's all over the news," a heavily accented voice replied in English. "Serves the bastard right."

Kloffman asked, "Do you know anything about it that could implicate AbaCo?"

"No." The guy sounded genuinely surprised. "We had no such orders. Besides, everyone would suspect us right away. We're not that stupid. Just do what you were sent to Washington to do and stay out of things that don't concern you."

Laura was surprised by the scorn in this Klaus guy's voice. That didn't sound anything at all like the respect due a genuine CEO. She glanced over at Nick and he was frowning, too. Apparently, Werner was telling the truth about being a figurehead.

"I'm sorry to bother you, Klaus."

The German ended the call. "Satisfied?" Kloffman spit out.

She answered, "Not yet."

"Look. I have children of my own. I would not hurt your son." As her gaze hardened, he added in desperation, "Why would I kidnap your boy? The trial's going to be stopped anyway."

Laura started, and it was Nick who leaned forward and said smoothly, "Who did you cut the deal with, Werner?"

"The CIA."

Laura was stunned. Her own agency had sold her out?

Thankfully, Nick didn't miss a beat and nodded beside her. "Of course. I'll bet you've held a few prisoners for the agency, maybe given them a heads-up where certain shipments were headed. You scratch their back, and now you've called in the favor and forced them to scratch yours."

"Exactly," Kloffman exclaimed, obviously relieved that Nick was on the same page. "In another day or two, the federal prosecutors will announce that national security could be compromised by proceeding with the case, and all charges will be quietly dropped. I have no need to kidnap your boy to silence you."

Then why did Meredith and the shadow operators at AbaCo go after Adam? Petty revenge? The question still remained as to how they'd managed to move so fast against her heavily defended estate. It just didn't add up in Laura's gut. She was missing something major, here.

Nick, bless him, was carrying the conversation while her mind stayed frustratingly blank. He asked the German, "When will the announcement be made stopping the trial?"

"Two days from now."

Laura's heart sank. If AbaCo was behind his kidnapping, they had two days before Adam's life became irrelevant to his kidnappers. How were they ever going to find him in so little time? Worse, if the trial was dead in the water, she and Nick had no leverage whatsoever to force this man to help them find Adam. Unless…

She leaned forward. "Werner, here's the deal. Even if the trial is halted, Nick and I aren't going to stop. We're going to go public with everything we have on your company. We'll use the media to full advantage, and with what we've got on AbaCo, we'll destroy the company. In fact, we can probably do a more effective job of ruining it without the constraints of a trial to tie our hands. Do you believe me?"

Kloffman stared at her for several long seconds. Finally, he said heavily, "What's it going to take to stop you from doing that?"

He might be a figurehead, but he undoubtedly liked his paycheck. He also seemed to understand that, as the figurehead, he'd be the sacrificial lamb.

Nick replied gently, "Save yourself, Werner. You don't strike me as a bad type. Don't let Meredith and her cronies drag you down with them."

"How?" Werner snapped. "Who'll believe me?"

"Why wouldn't people believe you?" Nick asked. "I'm living proof that someone at AbaCo is up to no good. And there are others who have been victims of the company."

Werner shook his head. "You don't understand. It's not about the prisoners they keep. It's about the cargo."

Nick glanced at her. Werner seemed inclined to talk to Nick, so she nodded subtly at him to take the lead. "What about the cargo?" Nick asked.

"AbaCo has become the freight carrier of choice for every nefarious group you can think of—drug lords, weapons dealers, terrorists, slavers, illegal lumber smugglers, you name it."

Nick paled beside her. It had to be painful to hear that his family's firm had fallen so far. "Do you have proof?" he asked hoarsely.

Kloffman hesitated one last time, and then he capitulated all in a rush. "I've been collecting it for years. Bit by bit. I had to be careful. But I've got cargo manifests, incriminating emails from customers, shipping documents, even financial records."

"Why haven't you taken it to the authorities before now?" Nick queried.

"What authorities?" Kloffman answered bitterly. "The same ones who are also using AbaCo to do their dirty work? How do you think the CIA gets weapons and supplies to the various regimes Uncle Sam can't publicly support?"

The three of them fell silent.

Laura eventually broke the silence. "Who within the company does the dirty work?"

"The Special Cargo division," Kloffman answered promptly.

That made sense. The people on trial for kidnapping Nick came out of that group. But the Feds had been combing through that division's records for most of the past year and not found anything to indicate that AbaCo was engaging in widespread criminal activity.

"Do you have access to their real records, then?" Laura asked curiously.

Kloffman nodded eagerly. "I've been copying everything for the past three years." He added sourly, "They didn't even bother to restrict my access to the accounts. They think I'm too stupid to notice what they're up to."

Nick made a commiserating sound, and Werner shared an aggrieved look with him. Nick really was incredible at garnering empathy and trust from the German. He asked gently, "Do you have copies of these records with you? If you wouldn't mind sharing them with us, I swear to you we'll see they fall into the right hands."

Kloffman reared back sharply. "No way. They'll kill me."

No need to ask who "they" was. Nick said soothingly, "Not if they don't know who the source of the leak was. I give you my word of honor we won't reveal where or who we got the information from."

Kloffman didn't look convinced. Laura spoke quietly. "Somebody has kidnapped our son. He's six years old. And he's going to die if we don't find him. Soon. Please help us, Herr Kloffman. I promise we'll help you."

He nodded slowly. "I will give you everything I have. Maybe you can find something about your boy."

Laura rose to her feet eagerly and Nick did the same.

"I'm sorry, but I don't have the files with me. I keep them in a safe place."

As would she in the same situation. So. It was going to require a leap of faith on their part, too. "Of course, Herr Kloffman. How soon can you get us a copy?"

"Twenty-four hours, maybe."

A whole day? Her gut twisted in dismay. But it wasn't like she had any choice in the matter. "Please hurry." Desperation crept into her voice. "He's so little...."

Kloffman squeezed her elbow reassuringly. "I shall do what I can to help, *Fraulein*."

She nodded, too choked up to say any more. Nick quietly traded contact information with the German and then guided her to the front door.

"A word of advice, Kloffman," Nick commented as he reached for the doorknob. "Convince whoever's actually running the show to sell off the pre-1970 ships before you have a major accident. Dump the Euro debt and invest in new, Norwegian-built, fast ships."

Kloffman stared. "I beg your pardon?"

Nick shrugged. "Spiros Shipping has been in my family for three generations. And it's being run into the ground. Stop thinking about short-term profit and look to the future before you destroy my company."

The German stared, flummoxed. “Assuming I still have a job in a week, I’ll try.”

“Thank you for your help, Herr Kloffman,” Nick said soberly as he opened the front door. “We are in your debt.”

Out of reflex, Laura reached for the light switch and turned off the porch light as she stepped outside. The night was dark and cold, and she was more terrified than ever of the forces that had taken her son from her.

Chapter 9

Nick's breathing still hadn't returned to normal, and he'd been driving as fast as he dared back toward the estate for nearly a half hour. His company had become a major crime syndicate, compliments of a wife he didn't remember? Why on God's green earth had he ever married the woman? He supposed it didn't matter, now. The deed was done, the damage cascading down on everyone he loved.

Laura burst out, "Do we dare trust him? With Adam's life?"

"I think we should," he answered.

"Why?"

He shrugged. "The time may come when we need Kloffman to hesitate before he calls his dogs down on us or Adam. I think we gave him good reason to hesitate."

Laura sighed beside him. "You're right, of course. I'm just not capable of thinking that clearly right now."

He glanced over at her. "You're not supposed to be

thinking clearly. You're a mother. You're allowed to be panicked."

"But Adam needs Super Mommy." Laura's voice cracked, sending a glass shard of pain through him. How was she ever going to move past the fact that he'd done this to their child? Even assuming Adam returned home safe and sound—and he refused to consider any other possibility—how were they going to move forward as a couple?

He asked slowly, "Do think you'll ever forgive me for all of this?"

She stared across the dark interior of the car at him a long time before she answered. "I don't know. After you lied to me in Paris and then spent the past year knowing you were living under an assumed identity and never told me, I don't know how I'm going to trust you again."

If only he could remember why he'd deceived her in Paris! For the first time, he regretted not really trying to work with the doctors who'd attempted to help him regain his memory.

"Now what?" Laura asked.

What, indeed? He was as stymied as she was and hated feeling this helpless. He'd felt this way in his box and had vowed never to be at anyone's mercy again. No, this time it was his son's life on the line. His control threatened to crack. Swearing silently, he fought off the urge. Laura needed him strong. Adam needed him strong.

"I don't have a lot of contacts in the crime world," Laura commented, "but I'll put out some feelers. See if anyone's heard anything."

"I'd lay odds that whoever kidnapped me grabbed Adam, too," Nick declared. "I'd love nothing better than to get my hands on that person and wring their neck."

"You only want to wring their neck? I had something slower and more painful in mind," Laura replied.

He shrugged. "I got you and the kids out of the deal. I learned things about myself in that box I'd have learned no other way. Things that have changed my life—changed me—dramatically for the better. Yes, the experience sucked. But, at some point, I have to get over it and get on with my life. I'm not kidding when I say that part of my past is over and gone. I don't dwell on it."

"I'm not so altruistic," Laura muttered.

"You can sit around hating your life and bemoaning all your problems. Or you can accept that everyone has them and get on with dealing with yours in a positive frame of mind. I'm not saying life can't be hard as hell. But it is possible to find joy in small things in the midst of all the bad stuff. I have my kidnapper to thank for making me understand this."

"Will you be so philosophical if we find out he or she is behind Adam's kidnapping?"

"I'll kill him." He added grimly, "And I'll be entirely philosophical about it afterward."

Laura smiled reluctantly and reached over to put a hand on his leg. He took a hand off the steering wheel and covered hers.

"We'll find Adam," Nick murmured. "Just keep the faith." Why did it take something so awful to bring them together like this? How was he supposed to feel anything other than too guilty to breathe when he was finding Laura again in the midst of losing his son?

The house was in an uproar when they walked in. Marta had gone upstairs for Ellie's 2 a.m. feeding and one of the FBI agents had discovered their disappearance.

The FBI agent-in-charge, a guy named Cal Blackledge, was not amused and chewed them up one side and down the other. Nick blandly explained that the two of them had needed to get away for a little while, to be alone and share their grief without an army of onlookers. Blackledge didn't look convinced, but Nick and Laura stuck to their story, and there wasn't much the FBI man could do about it.

As their chewing out was winding down, another FBI agent rushed into the kitchen. "You just got a message from who we believe to be the kidnapper."

Laura's coffee mug slipped out of her fingers and shattered into a hundred pieces all over the floor. Nick moved for the door nearly as quickly as she did, but Blackledge still got to Laura's office first. When Nick stepped into the spacious room, a team of people was huddling in front of her computer. They moved aside, and Laura slipped into her desk chair. He watched eagerly as she clicked on the email message.

Your son and his nanny are safe. They will stay with me until you testify against AbaCo. When those bastards are put away for good, then you can have your son back. Do not fail, or else.

Laura looked up at him in shock, the thought plain on her face the same as the one he was having. *The kidnapper was an enemy of AbaCo's?*

He asked, "What's the kidnapper going to do when the government announces that it's going to drop its charges?"

Laura paled and started to shake. He knew the feeling, dammit. They had two days until Adam's life was forfeit. Two days to find and save their son.

Nick had faced some scary crises in his life, but nothing compared to this. His son's life was in mortal danger. Seeing the threat on the computer screen before him made it real in a way it hadn't been until now. Nausea ripped through him.

"There's a video attachment," one of the FBI agents announced.

Laura clicked on it. A picture of their son smiling up at the camera flashed onto the computer monitor. The video rolled and Adam placed a bright red leaf into what looked like some kind of scrapbook. "Look at my pretty leaf," he announced in his clear, sweet voice.

Lisbet's voice came from off camera. "Tell Mummy and Daddy we're doing fine and that you're safe and warm and well-fed. Tell them Joe has been *très* kind to us."

Adam nodded. "I'm learning all kinds of neat things about nature. But I miss you. Joe says you're fighting the bad man for him. Hurry up and win. I want to go home."

A sob escaped Laura and she turned to Nick, burying her face against his side. He gripped her shoulder so tightly he was probably hurting her. But he couldn't help himself.

The FBI agents went into high gear around them.

"Identify that leaf."

"Nature. He's being held in a rural area."

"Joe. Get a list of disgruntled former AbaCo employees."

"The child turned the page in that album. Can we digitally enhance the leaves on the second page?"

"Analyze the grain of the floorboards. They look old. Rough. Maybe in a cabin of some kind."

The words flowed past Nick, but the only ones that stuck were the final ones in the note. Do not fail or else.

Or else.

Laura lifted her head. "Lisbet used the French word for very, *très*. She doesn't speak much French. She was signaling us that the kidnapper is French or speaks French."

Blackledge snapped, "Make that a list of French former AbaCo employees."

A flurry of phone calls took place around them while

Laura replayed the video over and over, presumably looking for more clues. Or maybe she just needed to see Adam's face. It was both sweet relief and stabbing pain to see him. He might be safe for now, but that *or else* hung heavily over the little boy.

"AbaCo is refusing to release any employee lists to us without a subpoena."

"Then get one," Blackledge snapped.

"That's going to be a problem," someone replied. "They'll have to release information about their American staff to us, but not their overseas employees."

Blackledge frowned. "The French courts are notoriously slow, particularly when it comes to cooperating with Americans. We're not exactly at the top of France's list of allies these days. If AbaCo refuses to cooperate, it's going to take too long to get what we need."

Nick said sharply, "Spiros Shipping had a major office in Paris. AbaCo probably still uses it."

"Do you think Kloffman—" Laura started.

Nick cut her off gently. "Why go to the top when you can go to the bottom?"

She frowned at him and he explained, "I ran Spiros Shipping for well over a decade. I'm betting Kloffman didn't fire every one of my old employees when AbaCo took over. People who used to work for me must still be there."

"What good does that do us?" she asked.

"My family believed strongly in knowing every employee and in building trust and loyalty among them. If I can find some of the old staff, they'll help me."

She pulled out her cell phone and slapped it into his hand.

"Let's see if they bothered to change the phone numbers," he muttered. He dialed the international number for Spiros Paris and was pleased when the call went through.

"AbaCo Shipping," a female voice said in his ear.

"Marie? Marie Clothier? Is that you?"

She switched into English to match his. "*Oui.* Who may I ask, is this?"

"Nick—" Then he corrected, "Nikolas Spiros."

The woman took off in a spate of excited French he only half caught. When she'd finally wound down, he said, "Look, Marie. I need your help. My son has been kidnapped and we're trying to figure out who did it. I need a list of all the employees fired from the Paris office since AbaCo took over. Is there someone left from the old days who would do that for me? Quietly and quickly?"

"But of course. Let me connect you with François Guerrard."

Nick laughed. "He's still working? Why didn't he retire years ago?"

"He would have if AbaCo hadn't cut our pensions so badly."

"Ahh, I'm sorry. I suppose it goes without saying that it would be best for you if you didn't mention this little call to anyone at AbaCo?"

She laughed wryly. "That would be correct, sir. Ahh, it is so good to hear your voice again. I never believed what they said about you—"

He gently cut off what was likely to become a lengthy monologue from the talkative woman. "Thank you, Marie. I'm afraid I'm in a great hurry. We need to find my son."

"Of course, Monsieur Nikolas. I shall pray for him."

In a few minutes, a list of fired employees was sitting in his email inbox. Blackledge printed it out and his people went to work tracking down every single person on the list. Nick and Laura stayed out of the way and let the FBI invoke its formidable connections with Interpol to do the job.

The leaves were identified as belonging to plants indigenous to the mid-Atlantic states. Nick supposed knowing Adam was in one of a half-dozen states was better than nothing, but not much.

Laura spoke to Nick thoughtfully. "Why did Lisbet make a point of saying they were warm? It has been unseasonably warm all over the East Coast this past week. Is there somewhere substantially colder within this region that would prompt her comment?"

"Mountains or a coast," Nick replied.

Laura turned to one of the FBI agents. "Would those leaves we saw be more likely to grow at high elevations or near the ocean?"

"The second leaf is a bush that tolerates salt spray well, ma'am."

"The shore it is," Laura announced.

Blackledge nodded his agreement. "You sure you don't want back into this business, ma'am?"

She laughed without much humor. "Just get my son back so I can be a mommy."

Nick put an arm around her shoulders and was gratified when she leaned against him. Within the hour, hundreds of law enforcement officials were combing the woods of coastal Virginia, searching for an isolated cabin. It was a needle-in-a-haystack hunt, but he appreciated the effort nonetheless.

A command center was set up in their living room to coordinate the various search teams, and he and Laura were only in the way. They eventually retreated to their suite to let Blackledge's team do its job.

It was late afternoon when Nick's phone dinged to indicate an incoming text message. He checked it quickly. "Kloffman. He wants to meet us in Washington tonight. Says he'll have what we need then. Do you think Agent Blackledge will lynch us if we sneak out again?"

She answered gravely, "I do. I'd suggest we tell him what we're up to this time." Their gazes met in mutual understanding. This was one of those times when no words were necessary for them to communicate perfectly.

Nick nodded. His thoughts drifted to his wife, Meredith, and the roadblock she represented to his future with Laura. "You do know that the minute I'm clear of her, I'm going to ask you to marry me, right?"

"And you're so sure I'll say yes?" Laura replied tightly.

He stared, thunderstruck. "You wouldn't marry me?"

"Nick, my son is gone. Everything I thought I knew about you turns out to be a lie. You have a *wife*. You cheated on her with me in Paris."

"Everything I know of her says I barely knew her and she no doubt married me purely for my money. There's no way it was a love match."

"I don't care how good or bad she was. You broke your marriage vows. I have a problem with that."

"I don't remember any of it," he replied with barely restrained frustration. "I can't imagine ever having married her. And even if I actually thought it was a good idea at some point, I'm not that man anymore."

"It's a lot for me to accept on faith."

"Laura, I love you with all my heart. Adam *will* come home safe and sound. This crisis will pass, and I'll still love you. I'll love you till the end of time."

"Is love enough?" she asked in anguish. "I'm not so sure."

"Love is everything," he replied with a desperate calm that belied the panic beneath.

Without replying, she turned and walked out of the room. His heart broke a little more. He had to find a way to put his family back together. There *had* to be a way.

How was it she could feel like she was drowning even though she wasn't even in water? Laura's world had come apart and she didn't have any idea how to put it back together again. She'd have thought her stress would have gone down slightly after the note from the kidnapper. The FBI profilers were confident that Adam wasn't in any immediate danger, and whoever had him was on their side in the fight against AbaCo. That had to count for something, right?

But instead, she could hardly function. Her thoughts were disjointed, she was unable to plan anything, and even the smallest of tasks overwhelmed her. Only Ellie kept her sane. The infant adhered to a steady schedule of eating, cuddling, and sleeping, and Laura was immensely grateful for the infant's rhythms.

It took twice as long as usual, but eventually, Laura formed a plan of action. First on her agenda was to contact some people at the CIA and see if Kloffman's claims were true. Had the agency cut a deal with him to block the AbaCo trial from going forward in the name of national security? If so, she planned to pull every string she had at her disposal to get the CIA to delay making the announcement for a few more days.

Laura slept restlessly in the recliner in Ellie's room, waking up a little after dawn. She pulled out her cell phone and dialed a familiar phone number. The CIA operator forwarded her call to her old boss.

"Hi, Clifton, it's Laura Delaney."

"I wondered how long it was going to take you to call me."

"So it's true? There's a deal to stop the AbaCo trial?"

"You know I'm not allowed to comment on such things, dear."

"And you understand the life of an innocent child is on the line?"

He sighed. "I do. I was so sorry to hear about the kidnapping. Is there any ransom demand?"

She replied sharply, "Why, yes. There is. The kidnapper is insisting that Nick testify against AbaCo and bury them, or else."

Heavy silence greeted that announcement. It was all the answer she needed from Clifton. The CIA had, indeed, cut a deal with AbaCo. "When is it going public?" she asked. "And don't tell me that information is classified. We have to find Adam before the news is released."

"Close of business today."

It wasn't enough time! "You have to delay it. We have to find my son first!"

"I understand, Laura. I'll see what I can do. But I can't make any promises."

She hung up, staring in dismay at the happy clouds and dancing unicorns on Ellie's pink walls. Adam was running out of time.

The FBI upped the man power over the course of the day, redoubling their efforts to locate Adam, but to no avail. Wherever the kidnapper was hiding him, he'd picked his spot well.

It was afternoon when another email came to her Laura Delaney address from the kidnapper. She raced downstairs and into the office to see it. Nick was already there, and he smiled encouragingly at her. Did that mean there was good news?

She sat down at her desk and read the note:

Thought you might like another video to know your son's okay. I promise I won't hurt him as long as you do the right thing and send AbaCo to hell where it belongs.

The attached video showed Adam playing some sort of pick-up-sticks game with Lisbet and squealing with laughter. For a kidnapping victim, he looked shockingly hale and hearty. The FBI team observing with her murmured in surprise.

"What?" she looked up at the faces around her in concern.

Blackledge shook his head. "This is the damnedest case. I've never seen a kid having the time of his life being kidnapped."

"Stockholm syndrome?" another agent suggested.

Laura frowned. Stockholm syndrome was when kidnapping victims began to sympathize with their captors. It was an involuntary psychological reaction to the threat of dying.

Blackledge replied, "I don't think so. The kid and nanny look like they're genuinely having a ball."

Laura asked, "Are they just making the best of a bad situation?"

One of the other analysts leaned forward, watching a playback of the tape. "They're showing no stress-related body language. The muscles of the nanny's face are relaxed and open, and see the way Adam's lounging, here? He's not taking any sort of self-protective posture. These two feel completely safe with their captor."

Another agent piped up. "In both notes, the kidnapper has made a point of reassuring the parents that their son is safe and in no danger as long as things go his way. He used the phrase 'I promise' in the latest one, indicating he has a strong sense of honor and right and wrong. His word matters. As a profiler, I have to say I don't think this guy has any intention of harming either of his victims. That's not to say he won't snap at some point and change his mind. After all, he's enraged enough at AbaCo to have taken the drastic action of kidnapping someone. So, he does have a breaking point."

Laura made a sound of distress. "And we're going to see it when he finds out the trial's not going to happen at all."

The call from Laura's CIA contact came in just a few minutes before five o'clock. The look of abject relief on her face said it all: they'd gotten their extension on the announcement that the AbaCo trial had been suspended.

She put down the phone and said, "He's got a firm commitment to delay twenty-four hours and a tentative agreement to postpone the announcement for up to forty-eight hours beyond that. It was the best he could do."

It wasn't perfect, but it was better than nothing. He and Laura could breathe for another few hours. Her shoulders slumped in front of him and it was all he could do not to gather her up, carry her upstairs and make love to her. Anything to escape this endless nightmare for just a few minutes. But no way would she agree to such a thing. Regretfully, he turned his attention back to figuring out something, anything, to do to help find Adam.

He said thoughtfully, "You know, the kidnapper keeps emphasizing burying AbaCo, not necessarily the trial itself. You already said it to—" he broke off sharply. Mustn't mention their extracurricular visit to Kloffman.

He continued in chagrin, "You said it to me. What if, instead of testifying, I go on a media blitz to tell my story and slam AbaCo all over the airwaves? Done properly, I could probably tank the stock price and get the senior leadership fired. I could mire AbaCo in scandal so deep they'll never recover."

Laura turned around and looked up at him doubtfully. "If you do that, you'll sacrifice a shot at a legitimate trial at some future date. You'd be giving away your chance to get justice for the crimes committed against you. Maybe you just launch a campaign to overturn the sale of Spiros Shipping and get it back."

Nick shrugged. "If I get my son back, who cares about justice or shipping companies? Even if they skate on the kidnapping charges, you have to admit there'd be a certain justice in destroying the reputations of AbaCo's senior leadership and wrecking the company."

Laura winced. "How many people would you put out of work? Do you think you're capable of destroying the business your great-grandfather built and your entire family poured its heart and soul into?"

Nick had to unclench his jaw to grind out, "How can you ask that of me? Do you really think I'm that shallow and materialistic? He's my son. Nothing on earth is more important to me than him."

Laura scowled back at him.

It was one thing to know they were both just lashing out in their stress and panic, but it was another thing entirely to stop the unreasoning fury bubbling up inside him, demanding that he yell at someone, anyone, in his agony. He knew Laura was feeling the exact same way. But it was still hard not to turn on her. They *had* to maintain a unified front. Work together. Adam's life depended on it.

Blackledge broke the heavy tension between them. "May I remind you that a massive manhunt is in progress as we speak? Let's not give up on the idea of finding and rescuing your son outright, shall we?"

Laura glanced over at Blackledge in chagrin. He was right. But it was so in her nature to have a plan B in case the main plan failed, and a plan C if plan B didn't work out, that she couldn't help coming up with contingencies for the crisis at hand.

The second video had put her mind a little more at ease. It was a good thing for a mother to know her child wasn't scared or in pain. And thank goodness Lisbet was still alive and with him. She'd protect Adam with her own life, Laura had no doubt. But there was still the dilemma of how to proceed, given that they weren't ultimately going to be able to meet the kidnapper's demand in a court of law.

Nick's thoughts must be running in the same vein, because he said soberly, "It would be a calculated risk to launch a media war against AbaCo. Maybe it would satisfy the kidnapper, maybe not. And if not, we'd have blown our shot at a trial that would satisfy the guy. What do you think about it, Laura?"

She looked up at him thoughtfully. "I think Agent Blackledge is right. Let's allow the manhunt to play out while we see what our…friends…can come up with now that we've got a few more days to search for Adam." She looked at him significantly. *And in the meantime, they'd meet with Kloffman.*

Nick nodded resolutely. "Done."

She touched his hand lightly, silently thanking him.

He responded, "In the mean time, how do you feel about heading up to Washington for the night?"

She nodded and glanced over at the FBI agents within

easy earshot. "You know me well. I'm starting to feel claustrophobic just sitting around here. I'd like to be close to Langley in case I have to twist some arms in person tomorrow. I'll go pack a bag for Ellie."

Nick nodded briskly. "I'll call the hotel and have them arrange for a babysitter."

Blackledge snorted. "Are you kidding? You're bringing along an FBI agent to guard your baby."

Laura glanced at Nick in chagrin. He said smoothly, "Excellent idea, Agent Blackledge. I'll call the Imperial Hotel and get us all a suite."

The FBI man nodded. "Morris, you've got kids, right?"

Agent Morris grinned. "Yes, sir. Five. I'm fully checked out on diapers."

"Perfect," Laura announced. "We'll leave in an hour."

Ms. I-can-handle-anything, I'm-totally-in-control vapor locked when it came time to choose a dress to wear to dinner. It was the darnedest thing. Laura stood in front of the hotel closet, staring at the dresses Marta had packed for her, mostly conservative business wear appropriate for a mother who was deeply concerned about her child's safety. And for the life of her, she couldn't choose one. It was as if her brain just shut down.

Nick stepped out of the bathroom, fresh from a shower, wearing dress slacks and no shirt, toweling his hair dry. He looked at her in concern from under his towel. "Everything okay?"

The man really was observant. "No," she wailed. "I can't decide what to wear."

He moved swiftly to her and gathered her into his arms. Smart man. He knew something was seriously wrong if such a little decision was hanging her up. His body was warm and humid against hers and smelled of his expensive soap.

He murmured into her hair, "You're doing great. I have no idea how you're holding it together the way you are. Just a little while longer, and we'll get him back. Courage, darling."

"I think I'm all out of courage," she whispered.

"Then borrow some of mine. Remember that Adam's happy and safe and the kidnapper has promised not to hurt him. We'll find a way to meet the kidnapper's demands. And Werner Kloffman's going to help us do that. He'll give us his files, and we'll be one step closer to getting our son back. But the first step is to pick out a dress and put it on."

Wise advice. Just take this one moment at a time, one simple task at a time.

He turned with her still in his arms to face the closet. "I've always liked you in blue. How about this one?" He pointed at an elegant, navy-blue suit dress.

"It's not very sexy," she said in a small voice.

He laughed. "Sweetheart, you could wear a burlap sack and a paper bag over your head, and I'd still find you sexy."

She sighed. "You do have a golden tongue. I don't know if you mean a word you say, but you say all the right things."

He kissed her forehead lightly. "I don't say them to anyone but you, so I must mean them."

She let him help her slip on the dress. He zipped it for her, and the perfectly tailored garment hugged her body with its slim lines. Nick left to finish dressing, and she pulled her hair back into a quick French twist. She added stockings and conservative high heels to the ensemble but stopped short of adding a pearl necklace to the outfit. She didn't want to look like her grandmother, after all. She tugged the dress's V-neck wider open and tightened her bra straps to increase the undergarment's lift. There. Definitely non-granny cleavage.

She smiled at Ellie who was playing in the middle of the big bed. "Sweetie, you do wonders for Mommy's assets."

The baby burbled back. Verbal early, Ellie was. Must be a girl-baby thing. She scooped up the infant and inhaled deeply of her fresh baby scent. "Mommy's going to go torture Daddy with this naughty dress for a few hours. It's going to be loads of fun. Be good for the nice FBI agent, okay?" She blew a raspberry against her daughter's tummy and laughed when Ellie squirmed and gave her a sweet, gum-filled smile.

Agent Morris poked his head through the open door. "Mr. Cass is ready whenever you are."

She nodded at the man. "Ellie just ate. She should be good for at least four hours. There's a bottle in the fridge just in case, and she should go down around 10:00 p.m. Order whatever you want from room service and watch whatever you want on TV." She added dryly, "And no boys in the house, please."

The agent grinned. "You forgot to ask me if I have a current CPR license and a babysitting certificate from an accredited after-school program."

Laura laughed. "I'm not paying you that much."

Morris looked around the plush suite. "Hey, this is the best babysitting gig I've ever landed. You and Mr. Cass have a nice evening. Ellie and me, we'll get along just fine." He patted the bulge on his right hip and added grimly, "Mr. Glock and I will see to it that nothing happens to your little princess on my watch."

Laura nodded, abruptly serious. "Thank you."

She stepped out into the living room and Nick made an appreciative sound. "You're stunning, Super Mommy."

She made a face. "I'm not feeling very super at the moment. I feel like I'm hanging on by my fingernails."

"Well, you're doing it with style. You look fabulous."

She rolled her eyes. "We've been over this before. I'm the thirty-year-old mother of two."

"That's correct. You're everything I've ever dreamed of and more."

Her heart melted a little. It would be so easy to ignore his trespasses from the past. To fall into his beautiful blue gaze and forget everything else. *Exactly the way she had for the past year.*

Like it or not, she had to face up to the fact that their current predicament wasn't entirely Nick's fault. She'd been as guilty as he of ignoring the past and pretending that nothing bad could be lurking in that giant memory gap of his.

If she lost herself in him and his damnably magnetic charm again, she'd regret it as sure as she was standing here. Someday reality would rear its ugly head again, just like it had this time, and bite her. Who would get hurt the next time? Her? The kids? All of them?

It was time. She and Nick had to confront the past head-on and make peace with it once and for all. They had to do it for their children…no matter what the cost to the two of them.

Chapter 10

The place Kloffman had picked for their meeting was dark and quiet. The booths had tall dividers separating them and plenty of privacy. Laura sighed beside Nick as they stepped inside.

"What's wrong?" he murmured.

"Too easy a place to do surveillance. Not a good spot for a clandestine exchange."

"Really?"

"Loud, rowdy, and crowded is a better venue. It's impossible to eavesdrop more than a few feet away, there's lots of noise pollution to foul up directional microphones, and people are hard to keep track of in a big crowd."

It made sense. And she was the former spy, after all.

She continued, "Our best bet is to get in and get out of here, fast."

"We'll just order drinks, then. We'll get what we came for and leave immediately," he replied.

She nodded beside him and pasted on a pleasant smile as

the maître d' approached. They were led to a booth near the back of the place, and Kloffman was already there, looking impatient. Nick smiled to himself. Typical German. If the guy wasn't five minutes early, he considered himself late.

Kloffman stood as they approached. Laura took his hands and greeted the German warmly. Quick on the uptake, Werner kissed her cheek and ushered them to the table like they were old friends. A waitress took their drink orders and left. Finally. They were alone.

Laura leaned forward and murmured past a warm smile that kept her lips from moving in any significant way, "Do you have the files?"

"Yes, my dear, I do." He brought out a small box from under the table, gaily wrapped in hot-pink paper and tied with a wide white ribbon. A white bow nearly overwhelmed the fist-sized box.

"How delightful!" Laura exclaimed. "You shouldn't have brought me a gift. Now I feel bad for not bringing you anything."

Werner laughed back. "My wife insisted. She said you should open it when you get home."

Laura duly tucked the box beside her on the banquette. She then led the conversation deftly into a discussion of how Werner's grown children were doing, and what he'd thought of Southeast Asia, where he'd taken a recent vacation. Nick was impressed. How she knew that about the German executive, he hadn't the slightest idea. Or maybe she'd just made it up and Werner was adept at following along with her patter.

Nick forced himself not to look around the place, not to check for listeners or watchers. He leaned back, looping an arm over the back of the banquette and smiling at Laura like a proud husband enjoying his attractive and effervescent wife. It wasn't hard to act besotted with her. He *was* besotted with her.

In due course, he and Werner argued good-naturedly about who would pick up the tab for the drinks, and he ultimately let Werner pay the bill. With a promise to stay in touch and come visit Werner in Germany soon, Nick and Laura stood up to leave.

And just like that, the entire records of AbaCo's Special Cargo division for the past several years were in their possession.

Nick hailed a cab and Laura climbed in as he held the door for her. He settled in the seat beside her. "Now what?"

"When we get back to the hotel, we open his gift and see what he gave us," she answered lightly, glancing warningly at the back of the cabbie's head.

He supposed she had a point. They couldn't be too careful at this late date. He relaxed and watched the city lights pass by outside. Washington really was a lovely city, a gracefully aging lady.

Agent Morris was on his feet, gun in hand and leveled at their chests, when they walked through the door to their suite. Nick nodded his approval as the guy lowered his weapon.

"You two are back early. Everything okay?" the FBI man asked.

Laura shrugged. "I made it through cocktails, but I'm not comfortable being away from Ellie. I convinced Nick to bring me back here for a quiet dinner in our room."

Morris nodded in sympathy. "How about I go take a nap with our little princess? Then I'll be in good shape to stand watch through the night. And in the mean time, you two could probably use a little privacy."

As the agent retreated, Nick called room service and ordered dinner.

He joined Laura at the desk in the corner of the living room as she booted up her laptop and plugged in the thumb drive she'd found inside the gift box. A long list of file names scrolled across her screen.

"How's it look?" he asked.

"If the files contain what their titles suggest they will, we've got a whole lot of dirt on AbaCo we didn't have an hour ago."

"Anything jump out at you that might have something to do with Adam's kidnapping?" he asked.

She typed quickly. "I'm going to do a sort for files created in the past year. The start date for the search will be the day you were released."

She undoubtedly didn't mean for that subtle note of blame to enter her voice, but it did. His gut twisted at the notion that his liberation was in some way the cause of Adam's predicament. He had to make it up to the boy, and to Laura. Adam *had* to be okay.

As she continued to type in what looked like a long list of random words, he asked, "What are you doing now?"

"Setting up keywords for the computer to search for within the files. The guys at AbaCo aren't likely to run around talking about kidnapping openly. They'll use euphemisms like 'picking up a package' or 'moving perishable goods.'"

Nick snorted. He'd felt like perishable goods plenty of times, sailing around in that damned shipping container. Laura threw him an apologetic glance.

"I've also set up a sorting algorithm to copy and organize all the content on this drive. It'll take a few minutes to run." She sighed heavily. "In the meantime, I think you and I need to go over the events from immediately before your kidnapping."

He jolted in alarm. "But I don't remember—"

"Yes, but I do. I thought I'd tell you everything I can remember and see if it jogs any memories for you or if you remember anything about some detail that might be important."

Her suggestion made sense, but why did she sound so reluctant to revisit what had supposedly been a torrid and thrilling affair? "You're making me nervous. What's so terrible about our time together in Paris that you haven't told me?"

"You truly don't remember any of it?" she asked in a small voice.

"Nothing. I'm sorry."

She waved off his apology and took a deep breath. "You saved my life the night we met."

"What?" Shock poured through him. "How?"

"My CIA field partner and I were attacked and you came out of nowhere. You grabbed our elbows and told us to come with you or die. Kent shook off your hand and demanded to know who you were."

Nick frowned. "I thought you types worked alone. You had a partner?"

Unaccountably, she blushed slightly. "Certain operations were best suited for couples."

Ahh. Damn. But it wasn't like he was in any position to cast the first stone at her. He had a wife floating around in his past. Of course an extraordinary woman like Laura had other men in her life. He asked as lightly as he could manage past his abruptly hoarse throat, "Were you two a couple?"

"Were. Past tense by then. The demands of keeping our roles as coworkers and lovers separate was too much strain on the relationship."

"Why did I grab you two?"

Laura frowned. "It was late at night. It had been raining

and the streets were mostly deserted. We were in the *Quartier Latin*—the Student Quarter. Lots of winding little streets and alleys. Several men had just come around a corner about a block ahead of us, and you materialized by my side. You must have come up from behind us. When Kent jumped away from you, you wrapped your arms around me and yanked me into an alley."

"Why did you come with me when your partner didn't?"

She smiled a little in recollection. "You were extremely handsome. Not many girls would mind having a man like you throw your arms around them and drag them off."

Nick frowned, scouring his mind for the slightest recollection of what she was describing. He came up blank. Frustrated he asked, "Then what happened?"

"I heard a noise in the street. Then a scuffle. Kent shouted something. It sounded like the beginning of my name. Then it cut off. And then nothing more."

"What did you and I do?"

"At the first sound of fighting, you pulled me down the alley. By the time Kent went quiet, you didn't have to pull me anymore. You had a car not far away and we drove off into the night. The rest is, as they say, history."

Misery filled her dark gaze and Nick moved quickly to embrace her. "Talk to me. What's so upsetting to you?"

"I left him, Nick. I abandoned Kent. I should have stayed and fought. Maybe the two of us could've bested whoever jumped him."

Oh, how well he knew the world of regret and self-recrimination. "Sweetheart, what's done is done. It's just as possible that the two of you would have lost that fight. Whatever fate met your partner could also have befallen you. There's no way of knowing. I assume you did your best to find out what happened to him?"

"The CIA and I turned Paris on its head looking for

him. But he was just…gone. Very much like how you disappeared. He's never been seen or heard from since."

Nick frowned. "Is there any chance he was kidnapped like I was?"

She shrugged. "I suppose. We know AbaCo held more prisoners over the years than the dozen or so they've released in the past twelve months. For all I know, there are more men and women just like you still floating around in international waters where law enforcement agencies can't touch them."

"Maybe we'll find the rest of them in the files Kloffman gave us."

"God, I hope so," she muttered.

Turning his attention back to Paris, he asked, "Do you have any idea how I found you that first night or why I pulled you out of there?"

"You refused to answer any of my questions about it and just said you 'had a feeling' there might be trouble."

He grinned ruefully. "I highly doubt I was psychic back then. I had to have known something."

She sighed. "That's what I thought. But every time I brought it up, we'd end up kissing and then…well, you know. My superiors thought we might be able to develop you into an asset once we learned more about you, so they told me not to press you too hard."

It was his turn to sigh. "I do wish I could remember falling in love with you the first time. I'm immensely grateful I got to do it again."

Her arms tightened around his waist. "I'm just grateful I found you. I swore I wouldn't give up until I did."

He murmured into her hair, "And it's that same stubbornness that's going to bring Adam home to us."

"From your lips to God's ears."

He lifted her chin lightly, sealing her words with a kiss.

He'd meant for it to be a simple gesture. Harmless. But instead, her arms wound around his neck, and with a sound of need in the back of her throat, she was suddenly all over him. And her desperation was all the excuse his needed to cut loose.

His arms came around her fiercely, lifting her off her feet and crushing her against him. They traded frantic kisses, tongues clashing as their hands ripped at their clothing. Never breaking the chain of heated kisses, they stumbled toward the master bedroom. He kicked the door shut with one foot as she dragged him by the open shirt toward the bed. They fell across the mattress, and his hands plunged into the deep V-neck of her dress, finding and seeking plump handfuls of female flesh. He shoved her clothing aside, his mouth fastening on one rosy peak. She arched up into him with a cry of need, filling his mouth with her bounty.

And then she was tearing at his remaining clothes, dragging his zipper down and freeing his rock-hard erection. He lifted his mouth away from her long enough to mutter, "How do you feel about three children?"

She laughed and fumbled in his back pants pocket, freeing his wallet, and fishing out the ubiquitous emergency condom inside.

He yanked her dress up and her panties down while she shoved his slacks aside and put on his protection. And then she grabbed his hips with eager hands, pulling him forward impatiently, her legs wrapping around him hungrily. He plunged into her heat, groaning at her tightness as she surged up around him.

It wasn't pretty or elegant. It was a fast and furious tangle of clothes and limbs and heavy breathing as they raced pell-mell for escape from everything to do with their real lives. It felt so good to lose himself completely in her, to sink into the pleasure of her body, to turn himself over to pure sensation, to turn off his mind completely and think of nothing at all. Just the blinding ecstasy of nerves shouting for release and the ever-more-urgent collisions of flesh on flesh as they both strained toward oblivion.

The cries started in the back of her throat, small at first, then building in intensity as her climax neared. He kissed her deeply, sucking up her pleasure hungrily. Their tongues took on the rhythmic movement of their bodies and the slick slide nearly pushed him over the edge. Her body went taut beneath his, arching up hard into him. He tore his mouth away from hers to stare down at her, reveling in the way her eyes glazed over and her breath stopped as a shattering orgasm broke over her. Her shuddering groan was the final straw. He plunged deep one last time as his own body exploded.

It was almost as if he passed out for a second. Everything went dark and peaceful and quiet, and nothing existed but shivering pleasure tearing through his body in wave after wave of exquisite, almost painfully intense, sensation.

Time lurched into motion once more. Laura was panting and her hair was a disheveled and entirely sexy mess around her face. Perspiration coated his bare chest, and somehow his shirt had gotten tangled up around his shoulders. Laura's dress was askew and her lips were pink and slightly swollen.

"We shouldn't have," she gasped.

"Why not?"

"Adam. Here we are having a good old time…wasting precious minutes we should be using to find him…so selfish…" She rolled away from him, yanking violently at her clothes, putting them back in place if not exactly to rights.

Who was she referring to when she spoke of selfishness?

Him? Her? Both of them? "Sweetheart, a little emotional release isn't a bad thing. We're both stretched to the breaking point—"

She cut him off with a sharp gesture of denial.

If he knew one thing, it was how to survive. And that meant being supremely selfish sometimes. Grabbing happiness whenever and wherever he could find it, hoarding it to himself, and reliving it greedily. He tried again. "You'll be no good to Adam if you don't take care of yourself."

"I'm fine. He needs me, and I let myself be distracted…. I can't believe you went there with your son's life on the line."

"I'm sorry. But I think you're underestimating how stressed out you were. Don't you feel even a little bit better?"

"No. I feel guilty and self-indulgent. If something happens to Adam, it'll be *my* fault."

"Laura." He took her by both shoulders and forced her to look up at him. "You did not kidnap him. You are not responsible for this. Don't take guilt onto yourself that is not yours to carry."

"Easy for you to say," she snapped. "You conveniently forgot everything in your life you should feel guilty for. You've got a built-in free pass."

He pulled back sharply. So. The truth finally came out. She did resent his memory loss, and she didn't forgive him for it. He'd long suspected she harbored hidden anger about it, but she was such a damned good actress, she'd never really let on how she felt.

He understood her perspective. Really. But it wasn't as if he could do anything about it. He was what he was, like it or leave it. And recent mind-blowing sex notwithstanding, apparently she'd rather leave it. Leave *him*.

He went cold from the inside out. It was as if he froze,

every cell and fiber of his being crystallizing in an agonizingly slow spread of needle-sharp pain. The muscles of his face froze, and he couldn't make a meaningful facial expression in that moment if his life depended on it. Only his thoughts continued to function, spinning fruitlessly round and round like a car doing donuts on sheet ice.

How were they supposed to proceed from here? Either she trusted him or she didn't. Forgave him or she didn't. Accepted him—all of him, his past and his problems included—or she didn't.

The verdict was in. His attempt to make a life with her and the kids was an epic failure.

His survival instinct kicked in. Must keep busy. Give himself small jobs to do. Count the ribs in the walls of his box. Check his food and water supply. Exercise and stretch. Press his eyes close to the small hole in one wall of the box. Keep his retinas acclimated to light. Think about the business plan for the new company he was going to start when he got out of here. Just. Keep. Moving.

Mechanically, he mumbled, "I wonder if our dinner's here yet." Take care of basic body needs first. Food. Water.

"I'm taking a shower," she announced, revulsion plain in her voice.

She wanted to scrub the feel of him off of her. The frost surrounding his heart hardened a little more, constricting painfully. He'd lost his son, and now her. The blow was almost more than he could bear. An urge to crumple to the floor, to curl up in a ball, to close his eyes and slip into the black abyss in his mind nearly overwhelmed him. He almost wished for his box. Things had been simple in there. Clear. Survive one day at a time. One sunrise to the next.

But this—this he wasn't sure he could stand.

He stood in the middle of the bedroom and stared at

nothing until he heard the shower water cut off. The sudden silence spurred him to motion and he stumbled out into the living room.

Laura emerged from the bedroom a while later. He had no idea how long it took her to dress. He pulled a chair out for her at the table their dinner had been laid upon. She sat down, silent, and he moved around to sit across from her. The rounded stainless dome over his plate had actually kept his fillet mignon lukewarm. The meat was tender and juicy. It probably tasted wonderful, but he couldn't tell. It all tasted like sawdust.

Laura ate quickly and then moved over to her computer to start cruising through the AbaCo documents. The search for Adam was all they had left between them.

He had files of his own to search. The ones he'd lifted from William Ward's desk after the attorney had been murdered. Maybe they'd have information in them that might lead to his son. Even the idea of such a project overwhelmed him right now. He needed to think more simply than that. Move to desk. Open laptop. Turn it on. Insert flash drive into USB port.

"What's that?" Laura asked suspiciously.

"The thumb drive I found in my lawyer's desk."

Her brows shot up in surprise. "I assumed you'd already looked through that and hadn't found anything worth mentioning."

He sighed. "I was avoiding it, actually. I expect there'll be information in here about my past, and I wasn't ready to face it until now."

The dishonesty of his words tore at his tongue as if it were being ripped off a frozen well handle. He still wasn't ready to face his past. But it wasn't like he had any choice. Adam's life hung in the balance, and he'd walk through the fires of Hell for his son.

Laura's gaze was dark and accusing.

The directory of files on William's secret storage device scrolled down the screen in front of him. It looked like a list of client names. Most of this stuff was probably highly confidential. He glanced through the list. Smith. Spangler. Spiros.

There he was. He clicked on his name.

A sub folder opened up and a list of files unfolded before him. He browsed the titles curiously. They mostly looked like business contracts. But on the third page of file names, one in particular caught his eye. It was a report from the same private investigator who'd been looking into the Nick Cass identity and found nothing. It was dated the day William had called and insisted Nick come to the Cape—the same day William had died. Nick abruptly felt as if he'd just been kicked in the stomach. Hard. Taking a deep breath, he clicked on the report and started to read.

"What did you find?" Laura asked from across the desk. Sometimes the degree to which she was observant made living with her damned hard. Or more to the point, made living with secrets around her damned hard.

He answered heavily, "I think I just found my prenuptial agreement with Meredith."

Chapter 11

What little breath Laura had left after the mood swings of the past two hours whooshed out of her. She felt like a washcloth that had been twisted and squeezed until every last drop of life had been wrung out of her. She was empty. Emotionally done in. Logic told her this was an extreme situation and not to make any major life decisions in the midst of the crisis. But the urge to sweep aside everything and everyone who stood between her and Adam was irresistible.

Nick began to read aloud. She exhaled carefully as he went through a ridiculously huge list of assets. Nikolas Spiros hadn't been merely rich. He'd been wealthy beyond imagining. And she had a pretty big imagination.

"Listen to this," he exclaimed. "If I die of unnatural causes, she gets nothing."

"As in zero?"

"That's correct. Not a dime. And in fact, she's required

to return any jewelry, clothing, cars, homes, or cash assets accrued during the marriage to my estate."

"Wow. Trust her much, did you?"

"Apparently not."

"Sounds like you thought she was a potential black widow even before you married her," Laura responded.

Nick was frowning, too. "It does beg the question, why did I marry her in the first place if I thought it was a good possibility that she'd try to kill me for my money?"

"Were you always that mistrustful of the women you dated?"

"It was an issue wondering if women wanted me for myself or for my wealth. But at some point, you have to take a chance and go with your gut. I may have gotten it wrong with Meredith, but I got it right with you…twice."

She brushed aside the overture. Adam was her entire focus at this juncture. But the mystery of Nick's marriage to a woman he clearly thought dangerous tantalized her. Was Meredith behind either or both kidnappings after all?

The man she knew—both in Paris and now—simply wouldn't have married a woman in whom he had so little faith. Surely Nick's core personality hadn't changed that much in the past six years. "Do you have any idea how you met Meredith?" she asked.

"No, I don't."

She asked cautiously, "Would you mind if I researched your wife a little?"

His gaze was open and honest, and he answered without hesitation. "Be my guest."

Thank God. He was finally willing, not only to face his past, but to let her see it, too. She minimized the AbaCo files and pulled up her favorite search engine. She typed rapidly.

In seconds, pictures of Nick and Meredith from the front

pages of the tabloids leaped onto her screen. "Attractive woman," Laura commented.

Nick shrugged. "Beauty comes from inside a person. *You're* attractive. From what I know of her, she has the heart of a snake. She may be well-groomed, but she is *not* attractive to me."

Laura might have smiled under other circumstances. But as it was, she kept typing grimly. "She was living pretty high on the hog when you met—designer clothes, expensive hotels and spas, jewelry running into hundreds of thousands of dollars..." She typed some more. "Did you know she was collecting art? It looks like she'd bought a couple million dollars' worth by the time you two hooked up."

Nick looked about as interested as if she'd told him the price of tea in China had gone up by a penny a pound.

Laura poked around some more, but then leaned back, perplexed. "I can't find the source of her money. She doesn't come from a wealthy background, and I'm not finding any indication she had a high-paying job. She had a high school education from an average school. No college. She wasn't a model. Several years prior to meeting you, she started tossing around the big bucks. She didn't appear to be dating any men who could've financed that sort of lifestyle. According to her tabloid appearances, she seemed to be picking up mostly good-looking toy boys and footing the bill for them."

Nick made a face. "Maybe she was a hooker."

Laura snorted. "Even high-end working girls don't pull down the kind of money she was spending. She was blowing through three to five million dollars a year."

"Was she running up a massive debt? Maybe she married me to dig herself out?"

Laura gestured with her chin toward his laptop. "Is

there any record of your attorney running a background check on her? My lawyer used to run one on all the guys I dated in college, and I didn't inherit anywhere near the wealth you had."

Nick scowled. "I seem to recall William checking out my girlfriends at university, and it drove me crazy."

"Did you tell him to stop?"

He laughed. "I doubt William would have listened to me. He was the executor of my father's estate and had the power to do pretty much whatever he pleased. As I recall, he didn't think I was exactly the most responsible young man on the planet."

"Was he right?"

"Absolutely. I was in my early twenties, good-looking, smart, and too rich for my own good. Girls flocked to me, and I had no problem taking advantage of that. William kept me on a stupidly tight financial leash. Good thing he did, too. I might have blown my inheritance before I grew up and got interested in the shipping business."

"What else could Meredith have been up to that pulled in so much cash?" Laura asked thoughtfully.

"No education. No fancy job. No modeling. No prostitution. No rich boyfriend," Nick ticked off. "She was either the secret mistress of someone extremely wealthy, or she was into something illegal."

Laura spent the next several minutes looking at Meredith's travel patterns over a three-year period. She found no recurring destinations. She even cross-checked the guest lists at various hotels and resorts Meredith frequented and found no pattern of any repeating guest at the same places. Tabloid references consistently called Meredith single and on the prowl. She appeared to subscribe to the theory of a new man in her bed every night. Laura even ran Meredith's name through the various intelligence databases that she had legal—and occasionally way off the books and not so legal—access to. There were no records or even rumors of the woman being involved with anyone. Nada.

Finally, Laura announced, "If she was having a secret affair, it's so secret I can't find any hint of it. I think the crime angle is all we've got left."

"Given what Kloffman says she's into now, it seems the likeliest scenario."

Laura nodded. "Okay. Let's assume she was already dabbling in crime. She comes to you with a plan to use your shipping company to expand her activities. Do you say yes or no?"

"Emphatically no," Nick replied firmly. "I always ran a legitimate business."

Laura nodded and continued her line of reasoning. "But she doesn't take no for an answer. She figures she can seduce you and gain access to your company that way. Either she figures she can do it behind your back, or once you're married, you'll go along with what she's up to and take the money and run rather than turn in your wife."

Nick pushed his laptop aside and propped his elbows on the desk. "But what if, after we were married, I didn't want to go along with her plan for Spiros Shipping?"

Laura picked up the thread of the logic. "Then she's got to get rid of you. But because of the prenup, she'll lose all control of, and even access to, the shipping company if you die."

"So, she has me kidnapped, tosses me on one of my ships, and has it sail around indefinitely in international waters with me aboard. For all I know, I might have been the first prisoner. Maybe she got the idea for selling high-end kidnappings from me."

Laura scowled. That woman had better hope her path never crossed Laura's. On behalf of all the families of the kidnapping victims, she was going to gouge the woman's eyeballs out with her bare hands.

"Surely I suspected something before I married her, or else I wouldn't have insisted on this crazy prenup."

"Is it possible you had in mind some sort of scheme to expose what she was up to and married her to find out what exactly she was involved in? Maybe to expose who her business partners were?"

Nick stared into space for a long time. It was painful watching him try to dredge up a memory that simply wasn't there. Finally, he huffed in frustration and his gaze focused on her once more. "Yes, it's possible. But I don't remember." He added in a rush, "I wish now that I'd cooperated with all those shrinks who tried to help me remember the lost years."

Laura jolted. She'd long suspected he'd stonewalled his doctors, but to hear him say the words aloud was a shock. "Why didn't you cooperate?"

He laughed shortly. Without humor. "I knew something really bad had happened during that lost time, and I was dead certain something even worse would happen if the docs uncovered it."

She had to give the man credit. He was one fine actor to have fooled all the physicians like that. But it did raise another and more disturbing question: What else wasn't he being square with her about?

It took her a moment to pick up the dropped threads of their conversation. "Okay, so you suspected Meredith of being up to no good. Maybe she was already using your company to ship illegal somethings."

He nodded. "But she was too careful, and I couldn't find out what she'd involved Spiros in unknowingly."

"Do you think it's fair to assume you were acting nobly to protect your company?"

He nodded. "My only recollections of Spiros Shipping are fond and proud. I can't imagine doing anything to sabotage it."

"Okay. We go with noble motivations. Would you have been willing to seduce Meredith to find out what she was up to?"

He nodded again, but slowly this time. "If my hobbies were any indication, I was a bit of a risk taker back then. I might have gotten involved with someone like her for the sake of my family's business. Hell, I might have done it purely for the thrill of playing with fire."

She tsked. "Nick, Nick. What did you get yourself into?"

"Apparently, I got myself into waters way over my head." He reached across the table to squeeze her hand apologetically. "I'm so sorry I sucked you into this mess."

Recollection of why they were having this conversation washed over her. *Adam.* His precious face, so much like his father's, swam in her mind's eye. Agony stabbed her.

A cold feeling settled in the pit of her stomach as a disturbing thought occurred to her. She frowned. "Do you think it's possible you knew who I was in Paris? Did you approach me because I was CIA and could help you take her down?"

A horrified look leaped into his eyes. "Surely not. Surely I wouldn't have used you like that. Maybe I found out you were getting too close to her and might ruin my investigation, or maybe you had come onto Meredith's radar and were in danger."

How could she have been so stupid in Paris? She'd been so swept off her feet by Nick's good looks and extraordinary charm that she'd never stopped to ask herself exactly why and how he'd blown into her life. What if it hadn't been happy coincidence at all? What if he'd been using her? Had their instant and explosive attraction been a lie? Had he really loved her at all?

Oh, God. And what about now? Had the past year been all about using her resources to hide from his enemies? About regaining his strength for another fight? Had their entire life together been a lie?

She reeled, both emotionally and physically, and actually had to grab the edge of the desk to steady herself. Nick was speaking again, and she struggled to focus on his words.

"…know what your partner was investigating? Did he maybe stumble across something having to do with Meredith's activities?"

She retreated into the mundane rather than dwell on the horror spinning through her mind right now. "We were investigating the Russian mob's activities in France. It's possible I didn't know everything Kent was doing, though. But I can find out." Using a dummy email account, she typed out a quick email to her old boss at the CIA asking if her partner might possibly have been investigating Meredith Black Spiros at the time of his disappearance. Clifton had also been Kent's supervisor. If anyone would know what Kent had been up to, it would be him. She hit the send button. Clifton's reply was almost immediate—he must be working late. Kent hadn't been working on anything else to his knowledge. No help there.

Her research on Meredith dead-ended for the moment, she turned her attention back to the AbaCo documents. Nick went back to reading legal documents from his lawyer's files.

She'd been perusing blindingly dull shipping documents and correspondence for about an hour when she sat up straight abruptly. She read the short email correspondence again—in Russian. Nope, she hadn't mistranslated it. Holy cow.

"Uhh, Nick? I know where your wife got her money."

He glanced up questioningly from his own computer.

"She worked for the Russians," Laura announced.

"What?"

"There's a message in here for her, in Russian. Kloffman made a note on the email that he didn't know what it was, but he was startled that a personal email for Meredith had accidentally made its way into AbaCo's files, and that it was in what looked like Russian. She apparently never let on to him that she speaks the language. I have to agree with Kloffman. It had to be a mistake that this got saved in an AbaCo archive."

"Can you read it?"

She smiled grimly. "I had a Russian minor in college."

"What does the email say? Is she a spy?" Nick demanded.

"I don't know. This could have come from the URS—the Russian security service—or possibly the Russian mob." She added dryly, "Not that it makes much difference one way or the other. The two organizations are firmly in bed with each other."

Nick stared. "Was she some sort of plant? A mole to get inside my company?"

"Maybe."

Or maybe Nick had made some sort of deal with the Russians and Meredith had been merely the instrument of its implementation. It was all well and good to spin Nick as the possible hero in the Paris scenario, but it was just as possible he'd instigated whatever criminal activities Spiros Shipping had gotten into. Maybe he'd been unwilling to add murder to the list and had saved her that rainy night as a selfish maneuver to protect himself. Or maybe he'd been trying to ingratiate himself with the CIA.

It was so maddening not knowing the truth! Did she dare trust him or not? By his own admission, he'd run interference on the doctors trying to discover the truth about his past. Had that, too, been a purely self-protective maneuver?

She had to believe his memory loss was real. Too many times over the past year, he'd casually reached for some memory in an unguarded moment and run into the black wall of nothingness. She'd seen the fear and frustration in his eyes when he didn't think she was looking. He hadn't been acting for her benefit in those moments, and he'd been absolutely consistent in his inability to remember even the smallest details of that time, even when he was half-asleep, distracted by the kids, or just surprised by a sudden question from her. No actor was that good.

Good guy or bad guy? Liar or victim? Who in the world was Nikolas Spiros/Nick Cass? She had to unravel the mystery fast or else their son might very well die.

She glanced up. Nick was frowning deeply, obviously trying yet again to pierce the black veil in his mind. "Anything?" she asked.

He shook his head. "How did she get away with being a spy, or at least some sort of Russian agent?"

That was an excellent question. Laura went back to her earlier computer screenshots of Meredith's childhood and early adulthood. Some or all of it could very well be faked. She studied the records carefully. If it was fake, it had been extremely well done. Which meant the URS was probably behind it.

Of course, working for the Russian government didn't exactly exclude Meredith from working for the Russian mob, too. Laura reached for her cell phone. "Let me make a few calls to Langley. I need to talk to the guys on the Russia desk about her."

Although she was no longer a CIA agent and her clearances had long been terminated, she was nonetheless considered to be a friend of the agency. In that capacity, people listened to the occasional tips she passed their way. And in return, they threw her a bone now and then. An anonymous male voice answered the line.

"Hi, my name's Laura Delaney. You can run my bona fides past Clifton Moore in the morning. He'll vouch for me. Please copy the following for immediate dissemination: I believe I have discovered a long-term Russian mole. A sparrow possibly, functioning inside and behind a major international cargo shipping company."

The man at the other end of the phone made a sound of surprise. Over the years, there'd been a lot of rumors about the KGB's vaunted core of operatives who used sex as a potent weapon of espionage. The men had been called ravens, the women, sparrows. But the talk had been mostly rumors and urban legends.

She continued briskly, "Her name is Meredith Black Spiros. I have reason to believe she is using the resources of AbaCo Shipping to engage in much more extensive illegal activities than the Agency is currently aware of. Her financials are highly suspicious. I recommend the Agency take a closer look immediately. I'm requesting any additional information available on her. Have you got all that?"

"Yes, ma'am. What is a good phone number and email address at which we can contact you?"

"Clifton Moore knows how to get in touch with me." Laura hung up the phone.

"Are you so sure that was a good idea?" Nick asked doubtfully. "If she's some dangerous spy, wouldn't she be really mad if you sicced the CIA on her? I mean, what if she's behind Adam's kidnapping? Lord knows, if she's connected with the Russians, she'd have access to the kind of resources to pull it off."

Laura shook her head, remembering Adam and Lisbet laughing on the floor. "Lisbet worked for a Russian family before I hired her. She speaks some Russian. She'd know if she were being held by one and would have used some sort of Russian word out of context instead of a French one."

Nick studied her intently. "Are you willing to bet our son's life on it? Because that's what you're doing."

None of her mommy-warning intuitions were firing. Was it possible that Meredith's true identity and Adam's disappearance were not related? One thing she was sure of: Whoever had Adam was out for AbaCo's blood, not Meredith's.

Nick surged up out of his chair. "You could've made a terrible mistake by calling Langley."

"I did my job," she retorted sharply.

"You're not a spy anymore. You're a mother. And you may have just endangered my son even more than he already is."

They glared daggers at each other, as much frustration glinting in his eyes as roiled in her gut. "I wasn't being impulsive or reckless," she snapped. "As a citizen, I have a duty to report a national security risk to my government."

"It's pretty arrogant of you to decide that all by yourself, don't you think? He's my son, too."

"And where were you the first five years of his life?" she shot back. She regretted the words the second they were out of her mouth, but once said, they couldn't be unsaid.

"It's not my fault I was locked in a box that whole time!

I didn't know I *had* a son. And even if I did, there isn't a damned thing I could've done about it."

He was right. But he also had no idea what it had been like, having no clue where he'd gone or why he'd just disappeared like a puff of smoke from her life. In spite of her determination to find him, she had to admit—if she was being brutally honest with herself—that part of her had been furious at Nick during the long years of his absence.

She'd been left at home to wait and worry and raise her son as a single parent. To dodge the difficult questions about who and where his father was when Adam got old enough to start asking. It hadn't been easy keeping her act together, and for the first time, she admitted to herself that she'd hated Nick a little for it.

In fact, she still hated him a little for it. She knew intellectually that he'd been through no picnic himself. That five years of captivity had nearly broken him mentally, physically, and spiritually. Maybe she just wanted a little acknowledgement from him that she hadn't had an easy path to walk, either.

She was being selfish. Immature. Downright stupid. But she was also too exhausted to keep up the Super Mommy façade any longer. She wanted Adam back, and she wanted all this crap from Nick's past to go away and leave her and the kids alone. Was that too much to ask? Was that selfish of her? Maybe. But she couldn't help it. That was how she felt.

Finally, as physical and mental exhaustion claimed her, she crawled into the big bed in their room. Nick joined her in tense silence. Thankfully there was little chance of a repeat slip between them like earlier.

She lay in the dark for long hours beside him, listening to his deep, even breathing. And everywhere her thoughts turned, she only ran into questions and more questions. Thing was, she was an answer kind of gal. If she didn't start getting some of those soon, her head was going to explode.

"Why don't you two crazy kids go out for breakfast?"

Nick glanced up at Agent Morris and smiled. "While I appreciate the sentiment, I think Laura and I would rather get straight to work finding our son."

"The FBI's doing everything in its power to find Adam. We're not exactly schlubs when it comes to that kind of thing, you know."

Nick answered smoothly, "And we appreciate all your efforts. But we can't help using all of our personal resources as well."

Morris nodded in commiseration. "If it were my son, I'd be doing the same thing. Do you need me to keep an eye on Ellie while you two run around this morning?"

"Actually, that would be incredibly helpful."

"All right, then. I'll hold down the fort here."

Laura emerged from the bedroom just then and Nick glanced up at her cautiously. He didn't blame her for being in a volatile emotional state, but frankly, he didn't have any idea what to expect from her this morning.

Frustration scored across his skin like the tines of a fork—sharp enough to hurt, but too dull to make a nice, clean cut. He was not accustomed to feeling so damned helpless. Even when he'd been at the complete mercy of his captors, he'd never succumbed to the ever-creeping sense of helplessness. He'd controlled his own schedule, tracked weather patterns, exercised, and engaged in any number of mental activities to stay sane. At least until he got so debilitated that he couldn't do it anymore. But that had only been near the end. Not long before Laura and her friends rescued him. All else aside, he'd always be grateful to her for that.

"How did you sleep?" he murmured to her.

She shrugged. Which meant she hadn't slept at all. He followed up with, "Come up with any new ideas while you were staring at the ceiling all night?"

"I've got to go to Langley this morning. I need to make sure the Agency delays the announcement about the trial like it said it would. And while I'm there, I'll find out what they've got on your wife."

Uh-oh. Meredith was "his wife" this morning. He winced and muttered, "I prefer not to think of her that way. She will be my ex-wife as quickly as my law firm can file divorce papers."

Laura merely pressed her lips together as she poured herself a cup of coffee.

"Shall I drive you?" he asked in resignation.

"If you like."

"Agent Morris has volunteered to babysit Ellie for us."

Laura turned and thanked the FBI man warmly. Okay, then. So this morning's chill was reserved for him. Nick sighed and stood up. "I'm ready to go whenever you are."

The morning traffic had mostly thinned out by the time they reached the heavily wooded Rock Creek Parkway. In thick silence, he guided the nimble BMW along its winding curves. Without warning, the GPS screen mounted in the middle of the dashboard shattered, and his hands jerked on the steering wheel in shock.

"Shooter at six o'clock!" Laura bit out, turning in her seat while she fumbled at her purse.

No kidding. He stomped on the accelerator and glanced in his rearview mirror. Sure enough, a small round hole had appeared in his rear window, a spiderweb of cracks radiating outward from it. A silver sedan matched his acceleration behind them.

As soon as he spotted a break in the oncoming traffic, he ordered, “Hang on.”

Slamming on the brakes, he yanked the hard left on the steering wheel, came off the brakes, and floored the accelerator as the Beemer screeched around in a sharp one-eighty turn. His side window shattered, showering him with tiny chunks of tempered glass. He ducked, but grimly kept his foot on the gas. As tires screeched behind him, their car roared down the Rock Creek Parkway in the opposite direction.

The BMW wove in and out of traffic, startling drivers and leaving a trail of irritated horn honking in their wake. The good news was the frightened drivers had mostly been forced to brake hard to avoid his driving tactics, and in so doing made themselves an even more difficult obstacle course for their pursuers to wind through.

It took a few minutes of entirely reckless driving on his part, but eventually, Laura announced, “I think we’ve lost them. Time to get off this road.”

Nick took the next right turn slowly enough not to lay down any tire marks and accelerated down a side street in northwest D.C. Brick row houses flew past in a red blur. He turned a few more times, and eventually, eased off the accelerator. He guided the car west until they hit the Beltway and followed Laura’s instructions until an unobtrusive sign for CIA headquarters came into sight.

“Correct me if I’m wrong,” Nick said, “But did someone just try to kill us?”

She replied dryly, “In my experience, when someone’s shooting a gun at you, they generally want you dead, yes.”

He grinned reluctantly.

“You just missed the turn!” Laura exclaimed.

"Think about it. No one tried to kill us until you called the CIA and told them Meredith is a Russian agent. Doesn't the timing of this morning's attack make you a little suspicious? You wanted to know if the CIA's involved with her? I think you just got your answer. Either that, or there's a leak inside your precious agency, and Meredith and Aba-Co's goons found out we're on to them." And wasn't that a hell of a choice? Meredith was either a double agent herself or working with one inside the CIA.

Laura stared across the damaged car at him in dismay. "If it's someone in the CIA, we've got to get off the road. Hide. They'll order the FBI to find us. And that bunch has massive resources for tracking fugitives." Her voice dropped into a tone of horror. "Ohmigosh. We've got to get Ellie. *Now.*"

His heart began to pound. No. God, no. Not his baby girl, too.

Nick yanked out his cell phone. "Agent Morris, listen to me. You've got to get out of there. Fast. Someone just tried to kill us. Head back to the estate and we'll meet you there. And don't take new orders from anyone else. I'll explain when you get to the house. Got it?"

"Did he agree to do it?" Laura asked tightly when Nick disconnected.

"Yes."

She sagged in her seat, her face gray. She looked as close to breaking as he'd seen her since this whole mess started.

"Let's go home," he said quietly. He opted not to switch out his Beemer for a new car. It would take too much time. Right now, he just wanted to get them to the estate, surrounded by Laura's state-of-the-art security system and a houseful of hopefully untainted FBI agents, and get Ellie back under their protection.

Laura nodded wearily as he pointed the car south.

What had they stumbled into the middle of? How big was whatever conspiracy they'd uncovered? They knew for certain that someone in the CIA was in bed with AbaCo—Kloffman had confessed that to them. But did the Agency know AbaCo was being run by a Russian operative? Was the CIA being duped? Or was it using AbaCo with full knowledge of its shenanigans for the Agency's own advantage?

From what they'd learned of Meredith to date, his best guess was that the woman was playing everyone against each other and raking in piles of profits in the meantime. The question was did everyone else know what she was doing? Were they all looking the other way because they needed her to do their dirty work? Or was there some sort of sinister conspiracy to protect her and the illegal shipping she would do for anyone?

How deep into the government did the complicity go? Did it reach beyond the CIA? Into the FBI even? Was the FBI legitimately trying to find their son? Or was the whole search for Adam nothing but smoke and mirrors, a ploy to shut them up while Uncle Sam covered its tracks?

This mess was slipping away from them. And Adam was going to end up caught in the cross fire. Sick certainty of it roiled in his gut.

For that matter, Laura was slipping away from him, too. Faster than the tide rolling out on the beloved beaches of his home. She doubted him. Doubted his honesty. Doubted his motives—both in Paris and now. Not that he blamed her. The circumstantial evidence didn't look good for him. If only he could *remember*.

The doctors had told him that if his memories didn't start to spontaneously return on their own within a few months of his release, they were probably gone for good.

He'd thought that was just fine until this mess blew up in his face. Now, it was coming back to haunt him in a big way.

His son was gone. His daughter was possibly in the enemy's hands. Laura hated him. His attorney had been murdered, and now someone had tried to kill him and Laura. It was as if a net had snared him, drawing tighter and tighter until he couldn't move. And even knowing full well what was closing in around him, he couldn't find a way out of the trap.

Mile by mile as he drove into Virginia, he felt Laura pulling away from him. The more time she had to think, the farther she withdrew. And there wasn't a thing he could do to stop it. He didn't remember what had happened between them in Paris or why; he had no explanations for her. And he refused to make up some glib lie. She deserved better than that from him.

Their life, their love, was unraveling before his eyes, slipping inexorably through his fingers. And no matter how hard he tried, he couldn't catch the falling threads. For the first time in his life, he felt truly helpless.

If only there were something she could *do!* This sitting and twiddling her thumbs, waiting around for some new development, was maddening to Laura. She needed some fact to uncover, some door to knock down—heck, someone to shoot.

Desperation was creeping up on her, choking her slowly but surely, and there was nothing she could do to hold it back. All of her avenues for finding Adam were drying up, and she didn't know where to turn next. Even during the long years of Nick's absence, she'd never felt this alone, this helpless, darn it. MysteryMom could use a dose of her own medicine. If only there was someone who could roll in and save her from this nightmare like she'd done for so many women before.

Her love for Nick had always been her rock, the touchstone she returned to when everything else in her life went to pieces. But now, she didn't have the slightest idea if it had ever been real. Had she built her life on a foundation of quicksand, after all?

She glanced over at him. He was staring ahead, his expression inscrutable. He was so beautiful to look at that it hurt, sometimes. And her son was a tiny carbon copy of the man. Adam reminded her so much of him that it was hard to separate her love for the two of them in her mind.

And now there was Ellie to add to the pie. She favored Laura a little more in her features, but she had Nick's dark hair and shocking blue eyes.

What had she done to her children? How were they supposed to grow up with an enigmatic ghost for a father? Would he stick around to see them grow up, or would his dangerous world suck him away from them again, this time for good?

How was *she* supposed to survive if he left? Her whirling merry-go-round of thoughts screeched to a halt and stuck on that one. She might be furious at him for endangering their son, and she might be pushing him away for all she was worth right now, but she couldn't fathom his complete absence.

What *if* he left? The hell of it was that, for the life of her, she couldn't come up with an answer for that one. The idea of a life without Nick in it yawned before her as black and featureless as Nick's lost past.

When Nick had been gone before, people kept telling her to carry on for the sake of her son. And they were right up to a point. Even now, she knew she had to carry on for Ellie. But even she had a breaking point. And she was becoming increasingly concerned that she was reaching it. For better or worse, she loved Nick too much to survive without him. Too much to let go of him.

The two of them were headed for a crash, and there wasn't a darned thing she could do to stop this runaway train.

Chapter 12

Laura's heart was heavy as Nick approached the estate from the back entrance. He parked the damaged BMW at the far end of the garage behind the SUV Marta usually used to go shopping and run errands, and she followed him silently into the house.

"Is Agent Morris back with Ellie?" she asked with a casualness she did not feel.

"Not yet, ma'am," one of the FBI agents at the kitchen table answered.

"Any news?" she asked the men.

"No, ma'am. But Agent Blackledge wants to talk to the two of you."

Laura caught Nick's faint frown and matched the expression. They stepped into the library and Nick asked shortly, "What's up?"

The FBI supervisor looked up from a computer. "I need you two to stay in closer touch with me. In fact, I'd prefer it if you stopped your gallivanting around altogether."

Her warning instincts went on full alert, shouting frantically at her. They weren't exactly out partying the nights away. They were trying to find their son. What was going on, here? She prevented herself from blurting the question sharply, but still asked, "Why?"

Blackledge's gaze went opaque. Unreadable. Whatever he says next is going to be a lie. "We're kicking the investigation into high gear and events are likely to move faster from here on out."

"Does that mean you have new information you think will lead you to Adam?" Nick asked with a casual calm that was completely at odds with his keen, assessing gaze.

"We have resources well beyond what I can share with you," the FBI man answered with false warmth. "I'm sure you understand."

Okay, her warning instincts were screaming at her, now. First, the attack on them in Washington, and now this sudden evasiveness from the FBI agent in charge of Adam's recovery? She was dead certain the two were related. How deep into the U.S. government did AbaCo's tentacles reach?

She risked a look at Nick. A pleasant smile was pasted on his face, but he'd gone faintly pale. A person had to know him well to spot it, but he was as freaked out as she was. Not good. Very, very not good.

"Honey, I'm a little dizzy. Do you think you could help me upstairs?" she said wanly. "I think I need to lie down."

Nick, ever quick on the uptake, took her elbow solicitously. "You haven't been resting enough, darling. I know you're panicked, but you have to trust Agent Blackledge and his men. They're doing all they can. And if anybody can find Adam, it's the FBI."

He led her slowly from the room. As she left, she glanced out of the corner of her eye at Blackledge's turned back. His shoulders had come down from around his ears. Good. He'd bought their act.

When the bedroom door closed behind them, Nick opened his mouth to speak, but she waved him quickly to silence. He nodded, his expression grim. Instead, she said, "Do you think you could get a cold cloth for my forehead, and maybe some aspirin? I'm starting to develop a terrible headache."

He headed for the bathroom while she went to her closet and opened the safe there. It contained, in addition to the usual jewelry and back-up copies of important personal documents, an array of paraphernalia from her days as a spy. She pulled out a sensitive electronic scanner and checked their room in minute detail for any sign of bugs or cameras.

It was clean. She nodded at Nick. "As long as we keep our voices down, we can speak freely."

Nick blurted under his breath, "What the hell's going on with Blackledge? Why the sudden stonewalling?"

"I'm afraid you were right earlier. My call to the CIA about Meredith and AbaCo has upset someone. A lot. Enough to reach into the FBI to mess with the investigation of Adam's kidnapping."

Nick spoke thoughtfully, "I don't think Blackledge was involved in it before. He was legitimately trying to find Adam until this morning. I think this interference comes from above his pay grade."

"I have to agree with you."

"That means we can pretty much kiss off getting any significant help from the U.S. government from here on out with finding Adam. We're on our own."

The sense of isolation she'd been feeling before slammed into her even more forcefully. Tears, hot and infuriating because she had no time for them, filled her eyes. She swore at herself under her breath.

Nick was there in an instant, his arms strong around her. "We'll figure this out together. We're both smart and experienced at these sort of games. Besides, I promised Adam I'd keep him safe from the bad man."

"I'm not so sure the bad man has him," Laura mumbled against his chest.

Nick froze, arrested by the observation. "You know, that's a very good point."

She looked up from where she was smearing mascara on his white dress shirt. "How's that?"

"I think we may be on the same side as Adam's kidnapper in this whole mess. I wouldn't go so far as to say he's done us a favor by pulling our son out of harm's way, but there may be an element of truth to that. If the kidnapper's not associated with the CIA, FBI, or Meredith, he may be safer with the kidnapper right now."

"Oh my god," she breathed in horror. "The FBI has Ellie."

She couldn't help it. She started to shake, and then to cry. Not her baby, too. Her legs collapsed, but Nick caught her against him. He bent down, scooped her legs out from underneath her and carried her over to a big armchair by the window. He sat down, cuddling her against his chest like a baby, herself.

No matter how bad things were between them, they were both worried parents. They would always have that in common. And right now, she wasn't strong enough to turn down his emotional support.

Nick murmured soothingly, "As long as we play along with them, I can't imagine they'll keep her from us. We just have to pretend that everything's okay until Agent

Morris gets here with her." His eyes lit up. "In fact, I have an idea. Blackledge is a single guy, right?"

Laura nodded.

Nick grinned. "Even better." He dug out his cell phone and dialed quickly. "Agent Blackledge. It's Nick Cass. Do you have an ETA on Agent Morris and our daughter? My wife is getting…uncomfortable…you know, nursing mother…to pump or not to pump…"

She smiled in spite of herself at the awkward sputtering suddenly coming from the other end of the phone.

"Twenty minutes? Thanks," Nick said. "If you could have someone bring her up right away…"

More sputtering. Nick hung up. "There you go. Twenty minutes."

To pass the time, Laura climbed out of Nick's disturbingly comfortable lap to check her email—the private one she hadn't told the FBI about. A familiar name caught her eye as she scrolled down through various junk mails to it. "I got a message from Clifton Moore."

Nick tensed. "What does he have to say?"

Foreboding filled her as she opened the short message and scanned it rapidly.

Federal prosecutor will announce suspension of trial in a press conference at 8:00 a.m. tomorrow. Be sure to put eyes on it.

"Not so soon!" she gasped.

"What?" Nick moved quickly to her side and read the message for himself. He swore quietly. "We're out of time. We've got to *do* something."

She added tightly, "'Eyes on' is an old code phrase between Clifton and me. He's telling me my investigation is compromised from inside the Agency. We can't trust the CIA."

"We sure as hell can't trust the FBI, either," Nick replied.

She looked up at him in dismay as the totality of their isolation struck her. "We're completely on our own. If we're going to find Adam and rescue him, it has to be now. We have until 8:00 a.m. tomorrow morning."

"It's time for Daddy Finders Inc. to become Adam Finders Inc. To heck with the government. We'll find him ourselves."

Panic rolled through her, a wild storm riding a wind of despair. "I can't do this," she whispered.

"Maybe not alone," Nick replied firmly. "But together we can do this. We're both highly intelligent and extremely motivated. Between the two of us, we have massive resources outside the U.S. government. The first order of business is to find somewhere safe to leave Ellie tonight." He ticked off the requirements on his fingers. "She needs to be out of the house, with someone we trust, and whom the government won't know to look for."

Laura nodded, mopping tears from her eyes that threatened to spill down her cheeks. Nick was right. She couldn't fall apart now. Adam needed her. Needed *them.* And goodness knew, they couldn't drag Ellie all over the countryside when they went after Adam. Memory of that awful chase through the Cape Cod woods with men shooting at them and Ellie screaming her head off flashed through her mind.

She announced suddenly, "I know just the person. Emily Holtz's mother lives not far from here. Emily's the woman who helped rescue you from the ship."

Nick nodded. "I remember her well."

"Her mother, Doris, is as fierce as a lioness when it

comes to protecting her cubs. She was the woman in the safe room with Adam the night we rescued you and brought you here. She protected Adam when your kidnapper tried to recover you."

"Sounds perfect. Now we just have to figure out where Adam is."

He made it sound so easy. She'd been wracking her brains for days as to how to identify and find Adam's kidnapper to no avail. How to begin? A comment Nick had made earlier came back to her. Laura said thoughtfully, "You said before that Adam's kidnapper is on the same side we are. Let's follow that logic for a moment. Expand on what you meant by that."

Nick answered, "The kidnapper's mad at AbaCo. He wants to see them buried. Why? What did AbaCo do to him? If we could figure that out, it might give us a clue as to who he is."

Laura looked up into his eyes hopefully and continued the logic. "He knows AbaCo's been doing things that can get the company in serious trouble. Which means he's either in the Special Cargo division or has done work for it."

"Why is he taking action now? Why not earlier? Has he seen something that goes beyond what he can stand morally without taking action?"

"It probably isn't smuggled stuff in boxes that's got him so riled up. AbaCo's been doing that for years. Whatever goaded him to action is something new. Something appalling to anyone with a smidgen of conscience."

Nick added grimly, "Humans locked away in boxes for years on end might make him mad enough to act. And it might explain why he chose me specifically to put the screws to. He figures I'm as mad about that as he is. He can trust me to tear AbaCo apart with the vigor he thinks the company deserves."

Laura continued eagerly, "So instead of searching the entire AbaCo employee roster for fired employees, we should look for someone who's left the Special Cargo division recently under any circumstances. Maybe retirement or just quitting. The FBI's investigation of fired employees might not have been broad enough."

Nick rose as well. "And we just happen to have the Special Cargo division's complete personnel roster for the past few years, compliments of our friend Kloffman."

She raced over to her laptop and reached for the keyboard.

Nick said sharply, "Are you sure the guys downstairs won't see what you're doing on that?"

"Good point. Let me deactivate my wireless access and throw up a couple of extra security protocols."

"Maybe you should wait until Ellie's safely with us," he suggested gently.

She lifted her hands away from the computer, frustrated. "Waiting is so hard," she whispered.

"I got pretty good at waiting in my box," Nick murmured. "Come here."

As conflicted as she was about him, she wasn't about to pick a fight with him now. Adam's life depended on the two of them setting aside their differences and working together. Reluctantly, she sank into his lap and had to admit it felt shockingly nice.

He murmured, "I used to think about the vacation I would take when I was freed. I would imagine it down to the smallest detail. Where shall we go as a family when we're all back together?"

A family. Oh, how she liked the sound of that. If only it could be. She turned her attention to his question and replied, "You have to ask? We have small children. There's only one place on Earth to take them."

Nick laughed. "Orlando, here we come." He continued, "Shall we wait until Ellie's a little older or go right away?"

"Both, I think."

He nodded encouragingly. "Now you're getting the hang of it. What will we do first with the kids?"

They spent the next several minutes planning the details of their vacation. Although it did help her pass the time while they waited for Ellie's return, a little voice in the back of her head wondered if any of them would ever get to take the trip. She mustn't think that way!

A knock sounded on their door. Laura leaped out of Nick's arms and threw the portal open. A smiling Agent Morris stood there with a bundle of pink fuzzy blanket in his arms. It was all Laura could do not to fling herself forward and tear her daughter away from the guy. As it was, a sob shook her as the man handed her daughter over.

Nick thanked the agent quietly and closed the door as she retreated to their bed and unwrapped her daughter to perform a count of every last finger and toe. The infant was perfectly fine and thankfully hungry.

She nursed Ellie while Nick activated additional security protocols and opened a search algorithm on her laptop following her instructions. The three of them sprawled on the bed together, with the computer between them. Over the baby's dark head, she helped him build a mini-program to search the Special Cargo division's detailed personnel files.

Nick hit the enter key. The computer would eliminate all females, all non-French-speaking men, and all deceased employees in the Special Cargo Division. Then it would search for employees who'd left the division recently for any reason, rank ordering them according to when they'd left AbaCo. In a few minutes, a list of names scrolled down the screen.

Nick commented, "Unless our guy was some sort of contract longshoreman who didn't actually work for AbaCo, I'd lay odds our kidnapper's on this list."

She nodded resolutely. "Now we just have to figure out where all these guys are. The one we can't account for is our kidnapper."

"Easy as pie," Nick retorted. "We'll both work on it, and it'll go faster."

It didn't turn out to be quite that simple, however. The two of them spent the rest of the afternoon working on their respective laptops, hunting down the whereabouts of dozens of former and current AbaCo employees. His knowledge of the company's personnel record system turned out to be invaluable. Laura hacked into AbaCo's current Human Resources records, and he navigated rapidly to the address list used to mail various pension checks and insurance information to former employees. By eliminating those people who lived outside of North America, they removed over half the suspects from their list.

At about dinner time, someone knocked on their door. They hastily closed their computers and Nick opened the panel. A female FBI agent stood there. "Would you like us to send up some food?" she asked.

"Yes. That would be perfect," Nick murmured, turning on the charm. Laura watched in amusement as the agent blushed. She knew the feeling. The guy was impossible to resist. "Any new information?" Nick asked.

The agent stiffened fractionally and threw a glance in Laura's direction. "No, sir. I'm sorry."

Nick shut the door and pressed his ear to it, presumably to listen to the woman's retreating footsteps. He turned sharply. "She was lying."

Amused, Laura asked, "You're good at telling when women are lying to you?"

He answered sourly, "It comes with the territory when you're a reasonably eligible bachelor."

She laughed lightly. She had no trouble imagining the legions of women who must've thrown themselves at him over the years. More seriously, she asked, "Do you think she suspected anything?"

"No. You looked appropriately wan and distressed when she checked you out."

Laura snorted. "You're not the only good actor in this family."

He rolled his eyes at her, but accepted the compliment. If, indeed, it was a compliment at all. They traded a look of complete understanding. The two of them were cut from the exact same cloth. They did what it took to get the job done, and neither of them took life lying down. They went out and got what they wanted and didn't wait around for things to come to them. And right now, they wanted their son back.

She said quietly, "Shall we press on with our investigation?"

He nodded and gestured for her to precede him back to the table and their laptops.

"I think it's time to add a few more parameters to our sorting program," she announced.

"Like what?"

"People who are living on the east coast of the United States."

"We may exclude the kidnapper with those parameters. For example, the guy could live in California but have traveled here for the express purpose of kidnapping Adam."

Laura replied thoughtfully, "Setting up the logistics of a successful kidnapping takes time. The guy had to prepare a hideout, lay in supplies, figure out how to get into this house. I think he's been in this area for some time."

Nick nodded. "Your logic is sound."

"We're running out of time. We're going to have to take a few chances, follow our guts, and hope we're right."

He replied soberly, "I'd bet my life on your gut instincts."

"All right then. Let's finish this thing."

"Thank God," he replied fervently. "I can't stand waiting around anymore."

She texted Doris to ask if the woman would watch Ellie while Nick modified the search program. Doris responded almost immediately that she'd be delighted to babysit Ellie. As Laura was replying that they'd be at her home sometime later in the evening, Nick's computer beeped.

Laura got up and moved around to see what their revised search-and-sort program had turned up. Five names blinked on his screen. Now they were talking. That was a much more manageable list of suspects.

Nick piped up. "Can you check and see if any of these five remaining guys have bought land nearby in the last few years?"

She nodded, liking his logic. They knew from the videos that Adam was being held at a cabin of some kind, likely surrounded by woods to explain Adam's leaf collection. She ran a search and came up with nothing, however.

Nick frowned. "Can you search farther back? Maybe our kidnapper bought land and held it for a while before he built a cabin on it. Or maybe he's had it for a long time."

Again, frustratingly nothing. Her head was starting to throb. This line of research had to pan out. They didn't *have* anything else.

Nick spoke again. "How about searching county tax

records for the surnames of these guys? Maybe the land's been in the family for a long time."

She frowned. "Not every county has digitalized its tax records. But it's worth a try."

They got a list of hits, maybe twenty properties in all. She dragged the addresses to a map program and a series of pinpoints popped up on a map of the mid-Atlantic region. She commented, "One of the leaves in Adam's collection came from a bush that grows well near salt air. So let's assume he's near the Atlantic coast. That leaves us with these four locations."

They tried several more search programs, and nothing they did could narrow down which property was the likely hiding place of Adam's kidnapper. There was no help for it. They were going to have to check out all four. It was going to be a long night.

As she packed an overnight bag for her daughter, Laura's maternal urges protested at leaving Ellie with Doris. But she knew it to be the best thing. She had no right to endanger an infant, and furthermore, tonight's activity would require stealth. And as she knew from personal experience, crying babies did *not* qualify.

She and Nick waited until Ellie had nursed and was deeply asleep to put their plan into motion. Laura loaded Ellie's spare baby bag with pistols, ammunition, and a small pair of night vision goggles. She opened the safe in her closet and threw in nearly a hundred thousand dollars in cash, too. It was mostly hundred-dollar bills bundled into five-thousand-dollar stacks. In her experience, when bribing someone—like a kidnapper—cold, hard cash had a much more visceral and powerful impact than a check or electronic wire transfer.

She snuck down the back staircase to the kitchen with a sleeping Ellie in her arms. Right about now, Nick should be making a rueful request to Agent Blackledge to be allowed to go to the store and get tampons for Laura. She'd predicted that none of the all-male FBI team on duty tonight would volunteer to run the errand for him. From her perch in the shadows a few steps above the kitchen, she vaguely heard Nick grousing about three women living in a house this size and not managing to have a tampon among them. Grinning to herself, she told Marta what she and Nick were up to and slipped quickly into the darkened garage.

Nick joined her in a few moments. In keeping with the errand guise, Laura and Ellie laid down in the cramped backseat of the hybrid car the staff usually used for small errands.

"Any problems?" she murmured as the car backed quietly out of the garage, its electric motor ghostly silent.

"Nope. Just the word tampon terrified them all into catatonia," he chortled.

"Works every time on bachelors," she declared as she installed Ellie's car seat and tightened the straps holding it in place. She eased the baby into the carrier and breathed a sigh of relief when the infant didn't wake.

"Then I guess I'm not a bachelor anymore," he commented. "Female stuff doesn't scare me. Good thing, too, now that I have a daughter."

Did that mean he was planning to stick around for his kids' lives, then? The vacation to Disney World wasn't merely an exercise in mental distraction? Her initial reaction was relief, but hard on its heels came doubt. Could she trust him to follow through? Would he breeze in and out of their lives when it was convenient for him? Throw some money at the kids to buy their love and then take off again? Or would he be there for the long haul? For the doctor's visits and homework and myriad decisions that came with raising a child? Would he be there for her to lean on? To talk over parental concerns with? Did she dare share the burden with him and risk yet another disappointment?

The drive to Doris's house didn't take long. The older woman was thrilled to have a baby to spoil rotten, and her husband looked satisfyingly grim and confident when Laura relayed that there might be a threat to Ellie's safety if anyone found out the baby was here with them. Nick approved of the well-oiled shotgun Doris's husband pulled out and leaned against the wall inside the front door.

While Doris cooed at Ellie and pronounced her the cutest baby ever, Laura looked stricken. Nick put a comforting arm around her shoulders. "She'll be fine, darling. Tonight, Adam needs us."

He was right. With a last kiss on Ellie's forehead, Laura turned away from her daughter. "Let's do this," she announced soberly.

Nick nodded back equally soberly, his hand straying to the hip of his jacket, where she knew a pistol was concealed. She sincerely hoped it didn't come to that.

Chapter 13

Nick drove. Once they were alone, the research done, a plan of action in place, the temporary truce between them evaporated. Just like that, all the questions about their relationship circled them like vultures, waiting for the death of their love. Not yet. They had to rescue Adam first. Then the rest of it could fall to pieces. Thankfully, the act of steering the car along increasingly narrow and rural roads was calming. It distracted him from the mistrustful look in Laura's eyes, from the way she pulled back slightly whenever he reached toward her. He stared at the dark ribbon of asphalt before him bleakly. He'd lost everything and everyone in his life once before and survived it. A vision of Adam laughing at race cars flying across the playroom taunted him. Ellie's baby burbles as she snuggled close to him. Laura's face, transported in ecstasy as they made love—

Nope. It would kill him this time.

"What can I do to make things right between us?" he finally asked into the heavy silence between them.

Laura glanced over at him, startled. She answered slowly, "How am I supposed to trust you when you've kept so many secrets from me?"

"The only secrets I'm keeping from you now are the ones I can't remember. I'd tell them all to you if I knew what they were," he replied in frustration.

She shrugged. "It's not enough. I need to know the children and I will be safe from whatever or whoever else lurks in your past."

"It's not like your past is entirely free of dangers, either," he retorted. "Life is never a certain thing. You have to take it as it comes, for better or worse."

She made a sound. He couldn't tell if it was distress or disgust. "I don't recall promising any for better or worse with you."

"I'd have married you months ago, but I didn't know if I was already married or not. The only reason I didn't propose was because I was afraid to become a bigamist."

"Then why didn't you find out?" she snapped. "You knew your real name. A simple search on the internet would've revealed whether or not you were married."

"The only thing I knew for sure was that stirring up my past would be dangerous. And it turns out I was right. I knew the best and only way to make sure you and the children were safe was to lay low. And I was right about that, too."

Laura was silent beside him, but the turbulence of her thoughts buffeted him.

"I love you," he declared. "You say you love me. Why does it have to be any more complicated than that?"

"Because it's not enough to love someone. A long-term relationship takes more than that."

"Like what?"

"Trust. Friendship. Openness. Respect."

"Haven't we had all of those this past year?"

She exhaled hard. "And were any of them real? Did you trust me enough to tell me who you really are? Were you open with me about what you do remember of your past? Did you respect me enough to tell me there might be dangerous secrets in your past?"

"I was trying to protect you and the children! Doesn't that count for anything?"

"And look how well you did at that," she replied with a hint of bitterness in her voice.

Her words were a scalpel slicing into his heart. She was right. He'd failed them all. Adam was in mortal danger, their daughter was hidden with a stranger, and Laura was on the verge of falling apart. He had to make it right. But how? If she wouldn't give him a chance, what was he to do?

The one thing he wasn't going to do was give up. He'd fight with every breath in his body to keep his children safe and win back the woman he loved. No matter how long it took or what he had to do. He gripped the steering wheel with renewed resolve. There *had* to be a way.

They approached the first cabin on foot, creeping through the woods in taut silence until they were able to peer in the windows cautiously. The tiny building turned out to be deserted. A quick look through the filthy glass panes revealed a thick layer of undisturbed dust over everything in the structure's interior. No one had been here for months.

They drove for another hour of strained silence to the second cabin. As they neared the isolated road that, according to the GPS, dead-ended at its front door, he turned off the headlights and guided the car slowly through the darkness. It coasted forward in near total silence, only the crunch of gravel under the tires disturbing the night.

"Stop here, and turn the car around," Laura instructed. "We'll go the rest of the way on foot."

He nodded and jockeyed the car back and forth, turning it to face the way they'd come on the narrow, one-lane road. No doubt she was setting them up for a fast getaway if things went bad. Always thinking several steps ahead, Laura was. He wondered if it was trained habit or intuition that led her to make the suggestion.

He had to shove his door open through a tangle of brambles and weeds. Thorns caught at his legs, and he picked his way carefully through the dangerous mass, stomping it down as he went in anticipation of his return. An apt metaphor for his entire life, right now—jumping on thorny problems in a futile effort to keep from being hopelessly snared by them.

"Did Super Mommy bring the diaper bag of doom?" he murmured.

Laura smiled reluctantly as she pulled night vision goggles out of said diaper bag and donned them. They made her look buglike. "I'll take point."

He fell in behind her, amused at the abrupt shift from Super Mommy to Super Spy. He'd been on a half-dozen photo safaris in Africa, and creeping through the woods at night like this reminded him strongly of trying to get close-up pictures of lions in the Serengeti.

Laura stopped and pointed ahead. He looked forward over her shoulder and spotted the vague outline of a man-made structure ahead. "There it is," she breathed.

Stealthy creeping came naturally to him as they eased toward the cabin. Laura paused in the shadow of a broad, bushy juniper and he moved up close behind her. They were looking at the back of the cabin. A small porch stuck out, one side of it dominated by a large, stacked woodpile. On each side of it was a window. Both windows were boarded over with plywood, and no light crept around the edges of the boards.

Laura took a hard look around the clearing, and then signaled him forward. They sidled up to the porch. Nick took each step one at a time, gently easing his weight onto each foot to minimize creaking. Laura did the same. She gestured for him to press his ear to the door while she watched his back. He nodded his understanding.

The wood was rough and cold against his ear. Holding his breath, he concentrated hard. He thought he heard a scrape inside. A shuffle of sound. His adrenaline spiked hard, and abruptly his heart pounded like a bass drum in his ear.

"Someone's home," he mouthed silently.

Laura nodded, the movement jerky as if she was tense, too. She eased down off the porch by slow degrees. It was nearly impossible to restrain his impatience behind her. But he understood the drill. Ten minutes of slow stealth now was better by a mile than an injured child—or worse.

They backed into the woods to crouch behind a stand of brush and confer quietly.

"Now what?" he asked.

For the first time he could ever remember, he saw indecision on Laura's face. The sight tore at him as little else could. A mother terrified for her child's safety was a terrible thing to see. He reached out to squeeze her hand.

"We have to make contact with the kidnapper, but we can't freak him out. We don't want to scare him into doing something rash."

Nick nodded. "Sounds reasonable."

"But I don't know how to do this. I know how to perform surveillance on secure locations, how to break and enter practically anywhere, but I have no clue how to initiate a conversation."

"How about we knock on the front door like we did with Kloffman?" Nick suggested.

Laura blinked. "You think that would work?"

"I think it would if you do it. A woman's voice is a lot less intimidating than a man's. And if he recognizes you, he knows you would never do anything to endanger your son."

She nodded, thinking hard. "I'd have to make the approach alone. Unarmed."

Alarm ripped through him. "Now wait a minute. Let's not get carried away, here. I don't want anything bad to happen to you."

She gave him a sad little smile. "Something bad already has. My son's been taken from me."

Granted. Still, the idea of risking her life, too, appalled him.

"Have you got any better ideas?" she whispered.

They had no phone number, no email, no other less-direct method of talking to whoever was inside that cabin. "I guess you're knocking on the door," Nick allowed reluctantly. "But be careful."

It was her turn to squeeze his hand. "Count on it. And hey. For all we know, this isn't the right place. Some hunter out here for a vacation may open that door."

A tiny part of him hoped that was true for Laura's sake. But mostly he hoped she was wrong. Time was running out on them to find their son.

Laura took a deep breath. She couldn't ever remember being this scared—not in her career as a spy, not when she'd gone into labor with her first child, not even when she'd executed the daring rescue of a prisoner who turned out to be Nick. She shook from head to foot and couldn't seem to control her knees properly.

All she had to do was walk across that little clearing, knock on the door, somehow gain the trust of the kidnapper, convince him she and Nick were on his side, and inquire politely as to the return of their son. What could be easier?

Unfortunately, her training permitted her to think up a thousand things that could go wrong with that simple little plan, many of which ended with Adam's death and/or hers.

"If it feels bad, back out," Nick whispered. "Trust your instincts. They've never led you wrong."

Hah. If only. She'd followed her instinct to trust Nick in Paris and had lost her partner because of it. She'd followed her instincts not to push Nick about his past, and look where that had gotten all of them.

She rose to her feet and handed over her pistol to him. The diaper bag she kept with her. If nothing else, maybe she could use the cash inside it to buy Adam's release.

"The diaper bag is the perfect touch," Nick nodded. "It disguises Super Spy perfectly as Super Mommy."

If only she truly were either one of those alter egos. Maybe they wouldn't be in this mess. She was beyond tired and scared and simply doing what she had to do for her son. And after all, wasn't that what all mommies did every day?

"Here I go," she muttered.

"I love you. Be strong," Nick murmured back.

Right. Strong. For Adam. She squared her shoulders and stepped into the clearing.

Since she was planning on announcing her presence anyway, she didn't make any attempt at stealth until she reached the porch. Out of long habit, she eased up the steps so they wouldn't creak. This was it.

She dared not stop to think about it or she might very well chicken out. She raised a fist and knocked quietly on the front door. The faint noises from the other side of the panel stopped abruptly and entirely.

"Hello!" she called out quietly. "It's Laura Delaney. I'm alone and I'm not armed. I'd like to talk to you about what you know about AbaCo. I think we might be able to help each other."

The pause on the other side of the door stretched out. She waited. And waited.

Oh, yeah. She and Nick had definitely found the right place. Elation frosted the edges of the tension gripping her.

Finally, a noise sounded just on the other side of the door. Perhaps a floorboard creaking.

"I have a diaper bag with me," she said carefully. "I'm going to set it down beside me on the porch. I'm clasping my hands behind my head. I won't move, I promise. If you'd like to search me and the bag, that's fine."

Another long pause. But this time, it was broken by the sound of a bolt opening. Her knees all but gave out from under her. *Please, God, let Adam be on the other side of that door.*

The door opened an inch. No surprise, the barrel of a shotgun poked out first. And then an eye. Its owner showed a sliver of iron-gray hair and rough, tanned skin.

A gruff voice ordered, "Step back from the door."

She did as ordered.

"Now open the bag. Tilt it so I can see into it."

She knelt slowly and unzipped the pink, quilted bag.

A low whistle came from inside the cabin. "Whatchya planning to do with all that cash?"

"Give it to you if you want it."

The door opened wide to reveal a short, burly man. He looked to be in maybe his mid-sixties, with a grizzled gray stubble covering his jaw. He wore a flannel shirt over massive shoulders with the sleeves rolled up to show forearms corded in muscle. Nick had been right, after all. This guy had been a longshoreman—she'd bet her life on it. She'd also bet he'd seen something on AbaCo's ships he couldn't live with.

He took a step forward and patted her down with awkward, but thorough, hands. He muttered an apology as he handled her more private places.

"Do you want me to dump out the money so you can see there's nothing dangerous underneath it?" she asked.

"Naw, you're not that dumb." He gazed sharply around the clearing, no doubt looking for a trick. "Get inside," he said roughly.

She stepped into the cabin's living area and looked around quickly. No sign of Adam. Her heart thudded to her feet. Had she and Nick been wrong about this place? Was she wasting her time here?

Her host raised his voice and called, "You can come out."

The bedroom door opened cautiously, and two pairs of eyes, one high and one low, peered out. The door panel flew open and a small, dark-haired projectile launched itself at her. "Mommmmeeeeeeee!"

Tears were streaming down her face by the time Adam flung himself into her arms, nearly knocking her over. He clutched her neck until she almost choked, and she didn't care in the least. She hugged him back as hard as she could, and he finally squirmed in protest. She loosened her grip a tiny bit, but not much.

"I knew you'd find us!" he babbled. "This is Joe, and he's been really nice. He said you and Daddy were helping him and would come for me when the bad man was beaten. Did you win? Is Daddy okay?"

She made eye contact with the older man over Adam's head. "That's what I'm here to talk with Joe about." Her gaze shifted to Lisbet, who'd stepped into the room more sedately than the boy.

"Are you all right?" Laura asked the nanny.

"Yes. Joe's been a perfect host. We're both fine."

"I can't thank you enough for taking care of Adam," Laura tried to say calmly. Except the words provoked a new rush of tears down her cheeks.

"I treated him as I would my own son, ma'am."

Laura nodded, too choked up to say more.

"Took you long enough to find us," Joe rumbled. He set the diaper bag down on the kitchen table. "Didn't you bring any help with you? I was counting on that."

Huh? Laura stared at the man, bemused.

"You don't think this thing with AbaCo is over, do you?" he snorted. "They don't give up that easy. You of all people should know that."

"What are you talking about?" she asked in alarm.

"You led their goons to us, of course."

She frowned. "We weren't followed. We made sure of it."

Joe pounced on that. "We who? Who's out there?"

"Nick's in the woods. It's just the two of us."

"Damn. No FBI? No cops?" Joe demanded.

He sounds disappointed! "I don't understand."

"You better get your fella in here. We need to talk," Joe said cryptically. As she stared, he waved an impatient hand. "Go on. Go get him. I'll wait."

Still carrying Adam, who was attached to her like a leech—and that was just fine with her; she didn't feel like letting go of him for a good long time, either—she headed for the front door.

She stepped onto the porch and called out, "Nick. It's okay. You can come in, now."

His tall form materialized out of the trees. He strode forward, then broke into a jog, and then into a run. He bounded onto the front porch and wrapped both her and Adam in a rib-cracking hug. He buried his face in her hair, and she felt the shudder of a sob wrack his body against hers. Adam's grip shifted from her to Nick, but she didn't begrudge the two of them the hug.

"Daddy! I *knew* you'd come for me. I missed you. I got more leaves for my album. And Joe showed me how to tie knots and build a fire and all kinds of cool stuff. Will you take me camping when we get home?"

Laughter replaced Nick's silent relief in shaking him. "Sure, buddy."

"Y'all want to bring the love fest inside?" Joe said from the doorway. "We gotta talk. And if I don't miss my guess, we ain't got long."

Nick frowned and glanced down at her.

"He thinks AbaCo has followed us. He's disappointed that we didn't bring the cavalry along."

They stepped inside and Nick closed the door behind them, asking grimly, "Did you tell him we think the cavalry's been infiltrated by AbaCo?"

"We haven't gotten to that part, yet," she answered ruefully.

"What're you two talking about?" Joe blurted.

"We think a few individuals in the CIA and the FBI work for AbaCo."

"Come again?" the older man demanded.

Reluctantly, Laura set Adam down. "Do you think you could go get your leaf album for us? Mommy and Daddy need to talk to Joe for a minute. And maybe the two of you should pack your things."

Lisbet nodded in silent understanding of the unspoken request to keep Adam out of earshot and took him by the hand.

Laura followed the men over to the rough wood table in the corner and sat down in the chair Nick held for her.

"What's up?" Joe asked shortly.

She leaned forward and asked gently, "Are we correct in guessing that you don't like AbaCo any more than we do?"

"Those bastards are killing folks. Locking 'em in boxes till they die and then tossing them overboard like trash. I don't care how bad a thing a man done, nobody deserves that."

They'd been spot-on in their assessment of Adam's kidnapper. She made eye contact with Nick and he nodded back.

She leaned forward. "As you anticipated, your kidnapping Adam spurred the two of us to turn over a few rocks with AbaCo's name on them. It turns out the person or persons running AbaCo are a front for a Russian operation. We don't know if they're Russian intelligence or Russian mob, but either way, AbaCo's doing their dirty work."

Nick picked up the thread. "It turns out they've got agents inside our government. When Laura and I poked in the wrong places, they tried to kill us."

She added, "And they've pulled strings to get the AbaCo trial called off. That will be announced at a press conference in the morning."

Predictably, Joe surged up out of his seat, swearing furiously, and paced the small room in agitation.

"But all is not lost," Nick explained quickly. "In fact, this may work to our advantage. We can take our accusations to the media now, without the trial restricting what we can say. And Laura and I have collected a ton of damning data on AbaCo." She watched as Nick's gaze went black and genuinely furious. "We can bury those sorry bastards so deep they'll never come up for air. I swear to you, I will take them down."

Joe shook his head. "You don't understand. You have no idea how powerful these people are. How ruthless. They'll kill us all. You were supposed to bring an army with you to get the boy. Enough force to get us out of here alive and into protective custody while the Feds catch AbaCo's thugs who were sent here to silence us and prove they're up to no good."

Laura jolted. "Is that what this is about? You need protection from AbaCo? All you had to do was ask us. We'd have given it to you."

"You ain't big enough to take these guys. Hell, they messed up the U.S. government."

She frowned. "Not the entire government. I still know plenty of people whom I trust completely. People who can make you disappear. Give you a new identity. You'll be completely safe."

Joe snorted. "Like the U.S. Marshals are gonna be immune to these guys if they can get inside the CIA and the FBI? Besides, I'm a felon, now. The Feds would never help me."

The man had a point. Several, in fact.

Nick studied the older man intently. She tried to guess where Nick's thoughts were heading.

"So, here's the deal," Nick finally announced bluntly. "We owe you one for pulling Adam out of the middle of this mess and keeping him safe while we investigated AbaCo. And there's no law saying we have to press charges against you for kidnapping. What do you want from us?"

Joe looked startled. "You ain't mad at me?"

Nick shrugged. "You scared the hell out of us and nearly killed Laura when she found out Adam was missing. But you did protect him whether you meant to or not."

Laura gave Nick an approving look. He was making allies with Joe. Putting the three of them squarely on the same side of the fight.

Joe sat back down at the table. "The way I figure it, AbaCo's thugs are on their way here now if they're not already outside."

"How's that?" Laura asked sharply.

"Of course they followed you. They know how good you are at finding lost stuff. Any idiot knows you'd go after your own kid like a madwoman. Of course, you're gonna find him. All they gotta do is bug your house, track your cars and wait for you to lead them to me."

"Why are you so important to them, Joe? What do you know?"

"It ain't what I know. It's what I got."

"And what's that?"

"Video. And not just any video. I was a security technician on a couple of AbaCo's big container ships based out of the Paris office. What with pirates and all, you'd be surprised how high-tech security is on those ships. Almost as good as your house, ma'am. Took me a few weeks to figure that system out."

Nick leaned forward eagerly. "What *have* you got?"

Joe grinned broadly. "I got your ever-lovin' wife on tape bringing you down to the container ship, *Veronique*, and telling the boys to lock you up an' never let you out. She's some piece of work, that woman."

Nick lurched in his seat. "You're kidding."

"Nope. She was with a bunch of Russkies. Talkin' Russian. But see, my first job was on a Russian oil tanker and I *govoreet* me a little po russkie."

Satisfaction surged through Laura. If Joe was telling the truth, that footage would be enough to break not only AbaCo, but Nick's wife. Startled, Laura realized that was actually jealousy roiling around in her gut, purring in satisfaction that Meredith Black was about to go down in flames. "How does AbaCo know you've got the tape?" Laura asked.

"They inventory the hard copies every few days. They're read-only—takes special equipment to burn copies—so I had to take the original with me when I left. They've been trying to find me ever since."

"Have you got copies of these videos now?" Laura asked the older man.

He nodded. "Had 'em made before I snatched your boy. But who's gonna listen to a guy like me? I'm a nobody. An' I figure AbaCo'd take me out long before I convinced anyone to take me serious. But you two. You're all rich and educated and got fancy connections. Folks'll listen to you straight away. I had to make sure you testified against them bastards."

Sadly, he was probably right.

"If you'll hand over a copy of that tape to me," Laura said earnestly, "I swear to you we'll make sure the right people see it."

Joe started to speak, but raised his hand abruptly, signaling them to be silent. Laura went on full alert. What had he heard? She'd been so focused on the implications of Joe's evidence she hadn't been listening carefully.

The older man got up and moved toward the front window. For a husky man, he moved quietly. Joe reached for the curtain to peek out and murmured over his shoulder, "Turn off the lights in here, and turn on the bedroom light so whoever's out there will think we're moving within the house and not suspicious of noise outside."

Nick did as the man ordered. Laura moved to the left-hand window, and Joe took the right one while Nick went to the back door to peer out.

"Report," Laura called out quietly.

"I think I see a couple of guys off to the southwest a bit," Joe muttered.

"I've got at least one on my left," Laura said.

"Either they're better than I am or no one's back here," Nick replied quietly.

"I told you they'd track your car. Looks like I was right. We gotta go," Joe grunted. "Get Lisbet and the boy."

Laura lurched. "We don't know who's out there. How many people are there? Are they armed? Here to help us?"

Joe scowled. "Don't be stupid. Them's AbaCo's men out there. His wife's flunkies." Joe jerked a thumb in Nick's direction.

"I'm fairly certain I married her in order to trap her into revealing her schemes," Nick replied a shade defensively. "I have no recollection of her, and believe me, I'm divorcing her as fast as humanly possible when we get home."

Laura thought fast. Worst-case scenario, Joe was exactly right. And given how the last few days had been going, she was inclined to expect the worst case. They needed an escape plan. Clearly, charging out the front door with her son and putting him in the middle of a firefight was out of the question. They had to go out the back and pray it wasn't a trap.

"Our car's out the back and through the trees maybe a quarter-mile away. It's parked on a dirt road that runs north-south. Do you know it, Joe?"

"Yup. Long ways to go with shooters chasing a person."

"We could use a diversion," Nick commented.

"We don't have the resources to mount one," she replied grimly.

Joe piped up. "We got this cabin. What say we make a fireball of it?"

It could work. Particularly if they took out a couple of the people currently lurking outside, too.

Laura stepped away from the window and poked her head into the bedroom. "Lisbet. Adam. Put on the darkest clothing you have with you. Quickly. Leave everything else behind."

Nick was already yanking open kitchen cabinets looking for supplies.

"Don't bother," Joe bit out. "I got nothing like you need. I knew a little kid would be here. I took out the dangerous cleaning supplies and the like."

While the mommy part of her was grateful for his consideration for Adam's safety, the spy within her lamented the lack of good household chemicals for improvising a bomb. Hmm. A bomb…

She had an idea. "Joe, have you got an electric fan, by any chance?"

"Yeah, actually. This place ain't got air-conditioning, and it can get a mite stuffy in the afternoon."

"I need it. Quickly."

The older man nodded and disappeared into the bedroom.

She raced to the front door and rummaged in the diaper bag. "Any movement out back?" she asked Nick tersely.

"Nope."

"They're probably doing the same thing we are. Trying to figure out how to get inside and take us all down."

Nick retorted bitterly, "Yeah, but they'll bring in commandos wielding automatic weapons and it'll be lights-out for us."

He was right. If they didn't get moving soon, this confrontation was going to be over before it began. They needed to even the odds. Fast. She fumbled in her pocket, pulled out her cell phone and dialed rapidly.

"What're you doing?" Nick blurted.

"Calling in the cavalry."

"But—"

"Not the CIA or the FBI. The local sheriff."

A female voice spoke in her ear.

"9-1-1. What's your emergency?"

"There are a bunch of men outside my place." She gave the woman the address quickly. "They've got guns and a rope tied into a noose. I think it's the Ku Klux Klan. They're coming to lynch me. Hurry!"

Laura stuffed the phone in her pocket.

"The KKK?" Nick asked doubtfully.

"It was the most inflammatory thing I could think of. No lawman wants somebody lynched on his watch. The sheriff will call in every deputy he's got and probably every one in the next county over while he's at it. There'll be a half dozen men here in minutes and fifty guys with shotguns here in a half hour. And they'll know these woods."

Nick grinned as Joe stepped into the living room carrying an old-style floor fan, the round kind that oscillated from side to side. Perfect.

Laura nodded. "I need string or twine if you have it, and a manilla envelope."

"String I got. But I don't mail nothing from here."

She eyed a high shelf beside the front door. "That's okay. I can improvise." Heck, her whole crazy idea was a massive improvisation.

Lisbet and Adam stepped into the room.

Laura pulled a small jar of petroleum jelly and a plastic

bag of cotton balls out of the diaper bag. "I need the two of you to mix these together as thoroughly as you can."

They set to work and she turned to Nick. "I need you to rig a string to the front door. When AbaCo's people open it, we'll need to knock over this can of baby formula." Thank God she'd never gotten around to pulling the sample can from the hospital out of the bag and had been in too big of a hurry earlier today to take it out.

Nick frowned, and she explained. "Non-dairy creamer is extremely flammable when it's dispersed in air as a cloud of powder. Ellie's baby formula is largely made of the same stuff."

Joe started to chuckle. "I worked at a grain elevator when I was a kid. We lived in fear of the dust from wheat or corn catching on fire. Would've blown the elevator sky high."

Laura nodded. "Same principle. We'll set up this electric fan under that shelf. When AbaCo's guys open the front door, Nick's string will dump the can of baby formula down on the fan, which should disperse the formula in a cloud throughout this room."

Nick added, "And then we use the cotton balls and petroleum jelly to provide a fire to light the stuff, and kaboom—"

Laura grinned as his eyes lit up.

"—Super Mommy saves the day," Nick finished.

"That's the idea," she muttered as she positioned the electric fan. "How's that cotton coming?"

"Done, ma'am," Lisbet answered.

Laura pulled out one of Ellie's bottles and quickly stuffed the petroleum jelly soaked cotton balls inside. She bit the end off a nipple and pulled some of the cotton out the tip. "Voila. One non-dousable candle to light off our explosion."

Nick frowned. "Will it be hot enough to ignite the powder?"

Joe answered for her. "Hell, yeah. The slightest open flame around flour dust will set the stuff off."

Nick and Laura finished setting up their trap, and in a few minutes, it was ready to go. She would have loved to test the string on the door, but they didn't dare. They'd get one shot at this thing.

Joe checked out the back door one last time and gave Laura a thumbs-up just as Lisbet announced from one of the front windows, "I think I see someone moving out there. It looks like he's coming this way."

"Time to go," Nick announced grimly. "I'll carry Adam. How do you feel about piggybacking with me, son? Can you hang on if I run really fast?"

Adam nodded, his eyes big and dark with fear. The child was far too perceptive for his own good sometimes. He knew they were in trouble.

While Joe, Lisbet, Nick and Adam headed for the back door, Laura took one last peek out the front window. A shadow slid from one tree to another right at the edge of the small clearing, no more than fifty feet from the house. Yup, whoever was out there was on the move.

She carefully lit the baby-bottle candle with a match. It gave off a bright, steady flame. The thing should stay lit for at least an hour. Although she doubted it would have to burn for more than a few minutes, given how close those people outside were. She raced for the back of the tiny cabin.

"Okay," Nick murmured. "From here on out, we move slow and silent."

There were nods all around as he eased open the door. Crouching low, he moved out into the dark. Joe and Lisbet followed and Laura brought up the rear, closing and locking the door quietly behind her.

Laura picked up a twig off the porch and jammed it into the key hole, breaking it off inside the lock. There. Now no one could pick this lock and gain entrance from this direction, limiting them to the front door and their trap. Super Mommy had done all she could to buy them an escape.

Chapter 14

Nick forced himself to breathe slowly, inhaling and exhaling on a steady three count. But it was damned hard to stay calm out here in the dark, all exposed like this. The fifty feet or so to the nearest trees seemed like a thousand miles as he eased one foot after another forward slowly, doing his best not to shuffle any leaves.

Each little noise from someone in the group made him wince, but there was nothing they could do for it. It wasn't like anyone besides Laura was a trained operative. The pistol clutched in his right hand felt heavy and foreign all of a sudden. He'd shot on target ranges before, and was even a half-decent skeet shooter. But the idea of gunning down another human being rattled him.

He clenched his jaw grimly. He'd do whatever it took to keep his son and his woman safe. Even if that meant killing someone.

Laura moved off to the left a bit, and Joe slid off to the

right a little ways. Nick squinted into the darkness, trying to remember which trees he and Laura had come from between before. They couldn't afford to miss the car by much.

Lisbet stumbled slightly in front of him and crunched loudly in a pile of dead leaves. Laura gestured sharply with her hand. Even not knowing any fancy hand signals, it was clear she wanted them to stop and get down. Nick dropped onto his haunches. Adam's feet must've touched the ground, because the child's weight around his neck suddenly eased. Nick reached back to pat his son reassuringly on the shoulder.

Laura was crawling now, and Lisbet imitated her employer. Nick duckwalked awkwardly, unwilling to commit to being on his hands-and-knees and unable to protect Adam quickly if need be.

Joe moved farther off to the right and was first to reach a stand of brush. His bulky silhouette disappeared from sight. Then Lisbet slipped behind a tree trunk. And finally, tree branches closed in around him and Adam. They were far from safe, but he felt better with someplace to hide.

Ka-boom! Boom!

Bright white lit the forest around them like day as a wave of heat slammed into his back. The propane tank beside the cabin must've blown, too. Adam cried out in terror and buried his face against the back of Nick's neck.

"Run!" Laura screamed.

Nick spared one glance over his shoulder and saw a half-dozen weapon-toting men streaming around the flaming remains of the cabin. He turned and ran for his and Adam's life. He'd hate to see how many men would've come after them were it not for the explosion. Flaming bits of debris began to rain down around him, sizzling as they hit damp leaves. Hot embers on his face felt like needles stabbing him, but he ignored them and just kept running.

A gunshot exploded off to their right. Crap. That sounded like Joe's voice grunting in pain. Was he hit? It wasn't like Nick could stop and check on the guy. Adam's arms tightened even more around his neck. *Hang on, son.*

Nick caught up to Lisbet, who waved him to go ahead of her. The young woman was fast, but not very good at seeing and dodging tree branches and brambles. Not that he was much better. He was just willing to slam into and through any obstacles in his path at this point.

"This way," a female voice panted off to his left.

Laura. He veered toward her.

"Joe?" she gasped as he fell in beside her.

"Haven't seen him," Nick grunted back.

"We need that video."

"We can't stop for him," he retorted.

She didn't answer, but merely turned even more to the left. He followed in grim silence, glad that it sounded like Lisbet was keeping up with him leading the way.

When Laura screeched to a halt seconds later, he barely managed not to slam into her. Lisbet did slam into him. Adam let out an *oomph* that was all too audible in the sudden silence.

Laura signaled something. She pointed at her eyes then out into the woods and then held up three fingers. Three men off to their right, maybe? The pistol in his hand crept up into a firing position. He peered into the trees and shadows desperately. As much as he didn't want anyone to be out there, he almost hoped he'd spot someone so he could shoot them.

Laura held up four fingers. Then five. He didn't need to see the distress lining her face to know they were in serious trouble. They were out of distractions, and as best he could tell, they weren't even close to the car, yet. Too bad they couldn't just pay these guys off to go away. Pay…

Crouching, he slid over beside Laura. She looked at him questioningly, and he pointed at the diaper bag flung over her shoulder. Frowning, she handed it to him. He reached inside quickly and pulled out a bundle of hundred-dollar bills, sliding off the paper ring holding it together. Quickly, he scattered the bills on the ground around them.

Laura smiled briefly and got into the act, yanking out handfuls of cash. They started moving again, sliding slowly from shadow to shadow, spreading handfuls of bills all around them.

He didn't actually expect their pursuers to abandon the chase and go on a money hunt, but perhaps the incongruous sight of thousands of dollars in cash lying on the ground and clinging to leaves and branches would at least give the men pause. And they were playing a game of seconds right now.

The money ran out all too soon, and Laura took off running again. He and Lisbet followed.

The women were panting nearly as hard as he was. The woods stretched on interminably before them with no sign of that dirt road and their vehicle. Had they gone the wrong direction? Missed the car entirely?

His thighs and lungs were burning, and Adam was starting to feel like he weighed a hundred pounds. Not that Nick minded. He'd have gladly carried his son if he weighed a thousand pounds.

Without warning, a sandy track opened up before them. The road. Praise the Lord.

Laura paused, looking right and left, and took off running to the left. The footing was firm and free of obstacles, and her stride lengthened. Nick stretched out his long legs into a full run. Lisbet was falling behind a little, but he couldn't stop for her any more than he could for Joe. His first priority was to get his son out of here safely.

He thought he recognized a clump of brambles and bushes from before. They were getting close to the car, now.

And that was when the apparition rose up in front of them, standing in the middle of the road, an automatic weapon pointed directly at them. Laura pulled up, breathing hard, and he did the same. Lisbet stopped just behind him, and he felt the woman's hands go around Adam's waist, preparing to grab the boy and take off with him if necessary. If they lived through this night, he was going to make that nanny a very rich woman for her loyalty to Adam.

"My God," Laura breathed. "Kent? Is that you?"

Kent? Her old CIA partner? The one who'd disappeared in Paris the night he and Laura met? Nick peered into the darkness. A shock of recognition rolled through him. He'd seen this guy before. In Paris. Six years ago. A flash of a darkened street, wreathed in shadows not unlike these ones, came to him.

Nick didn't know if he was more staggered by the fact that he'd remembered something from the lost years, or the fact that he suddenly and certainly knew exactly why he'd been in that alley in Paris. Nick had found out that a young, beautiful CIA agent's partner had defected to the Russians and was setting her up for kidnapping. *Laura had been the target that night in Paris.* He'd taken it upon himself to save her because it would be a rush to play James Bond and because he thought she was hot.

"Hi, Laura. You're looking good," the Russian double-agent said casually.

"I thought you were dead," she exclaimed. "I'm so glad you're alive. Where have you been?"

"Long story."

Nick snorted. "Is that what they call treason these days? A long story?"

Laura glanced at him in shock and dawning comprehension. She looked back at her old partner in dismay. "How could you? We were lovers. Friends."

Kent shrugged. "The money was a hell of a lot better on the other side of the fence."

"You sold Nick out for money?" she asked in burgeoning outrage.

Nick corrected gently, "He sold you out, not me. You were the target that night, Laura. Kent and Meredith were going to kill you."

She glanced over at him in horror, then over at her old partner. "No. We were going to meet an informant. And the guy turned on us. Kidnapped you."

"I was kidnapped because I knew too much. If it weren't for that crazy prenup, they'd have just killed me. Isn't that right, Kent?" Nick asked. He continued gently, "Kent works for Meredith. Tell her. Laura deserves that much from you. After all, you betrayed a woman who loved you."

"You loved me?" Kent asked sadly.

"Yes," she half whispered. "I did."

Nick interjected. "Look. We've got a small child with us. Let him and Laura go and you can have me."

"No!" Laura cried out, staring at him, aghast. "The two of you have to leave. I couldn't live with losing either of you."

Something big crashed out of the trees behind them just then, and Nick and Laura whirled simultaneously to face this new threat.

Nick grunted as a bloody Joe all but fell into him.

He caught the man and barely managed to keep his feet under the man's weight. Lisbet rushed forward to wedge a shoulder under Joe's armpit. Adam started to cry and Nick shushed him. The child buried his face against Nick's neck and continued to shake with now-silent sobs.

"They're coming," Joe gasped. "Did what I could. Go."

"We've got a small problem," Nick murmured to the older man. "Laura's old partner is between us and the car and pointing a big gun at us."

Laura was speaking again, her voice low and reasonable. "Let us go for old time's sake, Kent."

"Why should I?"

"You owe me one. I loved you, and I know you loved me at least a little. And Lord knows, you owe Nick one after locking him in a box for five years."

Kent frowned.

Nick added, pitching his voice to be calm and soothing, "He's just a boy. Let Adam go and we won't kill you."

The former spy seemed to consider that.

"Do you have children of your own?" Nick asked.

Kent shook his head in the negative.

Vividly aware that a whole bunch of bad guys would burst out of the trees any second and shoot them all, Nick explained with desperate calm, "You see, Laura and I are parents. We'll both die without a second thought to protect our son. And we both have weapons. As soon as you fire yours, we're both going to fire ours at you. You'll kill one of us, but you won't get us both before the survivor takes you out. Frankly, Kent, that's a trade I can live with because my son walks away alive and with one parent. How 'bout you, darling?"

She nodded resolutely beside him. "Yup. I'm good with that. Besides, these woods are swarming with law enforcement. You'll never get away from here if you fire your gun and draw them all with the noise."

Kent's weapon wavered.

Crashing noises and shouting came from the trees close by.

"It's now or never," Laura muttered under her breath.

"Let's go," Nick replied grimly.

The two of them started walking forward. When Kent didn't immediately shoot them, they picked up their pace. Broke into a jog. And then raced past the man, who took off in the other direction.

Nick spotted the outline of the car ahead.

Gunshots erupted behind them. Maybe the law enforcement types Laura had just lied about had, indeed, arrived. Ducking instinctively, Nick dived for the car. He shoved Adam in the backseat. Lisbet piled in after him and Laura pushed Joe in the other side.

Nick glanced up in time to see a figure in black racing toward them. For the second time in as many minutes, he recognized the face bearing down on him. The *female* face. Of his wife. Meredith Black-Spiros—criminal, traitor, and bitch. The person who had not only made his life hell for five years, but who had *threatened his son*. He could forgive all the rest. But not that.

Without hesitating, he swung his pistol to bear on her.

Meredith made eye contact with him as she pointed a wicked looking semiautomatic weapon in his direction. She grinned, a disdainful expression that said she knew full well he didn't have what it took to kill her.

Quickly taking aim at the middle of her chest, he double-tapped the trigger. The impact of flying lead slammed Meredith backward. She looked down at the wet stain blossoming on her chest in stunned disbelief and back up at him. For good measure, he sent two more rounds into her torso.

"In the immortal words of Arnold Schwarznegger," Nick snarled, "consider this a divorce."

Meredith's legs folded and she crumpled to the ground.

Nick spun, jumped into the driver's seat and punched the ignition button, Laura leaped in and, hanging out the window partway, fired her weapon at someone behind them.

"Gun!" she shouted at Nick holding out her free hand.

He passed her his weapon and she continued rapid firing out the window.

Nick stomped on the accelerator and the vehicle jumped forward. The Prius wasn't exactly a Formula One race car, but in a few seconds it was still faster than a bunch of guys running on foot. Between shots, Laura tossed her empty pistol into the backseat, and Lisbet dug out a spare clip from the bottom of the diaper bag. Joe slammed the new clip into the weapon and passed it forward to Laura when Nick's pistol clicked on empty.

The accelerating car bumped wildly and careened around a corner, finally getting up a good head of steam. The sound of gunfire retreated abruptly into the distance behind them. In a few more seconds, only the sound of the car's gasoline engine whining disturbed the sudden silence.

He drove a few minutes in tense silence while everyone else watched out the back window for pursuit.

Finally, Laura said tentatively, "I think we did it."

He glanced over at her, and the two of them traded looks of mutual relief and triumph. They had their son back. Their family was safe. *Their family.* God, he liked the thought of that.

"Uhh, sir, I think we'd better find a hospital rather

quickly. Joe's bleeding quite a lot back here," Lisbet announced.

Adam wailed at that. "Uncle Joe, don't die! I never had an uncle before."

Laura stabbed at the car's GPS system and gave Nick tense instructions to the nearest hospital while Lisbet performed what first aid she could in the backseat. No ambulance ever drove so fast, and perhaps no other Prius, as Nick coaxed every last ounce of power out of the hybrid engine.

Eventually, the bright lights of a small hospital came into view. Laura had already been on the phone requesting that medics meet them at the door. Nick spotted several nurses and doctors waiting as they pulled up.

The trauma team whisked an unconscious Joe out of the back of the car onto a stretcher and then away into the bowels of the emergency room. Adam cried softly in Lisbet's arms.

"They'll do everything they can for him, buddy," Nick assured his son gently.

The three adults and Adam trailed inside the waiting room and Laura headed for the admissions desk. "You need to call the police immediately," she told the attendant. "A whole bunch of men just tried to kill us. That's how our friend got shot. They'll be here soon with big guns."

Panic lit the woman's face and she snatched up a telephone and began babbling into it.

Nick put an arm around Laura's shoulder. "You do have a way of evoking strong reactions in people."

Smiling a little, she gazed up at him. "Do I do that to you?"

"You always have. Always will."

She turned into him, leaning her forehead against his chest. "I like the sound of that."

They stood together like that for a long moment, and he savored the rightness of her in his arms. No doubt about it, this woman was his entire world.

"Were you really willing to die for Adam?" she asked in a small voice.

"You even have to ask? Of course. He and you and Ellie are my family. The three of you are my whole world. I'd die for any of you. I *love* you." By that he meant all of them, but she was bright. She'd get that. "Laura, love is about all the things you said it is: trust and openness and respect. But it's also about sacrifice and protectiveness and taking care of those you love. Love has many, many forms of expression."

She went still against him. And by slow degrees, she finally relaxed in his arms. "You really don't remember Paris?"

"Funny that. Seeing Kent jogged a brief memory for me of the night we met. Enough to know he'd sold you out and was working with Meredith."

She jolted and pulled back to stare at him.

"If I got that back, maybe I can get more." He shrugged. "I'm willing to try if you're willing to wait for the truth before you condemn me and throw in the towel on us."

She frowned thoughtfully and he took that as a hopeful sign. At least she hadn't rejected the offer outright.

Several police cars streamed into the parking lot just then, light and sirens screaming. Laura stepped away from him to go brief the police.

It was a long night. They had to answer questions from the police for hours. Doris and Marta got calls to let them know all was well. Joe survived surgery to remove three bullets from his gut, but faced a long recovery. It went without question that he'd come back to the estate with them for that. After all, Adam had never had an uncle.

Laura was dozing in Nick's arms the next morning when an all-news channel announced that the trial of AbaCo Shipping had been suspended by federal prosecutors on grounds of national security. He woke up Laura to catch the end of the announcement, although it was moot at this point. Adam was safe and asleep with Lisbet in one of the examining rooms under police guard.

Nick was surprised, though, when the newscaster continued, "In other news, wealthy socialite, Meredith Black-Spiros was found dead last night in Virginia. The circumstances of her death are being withheld by police pending an investigation."

He jolted. "Will they send me to jail for killing her?"

"She pointed her weapon at you, and you had every reason to believe she would fire it. Trust me, it was self-defense all the way. Joe and Lisbet and I will all testify to it. No worries." She reached up to smooth the furrows from between his brows. Slowly, his clenched neck and shoulder muscles unwound.

Laura glanced up at him out of the corner of her eye. "What are your plans now that she's dead?"

Nick shifted so he could look down fully at her. "To marry you as soon as possible if you'll have me. After that, I'd like to work with those doctors of yours—cooperatively this time—to see if I can recover any more of my memories for you, so you'll know without a shadow of a doubt that I always loved you and only you."

She was silent for a long time, and then she said slowly, "I don't need a psychiatrist to extract that information from your mind for me to know it's true. I've known it deep down in my gut all along. I was just hurt and scared and worried about Adam. Can you forgive me for doubting you?"

"Truly?" he breathed.

"Pinkie swear," she avowed solemnly.

The explosion of joy in his gut was so forceful it hurt. Laughing, he answered, "Darling, there's nothing to forgive. I'm the one who needs forgiveness. I swear, everything I did, good, bad, or stupid, was to protect you and the children."

"I believe you. Only a man who loves his family would offer to sacrifice himself to save them like you did last night."

She leaned up to kiss him, and as always, he lost himself in her the moment their lips met. She was everything he'd ever wanted and more. How blessed was he to have found her not once, but twice in a lifetime?

"Uhh, Laura?" he mumbled against her mouth.

"Hmm?" she mumbled back, not breaking the addictive contact.

"You didn't answer my question."

"What question would that be?"

"Will you marry me?"

She leaned back to smile up at him. "I thought you'd *never* ask."

For some reason, his heart was pounding and his face felt like it was on fire. "Is that a yes?"

She laughed softly. "Of course, it's a yes. I was a goner from the moment you stepped out of that alley and saved my life."

His arms tightened around her. "You've got that all wrong. You saved me that night. You've saved me over and over, in fact. How can I ever repay you?"

"Love me and the children for the rest of our lives."

"And our grandchildren's and great-grandchildren's lives," he promised.

She sighed blissfully and relaxed in his arms. "What

are we going to do with ourselves now that our family is all safe and Super Mommy can hang up her diaper bag?"

Smiling, he replied, "That's one heck of a diaper bag I've got to live up to. I was thinking about getting my shipping company back and cleaning up its act. I'll teach Adam how to run it when the times comes."

"And Ellie," Laura added firmly. "This is an equal-opportunity family."

Nick smiled broadly. "I wouldn't have it any other way." He pondered with no small wonder what kind of woman Ellie was going to grow into with a woman like Laura to raise her. "What about you, darling? What do you want to do next?"

"First, I want to pick up Ellie and take my whole family home. Then I was thinking about going back into the daddy-finding business. It's a whole lot safer than tangling with kidnappers and double agents."

Thank goodness. He'd had all the excitement he could handle for a few decades.

Laura's cell phone rang and she dug it out. "Huh. It's Clifton Moore." She spoke to her former boss briefly. "You're sure about that?" A pause. "Okay then. Thanks."

Nick waited until she disconnected to ask, "What was that about?"

"His people have found Meredith's mole in the CIA. He was Kent's old college roommate, and he rolled over on her man in the FBI. They're both in custody and singing like canaries. She was Russian mob. It looks like we smoked out a whole network of arms dealers, human traffickers, and smugglers."

"Not a bad day's work, Mrs. Spiros," he murmured.

"Mmm, I like the sound of that." She snuggled more closely against him.

"Get used to it, darling. You're going to be hearing it for the rest of your very long and happy life."

"I love you, Nick."

He was never going to get tired of hearing that. Even if she spent a hundred years saying it to him every day, those words were always going to make him feel like the luckiest guy alive. And just maybe he was.

Epilogue

Laura glanced up from her computer as Nick entered her office. "Hi. How was the meeting today?"

"Couldn't have gone better. You're looking at the brand-new chairman of the board of AbaCo Shipping. And as my first act in the job, I made a motion to change the name of the company back to Spiros Shipping."

"Did it pass?" she asked eagerly.

"Unanimously." He came over to her desk chair and leaned down to nibble on her ear. Ripples of pleasure spiraled outward from her earlobe. If he wasn't careful, they were going to have that third child they'd been talking about soon rather than later.

He whispered in her ear, his lips moving deliciously against it, "Then, in another unanimous vote, the board appointed me CEO."

Beaming, she threw her arms around his neck and kissed him soundly. "Oh, Nick. That's wonderful."

"Are you busy this afternoon?" he asked, glancing significantly at her. Deliberately misunderstanding his intent in asking, she answered casually, "I got an email from Todd Blackledge. I was just replying to it."

"What did our favorite FBI agent have to say?"

"He's been reassigned to the New Orleans office. He got promoted to agent-in-charge of something or other. At any rate, he likes it down there. He mentioned a little problem he's having, though."

Nick massaged her neck under her hair just the way she liked it. She was going to be putty in his hands if he kept that up for much longer. She murmured, "Apparently, there have been several suspicious disappearances of babies down there."

"Is he investigating it?"

"There's no case, formerly. The local police are handling it. But he was wondering if maybe I could look into it. Unofficially, of course. See if I can turn anything up."

"I thought your thing was tracking down missing dads."

She frowned. "Yes, but these women's babies are gone. Many of them are single moms with no family or resources to track their children down. I know exactly how panicked and helpless they're feeling right now."

Nick's gaze met hers soberly. Neither of them would ever forget what it was like not to know where their son was or if he was safe. "I think you should help them."

"It might mean more time working for me. More time away from you and the children."

"I know you. If you might help a mother get her baby back, you won't be able to live with yourself if you don't try."

She tugged on his tie, bringing his mouth down to hers, and whispered against his lips, "Thank you."

"I can think of a better way for you to thank me—"

"Mommy! Daddy! You'll never believe what we saw at the zoo today!" Adam burst into the office with Uncle Joe in tow. The older man had fully recovered from his gunshot wounds and taken to his duties as bodyguard to Adam and Ellie like a fish to water. Lisbet followed more sedately, carrying a sleepy but smiling Ellie.

Nick scooped up Adam, exclaiming, "Pee-Yaw! You smell like an elephant. You need a bath!"

"With bubbles?" Adam asked eagerly. Even Ellie perked up at that suggestion.

Laura laughed and followed the entire entourage upstairs. "Now you've gone and done it, Nick. We'll be mopping up the mess for hours."

"Ahh, but you're so good at cleaning up messes," he retorted, laughing.

He wasn't too bad, himself. Between the two of them, they'd managed to put not only their family, but their romance, back together, stronger than ever. Laura stepped into the bathroom and laughed as a fistful of bubbles came flying her way.

"Oh, it's on now," she said, laughing.

Yup. Life didn't get any better than this.

* * * * *

OPERATION BABY RESCUE

BY
BETH CORNELISON

Beth Cornelison started writing stories as a child when she penned a tale about the adventures of her cat, Ajax. A Georgia native, she received her bachelor's degree in public relations from the University of Georgia. After working in public relations for a little more than a year, she moved with her husband to Louisiana, where she decided to pursue her love of writing fiction.

Since that first time, Beth has written many more stories of adventure and romance suspense and has won numerous honors for her work, including a coveted Golden Heart award in romance suspense from Romance Writers of America. She is active on the board of directors for the North Louisiana Storytellers and Authors of Romance (NOLA STARS) and loves reading, traveling, *Peanuts*' Snoopy and spending downtime with her family.

She writes from her home in Louisiana, where she lives with her husband, one son and two cats who think they are people. Beth loves to hear from her readers. You can write to her at PO Box 5418, Bossier City, LA 71171, USA or visit her website, www.bethcornelison.com.

To my mom, who is always ready to lend me a helping hand (or eyes to read a manuscript) and who shares my passion for books. I love you!

Prologue

"Push!"

Elise Norris squeezed her eyes shut, gritted her teeth and pushed through the contraction that wrenched her belly in an excruciating vise grip.

The nurse at her side held her hand and wiped perspiration from Elise's brow. "You're doing great! Almost there…"

"Now breathe. Catch your breath. I think the next one should do it." Dr. Arrimand peered at her over his mask and gave a confident nod.

As the pain eased, Elise rolled her head to the side to gaze at the ultrasound image of her daughter that was taped to the bed rail. The photo, which she'd carried in her wallet for weeks, had been her focal point throughout the delivery. In fact, her daughter had been her focal point for the past nine months. Longer than that. She'd been planning for, saving money for and praying for this day for years.

With a trembling finger, she traced the lines of the fuzzy picture she'd memorized in the past several weeks and smiled. Raising a child alone would be difficult. She had no illusions otherwise. But Elise had known she wanted to be a mother, wanted to raise a family, since she'd been a little girl herself. When she'd celebrated her thirtieth birthday without a husband with whom she could share the joys of parenthood, she'd researched sperm banks and set about finding the perfect donor to father her baby.

"It's okay, Gracie," she whispered to the ultrasound picture. "We'll be fine. You and me. We'll be a t-team." The last word of her pledge caught in her throat as another powerful spasm of pain ripped through her. Building quickly to a crescendo, the contraction stole her breath.

"This is it. Keep pushing!" Dr. Arrimand coached.

She clenched her teeth and concentrated on bringing her daughter into the world. All her physical strength and love were focused on the task. Minutes later, the nurse laid a pink-faced bundle in her arms.

Elise gazed into her daughter's eyes and fell instantly in love. The bond was powerful, emotional, solid. Her daughter. Her flesh and blood. Her dream come true.

With one finger she traced Gracie's nose and lips. "Hi, sweetheart. I'm your mommy. Oh, you're beautiful." She smoothed her daughter's tiny eyebrows and kissed her sweet forehead. A thin layer of hair the same shade of golden blond as Elise's crowned Grace's head, and she saw her own blue eyes reflected in her baby's cerulean gaze. "You're perfect. I love you."

Elise tugged on the pink blanket the nurse had swaddled Gracie in and freed her daughter's right arm. She lifted Grace's hand and studied the tiny fingers, perfect fingernails, delicate skin. "So sweet and little..."

Not wanting Grace to get chilled, Elise pulled the

blanket back around her daughter and noticed a small red pear-shaped birthmark on Grace's right shoulder. "Angel kissed," she whispered to Grace. "That's what my mom said about my brother's birthmark."

A pang of regret stung her heart. Had she lived, what would her mother have thought about her granddaughter, her namesake?

At her side, the nurse fumbled with the tubes of her IV.

"What's that?" she asked, spotting the syringe in the nurse's hand.

"This will help with the pain so you can rest." She injected a clear solution into the port and smiled. "Just another minute, Mom, then I need to take the baby to be checked thoroughly by the staff pediatrician."

Already the drug she'd been given made Elise woozy. She frowned. She hadn't asked for pain medicine. She wanted to be alert, savoring every detail of the experience. "I don't want to sleep. I want to be with my baby, to bond…"

She heard her speech slur slightly as her eyelids drooped.

"We'll bring her to your room later to breastfeed." The nurse scooped Grace from Elise's arms, and Elise felt a pang in her heart.

"Not yet. Give me… just another… minute." But Elise could barely keep her eyes open. She forced herself to stay awake long enough to watch the nurse whisk Grace through the door to the next room. As she disappeared from Elise's line of sight, her daughter gave a mewling cry.

Gracie...

Elise fought off the fog of sleep and blinked her surroundings into focus. The patient room at the small-town hospital was not lavishly furnished but was comfortable and painted a cheerful pale yellow. With a sigh she thought of the state-of-the-art hospital in Lagniappe, Louisiana, where she'd planned to give birth.

With her due date still three weeks away, she'd believed she'd be fine driving to the weekend crafts fair in the rural community forty-five minutes from her home. If she began having contractions, she could easily get back to Lagniappe. Or so she'd thought. But the best laid plans…

Her water had broken while she paid for an antique rocking chair, and the contractions had come hard and fast. Within ten miles, she'd been doubled over in pain and had pulled to the side of the road to call 911.

The local ambulance had arrived quickly—thank God—and she'd been rushed to Pine Mill Community Hospital in time for the delivery.

The window was dark now, telling her night had fallen, and she searched her walls for a clock. How long had she slept? A simple white clock over the door read eleven forty-five. Elise rubbed her eyes and worked to clear the cobwebs of drug-induced sleep to do the simple calculation. Grace had been born at 3:30 p.m., so…more than eight hours had passed. She groaned and found the call button on the bed rail.

Enough of sleep. She wanted to hold her daughter. Nurse her daughter. Memorize every inch of her daughter's face and hands and toes…

"Can I help you?" came the response to her page.

"I'm awake now, and I want to see my baby. Can someone bring her to me?"

Her request met silence then a hesitant, "Um, I'll…have the doctor come talk to you."

The doctor? Elise tensed, butterflies kicking to life in

her gut. She didn't like the uneasy hesitation in the nurse's voice.

"Is there a problem? Is my baby okay?"

"Dr. Arrimand will be in to see you in a moment, ma'am," a different, more authoritative voice said.

"But what about my daughter? I want to see her." No response. "Hello? Hello? I want my baby brought to me!"

Again silence answered her. She buzzed the nurses' station, but her page was ignored. Irritation and concern spiked her pulse. Elise threw back her covers and swung her feet to the floor.

If they wouldn't bring Grace to her, she'd go get her from the nursery herself. She was Grace's mother, and they had no right to keep her from her. If something was wrong, she deserved answers…now!

Her head spun as she pushed off the bed, and her body throbbed from the rigors of the delivery. Elise grabbed the bed railing to keep from falling. Black spots danced in front of her eyes, and she waited impatiently for her equilibrium to return. When the room stopped shifting around her, she tried again to make her way to the door.

"Oh, Ms. Norris! You shouldn't try to walk alone yet!" a nurse fussed as she bustled into the room with a blood-pressure cuff in her hands. She took Elise's elbow and steered her back to the bed.

Elise tried to shrug away from the nurse's grip. "I want to see my daughter!"

With a strength that overpowered Elise's post-delivery condition, the nurse guided her back to the bed. "Dr. Arrimand has been called. He's on his way, and he'll explain everything."

The cryptic response rang warning bells in her head. A bubble of panic formed in her chest. "What does he have to explain? What's wrong with Grace?"

"The doctor will—"

"No! Tell me now! What happened? Where's my baby?" Tremors of dread shook her.

At that moment, the dark haired doctor, now wearing a white lab coat instead of scrubs, stepped into her room and helped the nurse maneuver Elise back to the bed.

Elise drilled the doctor with a hard, frantic stare. "Where's my daughter? Why won't anyone talk to me?"

Dr. Arrimand took a step back from the side of the bed and cleared his throat. "I'm sorry, Ms. Norris, but while you were asleep, your daughter's heart..." He paused, pressing his mouth in a grim line, then sighed heavily. "...Stopped beating."

A chill washed through Elise, and she was sure her heart had stopped, as well. "Wh—what?"

"We did everything we could to resuscitate her, but... we couldn't save her."

The room tilted. Blood whooshed in her ears. Shock rendered her mute and unable to move.

This couldn't be happening. She had to be hallucinating from the drugs they'd given her. Surely she'd heard him wrong. They had the wrong person.

"I'm very sorry," the doctor muttered, eyeing her with pity.

No. Her baby was *not* dead.

No, no, no, no, noooo!

The denials in her head became a keening wail. Agony and horror rose in a suffocating wave, filling her chest, squeezing her throat.

Questions pounded her brain. What made her heart stop? Why couldn't they save her? Why had they waited to tell her? Where was Grace now?

But her heart ached too much to voice them. Shock

and grief made all but gasping sobs and tormented moans beyond her reach.

In the blink of an eye, her dream come true had turned into every parent's worst nightmare. Her baby was dead.

Chapter 1

Fourteen months later

Elise shuffled into the church fellowship hall and cast a wary gaze around the assembled group. The rich aroma of freshly brewed coffee scented the air, lending a warmth and welcome to what she expected to be a most uncomfortable environment—sharing her grief with strangers.

One of the women seated in the circle of chairs spotted her standing in the doorway and called to her. "Hello. Are you looking for the grief-support meeting?"

Elise took a reinforcing breath and nodded.

The woman stood and waved her closer. "Please, come join us." As Elise approached the circle of chairs, several of the men stood, as well, greeting her with smiles and nods of welcome, and the woman who'd spoken first took her hand and patted it. "My name's Joleen Causey. I'm the group facilitator. Welcome."

"Thanks. I'm Elise Norris." She gave Joleen an awkward smile, and when the facilitator motioned to a seat next to her, Elise sat on the folding metal chair. As the others introduced themselves in an onslaught of names she didn't even try to remember, she scanned the faces of the group gathered in the small circle and gripped the edge of her chair. Several elderly ladies gave her curious glances, two gentlemen with gray-streaked hair nodded in greeting, a couple about her age clutched hands and sent her wan smiles, and a raven-haired man she estimated to be in his early thirties met her gaze and flashed her a strained crooked grin. "Jared Coleman," he said.

Other than the couple who clung to each other's hands as if their lives depended on it, Jared Coleman stood out simply because he was at least twenty-five years younger than any of the other members. She wondered briefly whom he'd lost and how he'd wound up in this group.

She'd been told about the group by a neighbor who attended the church that sponsored the meetings. For six months, Elise had worked on gathering the nerve to attend this grief-support program. For someone who'd been looking out for herself most of her life, who had established her independence from an early age and prided herself on her efficiency, reliability and self-sufficiency, seeking help had felt like a defeat. But when the one-year anniversary of Grace's death passed, Elise had still been moving through her life in the same fog of pain and denial as she had the first week. While she knew she'd never forget the child she lost, she had to come to grips with Grace's death so she could move on in her life.

"Don't feel like you have to talk tonight if all you want to do is listen," Joleen said. "But if you want to talk about what brought you here today or anything else that's in your heart, please feel free. We're here to listen and support you however we can." She flashed another warm and encouraging smile, tucking a wisp of her blond hair behind her ear, and Elise nodded.

"I came tonight because…" She took a deep breath. "…Just over a year ago, my daughter died right after birth."

Across the circle, the young wife gasped. Elise's gaze darted to her, but the woman was sharing a sad look with her husband. A prick of envy poked Elise. At least this woman had someone to share her grief with. In the past months, Elise had felt more alone than ever.

Elise squeezed her hands into such tight fists, her fingernails bit into her palms. "I only had a few minutes to hold her before…" She paused, feeling a knot forming in her throat. "Anyway, I'm just having a hard time… handling it."

"Of course. Many people say losing a child is the hardest death for a person to experience. But you're not alone." Joleen gestured to the rest of the group. "We're all here to help each other."

Elise forced a thin smile of acknowledgment then stared down at her lap. She hadn't talked with anyone about Gracie in months, largely because she couldn't get through even a simple comment without getting choked up. And the instant her eyes got teary, her neighbors or her colleagues at the Lagniappe newspaper, where she was a staff photographer, would back away with stricken expressions, as if they expected her to dissolve into wailing histrionics.

Knowing that her grief made other people uncomfortable chafed. Since when was there a time limit on compassion for a person's loss? But since talking about Grace was difficult anyway, she'd soon learned to avoid the topic of her daughter. Would sharing her feelings about Grace and the unfairness of her loss be any easier here?

"We lost our baby, too."

Elise jerked her head up and looked at the man who sat clinging to his wife.

The wife had her mouth pressed in a tight line as if struggling not to cry, but her eyes held Elise's. In an even tone, the husband continued, "It's been six months now, and while coming here—" he gestured with his head to the group "—has helped, it's still hard, really hard, for both of us to deal with. So while I won't pretend to know what you are feeling, because everyone grieves differently, we know at least something of what you're going through."

The wife bit her bottom lip and nodded to Elise.

"My son Sammy died fifteen years ago," a white-haired lady next to Elise said, patting her arm, "and I still think of him every day. It gets easier with time, but a mother's love never ends."

Elise swallowed hard, fighting back the stranglehold of emotion rising in her throat. If she allowed her tears to come now, she was afraid she might not be able to stop crying. Had coming here been a mistake? How could she relive the horror of that day, the crushing sense of loss over and again by coming to this group every week?

When she scanned the faces around the circle again, her gaze met Jared Coleman's. His dark brown eyes were locked on her, and an odd expression of guilt or uneasiness shadowed his face.

"Do you and your husband have any other children?" Joleen asked, and it took a moment for Elise to realize the question was directed to her.

"Oh, I…I'm not married. And no, no other children."

Joleen gave her a sympathetic look. "I see. Well, the loss of a child can be hard on a marriage. Divorce, sadly, is common following such a tragedy."

The young woman across the circle nodded. "Greg and

I have promised each other to be open and honest about our feelings. This group is part of our strategy to make sure our marriage survives."

Elise shook her head. "No, I mean I was never married. I—" Elise stopped when the eyebrow of one of the older women across from her raised in judgment. She didn't owe this group an explanation of her personal choices. A pulse of anger for the woman's haughty attitude helped Elise get a handle on the burgeoning tears in her throat. Taking a deep restorative breath, she folded her arms around her midriff and sat back in her chair. She stared at the floor near her feet, second-guessing her decision to attend the meeting.

Joleen apparently read Elise's body language for what it was, a disinclination to say any more on the topic, and directed the next question elsewhere.

"Jared, earlier you mentioned that you'd had an especially tough day last week. Would you like to tell us what happened?"

Without raising her head, Elise angled her gaze up from the floor to glance at Jared Coleman. He met her eyes briefly before clearing his throat, shrugging a shoulder dismissively and shifting in his seat. "Um, I…" His gaze darted away, and he cracked the knuckles of one hand with his other.

His restlessness and reluctance to speak intrigued Elise. Especially since his guilty furtive glances toward her told her his discomfort sharing with the group centered on her presence. She made a point of averting her gaze, hoping to make him feel less on the spot.

"Isabel took her first steps last Wednesday," Jared said at last.

Around the circle, several of the women cooed.

Elise tightened her grip on her sleeves. First steps? Clearly Isabel was a baby. About one year old.

The same age Grace would have been had she lived.

Like a fist to the gut, a shot of renewed grief landed a sucker punch that stole Elise's breath. She sat very still, keeping her gaze on the floor, but she felt Jared's eyes watching her.

"As happy as I was about her walking," he continued, "it just brought home to me, again, all the milestones Kelly will never see."

Now the women around the circle made noises of empathy and shared sadness for Jared's revelation.

Elise made a few mental calculations. Jared was here alone. He apparently had a one-year-old daughter. Was the absent Kelly his wife?

He said no more about the situation, letting his feelings about the event go unspoken. In the ensuing silence, one of the older women launched into a story about missing her late husband during the holidays and family celebrations.

Elise hazarded a glace across the circle and found Jared's attention on her again. Instead of jerking her gaze away, as if she'd been caught peeking at something forbidden, she held his stare. More than grief over the story he'd just shared, she saw concern and guilt in his dark brown eyes. Guilt?

She was still pondering the reason behind his odd expression half an hour later when the group dismissed for refreshments. Elise had no appetite for the cookies on the table by the exit, but her mouth was dry, and she decided to stop for a cup of lemonade before she left. Her pause at the refreshment table gave Joleen a chance to catch up with her before Elise made her escape from the awkward meeting.

"I'm so glad you came tonight," she said, placing a hand on Elise's arm. "I hope you'll come back. Talking about your experiences and your feelings gets easier with practice, and having the support of people who understand what you're going through is invaluable."

How could anyone really know what she was feeling? Her grief seemed so personal.

Elise forced a smile. "Thank you." She made no comment on whether she'd return. The jury was still out on that. Even the little she'd said tonight had been painful to share. She drained her lemonade quickly, hoping to make a hasty exit before any other members of the group caught her in an uncomfortable conversation. Tossing her empty cup in the trash, she spun on her heel to leave…and almost collided with a broad chest belonging to a man with dark brown, soulful eyes.

"Hi," Jared said with a quick flash of a lopsided grin.

"Oh, uh…hi." Elise's heartbeat performed a stutter-step. He was much taller than she'd expected, and this close to him, she could smell a tantalizing hint of sandalwood.

He rubbed his palms on his jeans once before sliding his hands in his pockets. The rattle of keys told her he was fidgeting. "I'm sorry if I…made you uneasy or caused you more pain tonight."

She blinked at him and furrowed her brow. She wasn't sure what she'd expected him to say, but an apology was not on the list. "Pardon?"

"Talking about my daughter." He gave an apologetic wince. "When the Harrisons joined the group…" He hitched his head toward the young couple still chatting with an older lady at the circle of chairs. "…Kim would get upset when I talked about Isabel. I thought, maybe, since you'd lost your baby…hearing about my daughter would be…especially difficult." He pressed his lips in a taut line of regret. "If it was, I'm sorry."

Elise could only stare for a moment. His sensitivity to her pain was thoughtful and also…frustrating.

"I, um…" She shook her head in disbelief. "Thank you, but…I don't expect you to censor yourself to protect me. Sure, it hurts to hear about other people's kids and think about what might have been, but…that's not your problem."

He shrugged and frowned. "Maybe, but I'd hate to think you decided not to come back because my stories about Isabel upset you. Losing my wife was hard enough. I can't imagine how hard it would be to have lost Isabel, how difficult it must be for you and the Harrisons."

Pain shot through her chest, and she murmured, "It's been hell."

He pulled one hand out of his pocket and flipped it up in a gesture that said she'd proved his point. "And I don't want to make it worse."

She nodded, swallowing hard to force down the knot of emotion that had worked its way up her throat. "I appreciate that. But how selfish would it be of me to expect you not to say what you needed to about your daughter, if it helped you work through your own grief for your wife?"

He lifted his chin and cocked his head as if her comment caught him off guard.

Before he could say anything, she raised a hand. "Besides, I get a little tired of people avoiding mention of babies, and especially Gracie, my daughter, as if pretending she never existed would be easier for me, when really it's their own awkwardness they want to avoid."

She heard the bitter edge in her tone and bit the inside of her cheek. She hadn't meant to snap at him. Her frustrations with her coworkers and neighbors weren't his fault. But instead of taking offense, he smiled and nodded.

"Exactly. I get the same thing from my friends concerning my wife. As if any talk of spouses is suddenly taboo. I hate it."

His response surprised her. Something warm unfurled in her chest, releasing a bit of the pressure that squeezed her lungs. When was the last time someone had actually understood the tangled emotions she had over losing Grace? Even this tiny connection to Jared made her feel a little less alone. "Your wife must have died recently if Isabel is only a year old."

He nodded. "Nine months ago. Isabel was five months old when Kelly was killed by a drunk driver."

A spark of outrage fired through her. "A drunk driver. It's bad enough to lose someone to disease or an accident, but when another person's carelessness is to blame… that's—" She shook her head, fumbling for the right word to voice her dismay.

"Yeah. It is." He gave her a bittersweet smile, telling her he understood what went unsaid.

Empathy pricked her heart, and she felt another thread of connection form between them. His grief might be different, but they faced similar struggles.

"I'm sorry," she muttered, knowing how trite the words sounded. How many people had told her they were sorry for her loss? Enough that the platitude felt empty to her. Judging by his expression, he'd heard a lot of hollow phrases in the past nine months, as well. Well-meant words that did nothing to ease the ache in his heart.

Elise groaned and raised a hand to her face. "Ugh, did I just say that? Not that I'm not sorry about your loss, but—"

He chuckled softly and gave her an understanding look. "I'm sorry for your loss, too. There. Now we're even on banal expressions." He shrugged. "Although I've decided to cut folks a break. I don't think I'd know what to say to any of my friends if their wives died, either. Other than, *Man, that sucks.*"

They shared a wry grin. The flicker of humor in his dark eyes mesmerized her, and after a moment, she realized she was staring at him. He had the kind of face that held a woman's attention—square jaw, full lips, straight nose. As she shook herself from her trance, her pulse fluttered.

She adjusted the strap of her purse on her shoulder and sidled toward the door. "I should be going."

"Right. Well—" He offered his hand. "—It was nice to meet you, Elise."

"You, too." She took his hand, and his long fingers and warm palm folded around hers in an encompassing grasp. Firm. Strong. *Dependable.*

She let her hand linger in his, puzzling over the words that had sprung to mind. Thinking she could tell anything about his character from his handshake was preposterous. And of all the traits a man could be, why was his dependability what came to mind?

"Will you come back next week?"

His question roused her from her sidetracked thoughts.

Would she be back? Coming tonight had taken her weeks of preparation and building her nerve. "Maybe. I, um…"

He squeezed her hand before releasing it. "Maybe is good enough. No pressure. Just think about it."

And think, she did. All week. But not just about whether she'd return to the grief-support meeting. She thought about Jared Coleman. The way he'd lost his wife. His one-year-old daughter, who was walking. His dark, compassionate eyes.

When she weighed whether she wanted to return to the support group, her reluctance to open herself to the pain of rehashing Grace's death was tempered by a desire to see Jared again. The connection she'd felt with him had been real. Hadn't it? But was her interest in Jared about feeling less alone in her grief or about the flutter of attraction she'd experienced when he'd held her hand? She wasn't looking for a boyfriend, especially not one with his own baggage and a daughter who'd remind her every day of Gracie. So why did his lopsided smile keep drifting through her mind?

"Goodbye, Princess." Jared kissed his daughter on the top of her head as he moved toward the door the next Thursday night. "Be good for Grandma."

"She's always good. Aren't you, Isabel?" his mother asked as she helped guide Isabel's spoon to her mouth. Which was progress. "Will you be late?"

"Shouldn't be. The support group never runs later than eight o'clock. You know that." He shoved his arms in his jacket, then fumbled in his pocket for his keys.

"What I know is that you don't have any sort of social life," his mother said, and Jared groaned.

Here we go again...

"A handsome young man like you should be dating. It's been almost a year since Kelly died, and—"

"It's been nine months," he corrected, "and I'm not ready to date again. I may never be. No one can ever replace Kelly." He jangled the keys in his hand impatiently. How many times in the past few weeks had he had this same conversation?

"I'm not suggesting anyone replace her. But there are plenty of other women who have merits of their own. There's a perfectly lovely girl in my office who—"

He huffed a sigh of exasperation. "I can find my own dates, Mom."

"But you don't." She aimed Isabel's spoon at him to punctuate her point.

"Because I don't want to date. I told you it's too soon."

"A young man like you has…needs. Physical needs that—"

Jared shuddered. "Stop!" He held up a hand and marched quickly to the back door. "Do *not* go there."

He was *not* discussing his sex life with his mother.

"I'm just saying—"

"See you a little after eight, Mom. Good night!" He exited quickly and shook his head as he strolled to his car. He knew his mother meant well, but the idea of dating again stirred a sharp ache in his chest and an uneasy sense of guilt in his gut. Damn, but he missed Kelly so much some days he could barely stand it.

As he cranked his car's engine, he recalled the new woman who'd visited the grief-support group last week. Elise Norris. Her glossy blonde hair, bright blue eyes and sad smile had filtered through his thoughts at odd moments this past week. While he showered. While he tried to fall asleep. When he woke in the morning.

His pulse kicked up at the prospect of seeing her again tonight, and he frowned to himself. He'd just finished telling his mother that he wasn't ready to date. So why was he anticipating seeing Elise tonight with schoolboylike nerves?

Okay, yes, they'd had a certain connection in the few moments they'd talked, but that was hardly reason to get all worked up. On the heels of the anxious flutter, cumbersome thoughts of Kelly rose to quash any notion of pursuing his attention to Elise. Just five years ago he'd stood at the altar and promised to forsake all others for Kelly.

How could he think of another woman when Kelly hadn't even been gone for a year?

Raising his daughter had to be his focus now. Not finding a new wife.

Elise had almost made up her mind to skip the next support-group meeting when she remembered the Harrisons. Knowing that they'd also lost a baby made her want to reach out to them. If anyone could understand the hole in her heart, she guessed the young couple could. And maybe she could offer them some support, as well.

By the time she arrived at the meeting, there were only two chairs left vacant in the circle. As Joleen called a greeting to her, Elise headed for the chair closest to her, but before she reached it, one of the older ladies, who'd been getting a cup of coffee, took the seat. Which left one open chair. Next to Jared. She met his gaze as she approached the chair, and he flashed her the lopsided smile that had filled her thoughts throughout the week. Her stomach flip-flopped.

"Welcome back," he whispered to her as she settled next to him.

The sandalwood scent she remembered from last week filled her nose and stirred a warmth in her chest.

Joleen called the meeting to order and opened the floor to comments and discussion. Throughout the session, Elise tried to focus on what the other members were saying, tried to work up the nerve to share something that might be valuable to the conversation, but she found herself preoccupied with every movement, every sound Jared made. A grunt of sympathy for Mrs. Bagwell. A scratch of his chin. Crossing his arms over his chest. A heavy breath… of fatigue? Boredom?

When he shifted in his chair and her pulse scrambled,

she castigated herself mentally for her schoolgirl reaction to him. She couldn't remember ever being so hyperaware of a man in her life. What was wrong with her? She'd come to the support group for help managing her grief, not to find a boyfriend!

Elise balled her hands in frustration and made a concerted effort to pay attention to what Kim Harrison was saying. The death of this woman's baby was the primary reason she'd returned to the support group.

"...like Jared said last week. I think a lot about the could-have-beens. What her laugh would have sounded like, what her favorite food would have been, whether she'd have been good at sports." Kim looked over at Elise then. "Do you ever do that? Think about what your baby might have done, who she'd have been?"

Elise's breath snagged. "I...yeah. A lot. Almost constantly. When I'm not wondering what went wrong, what I could have done differently during my pregnancy that might have saved her, why this happened to me when she was my one shot at being a mother."

Mrs. Bagwell frowned. "Why do you think you won't have other children? You're still young."

Elise gripped the edge of her seat, startled by the older woman's question. Taking a breath for composure, she studied the woman's face and saw nothing but concern and confusion, not judgment. "Well, the procedure I used to get pregnant with Grace took most of my savings. Since I'm unmarried, not in a relationship and not into one-night stands, the chances of getting pregnant the natural way are pretty nonexistent."

Mrs. Bagwell seemed unfazed by her bluntness. "I see. I've learned, though, never to underestimate the surprises and twists of fate life can hold. Why, by this time next year, you could be happily wed and expecting again." The older woman punctuated her comment with a satisfied nod and sat back in her chair with a confident smile.

Elise could only gape, speechless.

"I suppose that's true," Joleen said. "Holding on to optimism is always a good thing, but let's look at some ways Elise can deal with the issues she's facing now. Kim, how do you handle those could-have-been thoughts when you have them?"

Kim glanced at her husband. "I talk about them with Greg. And here, with all of you. That helps. Sometimes I post my feelings to the online message board I've mentioned before." Kim directed her attention to Elise. "I'll give you the link. It's another support group I found. A message board for parents who've lost children whether to death or kidnapping or divorce. There's lots of information and links to great resources. You should look into it."

Elise nodded to Kim. "Thanks. I will."

The meeting continued, with the discussion turning to Mrs. Fenwick's late husband, before the group adjourned promptly at the end of the hour. As promised, Kim caught up to Elise by the refreshment table and handed her a scrap of paper with a URL printed neatly in pink ink.

"Here's the address for the message board. I know an online group seems impersonal, but the people are really helpful and sometimes it is easier to be honest about your feelings when you're not face-to-face with the people you're sharing with. You can be as anonymous or open with your identity as you want. I hope you'll try it."

Elise tucked the paper in her pocket. "Thanks. I'll check it out." She smiled her appreciation. This exchange of information, this opportunity to get to know the Harrisons, was exactly the reason she'd come tonight. Seizing the chance to speak privately with Kim, Elise cleared her throat and asked, "So…if you don't mind my asking… how did your daughter die?"

"I don't mind. In fact, I wanted to talk to you about it. Because of how your daughter died and all…" Kim said, leaning toward Elise and placing a hand on her arm.

Elise shook her head. "What does Grace's death have to do with your baby?"

Kim shrugged. "Maybe nothing. But I thought it was an odd coincidence is all."

"Coincidence?"

"Yeah." Kim's face darkened. "Our little girl died at the hospital, too. Just hours after she was born."

Chapter 2

Elise heard a buzzing in her ears, and her head swam. When her knees buckled, she groped futilely for something to brace against. As she stumbled back a step, she encountered the warm, solid wall of a chest, and a strong hand grasped her elbow, steadying her. The scent of sandalwood surrounded her, piercing her fog of shock. And she knew without looking who supported her.

"Elise?" Jared's deep voice rumbled near her ear.

"I'm sorry." Kim rushed forward, concern knitting her brow. "Maybe I shouldn't have said anything. I didn't mean to—"

"No. I…I'm okay. I was just…caught off guard. Everything about losing Grace just flooded back and—" She swallowed hard and blinked at Kim as the truth the woman had shared sank in. "Your baby died at the hospital, too? I…Was she premature?"

Kim shook her head. "Right on time. To the day. But

she apparently had a heart defect that our doctor missed during my pregnancy."

An eerie prickle nipped her neck. "Her heart stopped, and they couldn't resuscitate her," she whispered raggedly.

Kim blinked. "Yes. How did you—?" Her eyes widened. "You mean Grace—?"

Elise's voice stuck in her throat. The only sound she could make came out as a moan.

Behind her, Jared muttered a curse. "That sounds too suspicious to be a coincidence. The odds…"

"What hospital did you use?" Kim asked.

Elise struggled for her composure, sucking in a calming breath. "My labor started while I was out of town at a crafts fair. I went to a little hospital in Pine Mill…."

Kim frowned and shook her head. "No. We were at Crestview General."

Something like disappointment punctured the breath Elise had been holding. As tragic and macabre as the similarities in their losses were, hope had flickered briefly that she was on to some answers regarding Grace's mysterious death.

"So many times I've wondered if our baby would have made it if we'd been here in Lagniappe at St. Mary's where they have the PICU," Kim said.

"What-ifs are natural," Jared said quietly, "but you can make yourself crazy with them. Don't torture yourself, Kim."

She lifted a corner of her mouth in acknowledgment. "Easier said than done."

"Ready to go?" Greg asked, stepping up behind his wife.

"Sure." Kim turned back to Elise. "See you next time?"

Elise nodded and, still rather numb with shock, searched for her voice. "I—yeah. Bye."

As the Harrisons departed, Jared stepped around to

face Elise and dipped his head to get a better look at her expression. "Are you okay?"

Elise raked her blond hair back with her fingers. "I don't know," she answered honestly. "I really don't know what to make of this."

"It is pretty hard to believe. I mean, if this were 1811, maybe. But with modern health and medicine what it is, you'd think…" He stopped himself and shoved his hands in his pockets. "Well…anyway."

"The doctors should have been able to save her. That's what you were going to say, wasn't it?" Elise asked, meeting his gaze. Last week, she'd thought they'd reached an unspoken agreement to be candid with each other. His honesty about his grief had been at the heart of the connection she'd felt with him.

He furrowed his brow with a guilty look. "Yeah. Something like that."

She sighed. "Tiptoeing around delicate topics is so tedious. Can we agree not to play that game? We both know it serves no purpose."

He gave her a nod and a relieved smile. "Agreed."

"In that case, yes. I've got plenty of questions about why the doctors and modern medicine didn't save Grace. And now, in light of what Kim said about their baby dying the same way…" Elise lifted a trembling hand, flipping her palm up in frustration. "What am I supposed to make of that?"

Jared didn't answer. Instead, he glanced toward the kitchen area where Joleen was cleaning up the last of the refreshments. "Would you like to go somewhere? Get a cup of coffee?"

"I— Don't you need to get home? I'm sure babysitters are expensive."

"They can be. But my mom watches Isabel when I come

here." He paused and jingled the keys in his pocket. "I know Kim just dropped a bomb on you, and I don't want you going home alone to stew and drive yourself crazy over the news."

Elise lifted a corner of her mouth. "That's what I'd do. You're right."

"I'd be happy to be your sounding board for a while."

When was the last time someone had offered to just listen to her, let her vent and unburden her heart? Too long. Gratitude for his thoughtfulness tugged in her chest.

"I'd like that. How about Brewer's Café? It's just a couple blocks from here."

He gave a nod and a smile. "Meet you there in five."

Jared climbed behind his steering wheel and blew out a long, cleansing breath. What the hell was he doing? Hadn't he just told his mother tonight that he wasn't ready to date?

"Okay, so this is not a date. *Not,*" he muttered to himself as he gripped the steering wheel and stared out the windshield into the church parking lot. Despite his denials, guilt thumped a drumbeat in his chest. "You're just giving your support to another group member who had a shock tonight. It's not a date."

So why were his palms damp with sweat, and why was his conscience pricking him with images of Kelly in the last days they spent together?

Not a date. Not a date… He let the words repeat in his brain as he backed his car out of the parking space and pulled up behind Elise to follow her to Brewer's Café.

He recalled the look in Elise's eyes when she'd learned how the Harrisons' baby had died, and sympathy twisted inside him. No matter how conflicted he felt about meeting Elise for coffee, he wanted to be there for her tonight.

Elise was in shock and needed a friend. He could be her friend without it meaning anything else, couldn't he?

Of course. He released a deep breath. It was not a date.

"Tell me about Isabel," Elise said after twenty minutes of small talk. She cradled her mug of cappuccino, which had grown cold, and met his startled look with an encouraging nod.

"Are you sure? Doesn't hearing other people talk about their kids hurt?"

She sighed. "Of course it does. But am I supposed to avoid people with kids the rest of my life?"

He took a slow deep breath. "No."

"Do you have a picture of her?"

He chuckled, reaching into his back pocket for his wallet. "Seriously? You have to ask?"

She returned his grin. "A long shot, I know, but…"

He flipped open the wallet and turned it so she could see the bright-eyed cherub with blond curls. Elise's breath caught, and it took a moment to recover. Like all babies, Isabel was precious, but something about her sweet smile and chubby cheeks grabbed Elise by the throat.

"Wow," she rasped when she found enough air to talk. "Look at those curls. Believe it or not, I had curls like that when I was younger." She tugged on her straight hair and scoffed. "I'd kill for a few natural curls now."

"Those curls make for a pretty wild-looking bedhead after her naps, let me tell you," he said with a soft laugh. He flipped the picture to show her another more recent shot of his daughter. Two teeth peeked from her happy grin, and she wore a lacy white dress with a matching bow in her golden-colored hair. "This was at her baptism a couple months ago."

Elise admired the shot, fighting down the bittersweet

pang clambering inside her. Opposite the picture of Isabel was a picture of a raven-haired woman with olive skin and large almond-shaped eyes. Elise pointed to the woman. "Kelly?"

He nodded.

"She was beautiful."

"Thanks. I think so, too."

Elise bit her bottom lip in thought and studied the picture of Isabel again. "I'm trying to decide which of you Isabel favors more, but…"

"But…you don't see any resemblance to either of us. Am I right?"

"Well…"

"That's because she was adopted. Kelly couldn't have children."

Elise's gaze darted to Jared's. "Oh…I—" She didn't know how to respond, so she changed the subject. "So your family lives in town and helps you take care of Isabel. That's pretty handy."

"Yeah, most of my family is local." He closed the wallet and put it back in his pocket. "My mom and dad live across town, and I have a brother and sister-in-law, Michelle, who live just a couple blocks away. My sister-in-law is the one who keeps her while I'm at work." He tipped his head in inquiry. "What about you? Any family?"

"A brother who deigns to talk to his younger sister when I call him."

Jared arched an eyebrow. "He has something against talking to family?"

"Naw. He's just busy and doesn't think about calling his little sister. We're not especially close. After our mother died, our dad couldn't be bothered with raising kids, and we ended up in foster homes. Sometimes together, more often, not. I think he put an emotional distance between us as a defense mechanism. It hurts less to be separated from someone you only care marginally about."

Jared was quiet for a moment, studying her. "But clearly family is important to you. You make the effort to stay in touch with your brother."

She sighed and stared at the tabletop, idly tracing a crack in the top with her finger. "Yeah. And I was planning to raise a child alone, planning to start my family even if there was no husband in the picture." Jared didn't comment right away, and she glanced up when she sensed his reluctance to say what was on his mind. "Go ahead…ask. Remember, we promised to be candid with each other."

He flashed her a lopsided grin. "Right. I was just wondering why you never married."

"I actually thought I'd found Mr. Right a few years ago, but it turns out I was too late. His wife found him first."

He gave her an appropriately sympathetic groan.

"After that humiliation, I swore off dating for a while." She pulled a grimace then took a sip of cold cappuccino.

He grunted and cocked his head. "A loss to all single men. Any guy would be lucky to have a date with a lovely lady like you. I hate it when the jerks go and ruin things for the rest of us honest guys."

The comment may have been the standard polite response, but it still caught Elise off guard. She yanked her gaze up to him, and the warmth of his smile stirred a flickering pulse inside her.

"I—I wasn't fishing for a compliment." She chuckled awkwardly. "Really. I—"

Their waitress arrived just in time to save her from her fumbling. After refilling Jared's mug, their server left their check and bustled back to the counter.

"So…you want to talk about the elephant in the room

now? The reason I asked you here before you went home?" he asked.

Elise's gut tightened. "It's a lot to process. Accepting that Grace died of a freak heart condition hours after birth was hard enough. But to think the same type of thing happened to another couple in town within months of Grace's death is…spooky. Unsettling."

"Exactly." He furrowed his brow. "Did the doctor give you a medical explanation for Grace's death? Was an autopsy done?"

"Yes. As I understand it, there was. All they told me was she had a weak heart, and she died of heart failure. I know I should have asked more questions, but to be honest, I was kinda numb."

"I can understand that. I remember the shock that put me in a sort of daze after Kelly died. I got through it because my family rallied around me to help."

She gave him a wan smile. "You're lucky to have them."

"Yeah, I am." He gave her a nod and a smile that said he was counting his blessings. She didn't want to envy Jared for the support he had from his family, but the ache of loneliness she'd carried in her bones since losing Grace swamped her with a dizzying wallop.

Clearing her throat, she forged on, not wanting him to see how vulnerable and alone she felt. "So I've been thinking about asking the hospital for Gracie's medical file, but I've been putting it off because…well, I knew it would be hard. I'm kinda torn between wanting to know all the details to find some answers and shutting it all in the past and trying to move on."

He nodded, his gaze focused on her, letting her know he was listening. She knew he didn't have magic answers, but having him as a sounding board helped more than she'd expected. After months of carrying so much turmoil inside, having someone to listen to her ramble and unburden herself felt incredibly good, freeing.

"I mean, I know that, being a small hospital, they didn't have the neonatal ICU facilities that might have saved her. Like Kim was saying tonight about the lack of advanced care at Crestview General, I've wondered so often what would have happened if I'd not been out of town that day I went into labor."

He rolled one palm up. "Maybe that's all it is. Maybe babies die at smaller hospitals more frequently because of the limited facilities. I mean, years ago, women and babies died during childbirth pretty regularly."

She bit her bottom lip, considering his point. "Maybe."

"If I were you..." he started and waited for her to meet his gaze as if seeking permission to be so bold as to give unsolicited advice.

She locked onto the incisive spark in his eyes, hungry for whatever guidance he had. "Yeah?"

"I'd make some inquiries. See if there are reports of other cases similar to yours at that hospital. Compare what you learn to the mortality rate of bigger hospitals. Gather facts, look for a pattern, see what comes out in the wash."

"You don't think Grace's case was an isolated incident?" She narrowed an intent gaze on him. "You basically said as much earlier tonight...that Kim's loss was too similar to be a coincidence."

He spread his hands. "I don't know. I may have been talking out of turn. But yeah, my initial gut instinct said something fishy was going on."

Her heart beat an anxious tattoo. "Fishy as in...?"

He waved her off. "I don't want to speculate. Look, Kim mentioned an online community with a message board. That's a good place to start. Arm yourself with information."

"That I can do. Between the internet and my contacts through the newspaper, I think I can get plenty of information."

He arched one eyebrow. "You work at the paper?"

"Staff photographer," she said, turning the conversation to her job. Next, he told her about his position as foreman with a local, family-owned construction company. As they swapped stories about their work, education and acquaintances they had in common, the mood between them relaxed and fell into the time-honored patterns of a first date. Elise found Jared easy to talk to, and she experienced a tingling rush in her blood whenever he flashed his lopsided grin.

"Well, it worked," she said almost an hour later when she checked her watch. "Your pleasant company has kept my mind off what Kim told me tonight and saved me from sitting alone at home agonizing over what it could mean."

He gave her a satisfied smile. "Mission accomplished."

"I hope I haven't kept you too late."

He shrugged. "My mother might be a bit worried about what kept me, but as soon as she hears I was having coffee with an attractive lady, all will be forgiven. She's been encouraging me to start dating again."

A knot of regret tightened in Elise's chest. "Jared, I, uh…I'm not in a place where I…well, I'm not ready to date. I'm not looking for a relationship."

He nodded and raised a hand. "That's fine. I'm not sure I'm ready to date again, either. But…" He twisted his mouth in a thoughtful moue, and his eyes took on a devilish spark. "We don't have to tell my mother. As long as she thinks we might be an item, maybe she'll back off trying to fix me up with her single friends."

Elise scrunched her nose in a sympathetic wince and chuckled. "Oh, no."

"Oh, yes." A low, melodic laugh rumbled from his chest. "And let's just say, there is a reason some of her friends are still single." He rolled his eyes and whistled. "So the true nature of our friendship can be our little secret. Deal?"

She laughed harder, savoring the feeling. How long had it been since she had a reason to laugh? "So you want me to be your fake girlfriend?"

He pulled a face. "Well, we might not have to take it that far, but I'd consider it a personal favor if you'd be my excuse for not meeting Linda-from-accounting or Betty-from-her-scrapbooking-club."

She flashed him a sassy grin. "Yeah, and what do I get out of this deal?"

He leaned back in the booth and folded his arms over his chest. "An occasional cup of coffee, maybe dinner or a movie once or twice." He winked, and his cheek tugged up in a playful grin. "And, of course, my charming company and scintillating conversation."

"Gosh, I don't know…" She rubbed her chin and pursed her lips as if struggling with the decision, as if agreeing would be a hardship.

In truth, the hardest part of such an agreement would be *not* developing any romantic feelings for Jared. He was handsome, kind, thoughtful and funny. Exactly the kind of man she could fall for—if she were looking for a boyfriend. But, as alone as she felt most of the time, involvement with a man who had a one-year-old daughter would be…torture. Anguish. She was bound to form attachments to Isabel, painful reminders of what she'd lost, bonds that would add to her grief when they were inevitably broken. Because Jared wasn't looking for a new wife. He clearly still loved his late wife. Elise had already made the mistake of falling for a married man, and she wanted no part of a love triangle—even if the third party was a ghost.

"Wow," Jared said with a self-deprecating scoff when she hesitated a moment too long, "I didn't realize being my decoy was such an onerous favor to ask."

"Oh!" With a startled laugh, she shook herself from her thoughts and reached across the table to grasp his arm. "Oh, no… I was just thinking. I'd love to have coffee with you again. It's better than sitting home by myself stewing over tragedies."

He gave her a comically pained expression. "Ouch. Maybe I should quit while I'm behind."

She slapped a hand over her mouth, laughing softly. "That didn't come out right. I didn't mean…"

Shaking his head, he grinned and slid to the end of the booth, picking up the check as he stood. "Just say good-night, Gracie."

Gracie.

Though she knew he was quoting George Burns from his old radio show with his wife, Elise felt the blood drain from her face, and her heartbeat slowed. Jeez, she was a mess, if just the mention of her daughter's name still delivered an instant breath-stealing jolt.

Jared's face fell, and he dropped back on the booth bench, reaching for her. "Cripes, I'm sorry. That was thoughtless of—"

She covered his mouth with her fingers, and his warm breath tickled her palm. "Don't apologize. Remember—no tiptoeing around each other."

He wrapped his hand around her wrist and pressed a kiss on her palm. "Right."

The scratch of his five o'clock shadow on her skin sent a ripple of sweet sensation to her core. Inhaling deeply to steady herself, she mustered a smile for him and said softly, "Good night, Gracie."

* * *

Jared stayed in her thoughts as she drove home, and she caught herself smiling when she remembered his hand-kiss, his teasing, his dark bedroom eyes. Jared had been a pleasant distraction tonight, but as she parked in her driveway, her conversation with Kim replayed in her mind.

Two babies. Two hospitals. Two stopped hearts.

And Jared's muttered curse. *That sounds too suspicious to be a coincidence.*

The similarities in Grace's and the Harrisons' baby's deaths rankled, but what did she really know? She was no doctor. Maybe the sudden death of infants was more common than she knew. She'd heard of SIDS, Sudden Infant Death Syndrome, when babies died mysteriously in their sleep. Maybe Grace's death was related to that?

Information. As Jared suggested, she needed to gather some facts before she drew any conclusions that would serve no purpose other than making her paranoid.

She bustled into her house, a chill autumn wind following her inside. Her black-and-brown tabby, Brooke, greeted her and trotted into the kitchen, winding around Elise's legs as she begged for her supper.

"Hey, Brookie Wookie. Hang on. Dinner's coming." She fixed herself a cup of chamomile tea, poured Brooke a bowl of food, then set up her laptop. Placing her mug beside her computer, Elise typed *infant mortality rates* in an internet search engine. Within a few key strokes, Elise had learned that Louisiana's infant mortality rate of ten deaths per thousand births was higher than the national average. She also found breakdowns of infant deaths by race and region. The statistics, while eye-opening, didn't provide her the detailed information she wanted.

She rocked back in her chair, and Brooke took the opportunity to hop into her lap. She idly scratched Brooke's head and twisted her mouth in thought. Wouldn't a hospital's records be a matter of public information? Data on all births and deaths at a hospital would have to be reported to the government, wouldn't it? If she could get her hands on the records of Pine Mill Hospital, she could compare the information to the state and national average.

Reaching awkwardly around Brooke to type, she tried a more specific search for Pine Mill Hospital's yearly data, birth and infant-death totals, but hit a dead end. However the search terms *infant death* and *Pine Mill* led her to a two-year-old obituary in the *Pine Mill Gazette* for the infant son of a local couple.

Elise scanned the article with her heart in her throat. The baby had died of unknown causes just after his birth at Pine Mill Hospital. Her hand shaking, she hit Print to add the article to her file.

That made three infant deaths from mysterious causes within a matter of months, all in a small geographic region. Three that she knew of. How many more otherwise healthy babies had died tragically within hours of their births?

Did she dare contact the parents of the baby boy mentioned in the two-year-old obituary for more information? They could have heard of similar cases, just as she was learning of stories similar to Grace's. She didn't want to stir up painful memories for them without good cause.

As Jared suggested, perhaps her best move for now was to solicit information regarding similar cases. Remembering the online community message board Kim had mentioned at the grief-support meeting, Elise lifted Brooke off her lap and dug the scrap of paper with the URL out of her pocket. When she reached the home page, she created an account for herself and logged on.

On the first screen, she found a list of the most recent posts and replies. As Kim had said, the topics varied from posts about missing children, questions about legal rights and suggestions for surviving the holidays without your loved one.

She spent several minutes reading the various discussion threads and found the replies of the members to be both helpful and compassionate. No wonder Kim recommended the website. Elise sipped her tea and began mentally composing her introduction. Should she make an official request for information or simply explain what happened to her and see if it solicited replies of similar incidents?

After some thought, she chose to keep her first foray on the message board simple and see what came of it. She could always request similar stories later. At the end of her post, she gave a secondary email address she used for online shopping as her contact info. Taking a deep breath, she clicked the submit button, and her post vanished into the vast beyond. A few seconds later it appeared on the message board.

"Well, Brooke," she said, stroking the cat's back as the tabby rubbed against her leg. "All I can do now is wait and see who replies."

Jared tiptoed into Isabel's nursery and peered over the edge of her crib to check on his daughter before heading to bed himself. He could stand there for hours and never get tired of watching his little angel sleep. But as usual, the tenderness of the moment, Isabel's innocence and late hour were a potent brew that brought a pang of grief for what Kelly was missing. And for how much he missed Kelly.

Tonight, however, his memories of Kelly were tinged with a shade of guilt. He knew the source.

Elise.

He'd had a good time with Elise, had felt comfortable talking with her, had felt natural teasing her. And had been attracted to her. Powerfully so.

Maybe that was the root of his guilt. He'd had female friends while Kelly was alive, but his attraction to Elise seemed a bit like a betrayal of Kelly's memory. He knew he was being ridiculous. Moving on, dating again, didn't mean he loved Kelly any less or that he'd forgotten her. If the situation was reversed, he'd want Kelly to have a second chance for love and companionship. A life partner to help her raise Isabel. In his heart, he knew Kelly would say the same for him. But his attraction to Elise still left him off-balance somehow. He wasn't ready to start a new relationship....

Was he?

He brushed a wayward curl away from Isabel's cheek, and a pang tugged his heart. Maybe he was unsettled being around Elise because he knew how blessed he was to have Isabel, while Elise had lost her best chance to be a parent, had been stripped of the treasure he savored every day.

He shuddered when he thought about losing Isabel. One of the reasons he and Kelly had chosen the private agency they used to adopt Isabel had been the agency's assurances that the closed adoption process they employed meant the birth parents had forfeited all claims to Isabel. Their greatest fear had been to have one of the birth parents change their mind and try to take Isabel from them after the adoption closed. Just considering that scenario lit a fiery determination in his belly. He'd fight anyone who tried to take Isabel from him with every resource possible. Isabel was *his*.

Chapter 3

"Elise, I want you to go with Russell when he covers the ribbon cutting at the new monkey house at the zoo today."

Elise hurriedly minimized the website she'd been reading and spun in her chair to face her boss. The newspaper had rather lax rules about using the office computers for personal business, but she'd been checking for replies to her post on the Parents Without Children forum and wanted to protect her privacy.

"Be sure to get lots of shots of the mayor and town council members, not just the animals." The editor-in-chief put a sticky note on her desk with "zoo ribbon cutting—2:00 p.m." scrawled across it.

She moved the sticky note to her date book. "Yes, sir. Uh, Mr. Grimes?" she called before he could disappear back into his office. He turned and waited for her to speak.

She cleared her throat. "I'd like to do some kind of

special piece, maybe for a weekend edition, with a photo spread and feature article—"

"About the monkey house?" He frowned and propped his hands on his ample hips.

"Oh…no. No. About the people in the region. Small business owners. Veterans with interesting stories from the war. Maybe someone with an unusual hobby. Something with local color." *Something that might give me a better platform for my work than ribbon cuttings at monkey houses.* "I'd write the accompanying article myself."

"You can write?"

"I think I write pretty well."

He arched an eyebrow and grunted. "Since you used *well* correctly, instead of saying you write *good*—a pet peeve of mine—I'd be willing to consider it. No promises." He rubbed a hand across his mouth and chin as he thought. "Get me a specific idea and sample copy, and we'll talk."

"I will. Thank you." She smiled to herself as she turned back to her computer. As much as she loved photography, she knew the newspaper was struggling. Too many people had started getting their news online or from television. Rumors of staff cuts had been circulating, and she wanted to showcase her other talents and prove herself useful to the higher-ups. And she aspired to doing more with her photojournalism than snapping shots of the mayor glad-handing at ribbon cuttings.

A face appeared over the partition between cubicles. "Are you trying to put me out of a job?"

She glanced up at Russell Prine, the features editor, and shook her head. "No one could replace you, Russell. Why, I'd be surprised if your piece on the garden club's bazaar doesn't win a Pulitzer."

She flashed a teasing grin, and he rolled his eyes. "Very

funny. So, Miss Snark, want to ride with me to the big zoo shindig?"

"Sure. Thanks."

"I'm leaving in an hour." Russell disappeared again behind the cubicle wall, and Elise opened the web page for the forum again.

She had her first three replies. Holding her breath, she opened the first one.

Elise arrived at the grief-support meeting early the next week. She was eager to tell Jared what she'd learned so far, and, if she was honest, she had been looking forward to spending more time with the charming widower. She scanned the room but saw no sign of him. Yet.

Having skipped dinner, she swiped a couple of cookies from the refreshment table before she took a seat in the circle, carefully choosing one that had an open chair next to it where Jared could sit. She nibbled a cookie and watched the door for him to arrive.

Good heavens, you're acting like a scheming teenager with a crush. She gave her head a shake. For someone who wasn't interested in a relationship, she'd certainly spent a lot of time anticipating the meeting tonight and thinking about Jared Coleman.

"—Are you tonight?"

Elise snapped out of her daze when she realized Mr. Miller was speaking to her. "Oh, I'm sorry. What did you say?"

The older gentleman grinned. "I asked how you were doing, but since you were smiling, I'll assume you're doing well."

She'd been smiling? "Oh, yes. I'm doing pretty well. And you?"

Mr. Miller used her rhetorical inquiry as an excuse to

regale her with his medical history with an emphasis on his current arthritis issues. Elise patiently listened, trying to act interested in what the man was telling her about his knee-replacement surgery, while sending furtive glances toward the door.

When Jared appeared, a small sigh of relief escaped from her before she saw what was in his arms and she caught her breath again. *Isabel.*

He had a large diaper bag over one shoulder, and his golden-haired daughter perched on his hip as he talked to Joleen. Mr. Miller's monologue faded to a drone as Elise stared, her heart in her throat. She'd been eager to see Jared again but totally unprepared for seeing his daughter. Who was the age Grace would have been. Who had her thumb in her mouth and her head tucked shyly on Jared's shoulder. Jared gestured to Isabel then to the door.

Elise bit her bottom lip. Was he leaving? Had something happened?

Joleen shook her head and waved him toward the chairs with a smile then tickled Isabel's leg. Jared nodded and started toward the circle, his gaze latching instantly on Elise's. The smile that lit his face as he approached fueled a giddy kick in her pulse.

Oh, Elise, you are in trouble.

"Hi," he said. "Anyone sitting there?" He hitched his head toward the chair beside her.

"You." She reached for the diaper bag and helped him get settled. "No babysitter tonight?"

The older ladies sitting nearby cooed and grinned at Isabel as he took his seat.

"Michelle has the stomach flu, and my parents had plans. If my having Isabel here makes you uncomfortable, I don't have to stay."

Her heart squeezed as she caught a whiff of baby powder

mixed with Jared's sandalwood. If she needed a reminder of why falling for Jared was a bad idea, the sharp-edged longing that knifed through her gut as she inhaled Isabel's sweet scent sent a clear message. She wasn't ready to be around Jared's daughter, a too-poignant reminder of her loss.

But Elise cleared the knot of emotion that stuck in her throat and shook her head. "No, don't go. She's fine. I—"

"Kee," a tiny voice said, halting Elise mid-thought.

She dropped her gaze to Isabel, who stared at her with wide blue eyes and pointed a chubby finger at Elise's lap.

"What?" Elise glanced to Jared for help interpreting.

"She sees your cookies." He shot her a lopsided grin. "What can I say? My girl's got a sweet tooth."

"Kee!" Isabel said louder, eliciting another round of adoring sighs and grins from the older ladies.

"May she have one?" Elise asked, picking one of the sugar cookies off her plate.

"I suppose. She had a pretty good supper."

Her pulse pounding, Elise extended the cookie to Isabel, and the toddler's eyes lit with delight. She gave Elise a shy, four-toothed grin as she accepted her offering.

"Shall we begin?" Joleen said, calling the meeting to order.

Though she was well-behaved, Isabel proved a huge distraction for Elise throughout the meeting. First Elise watched, mesmerized, as the little girl gummed the sugar cookie to oblivion. Then, when the first cookie was gone, Isabel sent Elise a wide-eyed look that clearly asked, "More?"

Elise darted a glance to Jared, who seemed engrossed in what Joleen was telling Mr. Miller, and she furtively slipped another cookie to Isabel.

"Kee!" Isabel kicked her feet happily and flopped back against her father's chest to munch her treat.

Jared spotted the new cookie and raised an eyebrow at Elise. She returned a shrug and a guilty grin that won an indulgent smile from Jared.

After finishing her second cookie Isabel grew restless and wiggled free of Jared's lap. He grabbed for the back of her shirt to catch her before she toddled off, but she tottered straight to Elise's knees. When Isabel wobbled, Elise steadied the baby, who then grabbed Elise's pants with a cookie-smeared fist for balance. Her heart somersaulted, and warmth expanded in Elise's chest.

"Sorry," Jared said, reaching for his daughter.

Elise batted his hands away. "She's fine, Dad."

His look said, "Are you sure?"

Nodding, she smoothed a hand over Isabel's curls and met the girl's blinking blue-eyed gaze. The full feeling in her lungs gave a bittersweet twist. Maternal yearning clawed inside her, but she fought down the ache.

When Isabel held her arms up to her, a stab of tenderness and affection pierced her heart. Elise lifted Jared's daughter onto her lap and gave Isabel a friendly smile. Isabel glanced once to her father, as if for reassurance and approval, then leaned into Elise's chest with a shy grin. Spying the napkin that had held the cookies in Elise's hand, Isabel tugged at the corner and craned her neck to look for more treats.

"All gone," Elise murmured.

"Kee?" Innocent baby blues blinked at her.

"Sorry."

Isabel gave a sweet sigh of resignation and stuck her thumb in her mouth as she tucked her head against Elise for the last few minutes of the meeting.

Jared smiled at them as the meeting dismissed. "I think she's made a new friend."

"Bribery works wonders." She stroked Isabel's back and gave Jared a wry look. "The question is, would she have been as trusting of me had I not fed her cookies?"

Jared chuckled and lifted Isabel from Elise's lap. "Oh, I'm sure the cookies were the deciding factor. She's got a real sweet tooth, I'm afraid."

"Ah, a girl after my own heart." She watched Jared shoulder the diaper bag and remembered her eagerness to talk to him about her fact-finding efforts this week. "I did what you suggested about arming myself with information."

Jared glanced up from tugging a sweater onto Isabel's arms. "Oh, yeah? And?"

"I found some interesting things." She sighed. "I'd hoped we could get coffee again and talk about what I discovered, but…"

He glanced from her to Isabel and back to her. "Oh. Sorry. Can't tonight." He paused and drew his dark eyebrows together. "Unless…"

"Yeah?"

"You could follow us back to my place. I brew a pretty decent cup of coffee, and my mother brought over an apple coffee cake this morning."

"Oh, I don't want to impose." Going to a coffee shop for a chat was one thing, but visiting Jared at his house felt…too personal.

"No imposition. The coffee cake is low fat."

To buy herself time to think, Elise flashed a lopsided grin. "Low fat, huh? What are you telling me?"

He squeezed his eyes shut and chuckled. "I did it again, didn't I? I wasn't implying anything, I just—"

"I was kidding," she said with a laugh, compelled to

save him from his embarrassment. Then before she could talk herself out of it, she added, "Yes, I'll come. Thanks."

While Elise held Isabel, Jared keyed open his front door and led his guest inside. Isabel had fallen asleep in the car, and since he'd had the foresight, due to experience, to change her diaper and put her in her pajamas before he left the grief-support meeting, he only needed to slip her carefully into bed and she'd be down for the night. Fingers crossed.

"I'll take her," he whispered. "As soon as I get her in bed, I'll start a pot of coffee for us."

"Or…point me toward her room, and I'll put her down. One less transfer that risks waking her."

He nodded. "Good thinking. Follow me."

Jared showed Elise to Isabel's room and stood by the crib as she gently eased his daughter onto the mattress. Once she had Isabel positioned for safe sleep, Elise stroked his daughter's curls and ran a crooked finger along her plump cheek. "Good night, sweet girl."

Jared studied the poignant expression Elise wore as she gazed at Isabel, and his chest tightened. An all-too-familiar ache and gnawing guilt ate at him. How many nights had he stood here beside Kelly as she put Isabel to bed? How could it feel so wrong to be standing beside his daughter's bed with a different woman, and yet have it still feel so… right?

Elise would have made a terrific mother. Still would someday. He had no doubt that Elise would be given a second chance to have children of her own. Fate simply *couldn't* be so cruel as to deny this loving woman a chance to be a mother after all she'd already suffered.

Elise drew a ragged-sounding breath and made a hasty retreat from the nursery. Concern jabbed him, but before he pursued her, he spread a light blanket over Isabel, turned on the baby monitor beside her crib, and shooed Bubba, who'd been sleeping on the rocking chair, out of the room.

"Come on, Bubba," he said to the sleepy cat, who rubbed against his leg. "Dinner time."

Bubba gave a rather girlish meow and fell in step behind him as he headed down the hall.

He found Elise in the kitchen, filling the coffee carafe with water at the sink.

"You all right?" He stepped up beside her and angled his head to get a better view of her face.

She nodded. "Yeah."

But he heard tears in her voice, and her hand shook as she poured the water into the coffeemaker.

He turned and took the filters and coffee from the cabinet. Handing her a filter, he searched for the right words to comfort her. Knowing he had what she ached for but had lost sliced him with an odd sense of selfishness and guilty gratitude. Was this how survivors of a fatal accident felt about those who lost their lives?

"Elise—"

"It's not what you think." She faced him, and while her eyes were damp, she seemed remarkably composed. "Yes, I'm thinking about all I'm missing with Grace, but I got emotional because—" She sighed "—Isabel just looked so sweet and innocent. Peaceful. It was beautiful. I cry over things like sunsets and Christmas carols, too. I'm just a sentimental and weepy kind of girl. Sorry."

He eyed her through a narrowed gaze, gauging whether to buy her explanation. "Christmas carols, huh?"

"Well, not the upbeat ones, but 'Silent Night' gets me every time. And 'Away In A Manger.'" She held up a hand. "Don't get me started."

"I'll remember that." He stepped closer and wiped the moisture from her bottom eyelashes with his thumb.

She caught her breath, and her lips parted in surprise. He held her startled gaze, sinking into the fathomless blue of her eyes. Eyes like the ocean, deep and full of mystery. She grew still, except for slowly drawing her bottom lip between her teeth.

The action drew his attention to her mouth, and he acknowledged again how beautiful she was. Not in a high-maintenance, movie-star way, but in a softer way that he found far sexier. He wanted to taste the lip she nibbled, kiss away the haunted look that shadowed her gaze and made her appear so…vulnerable. It was that fragility that made him step back and drop his hand. He liked Elise too much to do anything to hurt her or ruin their budding friendship. Giving her his support and understanding as she negotiated the minefield of her grief was what mattered.

He cleared his throat. "Regular or decaf?"

She blinked as if shaking herself from a trance. "Uh, decaf, I guess." She flashed a wry grin. "Not that caffeine is the reason I can't sleep most nights, but why add fuel to the fire?"

"So why have you been losing sleep? What did you find in your research?"

"If you have a computer, I can show you."

"Sure, it's set up in my office. First door on the left." He hitched his head toward the hall. "Help yourself. I'll be in as soon as the coffee's brewing and I've fed the cats."

"You have cats?" She glanced around the floor.

"Why? Are you allergic?"

"No. In fact, I have one myself. I just…didn't picture you as a cat person."

"They were Kelly's when we married. They've grown on me." He put a can on the electric can opener and as soon as the motor whirred, Bubba and Diva trotted in from the next room and began circling his feet. Diva added a few loud meows, begging him to hurry.

Elise chuckled. “Wow, the black one is hungry. Hope she doesn’t wake Isabel with that racket.”

“Yeah, Diva’s got some pipes on her, doesn’t she?” He set the bowls of food on the floor, and the cats dived in.

“Diva?”

“Yep. And she lives up to her name. She can be a real prima donna, and she likes to hide Bubba’s toys.”

“The buff-and-orange one is Bubba, I take it?” Elise squatted beside the chowing cats and scratched Bubba on the neck. “Wow, his fur is really soft.” Before rising again, she gave Diva equal time, then dusted cat hair from her hands and glanced at him. “So…any passwords I need to get logged on?”

“Naw. It should be up and running.” He pried the lid off the can of coffee and watched over his shoulder as she headed out of the kitchen. Seeing another woman in Kelly’s kitchen, petting her cats, hadn’t been as strange or out of place as he’d thought it might. What did that mean? Was he finally moving past his wife’s death? How could he be when he still felt such a powerfully hollow ache in his soul when he thought of her?

And just how many scoops of coffee had he put in the filter while his mind wandered?

Jared groaned and eyed the grounds already in the basket, added one more scoop for good measure and started the pot brewing. When he reached the guest room, Elise had a message board open on his computer, and he pulled a chair over to the desk to join her. “Whatcha got?”

She tapped a few keys, and the screen changed. “This is the website that Kim told us about. There are lots of subgroups depending on what you are interested in learning about or getting help with. Depression, grief, single parenting, missing children, divorce, various support groups for medical conditions… It's a real hodgepodge."

"Looks like it," he said reading over her shoulder, trying to ignore the tantalizing fruity scent of her hair.

"I browsed the site, getting a feel for it for several nights, then the other day I posted about Grace's death in the hospital to both the grief group and the Parents Without Children discussion. Turns out the Parents Without Children board is mostly used by people who don't see their kids anymore because of divorce, but a few have had kids that died or were kidnapped or ran away."

Elise clicked a link to open that discussion page. "See, here it is. I had a few replies, most of them just commiserating and offering condolences, but one lady said that her sister had lost a baby right after birth a couple years ago." She opened that reply, and pointing to the screen, she faced him. "And get this…she was at the same hospital as me. Pine Mill Community Hospital."

Jared sat back in his chair, stunned. "Wow. This is eerie."

"And when I did a search for infant death rates, I found an article about another couple in Pine Mill whose baby had died just after birth. It's like an epidemic in that town! Three babies in just a couple years. And there could be more for all we know." Her eyes blazed with fervor, and her voice echoed her passion.

"Just being a devil's advocate here. Three babies in two years is tragic but…well, maybe it's not an unusual number. Did you find any stats on infant mortality rates?"

She sighed and faced the screen again. "Yeah, and Louisiana's rate is higher than the national average. But…

my gut is telling me something is off. Something is wrong at that hospital, whether it's negligence or foul play or…I don't know what."

Jared steepled his fingers and tapped them against his chin as he mulled over the information. "Yeah, but you'd think if something bad was happening—whatever it was—that the health department or the state licensing board or law enforcement or *someone* would have stepped in by now."

"You'd think." She frowned and stared at the floor, clearly lost in her own turbulent thoughts.

He studied the screen, rereading the reply she'd opened. "Hey, you have four new replies. Want to check them out?"

She raised her head. "I do?" Grabbing the mouse, she clicked the first of the new messages. More condolences. The second reply was a link to an article from the same lady whose sister had lost her baby with the comment:

Here's more information from the Pine Mill newspaper about my sister's baby.

Elise followed the link to the article, and her shoulders drooped. "Oh, looks like the sister's baby is the same one I read about. This is the same article I found in my search."

"So…just two babies in two years?"

"Plus Kim's."

"But she was at a different hospital." His comment earned him a scowl.

"Yeah, but… Are you having second thoughts? Even two at one hospital is too many. I bet if I keep looking, I'll find more cases like mine and Kim's."

The desperation in her tone bothered him, and he studied her fiery expression. "To what end?"

She blinked. "Excuse me?"

"Why are you looking for more cases like yours?" he asked carefully, his tone low and gentle. "Is it a need to feel you aren't alone? A mission to discredit the hospital? Are you thinking of building a class-action lawsuit?"

She furrowed her brow, looking a bit poleaxed. "I…I don't know. I guess that depends on what I find out." Her expression turned angry, and she folded her arms over her chest. "Besides, you're the one who said I should arm myself with information. So I am. Why have you changed your tune?"

"I'm not saying I've changed my mind." He wrapped his fingers around her elbow and met her glare. "I just want to be sure you know what you're getting into. Are you prepared for what you might learn? Are you willing to take action if you find misfeasance or malpractice?"

Her anger faded, her expression softening to despondency. She opened her mouth and closed it again without answering. With a sigh, she turned back to the computer and stared at the screen.

Jared watched her, his heart aching for her. He regretted having encouraged her to undertake what could end up being a painful and fruitless search for answers. Maybe there was no good answer to why her baby died. At least he could blame the drunk driver for taking Kelly from him.

After a minute, she moved her hand listlessly to the mouse. Her expression downcast and discouraged, she clicked open the next message to her. More condolences—along with a phone number to call if she wanted to buy insurance. *Sheesh.* Some people.

The subject line of the last reply read, "Your baby." Elise opened the message, and Jared read over her shoulder again.

Check your email. I may have information about your baby.

The message was signed MysteryMom.

"Huh." She shifted on her chair and cast a glance to him. "What do you suppose…?"

He shrugged. "Check your email." While she navigated to a new web page and accessed her email account, he pulled his chair closer to the desk so that he was beside her.

Elise scrolled through advertisements for refinancing her mortgage, fliers from stores and jokes from friends until she found the email from MysteryMom.

She opened the email and leaned closer to the screen to read.

Dear Elise, I read your post on the Parents Without Children message board with a heavy heart. Losing a child is every mother's worst nightmare, and the last thing I'd ever want is to add to your pain. But the circumstances of your story rang familiar to me, and I took the liberty of doing some digging. I have powerful contacts with access to reliable information about birth records and have made it my mission to help mothers like you—and I do think I can help you. Not wanting to raise false hope for you, I triple-checked my information before contacting you.

Elise, my sources tell me that your baby might be alive.

Chapter 4

Elise froze. She stared at the message while a numbing disbelief swept through her. With an odd buzzing in her ears, she read the email again. And again. It really said what she thought. Was Gracie *alive?*

A strangled noise between a gasp and a whimper rasped from her throat.

"Oh, my God," Jared groaned. "Ignore it, Elise. Just delete it. Some people are just cruel beyond belief."

His voice roused her from her stupor, and a jolt of adrenaline rushed to her head, clearing the fog of shock. In its wake, her entire body revived with turbulent chaos. Her limbs shook, her stomach roiled, her head spun. She cast a confused glance at Jared. "What?"

He waved a hand at the screen in disgust. "Some crackpot is just yanking your chain, playing on your emotions. You watch. The next thing he'll send you is a request for money to help him locate your baby. If it's not a scam, then it's some jerk who gets off on giving desperate people false hope."

She fought for the breath to speak. "You…don't think it's real?"

"No way." He met her gaze and frowned. "Wait, you're not taking this seriously, are you? The guy didn't even sign his name."

"Not a guy. A woman. MysteryMom," she rasped. A chill settled in her bones, and she shuddered.

Jared grasped her upper arms, pulled her to her feet and into his arms. "Dear God, look at you. You're shaking." He wrapped her in a warm hug and rubbed her back. "It's okay. I know this is upsetting. Don't let this guy get to you."

She curled her fingers into his shirt and fought to steady her breathing. "B-but…what if it's real? M-maybe Grace *is* alive."

"Ah, Elise, don't…" Disappointment and concern weighted his tone.

Her mind raced, hyped up on the adrenaline and the possibilities MysteryMom's email created. Common sense told her Jared was likely right. The chances that Grace was still alive were remote. The odds that this "MysteryMom" was a con artist were high.

But a voice in her brain wouldn't let her discount the email out of hand. A maternal instinct deep inside screamed through the doubts that if there was even a hint that Gracie was alive somewhere, she had to do everything in her power to find her daughter and bring her home.

Dragging in a fortifying breath, she pushed back from Jared's embrace. Still clutching his shirtfront, she held him at arm's length and raised her eyes to his. "What would you do if it were Isabel?"

He tensed and scowled. "That's not—"

"No, think about it. If Isabel were kidnapped and the police told you they were certain she was dead and to give up ever finding her—"

A look of horror darkened his face, and he recoiled. "Elise, don't be—"

"Then you got an anonymous email saying she *was* alive—"

Jared sighed heavily and took a step back from her, rubbing his face with his hands. "It's not the same."

"You'd do everything you could to find her, wouldn't you?"

He gave her a disgruntled scowl. "Of course, but we're not talking about—"

"And I have to believe this MysteryMom is right, even if all practical sense says it's impossible. If Grace is out there, I have to find her!" Her heart thumped a wild cadence as hope grabbed the coattails of her determination and swelled in her chest.

Grace. Alive.

The idea was staggering. Exhilarating. Terrifying.

Overwhelmed by the implications, Elise swayed and collapsed in the desk chair. "If it's true…I—I don't even know where to begin. I—"

A maelstrom of conflicting emotions ravaged her, clogging her throat and pricking her eyes with tears.

Jared blew out a breath and sat in the chair beside her. "I'd say the first step is to reply to MysteryMom and get more details. Ask her who her sources are, what information led her to her conclusion. Ask her for credentials you can check out."

She turned to him, blinking to clear her vision. "Does this mean…you believe it could be true? You've changed your mind?"

He reached for her hands and folded them between

his. "It means you're right. If I thought there was even a remote chance Isabel were alive, I'd move mountains to find her." His eyes darkened, and he furrowed his brow. "I can't say I'm happy about this, but if you pursue this, I'm behind you one hundred percent. I'll do whatever I can to help."

Elise flipped her hands and laced her fingers with his, clinging to him as if he were her lifeline, her only connection to Grace. "Thank you."

Elise left shortly after that, assuring Jared that though she was still shocked by MysteryMom's email, she would be fine tonight. If only she was as certain of the same as she convinced him she was.

When she got home, she pulled the email up on her laptop and hit the reply button.

Who are you? What information do you have? How do I know I can believe you or trust your sources? If this is a joke, you are one sick puppy.

She sent the message and was logging in to the Parents Without Children message board when a bell sound told her she had a new email. Returning to her email program, she found a notice from her internet server claiming her reply to MysteryMom was undeliverable. "The addressee's mailbox is full," she read aloud.

Sighing her frustration, she returned to the message board and posted, "To MysteryMom—You have my attention, but my reply to you bounced. What's your game?"

She read a couple more commiserating replies to her original post and pushed away from her laptop to start getting ready for bed. Not that she thought she'd get any sleep, but she had to be at work early the next morning for a staff meeting. She would give sleep her best shot.

Brooke was already curled in a ball at the foot of her bed, sleeping soundly, and she stroked the tabby's fur as she made her way to the bathroom. While she brushed her teeth, her mind turning over the tantalizing possibility that Grace was alive, she heard a chime from her computer. Curious what had popped up, she wiped her mouth and crossed the room to her laptop. An instant message window from the discussion board website had appeared in the bottom corner of her screen.

She sat down and read.

No game. I'm your friend. I think I can help you, but you'll have to trust me. —MysteryMom

Elise's pulse tripped, and she dropped heavily onto her desk chair. This was her chance to grill MysteryMom for information. Quickly, she tapped out a reply and hit the send button.

Trust you? I don't even know who you are.

A few seconds later, MysteryMom answered.

I'm afraid I can't tell you who I am. It would jeopardize my ability to continue my work on behalf of single mothers. Please believe that I am your friend, not a prankster. —MysteryMom

Elise scowled and typed, What work? You mentioned reliable sources gave you the information about my daughter. Who are your sources? How do I know your information is credible?

MysteryMom replied, I have contacts in all levels of local and federal law enforcement. In recent years, I've made it my mission, my purpose, to reunite children with their parents. It is my passion to do this work on behalf of single mothers. I have kids of my own, and I know the love a mother has for her child.

Elise's fingers hovered over her keyboard as she considered her reply. She wanted desperately to believe MysteryMom could help her, could prove to her that there had been a horrific mistake at the hospital after Grace was born. Had Grace been accidentally switched with another baby? It seemed unlikely with all the safety protocols in place at hospitals these days. And yet…

Elise typed, So what do you suspect happened to my daughter? What makes you think she is alive? What evidence do you have?

MysteryMom answered, Your case is a bit different from the others I've worked on. Usually I find a missing parent, but your post to the message board reminded me of a case I'd read about here in Texas. I asked my sources to do a little leg work, and we think we may be on to something big involving the hospital where your daughter was born.

Big… like what?

We're investigating the staff there and in some other hospitals in Louisiana.

For malpractice? A class action lawsuit? What?

It's best I don't say anything more until I have confirmation of the facts. I need more information from you.

Warning bells sounded in Elise's head, and she scowled. If MysteryMom asked for financial information, her social security number or other key facts that could lead to identity theft, Elise would know the woman—if, in fact, MysteryMom was even a woman—was a fraud, preying on her vulnerability as a grieving mother.

Elise responded, What kind of information?

MysteryMom asked, Were you given any drugs to put you to sleep following the birth of your baby?

Elise gasped, remembering the injection the nurse had put in her IV despite her protests. It was while she'd been in her drug-induced sleep that Grace had died. The back of Elise's neck prickled.

She answered quickly, Yes, I was.

Did you ever see your baby again after you were told she'd died?

Nausea swamped Elise's gut. MysteryMom's questions cut right to the heart of the issues that had bothered Elise the most about Grace's death.

Elise typed her response. No. They told me her body had already been sent to the morgue. I was devastated...hysterical over her death, and they kept me sedated until right before I was released from the hospital. I had a closed-casket funeral.

What reason were you given for her death?

Elise explained what she'd been told about Grace's unexplained heart failure and the hospital's lack of sufficient critical-care facilities for newborns.

MysteryMom didn't reply for several tense moments. Finally Elise typed, Does all this tell you anything? What does it mean?

It follows the pattern we've uncovered.

Elise's breath backed up in her lungs as she reread the reply. Pattern? The term implied numerous cases similar to hers. Could it be that something more than tragic coincidence tied her loss to cases like the Harrisons' baby and the other couple in Pine Mill she'd read about?

Elise asked, How many other women have you heard from?

I haven't personally worked any other cases like yours. But with your permission, I'll give your information to my contact who is working a similar case.

Elise chewed her lip. Did she dare venture down this path? Was she asking for trouble trusting MysteryMom or could MysteryMom help her work a miracle? She glanced at the copy of the ultrasound picture that she kept on her bedside table. Really, there was no question. As she'd told Jared, if even a slight chance of finding Grace alive and getting her daughter back existed, it was worth the risk. You have my permission.

She spent the next twenty minutes answering MysteryMom's questions about the exact day and time of Grace's birth, her birth weight and length. When asked about identifying birthmarks or other details that might help in the search for Grace, Elise described the small pear-shaped red mark she'd seen on Grace's shoulder.

Then MysteryMom replied, I need to go. I'll catch you up on what I find out in a couple days. Let's meet back here, same time on Sunday night.

All right. In the meantime, what can I do to help?

Sit tight. Be patient. Give my investigators the time and space they need to look into this. Okay?

Elise frowned. She didn't like the idea of sitting on the sidelines when there was so much at stake. She started typing, What if I just ask around about—

Before she could finish her reply, the star by MysteryMom's user ID disappeared, indicating she'd logged off. Sighing her frustration, Elise deleted her question and scrolled through their exchange. The same phrases jumped out at her again and buzzed through her brain. *Contacts in law enforcement. Follows the pattern. I've made it my mission.*

Elise sat back in her chair and realized she was shaking. The idea that Grace was alive, that she could actually get her daughter back, filled her with dizzying joy and a fiery determination and purpose. She would find out the truth about what happened to Grace, no matter what it took.

I've made it my mission, too.

Chapter 5

Elise couldn't wait a week for the next grief-support meeting to talk to Jared about her exchange with MysteryMom. The next morning after her staff meeting at the newspaper, she phoned Jared's house and left a message with his mother, who was filling in as babysitter while Michelle was sick. Her next call was to her brother, Michael.

"Are you sitting down?" she asked him.

"Why? What's up?"

"Grace might not be dead."

A brief silence followed in which she pictured Michael's stunned expression.

"What are you talking about? How is that possible?"

She filled him in on everything that had transpired in the past few weeks, including meeting the Harrisons, posting on the Parents Without Children message board and MysteryMom's shocking announcement. When she was finished, she waited for him to comment.

"Well?" she nudged.

"You can't be taking this whack job seriously, can you? You had a funeral. You buried Grace, Elise. All the wishing in the world is not going to bring her back."

His blunt disbelief gouged at her heart. "But what if she never really died? MysteryMom asked if I'd ever actually seen her body, and it sank in that I hadn't. I'd been mourning the fact I hadn't had a chance to say goodbye, but I'd never let myself believe that it could mean she wasn't really dead."

"Elise, she's dead. Hospitals don't make mistakes about that. They might make mistakes in diagnoses or amputate the wrong leg sometimes, but dead is pretty cut-and-dried."

"But MysteryMom implied there could be—"

"Elise, stop. I love you, and I know how much losing your baby hurt you, but this is crazy!"

"Do you?"

"Do I what?"

"Do you have any idea how much losing Grace hurt me? You never call to check on me, and heaven forbid you visit. Michael, you're all the family I have, and—"

"Oh, here we go again," he interrupted. "Look, I don't have a lot of time right now. I'm sorry this person has fed you this pipe dream, but that's all it is. Don't buy into it. Don't torture yourself with false hopes."

"But—"

"Bye, Elise." The line clicked dead in her ear.

She gritted her teeth and shoved down the disappointment that her only family could be so unsupportive. Maybe he meant well, but his lack of faith still hurt.

But Michael had had his feelings betrayed by their parents, too. He'd been shifted around from one foster home to the next and learned to guard his heart and hoard his trust like she had.

Her thoughts drifted to Jared, how he'd warned her MysteryMom could be a crank, as well. But even if he hadn't completely changed his mind about MysteryMom, he'd come around enough to support Elise in pursuing the possibility Grace was alive. She appreciated his backing more than he might ever know.

Jared's support meant even more to her the next Thursday night when she explained the turn of events to the grief-support group. After laying out the gist of what MysteryMom had claimed, she glanced from one face to the next around the circle. Expressions ranged from dubious concern to scoffing dismissal.

"Elise…" Joleen began, and by her tone, Elise knew she was about to be cautioned again about the unlikelihood that MysteryMom's assertions had any merit.

She held up a hand. "I know what you're going to say. I know how it sounds, but if there's a chance it is true, I have to follow up on it."

"Sometimes our grief is so great that we create alternate realities," Joleen said, clearly picking her words carefully, "or build our hope around fantasies that have no basis."

Elise sighed her frustration, and Jared, who had sat quietly beside her as she made her case, reached over and took her hand. He gave her fingers a squeeze of support, and her agitation calmed enough to hear Joleen out.

"Denial and bargaining are steps in the grieving process, but I'd be remiss if I didn't advise you to let go of this. You'll only prolong the healing process and hurt yourself more by indulging in this wild goose chase."

Tears of disappointment stung her eyes, and she blinked them back. Shifting her attention to the Harrisons, Elise asked, "What would you do?"

Greg shook his head and waved her off. "I don't want to speculate."

"Kim? If it turns out that Grace is really alive, it could mean your baby didn't really die, either."

Kim gasped and stared at her with an expression that was half horror and half hope.

"Elise, don't." Joleen's tone was firm and unyielding. "I may not be able to talk you out of following this destructive path, but do not sabotage Kim's or any other member's healing by poisoning her with false hope. If you do, I'll have to ask you to leave the group."

Stunned by Joleen's ultimatum, Elise opened her mouth, but words didn't come. She scanned the faces around the circle. Some seemed disappointed in her, others hostile. Jared gave her a penetrating look that begged her to drop the subject.

Clearly the bomb she'd dropped on the group had been emotional and controversial. She'd expected a strong reaction, but she'd hoped at least a few of the group's members would be supportive of her decision to trust MysteryMom and search for Grace.

Sharp-edged rejection and betrayal sliced through her, every bit as dispiriting as when her father had dumped her and Michael in a foster home and walked away. Pulling her hand from Jared's, she rose from her chair, her legs shaking.

"Elise?" Jared sat straighter, worry etched in his brow.

"I...h-have to go," she croaked.

"Elise, don't leave. Please." Joleen's expression had softened, and she motioned toward Elise's empty chair. "I'm sorry if I sounded harsh, but my job is to facilitate a healthy and productive conversation in managing our grief. I just can't, in good conscience, condone what I honestly believe is a counterproductive, even dangerous, mind-set on your part."

Elise backed toward the door. "I understand. No hard feelings, but…this is…it's something I have to do."

With that, she turned and hurried through the corridor of the church and toward the exit. She heard the scrape of a chair in the meeting room and the pounding of running feet behind her.

"Elise, wait."

She paused, hand on the door handle, tears stinging her sinuses, and let Jared catch up to her. "Everyone thinks I'm nuts for buying into MysteryMom's theory and pursuing her contentions. My brother called it a pipe dream."

Jared put a hand on her shoulder and turned her to face him. Cupping her chin with his palm, he stroked her cheek with his thumb. "I don't think you're nuts."

"Really? The other day, when I read that first email from MysteryMom, you said—"

"I know what I said. And I still have a few doubts about this whole crazy scenario. But…" He pulled her into a firm embrace, pressing a kiss to the top of her head. "I've thought a lot about what you asked me the other night. In your position, I'd absolutely do the same thing."

Elise's heart swelled. His admission was just the confirmation she needed to quiet her doubt demons. "Thank you."

"For what? I haven't done anything."

"Yes, you have. You've done more for me than you could imagine by supporting me in this." She tipped her head back and met his gaze. "I was beginning to question my own sanity."

He finger-combed her hair away from her face, then skimmed his knuckles along her jaw. His touch sent a heady sensation spinning through her. Her fingers tightened their hold on his shirt, and her breath stuttered from her lungs. She hadn't been held like this by a man in so long. After discovering her last boyfriend was married and had no intention of leaving his wife, the idea of investing her emotions in any kind of intimacy scared her. Her father, her foster families, her lover. She'd been burned too many times to allow anyone else close.

Then she'd fallen in love with the child growing inside her. Losing Grace had felt like the greatest betrayal of all. Fate had taunted her with the precious bond of motherhood, only to snatch it away in a soul-shattering instant.

She knew growing attached to Jared when she was so vulnerable was risky. But at that moment, she needed to revel in the warmth of his friendship. She needed to feel she wasn't alone.

"Do you want to go get a bite to eat?" he said, his voice a lulling murmur. "You can catch me up on what you've heard from MysteryMom."

"That would be a short conversation. When we chatted by instant message on Sunday, she didn't have much to report yet."

He hummed an acknowledgment. "When are you supposed to be in touch with her again?"

"Perhaps tonight, if she can get free. She said not to panic if I didn't hear from her. She promised to be online Friday if she got tied up tonight."

"I'd like to be there when you IM with her next time."

"We're not IM-ing until ten. Isn't that kinda late for—Mmm..." She sighed blissfully as Jared massaged the back of her neck with his fingers. She could feel her tension seeping from her taut muscles and leaving her weak and pliant in his hands.

"Late for...?" he prompted.

She rolled her head to the side, relishing the deep rub as he worked his way to the base of her skull. She peered up at him from half-shuttered eyes. "I don't remember. Lord, that feels so good. Don't stop. Ever."

A low rich chuckle rumbled from his chest. "Like that, do you?"

Elise closed her eyes. "Mmm-hmm."

"Can you access the IM from my computer?"

"I think so. We use the message board IM on the website I showed you last week."

Jared's hand stilled on her neck, and she opened her eyes, curious why he'd stopped the relaxing massage. His focus was riveted on her mouth, and his expression reflected an inner battle. He wanted to kiss her. She saw that much in the desire that darkened his eyes. But something held him back.

"Jared..." She could only manage a rasp, as longing and doubt squeezed her lungs.

Tightening his hold around the back of her head, he drew her closer. She held her breath as he brushed his lips against hers. Softly, tentatively at first, as if seeking permission. Sweet sensations washed through her, and she couldn't help the half moan, half sigh that he took as an invitation to deepen the kiss. Angling his mouth, he drew on her lips with a gentle persuasion and exquisite finesse.

She canted forward, leaning into him, into the kiss. Her world narrowed to the two of them and that moment. Any reservations she'd had fled, and a pleasant lethargy filled her body.

When he broke the kiss, he didn't back away. Instead, he rested his forehead against hers, closed his eyes and grew very still. Elise was grateful for the moment to collect herself. But when he continued to hold her without speaking, she sensed what was wrong.

"So...I'm guessing I am the first woman you've kissed since Kelly died."

He drew a deep, slow breath and released it. "Yeah."

"And it was…weird for you?"

He opened his eyes and levered back just far enough to meet her gaze. His brow furrowed as if he were mulling over her question. "Actually…what's weird is…it wasn't weird."

"No?"

"In fact it was…pretty great." He hiked up a corner of his mouth, and a dimple pocked his cheek.

Elise's pulse fluttered. "Then you're okay? You were quiet for so long I thought maybe…"

"I was regretting it?"

Her stomach swooped. "I was going to say something else but…do you regret it?"

He caressed the side of her face, and his smile grew. "No. I was praying that I hadn't offended you or scared you off. I know you're vulnerable right now, and I don't want to pressure you or take advantage of you."

His consideration touched her but didn't surprise her. Jared had already shown her in many ways that he understood her needs and her confused emotions. His patience and thoughtfulness earned him a little more of her respect and gratitude.

But consideration was not what she wanted in the wake of his earthshaking kiss. The crackle of her nerve endings told her how long it had been since she'd burned for a man's kiss. She slid her arms around his neck and tipped a coy grin his direction. "Did I complain?"

He lifted one eyebrow. "Hmm. In that case…" He tugged her close again and covered her lips with another toe-curling kiss.

Elise let herself sink into the sweet oblivion. She didn't stop to analyze what was happening. Something so elemental required no explanation. The spark of attraction she'd sensed between them had needed only a little help to be fanned into a bright blaze.

Jared stroked a hand down her back, his fingertip strumming the ridge of her spine and heightening the tingle already shooting through her. When his caress reached her waist, he slipped his hand beneath the hem of her sweater. The heat of his fingers against her bare skin sent shock waves to her core. When she trembled, he tightened his hold on her and pulled her flush against his taut muscles. Heat radiated from him in waves, cocooning her, and for a few moments, she was able to shut out the icy cold of grief, the uncertainty of her future and the ache of loss.

A door closed somewhere down the church corridor, and the click of footsteps on the linoleum floor reminded her where she was and that their privacy was an illusion. She jerked back from him, and Jared reluctantly released her.

"Elise?"

She pressed a hand to her swollen lips and drew a slow breath for composure. "Do you have decaf coffee at your house?"

He blinked and scrubbed a hand down his cheek. "I think so."

"Then I'll follow you in my car, and I'll catch you up on my week while we wait for MysteryMom to get online."

At Jared's house, his mother filled them in on Isabel's dinner and nap status, and while Jared walked his mom to her car, Elise joined Isabel on the living-room floor. On impulse, Elise had brought her camera inside, and she snapped a couple pictures as Jared's daughter gnawed on a wooden block and blinked her wide blue eyes at her visitor.

"Hi, Isabel. Do you remember me?" She picked up the

stuffed elephant beside her and walked it across the floor to Isabel's foot. "Elephant's gonna kiss you!" She made a silly smacking noise as she pressed the soft toy to the baby's cheek.

Isabel chuckled, then crawled closer to Elise. Grabbing fistfuls of Elise's sweater, Jared's daughter pulled herself up to her knees and studied Elise with an earnest expression. "Kee?"

Elise laughed. "So you do remember me, huh?"

Isabel plopped down on her diapered bottom and clapped her hands. "Kee-kee."

"As a matter of fact…" She reached for her purse, which she'd deposited on the sofa and dug in the bag for the snack pack of cookie bites she'd saved from her lunch. "Do you like shortbread?"

Isabel saw the foil packet, and her eyes glowed. "Kee!"

When Jared returned from the driveway, Elise had Isabel on her lap, and they were sharing a snack of shortbread cookies.

"And they say the way to a man's heart is through his stomach," she said around a mouthful. "I hate to think how your daughter might have rejected me if not for my bakery offerings."

"Ah, yes. My girl's a little cookie monster." Jared joined them on the sofa and held his hands out to Isabel. She refused to go to him. "Well, well. Somebody has made a new friend. You have a great rapport with her."

Elise grinned and hugged Isabel. "As long as the cookie supply lasts anyway."

But even before the cookies ran out, Isabel began whining and rubbing her eyes with sticky fingers.

"Gee, princess, it's kinda early for bed." Jared scratched his chin and gave Isabel a thoughtful look. "If I put you down now, you'll be up before the birds. Which means I will be, too."

Isabel rubbed a cookie-covered hand on her ear and wrinkled her nose as she fussed.

"Could she be coming down with something?" Elise asked. "I know I like to go to bed early when I feel bad."

"Well, Mom did say she's been cranky today and has a stuffy nose."

Isabel's whine escalated to a cry, and Jared shoved off the couch. "Okay, sweetie, let's get a bath."

Elise's heart melted hearing Isabel's mewling cry. "Want help?"

"Thanks, I got it." He must have seen her disappointment, because he hesitated. "But…you can rock her to sleep in a few minutes if you want."

Elise smiled. "I'd love that."

The next afternoon, Elise sat at her computer at the newspaper office reviewing the pictures she'd taken at a political rally earlier that morning. The task was taking twice as long as usual because her mind kept straying to her plans for that evening. MysteryMom had been a no-show the night before, so she and Jared had made arrangements to have dinner out then head back to his house to wait for MysteryMom's update at his computer.

Elise's mind was on Jared's kiss at the church the night before, her body humming with the same energy she'd experienced as he held her, when the editor-in-chief stopped by her desk, a cup of coffee in his hand. "Norris, Russell tells me his feature on the new art exhibit for next Saturday's edition hit a snag and needs to be bumped another week. This means there's room for your photo essay and feature piece, if you're still interested."

She sat straighter in her chair. "Yes, absolutely."

"Did you come up with any more ideas that weren't as lame-brained as your others?"

Cringing mentally at his critical attitude, she pulled out the notepad she'd been keeping her ideas on. "Well, the new library branch will be opening—"

"Boring."

"Uh, local breast cancer survi—"

"Been done. Often."

She took a deep breath to tamp down her frustration. "I heard about a man in town who was at Normandy on D-day. He's in a nursing home, but he's still quite lucid and according to his family has lots of stories about the war."

He sipped his coffee, and she held her breath.

"I like that."

A flutter of excitement stirred in her gut.

"But…"

She deflated.

"Russell can do that story on Memorial Day. We'll get the geezer to tell us all about his friends that died."

She prickled at her boss's reference to a decorated war hero as a "geezer" but bit down on the cynical retort that formed on her tongue.

"What else ya got?"

She sighed. "That's about it for now, but I'll keep brainstorming, and—"

"You do that. I'll be in my office when you have your breakthrough." Mr. Grimes strolled away, slurping his coffee, and Elise gritted her teeth.

At least he'd given her the green light to do a photo essay and write a feature. That was progress. Unless he was just yanking her chain, telling her she could do the article then nixing all her ideas to shut her up.

Russell popped up in his cubicle like a groundhog and

peered over the partition. "Don't let him get to you. He gets off on being a jerk."

Raking her hair back with her fingers, she blew out a breath of irritation. "I know he does. But this chance is important to me. I don't want to blow it."

Russell glanced over his shoulder toward Grimes's office then back to Elise. "Listen, all of your ideas have been good ones. Really. Just wait. He'll be assigning me the library story in a couple weeks and make it look like it was his idea."

Elise grunted and rolled her eyes. "That doesn't help me now."

"You'll think of something. My advice? Make it something that matters to you. Your passion for the topic will come through in your writing and in how you present the topic to Grimes."

She nodded. "Thanks. I'll keep that in mind."

Russell gave her a wink and disappeared behind the cubicle wall.

Something that mattered to her... She bit the cap of her pen and tried to shove aside her annoyance with her boss so she could think. When her phone rang, she answered mechanically, her mind miles away.

"Hi, I hope it's okay that I called you at work." *Jared.*

The sound of his voice sent her heartbeat into overdrive. She dropped the pen she'd been gnawing and turned her back to the newsroom, as if it would afford her more privacy. "No…I mean, yes, it's okay. What's up?"

"Well, Isabel's temperature for one. I hate to leave her when she's sick, so…about tonight…"

Disappointment plucked at her along with concern for Isabel. "I understand. Have you taken her to a doctor? What's wrong with her?"

"Probably just an ear infection. We're on the way to see the pediatrician now."

"Another time then? For dinner, I mean."

"Actually, if you're still game, I have a lasagna in my freezer that my mom brought over a few days ago. We can eat here, watch a movie, and I can keep an eye on the princess."

The princess. She smiled at his pet name for his daughter. "Sounds lovely. What can I bring?"

Elise hung up a few minutes later, having settled the new plans, and as she spun back to her computer, a copy of her ultrasound picture of Grace caught her eye. Her breath hitched, and the usual pang of longing and sadness bit her. Was anyone taking Grace to the doctor when she had an earache? Oh, what she'd give to be the one sitting up with her daughter when she was ill! Assuming MysteryMom was right about her being alive…

She shifted restlessly in her desk chair. Waiting for answers from MysteryMom was one of the hardest things she'd ever done. Elise needed to *do,* not sit on the sidelines. Especially something as important as—

She gripped the armrests of her chair as a half-formed idea popped into her head. Could she write an exposé on the questionable infant deaths? Without having fully decided what angle she'd take, she shot out of her seat and hurried to Mr. Grimes's office.

"I have an idea—" she started before realizing he was on the phone.

He held up a finger to say "wait a minute" and finished his call.

She gripped the edge of his door, and as she waited, doubts assailed her. MysteryMom had asked her not to get involved, not to do anything to undermine her contact's investigation. If she went to the hospital half-cocked, asking questions, would she blow whatever work MysteryMom had done?

As Grimes hung up, he shot her an impatient look. "All right. Dazzle me."

"I—" Her mouth went dry. How could she frame her piece in a way that wouldn't raise red flags but would still allow her to go behind the scenes at Pine Mill Hospital and snoop around?

Grimes steepled his fingers and rocked back in his desk chair. "Well?"

"I want to do…s-something at Pine Mill Hospital."

He stared at her blankly. Blinked slowly.

Okay, Elise, get it together. If you're going to get the okay for this assignment you have to sell it.

She cleared her throat. "With all the debate about health care in the nation recently, I was thinking I'd do a piece about a day in the life at a small-town hospital. So many small hospitals are struggling financially and…" He lifted one eyebrow, which she took as encouragement. "Just one day at any hospital is kind of symbolic of life as a whole…" Her idea began to jell, and as she warmed to it, her voice strengthened and passion infused her proposal. "I mean… life begins at a hospital in the maternity department, and we pass through again when we meet obstacles or have celebrations along the way…illness, accidents, the birth of our children—" *And the loss of our children.* She struggled to keep her composure as she plowed on. "And eventually, many times, we go to a hospital to die. The circle of life, right?"

She was drawing a breath to continue, when he waved a dismissive hand.

"Okay. Do it. Bye."

Elise blinked. "Really? I can do that story?"

"Are you deaf? Did I stutter?"

Excitement and relief pumped through her, and she flashed him a broad grin, ignoring his sarcasm. "Thank you!"

"I need it on my desk in a week."

A week. Her stomach clenched. She had to pull together a plan and get to work *pronto.* Step one, call the hospital administration and arrange access behind the scenes for her photo shoot and interviews with key employees. Dr. Arrimand, for one.

She dropped into her desk chair and pressed a hand to her swirling gut.

For the first time in more than a year, she was going back to the scene where her nightmare had begun.

Chapter 6

"Are you sure this is a good idea? Should I come with you?" Jared asked later in the week, his voice coming from her cell phone, which she'd set to speaker. Even when he wasn't there in person, the deep richness of his voice resonated inside her, kindling a tingling heat at her core.

Elise smiled. His concern for her helped calm the butterflies that swooped in her gut as she pulled into a parking spot at Pine Mill Hospital. "I'll be fine. Besides, I'm already at the hospital. I'm meeting with the chief administrator in ten minutes. He thinks my photo essay will be a great PR plug for the hospital, and he was thrilled to give me open access to any department I want to see."

"Just…be careful. Call me when you're done."

She could hear Isabel babbling in the background, and she felt a little catch in her chest. She drew a deep breath for courage and gathered her purse and camera bag from the seat beside her. "I will."

After locking her car, Elise stowed her keys in her purse and strode toward the front door, buffeted by a cool autumn wind. The volunteer at the information desk directed her to the office of the hospital administrator, George Bircham. The silver-haired man, who wore a suit that looked like he'd owned it since the 1970s, greeted her warmly and conducted the first several minutes of the tour himself. They'd visited the pediatric hall and the radiology lab first, while Elise clicked pictures and scribbled notes. Next, Mr. Bircham led her to the E.R. A shiver chased down her spine as she remembered entering the emergency room months ago, doubled over in pain as her contractions peaked. From the E.R., she'd been rushed upstairs to Labor and Delivery just in time for Grace's arrival.

"And unlike big-city hospitals where you may wait hours to be seen, our emergency-care department boasts an average wait of only eleven minutes!" the administrator bragged as his pager sounded. "I'm sorry, Ms. Norris. I have to answer this call." He flagged down a nurse who was leaving the cafeteria. "You work in Labor and Delivery, don't you?"

When the nurse nodded, Bircham introduced Elise and asked the nurse to show her around, let her take pictures and answer her questions.

"Thank you for your time," Elise said, shaking his hand then falling in step behind the nurse whose name tag identified her as Cheryl Watts.

Elise wiped sweat from her palms on her slacks as they rode the elevator to the second floor. When they reached Labor and Delivery, Cheryl led her to the nurses' station and introduced her to the nurses there. Elise snapped a couple pictures and asked a few innocuous questions to make the nurses feel more comfortable.

"What's going on here?" a male voice asked from behind her.

Her pulse jumped, and she nearly knocked over the coffee of one of the nurses as she spun to face the man in scrubs. *Dr. Arrimand.*

Would he recognize her? Remember her name?

Shoving down the swirl of nerves that danced through her, she stuck her hand out and pasted on a bright smile. "Elise Norris from the *Lagniappe Herald.* Mr. Bircham has granted me permission to photograph the behind-the-scenes operation here at Pine Mill for a feature article and photo spread about small-town hospitals."

He shook her hand and eyed her camera. "Bircham approved this?"

"Yes. I think he saw it as good promotion for the hospital. I'm planning a day-in-the-life piece."

The doctor lifted an eyebrow as if intrigued.

"I'd love to interview you for the article," she said as inspiration struck. Could she get any valuable information from him without arousing suspicion? She'd have to be careful, cagey.

"Dr. Arrimand, we're ready for you in delivery two."

Elise recognized the nurse who'd arrived to summon the doctor and flashed back to the minutes after Grace was born. She was the woman who'd injected her with the drug that had put her to sleep after only a brief time with Grace. When the nurse glanced toward Elise, the woman did a double take and frowned.

"On my way," Dr. Arrimand said. "I have to go now, but I can give you about ten minutes in around an hour."

"That's terrific. Thank you."

He started to walk away then turned back and aimed a finger at her. "I expect you to respect the patients' privacy. No pictures without their permission. Understand?"

"Absolutely." She could barely contain her relief as she watched him march down the hall. An interview with Dr. Arrimand was the next best thing to…

Her breath caught, and she hurried down the hall after the doctor. "Dr. Arrimand, wait!"

He paused and sent her an irritated look as she caught up to him. "I'd like to go into the delivery with you." Seeing a refusal coming from the darkening of his expression, she rushed on to explain, "The birth of a baby is so symbolic. I want to show how the hospital is there for the community from the beginning of life until the end and at major milestones along the way. I'll get the mother's permission, of course, and use the utmost professionalism and discretion in the angles I shoot."

"Dr. Arrimand!" the delivery-room nurse called from down the hall. She held a surgical gown out ready for the doctor to slip into.

"All right," he said, trotting away.

Elise followed at a jog, but was stopped at the door by the nurse. "You'll need sterile garb if you're coming in. The kits are on that shelf."

Finding the sterile coverings, Elise hastily donned the gown, shoe and hair covers, and a pair of latex gloves. When she entered the delivery room, the bright lights and antiseptic smell hit her with a cascade of memories. A tremor rose from deep in her core, and she fought the urge to flee.

The husband of the woman giving birth gave her a curious look. "What's with the camera?"

Seizing on the distraction and recalled to her reason for being there, she introduced herself and gave a quick summary of what she wanted to photograph. The couple agreed, and Elise began snapping pictures from the head of the bed.

Elise caught the moment Dr. Arrimand held the baby boy up for the couple to see for the first time and the moment the delivery nurse placed the swaddled infant in the mother's arms. Her hand trembled so badly as she photographed the family bonding that she was sure the pictures would be too blurry to use. Tears puddled in her eyes when the father bent to press a kiss on his new son's head.

She swallowed hard to clear the knot of emotion clogging her throat.

Oh, Grace, what happened to you?

"Congratulations." Her voice sounded choked as she set the camera aside and took out her notebook. "Do you have a name picked out?"

"Dillon Charles," the woman said, beaming proudly at the boy.

As Elise scribbled the name in her notes, the delivery nurse nudged her out of the way.

"Mom needs to rest, and we need to finish cleaning him up and give him a thorough health screening."

Elise held her breath, waiting to see if the mother was injected with any drugs. She watched as baby Dillon was passed to another nurse who placed a hospital ID on his ankle and laid him carefully in a clear bassinet labeled Baby Boy Thompson. Still no injection had been given to the mother. Elise was torn whether to follow the baby as he was rolled out of delivery to the nursery or stay with the mother to see what happened to her.

"When will the pictures be in the paper?" Dillon's father asked. "We want to be sure to get a copy…or ten."

Deciding what happened to the baby was the key to learning anything that would help find Grace, Elise backed toward the door, trying to keep the nurse with the baby in sight. "Uh…next weekend, I think. I—" She stepped into the hall in time to see the baby wheeled into the last room at the end of the corridor. "Thank you," she said in a rush, "for sharing your special moment with me…and our readers. I… Good luck."

She gave a little wave to the couple and hustled down the hall to the nursery. Through the plate glass window, she spotted the nurse unwrapping Dillon, carefully wiping him clean, and fitting him with a tiny diaper and blue cap. Next, she listened to his heart and lungs, and Elise clicked a few pictures through the glass. Lowering the camera, she watched the rest of the procedure until Dillon was returned to his bassinet and rolled into place next to the other babies. She chewed her lower lip with a strange sense of disappointment gnawing at her. Had she really been hoping to witness and document some egregious flaw in the delivery process? She would never want another baby placed in jeopardy the way Grace might have been, but how was she supposed to prove something was amiss at this hospital when everything she'd seen today seemed on the up-and-up?

She checked her watch and saw she had several minutes before her meeting with Dr. Arrimand, enough time to visit the morgue and ask a few questions. A chill shimmied through her. She dreaded the idea of seeing the morgue, but if her article was truly to cover the hospital's role in both the start and end of a person's life, a few pictures in the morgue were needed.

The coroner on duty, who introduced himself as Dr. Galloway, explained to her how he processed a body and which ones required an autopsy.

Clutching her pen so hard she thought it might break, Elise took notes on what he said. "Wh—what about babies? Are they handled any differently?"

The coroner gave her a sad smile. "Babies are always

sad cases, but no, they are treated the same as any other body we receive. Fortunately, the babies are few and far between. When we do get a child of any age, they stand out. That's a hard day at work."

"Can you tell me how many babies, newborns, you've had in the last two years?"

Dr. Galloway gave her an odd look, and she had to admit her question must have sounded morbid. "Only one or two off the top of my head. But Dr. Hambrick, the other coroner who works here, might have worked a case like that. Is it relevant to your article? I can look it up in our records if it's important."

Elise's nerves jangled, and she clutched her notepad against her chest like a shield. "Yes, please. I would like know."

He stepped over to a computer and logged in. "All babies or just newborns?"

"Just newborns." She bit her bottom lip as he scrolled through his records and sorted and filtered the information.

"Let's see…" He bent over the keyboard to study the results on his monitor. "In the last two years, we handled five babies that were less than a week old."

"Five?" Elise moved behind him to look over his shoulder at the screen. "Isn't that a lot?"

Dr. Galloway shrugged. "One seems like a lot to me."

"True."

He pointed to the monitor. "First one was stillborn, no autopsy run. The next three were significantly premature. No autopsies. And the last one…jeez, a one-week-old baby. Autopsy showed he died of shaken-baby syndrome."

Elise gasped. "How horrible!"

The coroner nodded. "I remember the case. The new mother was drunk at the time and couldn't get the baby to stop crying. Shook him so hard it caused brain damage and death. Dr. Hambrick had to testify at her trial. So sad."

Elise frowned. Where was Grace's record? "Are you sure that's all? Just those five?"

"Just those five?" He gave her a speculative glance. "A minute ago you said five was a lot."

"Well, it is…but…I just thought maybe…well, could that record be incomplete?"

"It's updated in real time. That's all the newborns under a week old that we handled."

Elise's head spun, and her knees shook so hard she had to sit down. The morgue had no record of Grace, with or without an autopsy. Was that more evidence the hospital had lied to her? Had given her false information about an autopsy being performed on Grace?

"Are you all right, ma'am?" Dr. Galloway narrowed a concerned look on her. "You look like you've seen a ghost."

"Oh, I…I just felt dizzy for a minute. I skipped lunch and…" Her voice trailed off as a new thought occurred to her.

Did the lack of a record on Grace support Mystery-Mom's theory that Grace was alive somewhere? Her pulse sped up, and a bubble of hope swelled in her chest.

"Can you print that page for me?"

He hesitated. "I'm not sure I—"

"Are you familiar with the Freedom of Information Act? By law, the public has a right to public records, including—"

He held up a hand to stop her. "But personal medical records are, by law, private. Since these records show only statistics, however, I guess it's okay. If you have a few minutes, I'll get it for you, but our printer is out of paper."

She checked her watch. She was due in Dr. Arrimand's office. "Can I stop back by and get it later? I'm interviewing Dr. Arrimand in just a few minutes."

Galloway's eyebrows shot up. "You managed to get an interview with Joe Arrimand?"

"Yes. Why?"

"He's not usually the talkative sort. Keeps to himself, doesn't socialize with the rest of the hospital staff much. And he's as busy as a one-legged man at a butt-kicking contest."

Elise had to chuckle at his simile. "I wouldn't have thought there were that many babies born here."

"Not just here. He also works at Crestview General and Clairmont Hospital."

Crestview. Where Kim had delivered her baby. A chill slithered through Elise as she processed the ramifications.

"Tell you what," he said. "I'll bring the copies to you. I'm headed out to dinner soon, so I'll stop by Dr. Arrimand's office with it."

With a grateful smile, she thanked Dr. Galloway for his assistance and hurried back upstairs to her meeting with Dr. Arrimand. She forced the new questions that buzzed through her brain to a back burner. She didn't need to be distracted or agitated as she interviewed Dr. Arrimand.

As she rode the elevator from the basement to the second floor, she checked her camera and discovered her memory card was full. Popping the card from its slot, she tucked it in her pocket and found a new one in her camera bag. She'd just clicked the new memory card in place when the elevator slid open.

Down the hall by the nursery's viewing window, a small crowd had gathered, laughing and cooing. Dillion's mother sat in a wheelchair in the middle of an adoring family, and his father received handshakes and slaps on the back.

Elise shoved aside her envy of the joyous occasion and

asked at the nurses' station for directions to Dr. Arrimand's office. The delivery nurse gave her a suspicious scowl, but Cheryl Watts escorted her down a back hall.

The doctor, still in his scrubs, greeted her more cordially than he had earlier and waved her toward a chair across from him. "I trust you're getting the information you need for your article, Ms. Norris. My staff tells me you've been taking lots of pictures."

"Well, photography is my first love and my regular assignment with the newspaper. But I was given special permission by my boss to write the accompanying article for this feature, as well, so that's the reason behind all the questions. I want to knock my boss's socks off, so that he'll trust me to do more features like this in the future."

Dr. Arrimand chuckled. "That's the spirit. How can I help you knock his socks off?"

She flipped open her pad to a fresh page and tapped her pen on it, thinking. As she had with the hospital administrator, Elise decided to start with few simple questions to put him at ease. "Tell me your favorite thing about your job. I mean…it must be so inspiring to be able to witness the miracle of new life every day, to see the joy of the parents and family…"

"Absolutely. That is the best part of the job." He went on to talk about a few of his favorite patients, the birth of his own children and the reason he chose obstetrics as a career. She asked him about his choice to work in the small-town hospital versus a larger hospital like the ones in Shreveport, New Orleans or Lagniappe.

"Well, I'm small-town born and raised. My father died when I was young, and my mother struggled to take care of us. We were as poor as dirt, but the town took care of us any way they could. I owe a lot to this town, and so in my own way, I'm paying back the folks who helped my family. Besides, I like living in Pine Mill, away from the crime and hustle and bustle."

Elise nodded, scribbling notes furiously. She furrowed her brow, debating the best way to phrase her next question. "Being a smaller hospital with less money, Pine Mill isn't able to afford some of the emerging technology and equipment. Do you find it frustrating having limited resources?"

He scoffed. "You make it sound like we're backward and out of date."

"Let me clarify. In the labor-and-delivery department, you don't have the critical-care facilities like St. Mary's in Lagniappe."

He turned up a palm. "And St. Mary's doesn't have the cutting-edge facilities to treat childhood cancer the way St. Jude does, and the Mayo Clinic has better facilities than a lot of places." He smiled. "There's always going to be a dog on the block with a bigger bone or a better doghouse. We do the best we can with what we have. Our patients get top-notch care for a hospital our size."

Elise opted not to press the issue, despite his politician-like deflection. She didn't want to raise undue suspicion about her hidden agenda. "Okay, we've talked about your favorite part of the job, helping bring babies into the world, but what about your least favorite?"

He laughed heartily. "Oh, that's easy. Paperwork." He motioned to his messy desk. "As you see I'm a bit behind in that department."

A knock on the door saved her from an awkward reply.

"Yes?" Dr. Arrimand called.

The door opened, and the nurse from the delivery room entered. "I'm sorry to interrupt." She cast a wary look toward Elise then hurried over to the doctor and bent at the waist to whisper in his ear.

The doctor's expression darkened, and he cut a quick, accusing look toward Elise. Had she not been watching the exchange with the nurse closely, she might have missed the telltale glance, but that brief sidelong glare told her she was the topic of the nurse's secret.

She sat forward in her chair, the nape of her neck tingling.

"You're sure?" Dr. Arrimand murmured in a low voice.

His nurse gave a quick, almost imperceptible nod.

"Okay, thank you, Helen." He leaned back in his chair, silently dismissing the nurse, and he turned back to Elise. The doctor was no longer smiling.

"Is everything all right?" she asked after several uncomfortable seconds of silence.

"Just fine." He leaned forward, bracing his weight on his folded arms, which he propped on his desk. His sudden shift felt aggressive, and Elise fought the urge to shrink back from his penetrating glare.

"Tell me something, Ms. Norris. What made you pick Pine Mill Hospital for the subject of your article? There are plenty of small hospitals in this corner of the state."

Adrenaline spiked in her, and her gut clenched. "Pine Mill Hospital seemed to be a fair representation of the kind of health care available in—"

"A fair representation based on what? Whose assessment?"

"Well, mine. I—"

"And what past experience do you have with our hospital?" He arched an eyebrow in query, his expression still stern.

Elise scrambled for an answer that wouldn't sound any alarms. What had the nurse told him that led him to grill her like this?

Her neck felt flushed. Her tongue dried, and when she

opened her mouth to speak, the words stuck in her throat. She paused long enough to swallow hard, aware the gesture gave away her nerves. She hated being the one on the hot seat.

She opted for honesty. He'd look her name up when she left anyway, if that wasn't what his nurse had already done. If she were to get caught in a lie, she'd cause more suspicion than being forthright…to an extent. "I was a patient here about a year ago."

"Is that so? Under what circumstances?"

She took a deep breath, gathering her composure. She needed to regain control of the interview. She was supposed to be the one asking the questions.

"How long have you worked at this hospital, Dr. Arrimand?"

"Twenty-one years. Why were you a patient here?" he volleyed back.

"I had a baby. Where did you work before coming to Pine Mill?"

His jaw tightened. "Boy or girl?"

"You didn't answer my question." Elise's heart was drumming so loud, she wondered if the doctor could hear it. He could probably see the frantic cadence as it hammered against her chest. "You also work at other small hospitals in the area. Is that right?"

Another knock sounded on the office door.

"What!" he barked to the visitor.

Dr. Galloway pushed open the door and stepped in. "Sorry to interrupt, Joe, but I promised these records to Ms. Norris."

"No problem." Dr. Arrimand's dark eyes stayed fixed on Elise. "We were finished here anyway."

Dr. Galloway held out the copies he'd made, and she

quickly stuffed them in the pocket of her camera bag, out of sight.

"Good luck with your article," the coroner said as he backed out of the office.

"Thank you." She forced a strained smile to her lips.

By the time she turned back to Dr. Arrimand, he'd risen behind his desk and folded his arms over his chest. "I'm afraid that's all the time I have, Ms. Norris."

Okay, she was getting the brush-off.

"Could we reschedule and finish the interview later?"

"That won't be necessary. I have nothing else to say." He stalked to his door and opened it. "You know the way out, don't you?"

And he was in a hurry to get rid of her. Interesting.

"I…yeah." She gathered her purse and camera bag, hiking both straps onto her shoulder as she made her way to the door. Maintaining her professionalism, she offered the doctor her hand to shake. "Thank you for your time."

He gave her fingers a perfunctory squeeze, flashed a false smile and opened the door wider.

Elise walked out, receiving a cool look from his delivery nurse, then headed for the elevator. Once the doors slid shut, she slumped against the back wall and released a deep breath. What had that been about? He'd morphed from amiable, if grudging, host to combatant in seconds. Because of whatever the nurse had told him.

Obviously they knew she'd had Grace there, and, quite possibly, they were concerned about a malpractice lawsuit. Or was there more to it than that? Did they realize Grace had died? Or rather that they'd *told* her Grace had died. She was more certain than ever that something nefarious, something *illegal* was going on at Pine Mill Hospital.

And Dr. Arrimand had a hand in it.

* * *

Elise hustled out to her car and put her camera bag and purse on the passenger seat next to her. As soon as she got home, she would post a notice on the Parents Without Children message board asking MysteryMom to contact her. MysteryMom's investigators needed to see the new information she had from the coroner, and Elise wanted MysteryMom to know about Dr. Arrimand's odd behavior. While the doctor's inhospitality didn't prove anything, every piece in this puzzle helped create a fuller picture.

She pulled out onto the rural highway and headed back to Lagniappe. The dashboard clock said it was still early enough for her to make it home by dinnertime. She could stop by Jared's, show him her pictures and get his opinion concerning the doctor's behavior.

And she could see Isabel before she went to bed. Her heart gave a joyful flutter. Jared's daughter had toddled her way into Elise's heart, and no one was more surprised than Elise. Not that Isabel wasn't precious and easy to love, but Elise had fallen head over heels for the pixie's slobbery grin and wide blue eyes. Somehow, instead of a painful reminder of her loss, Isabel was healing Elise's broken heart. And firing her resolve to find Grace. To find the truth that MysteryMom alluded to in her last email.

A loud *vroom* pulled her out of her deliberations, and she glanced in her rearview mirror to locate the source. A large silver pickup truck barreled down the road toward her. Judging from how rapidly the truck was catching up to her, she estimated the driver had to be pushing eighty miles per hour—a dangerous speed in most circumstances, but on this twisty two-lane road, such speed was deadly.

Gritting her teeth in disgust, she squeezed the steering wheel and prepared to take defensive maneuvers, if needed.

The idiot behind her might like to taunt death, but she had no desire to die today because of his foolishness.

Especially not now that she'd met Jared and Isabel.

The unbidden thought startled her, along with the gooey warmth that puddled in her gut when she thought of the father and daughter. Spending time with Jared and his daughter made her happy. For the first time since losing Grace, she had found the kind of joy that made her want to see what the new day would bring. She looked forward to the next time she could play with Isabel and share a bowl of popcorn and warm snuggles on the couch with Jared.

Elise chewed her bottom lip. Being happy was good, right? Then why did the idea of growing closer to the father and daughter fill her with such trepidation?

Her heart stutter-stepped. *The more you care, the more you have to lose.*

Behind her, the silver truck gunned its engine again and pulled alongside her. She sent a glare to the driver for his recklessness. Through the tint of his windows, all she could tell was that he was a heavyset man who wore a ball cap and dark sunglasses. He turned his head and met her stare.

Then veered his truck into the side of her car. Metal crunched and groaned. Her car lurched toward the shoulder.

Elise gasped and battled the steering wheel, keeping her car on the road. Barely.

The truck swerved again, crashing into her, shoving her until her right tires left the highway.

"You sonofa—What are you doing!" Panic sharpened her voice. Adrenaline spiked her pulse. Fear squeezed her chest.

He'd hit her intentionally. Even as the thought crystallized in her mind, the truck bashed into her again.

Sweat slickened her palms, and she pumped her brakes. The truck shot ahead of her when she slowed, and she breathed a sigh of relief. "Jerk."

But when she rounded the next curve, he was waiting for her. A chill streaked through her when she realized he was targeting her, not just randomly bullying. The truck's tires flung dirt and gravel from the side of the road as the driver wheeled back onto the highway. Neither speeding up or slowing to a crawl would shake him.

Finally, with trembling hands, she fumbled her cell phone out of her purse and dialed 911. Keeping the small phone between her cheek and shoulder was a challenge, but she wanted to keep both hands on the steering wheel. Ugh. Why hadn't she turned the phone back on the speaker setting before she left the hospital?

When the operator answered, Elise gave her name and approximate mile mark on the highway. "There's a truck, a silver quad-cab, and he's trying to run me off the road!"

Wham! The truck struck again. Hard. Her head snapped forward then back.

Elise dropped the phone as she fought to keep her car from careening off into the ditch. She muttered an unladylike curse that fit the situation. The cell phone lay on the floor of the passenger's side out of her reach.

Ahead, another sharp curve loomed, and signs proclaimed the approaching turnoff for Claiborne Lake. Her heart thundered.

Could she take the turnoff and lose the truck? She did a quick mental calculation. If she stopped on a side road, what would the guy do to her? She needed to find a populated place where she could have the protection and deterrent of witnesses. Just past the turnoff to Claiborne Lake State Park, a narrow two-lane bridge spanned the lake.

Surely, this maniac wouldn't keep up his game of chicken where they had no margin for error?

Nausea churned her gut. She had no such assurance. The driver was dangerous and completely unpredictable. Seeing the side road to the state park, Elise slowed to make the turn, but the truck slowed with her then pulled behind her.

He's preparing to follow if I turn, she thought.

But she was wrong. When she reached the road to the state park, the truck rammed her from behind, shoving her past the turnoff and into the scrubby weeds at the side of the road. Pulse racing and sour fear climbing her throat, Elise pulled back onto the road, determined to survive the madman's attack until she reached some sign of civilization and help.

But the truck driver had other ideas. As they approached the bridge over Claiborne Lake, he plowed into her back left fender, causing her front end to veer to the right. Off the road. Straight toward the embankment at the edge of the lake. Elise screamed when his intent became clear. He wanted her car to skid into the lake.

A jarring thump from behind. A free fall that made her stomach rise to her throat. And he'd achieved his goal.

Chapter 7

The nose of her car smacked the water, triggering her air bags and sending a jolt to her marrow. Elise's seat belt jerked taut across her chest with a bruising force. Her camera bag and purse flew forward onto the floor.

Once at rest in the lake, the car began sinking into the water, the weight of the engine pulling the hood down first. Elise coughed, choking on the powder released by the air bag. Stunned by the crash, she stared in disbelief as brown water crept toward her windshield. But as the initial shock faded and the reality of the danger she was in penetrated her fog, she rallied, flying into action. She had only seconds to get out of the car before it was submerged. Already the water level had reached her door, and the external pressure against the door was too great to open it. If she couldn't get out through the window soon, she'd be trapped. But the water had already shorted the car's electric wiring. The window wouldn't budge.

Jerking off her seat belt, she fumbled in her map pocket for the glass-busting hammer she kept there for just this type emergency. Before breaking her window, she grabbed her camera bag, purse and phone from the passenger-side floor. After zipping her cell in the waterproof camera bag and looping the straps around her neck, she took a deep breath for courage. She shielded her face from the window and gave the safety glass a firm whack with the spiked end of the hammer.

Shards of glass rained down and lake water, now at the base of her window, spilled into her car. Shoving the deflated air bag out of her way, she scrambled to hoist herself through the broken window. The jagged edges of broken glass sliced her hands as she fought her way out of the car. The chilly water soaked her clothes and stole her breath.

The car had landed only a dozen or so yards from the bank, and she began swimming in that direction as quickly as she could. The weight of her camera and purse dragged at her, and if she'd had farther to swim, she'd have ditched them rather than risk overtaxing herself before she reached shore. But her camera was her livelihood, and she wouldn't give it up if she didn't have to.

Finally after what felt like an eternity, she dragged herself up on the muddy bank and collapsed, panting. With trembling hands, she fumbled the zipper of the front pocket on her camera bag open and fished out her phone. *Please work!*

The screen lit when she opened it. Yes! Thank goodness for her waterproof camera bag. She prayed her camera had survived in good shape, too.

The crunch of footsteps in the dry leaves and gravel of the lakeshore roused her, and she glanced up to see who was coming. Sunlight backlit the man who approached, making it difficult to see his face.

But the large stick in his hand was clear enough. As was the pickup truck parked at the top of the embankment.

Panic swelled in her chest. A fresh surge of fear shot adrenaline to her limbs. She shoved to her knees just in time to see him swing the branch toward her in an arc. Elise gasped and raised her arms to protect her face, but the hefty stick cracked against her temple.

“Night, night,” the man said as she slumped to the ground. And the world faded to black.

After leaving another message on Elise’s voice mail, Jared tossed his cell phone on his kitchen counter and frowned. Where was she? What was taking so long?

“I knew I should have gone with her,” he muttered aloud.

“Da-dee?”

He raised his gaze to Isabel who wore a liberal coating of applesauce on her hands and face. So much for letting her feed herself. Had she gotten *any* of the food in her mouth?

“Whatcha need, princess?” Jared grabbed a rag from a drawer to wipe her mouth before joining her at the kitchen table.

“Da-dee?” she repeated, holding a bite of her hot dog out to him in her grubby hand.

The innocent offering stirred warmth in his chest, and he smiled at her as he swiped at her dirty cheeks. “No, thanks, Izzy. I’ll eat later. You finish your dinner.”

Isabel popped the hot dog into her mouth and chewed, looking like a greedy chipmunk with full cheeks.

On the counter, his phone buzzed, and he hurried over to answer it. *Elise,* his caller ID read, and he released a relieved sigh.

"Thank goodness. I was getting worried. What was the hold up?" he said by way of greeting.

"Jared..." Her voice warbled, and if he had to guess, he'd say she was crying.

His stomach pitched, and his fingers tightened around the phone. "Elise? What's wrong? What did you find out?"

"Someone f-followed me. R-ran me off the road."

Static crackled over the line, while his nerves jangled with alarm. "What? Where are you? Are you all right?"

"I guess. I may...c-concussion... hit me over the—"

"Elise, you're breaking up. Say that again. Did someone hit you?" Jared paced closer to the window hoping to get better reception, even though he knew the bad connection was likely on her end.

"Car's in the wa—" More static. "Stole my c—"

An icy ball of fear lodged in his gut. He might not know the specifics, but enough frightening words had seeped through the static to tell him Elise was in trouble, possibly even in danger. He flew into action, grabbing his car keys and jacket, even before he knew where he was going or what he was doing. He only knew Elise needed help, and every protective instinct in him shouted for him to rush to her rescue.

"...to call the police. He might come b—"

"Elise, where are you?" He glanced to Isabel and realized he couldn't take her with him. Not if there was even a remote chance of danger. He began calculating where he could leave Izzy as he did a quick wipe of her mouth and fumbled one-handed to unfasten the safety strap in her highchair. Michelle was still sick...

"Stranded...bridge over Claiborne L—"

Lake, he finished mentally. He pictured the highway to Pine Mill and remembered crossing Claiborne Lake about ten miles south of Lagniappe.

"I'm coming. I have to drop Isabel at my parents' on my way out, but I'll be there as soon as I can. Okay?"

"Hurry," she said, and the static couldn't mask the tears in her voice.

He scooped Isabel up and grabbed the diaper bag by the door as he rushed to his car.

Concussion. Stole. Stranded. The words taunted him, painting horrific scenarios in his mind as he backed out of his driveway.

Dear God, please let her be all right. He couldn't bear losing another woman he cared about.

The sound of a car engine and tires on gravel brought Elise's head up from where she huddled, shivering on the lakeshore. A sheriff's deputy stepped out of his cruiser and started down the hill toward her.

Relief whooshed from her in a heavy exhale.

"They're here," she told the 911 operator who'd insisted she stay on the line until the police arrived. She thumbed off her phone and struggled to her feet as the deputy climbed down the embankment from the road.

Although she was glad to see any help at this point, she really wished Jared was the one pulling off the highway to her rescue. She longed for his arms to hold her and for him to murmur soft reassurances that she was safe. She'd called him as soon as she came to from the blow to her head that had knocked her out. She'd shoved aside the nagging questions about what it meant that he was the person she'd turned to, the one she'd wanted most at her time of need. If she were growing too attached to him, counting on him too heavily, she could deal with the repercussions later. Right now, she needed his strength, warmth and friendship. The peace and security she felt when she was around him.

"Are you all right, ma'am?" the deputy called, eyeing her bleeding temple then the car in the water.

"Define *all right.* I'm alive and mostly unhurt, but I've got a goose egg on my head, my car's taking a swim and my camera has been stolen."

The shudder that rippled through her this time had less to do with her damp clothes than the reminder of having come to with a throbbing headache, only to find her camera missing. Not her purse or phone. Just her camera. Which told her plenty. The man who'd knocked her out hadn't been interested in robbing her. He'd run her off the road in order to get the camera. Or more specifically the pictures on the camera. From the hospital.

What had she photographed that he didn't want her to see or have evidence of? Whose feathers had she ruffled with her photo session and interviews?

"Did you hit your head when the car crashed?" he said, pulling off his sunglasses and gently probing her wound.

"No, the guy who ran me off the road clobbered me with a big branch."

The officer arched an eyebrow. "Pardon?"

Elise launched into the full story of what had happened. She was telling the deputy about waking up to discover her camera missing, when a second car pulled off the highway. She shielded her eyes from the sun and gazed up the embankment.

"Elise!" Jared called, hastily descending the steep slope at the side of the road.

She staggered past the deputy and flung herself into Jared's open embrace. "Oh, Jared, I was so scared."

Concern dented his brow. "You're bleeding."

"Could have been much worse." She pointed to her car, the front end completely submerged. Jared's face drained of color, and she knew he was thinking of the way Kelly died. "But you're here, and except for a headache, I'm okay. That's all that matters." She curled her fingers in his jacket and pulled him close. "Just hold me for a minute, and I'll be fine."

He wrapped a firm hug around her, strong and possessive. Protective. "Jeez, Elise, you have no idea the scenarios I was imagining driving out here. I only caught bits of what you were saying when you called, and—"

Tucked in his arms as she was, she felt the shudder that rolled through him, the hammering beat of his heart.

"Ma'am," the deputy said, "I need you to sign this accident report with your statement. Dispatch tells me an ambulance is less than five minutes away. They'll check your head wound."

"I don't need—" she started, shaking her head, and the pain that ricocheted through her skull silenced her argument. She raised a hand to the bump on her head. "Ow. Okay, you win."

She pulled reluctantly from Jared's arms and scribbled her signature on the bottom of the accident report.

"We'll let you know if we learn anything about the guy responsible." The deputy tapped his hat in parting and trudged back up the hill to his cruiser as the ambulance arrived.

"Hit-and-run?" Jared asked.

"Literally." She pointed to her head.

His eyes widened, and his jaw tensed. "You were assaulted?"

"And my camera was stolen. I think my questions at Pine Mill Hospital this afternoon rattled someone's cage."

"You think you were targeted? Why?" He held up a hand. "Wait. Tell me once we get you out of here."

He put a hand under her elbow and helped her up the hill to meet the EMTs. Good thing, too, because her legs were still a bit rubbery. She declined the ambulance transport, promising Jared he could take her to the E.R. instead.

Once they were on the road, she laid out the events of the whole day. "At first, everyone was excited to have an article written about the hospital. I got the chance to take pictures and even be present at a birth with none other than Dr. Arrimand delivering."

"Isn't he the guy who delivered Grace?"

"Yeah, and get this—he also delivers babies at two other small hospitals in the area."

Jared jerked his gaze from the road to her. "Including the hospital where Kim Harrison delivered?"

"Ding, ding, ding. Give that man a prize. Yep, Crest-view General where the Harrisons went, and Clairmont Community Hospital."

He returned his attention to the road and furrowed his brow. "Interesting."

"Dr. Arrimand was on duty while I was there. He was somewhat charming and friendly at first, and he granted me an interview, until…"

Jared arched an eyebrow. "Yeah?"

"His head nurse came in and whispered something to him. Then his mood changed dramatically. When I asked about the hospital's limited resources, specifically the critical-care facilities for newborns, he turned things around and began quizzing me on why I picked Pine Mill for my article and my past experience with the hospital. He became more and more closed off, and after Dr. Galloway brought me the reports he'd copied, Dr. Arrimand shut down completely."

"Who is Galloway?"

"The coroner. I learned some fascinating things from him, too, but the shift in Arrimand's behavior was what set off alarms for me. When Dr. Galloway left, Arrimand asked me to leave. When I asked about rescheduling to finish the interview, he refused."

"Sounds like he has something to hide."

"That's what I was thinking. And the mood change happened right after the nurse came in. What did she tell him?" she asked rhetorically as she stared out the window. "Then, as I was driving home, I was run off the road, and my camera was stolen."

Jared groaned, and his shoulders sagged. "So the thief has all the pictures you took at the hospital."

"Not exactly." She fished in her pocket and pulled out the memory card she'd taken from her camera earlier. "I have this."

Jared twitched a grin. "You're good."

"Well, it wasn't as much forethought or cunning as that the card was full, and I changed it. It doesn't have all the photos I took, but it has most of them." She took a deep breath and blew it out slowly. "What do you say we stick this baby in your computer and see what we've got? "

"After you get checked out at the E.R.," he said. "I would love to see if we can figure out what has the good doctor and his staff so worried."

Chapter 8

"You heard the doctor. You need someone to stay with you for a couple days," Jared argued as he helped Elise back to his car after she was released from the E.R. in Lagniappe. The hit to her head had caused a minor concussion, and someone needed to monitor her in case she experienced any side effects. "Because of Izzy, it's not practical for me to stay at your place. So you're coming to my house. Case closed."

"Jared, you don't have to—"

He stopped walking and caught her shoulders so that he had her full attention. "I want to. I need to be sure you're safe. I think it's obvious you riled someone with your questions, and they targeted you. I don't want them to have a second chance to hurt you."

Her face paled, and he pulled her into a tight hug.

"Do you have any idea how scared I was as I drove out to find you?" he murmured into her hair. After her swim in Claiborne Lake, she smelled slightly of fish and mud, but he didn't care. She was safe and relatively unharmed. "The thought of anything happening to another woman I cared about just—"

She tensed and lifted a querying gaze.

"What?" He traced her lips with a fingertip. "It surprises you that I care what happens to you? That you've become important to me?"

She ducked her head and leaned into him again. "I…I just— It's all just kind of overwhelming. Everything that's happened these last few weeks has my head spinning."

"You sure that's not the concussion?" He kissed her nose and gave her a half grin.

She groaned and closed her eyes. "I wish the painkillers they gave me would kick in. My head is throbbing."

A van pulled into the E.R. parking lot, and he guided Elise out of the van's path and to his car. "I don't mean to scare you, but you have to consider the possibility that whoever attacked you on the road might try to hurt you again."

She angled a dark frown at him as he unlocked the passenger door. "Yeah, it occurred to me."

"And what do you think they'll do when they realize they don't have the memory card from your camera?" She inhaled sharply and wavered on her feet. Drawing her back into his arms again, he rubbed her back. "They went to this much trouble to steal the camera. Do you really think they'll just give up?"

She shuddered, and he squeezed her tighter, wishing he could absorb her fear and shield her from any more pain. But ignoring the truth of her situation didn't serve any good. She needed to stay alert, take extra precautions, not turn a blind eye to possible trouble.

Elise tipped her head back to peer up at him. "I need

to tell MysteryMom what happened. I should send her the pictures I took, too."

"You can use my computer."

"No. If I'm going to stay with you, I need to stop by my place and pick up a few things. I'll bring my laptop."

Nodding, he opened the car door for her, and she slid carefully onto the seat. Elise directed him to her house but rode most of the way with her head leaned back and her eyes pinched closed in pain. At her house, he helped her to the door and took the keys from her when she fumbled them.

He unlocked her door, then stood back to let her enter first. A couple steps inside, Elise gasped and stopped so abruptly he nearly collided with her. "Elise? What—?"

Then he saw it. Her living room was in shambles, her possessions tossed from shelves and drawers, her sofa cushions upended. A cool draft drew his attention to the back door, which stood ajar.

"Oh, God. Someone's been here," she rasped.

She wobbled, and Jared quickly put an arm around her to steady her. "It looks like they were searching for something."

Her fingers clutched his wrist. "The memory card."

She was starting to hyperventilate, and he guided her toward a chair to sit down. "Breathe, sweetheart. Slow, deep breaths. I don't need you passing out on me."

"What if—"

A thump from the back of her house interrupted her, and they both tensed.

"They're still here!" she whispered, panic flooding her face.

"Stay here!" His tone brooked no resistance. Jared edged toward the hall, moving quietly. At the corner of the living room, he flattened himself against her wall out of sight and peered down the hall.

Another rustle drifted up the corridor. A shadow crept over the carpet. Jared tensed, adrenaline sharpening his senses.

Then a man in a gray fleece jacket stepped out of a back room, carrying her laptop. The intruder glanced warily down the hall then hustled toward Jared. Seeing no weapon in the burglar's hands, Jared swung out to block the man's escape. "Who are you? What are you doing here?"

Startled, the intruder halted. Briefly. Then he bared his teeth in a snarl and charged. He rammed Jared like a linebacker, his shoulder lowered to smash into Jared's chest.

Air whooshed from Jared's lungs, and he staggered back a step. Quickly finding his balance, Jared lurched for the intruder as the man tried to shove past him. With a wrestler's hold, Jared tackled the thief and used his weight to send the man to the floor. As they fell, Elise screamed, and Jared prayed she stayed back, out of harm's way.

He pinned the man down, grappling with him for the upper hand. In the struggle, Elise's laptop came loose from the intruder's grip, and Jared knocked the computer out of reach.

With his hands relieved of the laptop, however, the intruder was able to free a trapped arm. Before Jared could size up the threat, the man reared his arm back and landed a fist in Jared's jaw.

Jared had always thought the notion of seeing stars was hyperbole, but the pain that reverberated in his skull had him rethinking his belief. While he was dazed, the thief wrenched free and staggered to his feet. Jared scrambled to grab him. He managed to snag the bottom of the man's jacket, but the burglar shed the coat and darted out the back door.

"Jared!" Elise was at his side in an instant, gently probing his jaw with her fingers. "Are you all right? Your mouth is bleeding."

He dabbed at his busted lip and slowly moved his lower jaw side to side. "I'll live."

He rose to his feet, then helped her off the floor. "Call the cops. I have his jacket, and they can probably get DNA off it. And his fingerprints are going to be all over your laptop."

She shook her head. "He was wearing gloves."

"He was?" He tried to picture what he'd seen as he battled the intruder but had to admit he'd been preoccupied, trying to subdue the man.

She pulled her cell phone from her pocket and dialed. "Latex, like they wear at the doctor's office."

His gut clenched. "Or the hospital."

She met his gaze, acknowledging his comment with a troubled look, then turned her attention to answering the 911 operator's questions.

Jared dropped the jacket on a chair and went into the kitchen in search of ice and a towel for his jaw. As he assembled his ice pack, one thought played front and center in his mind. What would have happened to Elise if she'd come home to the intruder alone?

Somehow, Elise had poked a hornets' nest, and he feared the worst was yet to come.

After Jared finished answering the police officers' questions, he went in search of Elise, who'd finished her interview earlier and disappeared to the back of the house.

He followed Elise's voice to the back room and found her on her hands and knees, head down, bottom up, cooing to something under the bed. "Come on, baby. That bad man isn't going to get you. Come on, Brookie Wookie."

Brookie Wookie? Jared smiled to himself then tipped his head to admire the view of Elise's shapely fanny. When Kelly had gotten down on all fours like that to look under a bed or couch, he would give her a playful smack on the butt.

While Elise's derriere was a tempting target, he decided their relationship was not in a place he could take such intimate liberties, even in jest. But damn, she had a nice figure…

"That's a good girl," she said, backing up and pulling a tan-and-black tabby cat out from under the bed. She scratched the cat behind the ears and, hugging it close to her chest, kissed the tabby on the top of the head.

Jared pushed away from the door frame where he'd leaned his shoulder to watch and crouched beside Elise. He patted the cat's back. "Who's this?"

"Brooke. Can she come to your house, too? I don't want to leave her here alone."

"Sure." He flashed her a lopsided grin. "The more the merrier."

"Really?" She scrunched her nose skeptically. "You think your cats will mind?"

He grunted and scratched his chin. "Well, Diva will probably mind. She's earned her name. But she doesn't pay the mortgage. I do, and I say Brooke is welcome."

He put a hand under Elise's elbow and helped her to her feet while she cradled Brooke against her chest. On the bed, she'd already started filling a small travel bag with clothes and toiletries.

"I'll just go put her in her travel carrier," she said and headed out of the room.

Jared turned slowly, taking in the feminine decor, the personal touches that were uniquely Elise. Stepping over to her dresser, he studied an aged framed picture of a woman with two small children, a boy and a girl. Elise and her brother with their mother?

Next to the photo was a well-worn stuffed teddy bear with a ragged red ribbon around its neck, various bottles of lotion, perfume and nail polish, and a jewelry box, with its contents spilling out. His gut tightened. Had the intruder rifled through the box? It sickened him, infuriated him to think of the thug invading Elise's personal space, touching her private property, her most cherished possessions. If the intrusion bothered him this much, how must she feel?

He faced her bed and stared at the rumpled covers, picturing her lithe body wrapped in the silky sheets. Something pink and lacy peeked out from under her pillow. Heat flashed through him so hard and fast it stole his breath. He summoned the memory of the kiss they'd shared in the corridor outside the support-group meeting. Her lips had been warm and willing, sweet and soft. Desire coiled in his belly, and he gritted his teeth.

Cool it, Coleman. She's not looking for that kind of relationship. In fact, if what she'd told him the other night was true, she wasn't looking for any kind of relationship beyond friendship.

Huffing his frustration, he shifted his attention to her desk where drawers stood open with papers strewn about. Another spike of protective fury pumped through his blood. Nausea swamped him knowing the intruder had searched the space where Elise was at her most vulnerable, the room where she slept, where she let her guard down, where her secrets and heartaches should have been safe.

"Okay, we're ready." Her voice jolted him out of his musing. "Will you grab the bag on the bed?" She stood at the door with a pet carrier in her arms.

Brooke gave a plaintive meow from inside the cage.

Jared zipped her travel bag closed and hoisted it from the bed. He read her hesitation in her expression. "It's for the best, Elise. Especially now." *Now that someone has tried to kill you and has broken into your home.* The hollow, frightened look in her eyes told him the unspoken definition of *now* was understood.

He stepped closer to her and stroked a hand along her jaw, then cupped her cheek. "Elise, anyone trying to hurt you will have to come through me to get to you." He pressed a soft kiss on her lips and whispered, "I promise I will keep you safe."

"I'm afraid I didn't make a very good impression on your mother," Elise said, dropping wearily on the living-room sofa after she'd showered and changed clothes at Jared's house. "Coming in smelling like lake water and so rattled by the break-in, I could barely remember my own cat's name."

"Actually, she said she thought you seemed nice. Oh, and my brother and sister-in-law have invited you to come with me to their house next week for dinner." Jared handed her a mug of hot chocolate and sat down beside her. "The family is curious about the new lady in my life."

Isabel sat on the floor with a brightly colored set of rings that she fumbled to stack on a plastic post. Elise smiled when Isabel dropped a ring in place then clapped her hands, pleased with herself.

"Hey, good girl!" Jared cooed. He slid an arm around Elise's shoulders and tugged her closer. "There's a chicken casserole in the oven if you're hungry."

Elise shook her head. "No thanks." While sipping her cocoa, she spied Jared's orange cat sitting on the window-sill and asked, "Where are the other cats? They're getting along?"

"Well, Bubba didn't seem to mind having a visitor, but Diva is in a snit. She hissed and chased Brooke under my bed. I shut Diva in the laundry room, but Brooke has yet to come out."

Hearing his name, Bubba hopped down from the window and strolled over to the sofa. He sniffed Elise's feet then rubbed against her leg.

Isabel watched Elise bend over to scratch Bubba behind the ear. She squealed and pointed at Bubba. "Tee-tee."

Elise grinned. "Yeah, nice kitty."

"You speak baby? I'm impressed."

"Just one of my many talents," she said setting her hot chocolate on the coffee table. Tucking her bare feet beneath her, she leaned against the solid and reassuring warmth of Jared's chest.

"How's your head?" Jared strummed his fingers along her upper arm in hypnotizing strokes.

"The painkiller has kicked in and the hot shower helped relax me, so…I'm actually feeling okay right now."

He kissed her hair. "Good, 'cause I'm guessing tomorrow your muscles are gonna ache like the devil."

She groaned. "Probably."

"Ready to look at the pictures you took? Try to figure out what the thief didn't want you to see?"

Elise sighed and burrowed closer to Jared's warmth. "Not yet. I'm too comfy right now." She curled her fingers against his chest and pressed her ear over the steady thump of his heart. "After everything that's happened today, I just want to savor the quiet."

Isabel chose that moment to loose a high-pitched squeal of delight and bang the colored ring in her hand against the coffee table.

Jared chuckled, and Elise felt his laughter as a rumble

beneath her cheek. "What were you saying about the quiet?"

"Forget it. Quiet is overrated. I have too much of it at my house."

She watched Isabel inch her way wobbly step by wobbly step to the end of the coffee table then drop to her diapered bottom. Her target was clear as she started crawling toward Bubba. "Tee-tee."

A smile tugged Elise's lips, and she realized that the more she was around Isabel, the more she could appreciate, even cherish, the little girl's sweet innocence without a barrage of grief and regret over losing Grace. Was that because MysteryMom had instilled a hope in her that Grace was alive or because she was beginning to care for Isabel?

And what about her feelings for Jared? He'd been the only person she wanted beside her after her car had been run off the road into the lake. He was the one person who'd stood by her as she pursued MysteryMom's allegations. And in his arms was the only place she wanted to be at that moment. Cuddled with him, she felt safe after a perilous day, hopeful after the bleakest year of her life, and tempted to act on the attraction that smoldered between them. She was ready to put past romantic and family betrayals behind her and trust Jared with her heart.

"Well," he said, lifting her chin so that he could see her face, "you're welcome to come share the racket over here any time." He punctuated the invitation with a soft kiss.

Tendrils of desire unfurled deep inside her. Stretching closer to him, she deepened the kiss and sighed blissfully when he traced the seam of her lips with his tongue.

He whispered her name and tunneled his fingers into her hair to cradle her head between his palms. His kiss tasted like the creamy hot chocolate he'd been sipping, and she indulged in the sweetness of his lips on hers. Wrapping her arms around his neck, she wound her fingers in the hair at his nape and let her tongue tango with his.

He answered with a low growl of pleasure and eased her back on the sofa cushions. He followed her down, pinning her with his weight and the width of his shoulders. Rather than feeling trapped, she welcomed his embrace and the sense of shelter and protection his body provided.

She clung to him as he angled his mouth, his lips drawing deeply on hers and filling her with a growing hunger. With his taut muscles and hard angles pressed against her from head to toe, all her nerve endings were tingling and sparking, her body humming with tantalizing promise.

He smoothed a hand from her shoulder, over her breast and along her hip, his touch blazing a trail of fiery sensation. His caress held her so enraptured that she didn't notice the new presence by her head at first.

"Da-dee?"

Jared seemed not to hear the soft voice, but Elise angled her gaze toward the angelic blue eyes and slobbery grin at her eye level.

"Don't look now, but we have company," she said as he nuzzled her ear and covered the curve of her neck with nibbling kisses.

He continued nipping at her chin with toe-curling finesse and murmured, "Don't worry. She doesn't bite."

Elise chuckled and pushed against his chest. "Just the same, maybe we should put this on hold until after she's in bed."

He raised his head and gave Elise, then Isabel, considering looks. Arching an eyebrow, he sent his daughter a mock scowl. "Thanks for killing the mood, princess."

Rising to a seated position, he offered Elise a hand up, then smacked one last kiss on her lips before shoving to his feet. He scooped Isabel under the arms, tossing her a few inches into the air and catching her as she burst into fits of giggles and happy squeals. "Come on, priss, bath-time for you."

The father-daughter bond brought a smile to Elise's face, and a tender ache swelled in her chest.

Jared paused by the door to the hall. "If you're ready to start going through your pictures, I'll meet you at the computer as soon as I finish giving Isabel her bath."

Dragging herself off the couch, she crossed to the chair where she'd left her purse and dug the memory card out. "I guess I'm as ready as I'll ever be."

At Jared's computer, she inserted the program disk that would load her photo software, slid the memory card in the drive and began reviewing the shots she'd taken at the hospital. She scrolled through the images from radiology and the E.R. until she found the first pictures of the nursing staff at the maternity desk. Carefully she studied each face and the miscellaneous scenes she'd captured in the background of the shots. She searched for anything that she considered suspicious or worthy of the apparent concern she'd caused with her visit. She lingered over the photos of Dillon Thompson's birth, focusing more on what the doctor and nurse were doing than on the baby or parents. Frustration crept over her. Nothing seemed out of line. The birthing procedure followed the same regimen that she'd been through.

Except that Dillon's mother hadn't been drugged and put to sleep for the next several hours. And Dillon Thompson had been surrounded by family and friends in the hours following his birth.

The same twinge of envy that had poked her at the hospital needled her again. Would things have been different for her and Grace if she'd had a husband and parents, siblings and nephews all gathered in the hospital to welcome Grace to the world? To watch over her while Elise slept off the sedative?

Several minutes later, she heard the click of a door closing softly down the hall, and Jared entered the office with the baby monitor in his hand. "So have you come up with anything? What do the pictures show?"

"Nothing that stands out to me." She waved a hand toward the screen. "You're welcome to look, though. Maybe I'm missing something." She scooted out of the desk chair, and as Jared slid past her to take the seat, he caught her around the waist and planted a deep kiss on her mouth.

"Have I mentioned lately how glad I am that you're all right?" He brushed her cheek with his knuckles and searched her eyes with a hot, penetrating stare. Desire danced in the dark depths of his gaze, but she saw fear, as well.

Today, she'd revisited her nightmare by going to the hospital, the delivery room where she'd had—and lost—Grace. But Jared had also revisited the darkest day of his life when he'd heard she'd been in a car wreck. She knew his protectiveness, his insistence that she stay with him, had roots in that fear, in the memories of Kelly's tragic death.

"You have. And have I mentioned that I'm grateful for your help, so thankful that you were there for me today?" Elise wrapped her fingers around his hand and kissed his palm. The delicate scent that clung to his skin stirred a flurry of emotion in her chest. "Mmm, you smell good."

"Oh, yeah?"

"Yeah. Baby shampoo is one of the best smells in the world." She inhaled again, savoring the distinctive light scent. In the final days of her pregnancy, she'd stocked

Grace's nursery with baby shampoo and talc, lotions and washes. Following Grace's death, Elise had sat in the nursery, surrounded by the baby-fresh scents, and cried until her throat hurt. A bittersweet pang grabbed her, and she slipped away from Jared's arms to pace the floor.

Jared turned his attention to the computer screen and studied the pictures. "These are great pictures, Elise. Even if they don't show anything incriminating, your photo essay is going to be fantastic. You've captured such raw emotion on people's faces. Like this one, the little boy holding his arm against his chest."

She glanced over to see which shot he meant. "That was in the E.R. He'd broken it and was waiting to get a cast. He said what hurt most was knowing he couldn't play football again for a couple months."

"Well, you said you wanted to catalog all the stages and events of life that the hospital plays a part in. I'm sure this broken arm will stand out in that boy's memory the rest of his life." Jared clicked through a few more photographs and shook his head. Leaning back in the chair he linked his fingers behind his head. "Darned if I see anything worth running you off the road to steal your camera."

"You know, I keep going back to when the delivery-room nurse came in during my interview with Dr. Arrimand." Elise chewed her lip as she strolled across the floor and back restlessly.

Jared watched her from the computer chair. "You said earlier that was the turning point in his manner."

"He became stiff and suspicious and uncooperative, questioning me, clearly trying to get me to admit I'd been a patient. I figured it was pointless to deny the truth. He could have that information with a few keystokes anyway. Heck, that's probably what Nurse Ratched was telling him."

He grinned briefly at her movie reference, then furrowed his brow in thought. "Can you recall doing or saying anything to her that would have turned her against you?"

Elise shook her head. "On the contrary, she's the one who drugged me with the heavy sedative right after Grace was born."

"So…maybe whatever's happening over there…she's involved."

"A conspiracy?"

Jared turned a palm up. "I'd think there'd have to be a whole chain of people involved if records are going to be falsified, tracks covered, people deceived—"

Elise gasped. "The morgue records!"

Jared sat forward and shook his head. "What?"

"I started to tell you sooner but…remember I said Dr. Galloway came in and gave me some copies of the morgue's files?"

"And Arrimand clammed up completely after that and kicked you out?"

"Exactly. Dr. Galloway told me that only five newborn babies had been processed by the hospital morgue in the last two years." She explained everything that she'd discussed with the coroner and how his records proved that, if Grace had in fact died, there was no record to prove it. More evidence of the hospital's lies…or more specifically, Dr. Arrimand's and his head nurse's lies.

Jared gaped at her. "Where are those copies? I'd like to take a look."

She took a step toward the door. "I put them—" Elise felt the blood drain from her face, and a chill sweep through her. "Oh, my God." She pressed a shaking hand to her mouth. "I put them in my camera bag. Dr. Arrimand was right there. He saw me do it."

Jared shot out of his chair and closed the distance

between them. He steadied her with a hand on each arm. "Which means it might not have been your camera and pictures the thief was after at all, but the copies of the coroner's files."

"My proof that I was lied to about Grace, proof of a massive conspiracy." Elise drew a tremulous breath. "Proof that my daughter is alive."

Jared's grip tightened. "Dear God, Elise. If they know you're on to the scent of their conspiracy, whatever their game is, you're in more danger than you know."

Chapter 9

What were you doing at Pine Mill Hospital today?

Elise gaped at the message from MysteryMom that popped up in her instant-message window. No preamble, no greeting, no explanation of how she knew about Elise's trip.

She waved Jared over to the computer. "MysteryMom is online. Somehow she knows I was at Pine Mill today."

"How could she know that?" He settled beside her on a chair he'd brought in from the kitchen.

"I don't know," Elise said as she typed the same question for MysteryMom.

I just had a report from the agent who is undercover there. Your visit has really rattled some cages.

It has?

Yes. My agent found Dr. Arrimand and his nurse, Helen Sims, shredding documents and deleting files tonight. What were you thinking? I asked you to be patient and wait for me to report my progress to you. I asked you not to do any digging on your own that might cause suspicion.

Elise sat back in her chair, stung by MysteryMom's rebuke. Her fingers hovered over the keyboard for several seconds before she replied: I don't like being sidelined. I needed to do something.

No, you didn't. Your interference could blow a major investigation. We have several months and numerous resources invested, and before today, we were closing in on the evidence we needed to bring all the responsible parties to justice.

Acid filled Elise's stomach. What had she done?

More important, we were on track to trace what happened to the babies that were stolen and put up for adoption on the black market.

Black market. Elise froze when she read those words. The term *black market* conjured images of dangerous criminals and illegal weapons, espionage and dirty money. Could Grace have been a pawn in something so awful?

She glanced at Jared, whose face had lost some color as he read the instant messages with her.

"My baby was sold on the black market, Jared. My daughter!" She fought the hysteria that crept into her voice.

Jared wrapped his fingers around her wrist and gave her

a comforting squeeze. "You better tell her what happened to you, what you found out. She needs to know."

With a nod, Elise turned back to the keyboard. She explained everything to MysteryMom from the conception of her article and photo essay through finding the intruder searching her home.

MysteryMom made no reply for several minutes, long enough to make Elise worry. Finally, MysteryMom posted:

Do you have a friend you can stay with for a few days? I'm terribly afraid you've put yourself in the line of fire. Dangerous people could come after you again to silence you.

Icy tendrils of dread spread through her, and she shot Jared a horrified look.

He nudged her out of the way and typed, Yes, she can stay with me. I'll make sure she's safe.

Who are you?

Her boyfriend.

Elise caught her breath and raised a puzzled gaze to his.

"You have an objection to the term?" He tucked a wisp of her hair behind her ear.

Pleasant shivers chased through her from his touch. "I…don't know."

A muscle in his jaw twitched as he studied her, his eyes moving over her like a caress. "What would you call me? I think we both know we're more than friends." He leaned closer, brushing his lips against hers. "I'd like to be much more."

Heat suffused her blood as she imagined her naked body

twined with Jared's, the feel of his hands on her skin, his mouth exploring her most sensitive places.

"Jared..." she'd started when a new instant message popped onto the screen with a beep. She angled her head to read MysteryMom's reply.

Elise, you've been talking to other people about this?

Only Jared and my grief-support group. But everything we say there is in the strictest confidence.

In the delay before MysteryMom's reply, Elise could almost hear the other woman's groan and see her disappointed head shake.

Don't talk to anyone. If you want to be kept in the loop on our progress, it is essential that you follow my directions. With just one mistake, the whole operation could blow up in our face. I have people in precarious positions—dangerous positions if their cover is blown. We are so close to putting all the pieces together and dismantling the baby-selling ring.

A chill burrowed to her core. *A baby-selling ring.* She had thought Grace had been taken by a few warped individuals, but the scope of the evil that she'd fallen victim to shook her.

She typed, I'm sorry. I know that's probably too little, too late, but with my daughter's life on the line, I couldn't just sit on my hands. I had to *do* something.

I understand your restlessness. I'm a mother, too. But in my line of work, failure to follow orders can get you or one of your agents killed. It could be your life at risk if you don't back off and let us handle this. You've already made yourself a target with your questions today. These people have millions of dollars at stake. They won't take kindly to anyone disrupting their operation.

Elise shivered, and Jared slid onto her chair, pulling her onto his lap and wrapping her in his arms. She closed her eyes and soaked in the comforting strength and reassurance of his embrace, trying to absorb the magnitude of what was happening to her, what she'd unwittingly become a part of.

The beep of the IM drew her attention back to the screen.

I have to go now. I'll be in touch as soon as I have something to report. Stay safe and lie low. Okay?

Elise panicked. MysteryMom was her only link to Grace, and she was desperate for even the smallest piece of information about her.

Elise typed, Wait!

Yes?

Have you learned anything about Grace? Was she sold? Where she was sent? Who has her?

I don't know anything definite yet. We're getting close, but you must trust us.

Elise's stomach rolled. She wanted to tell MysteryMom how difficult it was for her to trust anyone. She'd already been betrayed by the people she should have been able to trust the most—her father, her lover, her doctor.

The icon beside MysteryMom's avatar disappeared, letting her know her secret advocate had logged off.

She continued to sit on Jared's lap, still and silent, absorbing everything she'd learned, everything that had happened. Having Jared's arms around her, his broad shoulder under her cheek, gave her a sense of security and stability when everything else in her life was shifting and shattering. He rubbed a warm hand up and down her back, comforting her the way she'd seen him calm Isabel. Tender. Loving.

"So what do you think?" she said finally.

He filled his lungs with a deep breath before answering. "I think you are lucky to be alive and… I'd like to keep you that way. I'll fix up the guest room for you."

"I mean, what do you think about there being a black market for selling babies? That's just so…mercenary and depraved." She gave an involuntary shudder, and he hugged her tighter, kissed her hair.

"Hence the term *black market.*"

She hummed her agreement distractedly.

"As horrible as it is, there will always be those who prey on vulnerable people to make a buck. These black marketeers know that couples who can't have children of their own sometimes get impatient or desperate. Maybe they've been turned down for adoption, or get frustrated with the red tape. When we decided to adopt, we met couples that were to the point they'd have paid any price and broken any law if they thought it would get them the child they wanted."

"Even if they knew the child they were buying had been stolen from her mother?"

He massaged her neck, working the tense muscles. "It's been a long, stressful day for both of us, and a warm bed is sounding pretty good about now."

She nodded stiffly, knowing that despite the weary ache in her limbs and her recent lack of sleep, she'd likely lie awake most of the night rehashing the day's events.

When she made no move to get up, Jared handed her the nursery monitor. When she gave him a puzzled look, he slid an arm behind her knees and another across her back, then lifted her as he stood. Cradling her in his arms, he headed to the hallway where he stopped.

She curled her fingers in the fabric of his shirt. "Where are we going?"

"That's up to you." He met her gaze, awaiting a response, but she could see from his expression that he was asking more than just which room to carry her to. Her answer spoke for what she wanted from their relationship. Did she trust him enough to become his lover? Did she still need time and emotional distance to sort out her feelings for him? Was friendship all she could ever give him?

She stroked a hand along the evening's growth of stubble on his chin and murmured, "Your room."

Her answer obviously pleased him, but his grin wasn't cocky or smug. Just…happy. And when she considered it, her decision brought her contentment and joy, as well. She'd already trusted Jared with her darkest fears, her deepest pain, her most private anguish. Sharing a physical intimacy with him felt ordained, predestined.

Jared laid her on his bed, pausing only long enough to remove his shoes and belt before he stretched out beside her and propped his cheek on a bent arm. "Unfortunately, I'm…not prepared for this."

"Not prepared? I take it you were never a Boy Scout?"

"Actually I was for a few years, but…the thing is, I haven't been with anyone since Kelly died, and we never needed contraception because she couldn't conceive."

"I see. So no condoms in the house?"

He pulled a face. "Sorry. If you'll watch Izzy, I can run out and get—"

"Wait." Elise looped an arm around his neck as he rose and chuckled. "You didn't ask me if I was on the pill."

He arched an eyebrow. "Are you on the pill?"

"No."

He frowned.

"But I use something even better." She pushed the waist of the borrowed sweatpants low on her hip to reveal her birth-control patch.

His gaze heated, and he traced the patch, then lower with his finger. "Nice."

He bent his head to kiss the skin she'd exposed to him, and Elise threaded her fingers through his hair. The scratch of his beard so low on her hip sent shockwaves through her.

"I like a woman who plans ahead." He moved his kiss to her navel and nuzzled her belly.

"Not that I've had any real use for it recently, but it helps ease my cramps each month." She winced and bit her lip. "Uh-oh, TMI?"

He raised an amused grin. "Don't worry about it. After all the diapers I've changed and baby spit I've cleaned up, nothing really shocks me anymore." He stretched up to give her a quick kiss on the mouth before hooking his fingers in her sweatpants and dragging them down slowly. He blazed a path with his mouth, an inch at a time, as he exposed more of her flesh.

Elise grabbed handfuls of the bedspread as he coaxed the sweats down her thighs and nibbled his way toward her knees. When he finally worked the pants down her calves and off her feet, already bare from her shower, he massaged her toes and her instep with deep rubs of his thumbs.

A moan escaped her throat, and she closed her eyes to savor the exquisite pampering. She'd never known her feet could be an erogenous zone, but as his ministrations continued, her body grew relaxed, and her skin sensitized from head to toe. Every touch as he worked his way back up her legs, caressing and tasting, sent shimmering tingles of anticipation to her core.

Most of her life, she'd fought stubbornly for control, to protect her heart and maintain her independence. After her father had abandoned her and her brother to a foster home, she'd been determined not to give anyone the power to hurt her so deeply again. Yet surrendering her body to Jared felt as natural as breathing. She didn't question why she instinctively trusted him, why his touch felt so… right.

But indulging the desire that had been growing between them didn't mean she would lose her head—or her heart—to him. Mind-numbing sex at the end of a hellish day was her right. She refused to believe her comfort level with Jared meant anything more than mutual respect.

As his kiss grazed the juncture of her thighs, she sucked in a rough gasp, and all rationalizations fled her brain in a wave of heady lethargy.

He freed one button at a time on the flannel shirt he'd lent her, parting the soft fabric and feathering his tongue over the skin he revealed. A thrum of desire and need coiled inside her as his slow seduction continued. He undressed her at a leisurely pace and treated every part of her to a tender caress and warm kisses. When she was naked, his gaze traveled over her with every bit as much heat and possessiveness as his fingers.

"You're beautiful," he whispered, scooting across the mattress to align his body with hers.

"And you're wearing too many clothes," she replied, hooking her legs around his thighs and cupping his buttocks with her hands.

"Hmm," he hummed capturing her lips for a deep, sexy kiss. "What should we do about that?" He used his thumb to trace her collarbone, then slid lower to circle her breast. Her nipples peaked, anticipating his touch.

Eager to feel his skin against hers, she fisted his shirt in her hands and dragged it over his head. He tossed the T-shirt aside, and Elise pressed her body closer. The pleasure of her breasts grazing the coarse sprinkling of hair on his chest electrified her already-crackling synapses. Her hands explored his back, savoring the contrast of supple skin over taut muscle.

Insinuating her hand between them, she began fumbling with the fly of his jeans. After a moment, Jared rolled beside her and finished the task, whisking his jeans and briefs off in one efficient motion.

When he moved back toward her, she planted a hand on his chest to stop him. Leaning up, propped on one arm, she drank in the sight of his lean torso and masculine physique. "You're rather beautiful yourself."

He arched an eyebrow. "Beautiful?"

She flashed him a saucy grin and trailed a fingernail up his thigh to his belly. "In the most he-manly way, of course."

"I th—"

Whatever he'd intended to say was lost in a hiss of pleasure, as she wrapped her hand around his heat and stroked the length of him. With a playful growl, he rolled on top of her and seized her mouth with a scorching kiss. He tangled his tongue with hers and settled in the V of her legs.

Elise raised her hips, increasing the friction of his body against hers. The clambering need inside her flashed hotter. She hadn't been with a man in years, but nothing in her experience equaled the powerful sensations that coursed through her, building, hovering just beyond reach.

Jared moved his attention to her breasts, drawing each taut peak into his mouth in turn. With one hand, he reached between them to caress her intimately, sliding a finger inside her. She gasped and thrust her hips off the mattress, ready to fly apart at any moment. "Jared!"

He needed no further coaxing. With a bold, sure stroke, he buried himself inside her, filling her and sending her into a dizzying maelstrom of sensation.

He gave a ragged groan and tightened his hold on her as she shuddered and pulsed around him. She clung to him, a knot of emotion clogging her throat, stealing her breath. Elise squeezed her eyes shut and swallowed hard, determined to shove down the ache that reached into her heart, refusing to attach any foolish romantic notions to their intimacies. Jared had made her no promises, and she had no right to expect any commitments from him. Tonight was about savoring the moment. About escaping reality for a few precious minutes. About sex.

When her body quieted, he began a sensual withdrawal, followed by a deep return glide. Just when she thought she'd pinnacled, he showed her a greater pleasure, a higher plane of ecstasy. His rhythmic lovemaking carried her higher, until they soared together to an earthshaking climax.

He held her close, his breath warm against her neck in the aftermath of their passion. Their bodies cooled, and he pulled a quilt around them, creating a cocoon that allowed her to pretend for a few minutes longer that nothing existed beyond this moment, this man, this peaceful contentment.

But a whimpering cry crackled over the baby monitor

on the nightstand, and Jared jerked from sated lethargy to parental attention in a heartbeat. "Sorry. Duty calls."

She gave him a hard deep kiss. "Don't apologize. If you didn't jump to tend to her, I'd have to rethink my association with you."

He grinned and flipped back the quilt, letting a wave of cold air into her snuggly cave. She shivered and slid to the edge of the bed. "Want me to go? Will she let me rock her, you think?"

He pulled on his pants and glanced at her. "Feel free to give it a try."

Elise threw on her borrowed clothes again and, with Jared on her heels, hurried to Isabel's room. The baby girl stood at the side of her crib, clinging to the side rail, mewling sleepily. When she saw Elise, she held out her arms and whimpered, "Mee-mee."

Elise's heart stopped, her breath stuck in her lungs. "D-did she just call me Mommy?"

Jared nudged her aside to approach the crib. "Sounded a little like it, but Mimi is what she calls Michelle."

Elise stepped forward, feeling foolish for her assumption. Why would Isabel think of her as a mother figure when she'd only seen Elise a handful of times? She drew a deep restorative breath, warning herself, *Don't start painting fanciful family portraits of yourself with this man and his child just because you slept with him.*

She watched Jared stroke Isabel's soft curls and murmur reassurances to her, and her heart melted. Painful longing, not only for the child she'd lost, but the family life she wanted, wrenched in her chest.

He lifted Isabel from the crib and turned to Elise. "Want to try rocking her?"

She nodded, not trusting her voice not to crack. She reached for the baby, and Isabel tucked her head under

Elise's chin, snuggling against her chest with the blind trust of the innocent. A melancholy mix of tenderness and regret speared Elise's soul as she settled in the rocking chair and patted Isabel's back.

Diva trotted in from the hallway and gave a meow that sounded surprisingly loud in the quiet of the dark nursery. By the glow of the nightlight, Elise spotted Bubba and Brooke lurking restlessly in the hallway. "Looks like everyone's up for a midnight snack."

Jared scooted Diva toward the hall door with his foot. "You seem to have things under control in here, so I'll go slop the hogs and…meet you back in bed in a few?"

The question mark in his tone told her he was as uncertain where they were headed with their relationship as she was.

And he was leaving the direction they took up to her. What did she want from him? Was she going to return to his bed for the cuddling and intimacy of sleeping in his arms? Or was she going to distance herself emotionally by spending the remainder of the night in her guest bed?

Diva rubbed against Jared's leg and yowled again impatiently. Elise felt as if the cat were rushing her, pressing her to examine her feelings for Jared, for Isabel, for her future. When had everything in her life become so topsy-turvy and confusing?

My sources tell me that your baby might be alive.

Yeah, that was the moment.

Elise pressed her cheek to the silky hair on Isabel's head, inhaled the sweet fragrance of baby shampoo and angled a glance toward Jared.

Jared was here and now. Real. Certain.

She grinned. "Yeah, I'll meet you in a few."

Chapter 10

An hour later, after making love to Jared again, Elise curled her body against his and trailed a finger down his chest. Settling her hand over the steady thump of his heart, she tipped her chin up to meet his gaze. "Will you tell me about how you adopted Isabel?"

"Sure." He brushed her hair back from her eyes. "What do you want to know?"

"Everything. Did you know her mother? Were you at her birth?"

He shook his head. "We don't know much about Isabel's mother, except that she was a teenager from Lake Charles who was eager to give her baby up for adoption so she could go back to being a teenager."

"So you've never met the girl?"

"No. On purpose. We used a 'boutique' adoption agency—" He drew quotation marks in the air with his fingers "—That specialized in closed adoptions. A friend of ours had heard about the agency through another couple that had used them."

"What made them a 'boutique' agency?" she asked, copying his finger quotations.

"You mean other than the exorbitant fees?" Jared remembered his shock when he'd first learned what the agency, Second Chance, charged for an adoption.

She tipped her head back to meet his eyes. "Their fees were higher than regular adoption agencies?"

"I'll say. Well, maybe not higher than international adoptions. I hear they can get pricey, too."

"So why pay it? What did you get for your higher fee?"

"Peace of mind, mostly. Most of the other agencies we talked to had some degree of openness to the adoption. A lot of the mothers wanted to be able to visit their child or leave the door open for the child to find them later if they wanted."

"You don't want Isabel to search for her biological mother when she's older?"

"Not necessarily. I guess I'll leave that up to Izzy when she's older."

"Then why the closed adoption?"

"Kelly was terrified that a few months after our adopting, the birth mother would change her mind and demand we return the baby. When we told people we were adopting, suddenly everyone had horror stories about couples losing their children to biological parents who'd had a change of heart."

Elise grunted. "Why do people do that? When I was pregnant with Grace, I was besieged with deliveries-gone-wrong stories and sick-or-preemie-baby stories." She sighed. "Little did I know I'd end up with my own nightmare to tell future mothers-to-be."

He squeezed her arm and pulled her closer for a kiss on

her head. "The same dark side of our human nature that makes people rubberneck at accident scenes, I guess."

"So how old was Isabel when you got her? Did you choose her or…did the mother choose you or…how did that work?"

"We drove down to Baton Rouge to pick her up when she was just two days old. We told the agency we didn't care what sex our baby was, so when she was born and brought to the agency's nursery, we were next on the list of approved couples waiting for a baby. We'd been on the list for about six months before we got the call." Jared grinned, remembering the day the call had come.

A kick of excitement spun through him, just as it had that day over a year ago when Second Chance had called. "We had only been up for a few minutes, and I was still making coffee. Kelly was in the shower. All I heard the woman say was 'we have a baby girl for you' and 'pick her up today.' We left the house so fast, Kelly's hair was still wet, my shirt was inside out, and we never drank the coffee I'd brewed. I'm lucky I didn't get a speeding ticket." He chuckled, and Elise angled a grin at him. "Although we joked about telling the cop we were having a baby if we were pulled over."

"That might have been a tough sell since Kelly wasn't pregnant."

"On the way home, though, I drove like a grandpa on a Sunday drive. I had precious cargo on board, and I wasn't about to run a yellow light or test the speed limits."

"I found myself driving slower and taking fewer chances in simple things when I was pregnant. I held the railing going down stairs, waited for longer breaks in traffic before crossing streets, and didn't develop any of my own film for fear the chemical fumes would hurt Grace."

She tugged her mouth in a lopsided grin and shook her head. "Silly, I know."

Jared combed his fingers through Elise's hair, gratified that she could smile when she shared memories of her pregnancy. "Not silly. It shows you care, and you were protecting your child."

Her eyebrows drew together in a scowl, and he knew immediately she was agonizing over her inability to protect Grace after her birth.

"You still use film in this digital age?" he asked to distract her.

"Sometimes. When I'm feeling artsy about my photography, I use film. I'll never give up my 35 mm if for no other reason than it was my first good camera as a kid. A gift from my mother. Sentimentality, you know."

"Absolutely. I still have my grandfather's slide rule he used for his engineering courses in college." He ruffled her hair a bit. "Don't know how to use it, but…"

She propped up on an elbow to gaze down at him with a speculative expression. "Why couldn't Kelly have children?"

"She had to have a hysterectomy when she was a kid. Her family was in a car accident, and her pelvis was crushed. She lost a kidney, too."

"Jeez. So she was in *two* major car accidents?"

"Mmm-hmm. One took her ability to have kids. One took her life." He twisted his mouth in thought. "I never heard her complain about her circumstances, though. She considered herself lucky to have survived that first accident, lucky her family survived. She focused on the positive. Always."

"She sounds like a remarkable woman."

"She was." His gaze dropped, and he added quietly,

"She was a good mother, too. She couldn't have loved Isabel more if she were her own flesh and blood."

Elise drew a hand along Jared's cheek, pulling his attention back to her. "So do you. I see it whenever you're with her."

He nodded, and a proud smile curved his lips. "She's my whole world. I don't know how I'd survive if anything happened to her." A second after he'd said it, he tensed, realizing how the comment sounded. "Jeez Louise, Elise," he said with a groan. "I did it again. I'm sorry. I can't seem to stop putting my foot in my mouth around you."

"And I thought I asked you to stop tiptoeing around me. I'm okay." She thought about MysteryMom's assurance that they were close to finding out what happened to Grace, and a smile ghosted across her lips. "Besides, I'm holding out hope that MysteryMom will help me get Grace back. Focus on the positive, right?"

He hugged her closer and kissed the crown of her head. "Right." Jared fell into a pensive silence then, staring up at the ceiling. When a frown puckered his brow, Elise propped herself on an elbow again.

"What? You look so serious."

He sighed. "I was just wondering…"

"Yeah?"

"About the people that might have Grace. If they bought a baby on the black market, they must have wanted a child pretty desperately. And…I'm guessing they've fallen in love with Grace as much as I have Isabel."

A chill slithered through Elise. She had purposely avoided thinking about the bond her baby might have made with some other woman and vice versa. Not that she didn't hope Grace had been well-loved and cared for, but because it created an ethical dilemma she hated to consider.

"How can I take Grace away from them if they're the only family she's ever known?"

"Exactly. I mean, I know she's your daughter, your flesh and blood, but…they've built their lives around her, formed bonds and—"

"We don't know that. I mean, I hope they have, but then I hope…Oh, God, Jared. What am I supposed to do? She's *my* daughter. I want her back."

"I know. I just…"

Elise shoved down the guilt that crept over her. "If they bought her on the black market, they have no legal right to her. I have every right to stake my claim to her and take her back." She clung to that precept, ruthlessly convincing herself she had nothing to feel guilty about. "I definitely want her back, and I'll hire a lawyer to do it if I have to."

Jared said nothing for a long time, and she could feel the tension and distance between them growing by the second because of her decision.

"That's what I thought you'd say." Regret hung heavy in his tone and, tossing aside the covers, he slid out of bed.

Elise sat up, holding the covers against her bare breasts. "Where are you going?"

He paused at the doorway, swiping a hand over his mouth as he sighed. "I, um…thought I'd check on Isabel."

But she saw his departure for what it was. An excuse. A need for distance. The first fissure in what could become a gulf that divided them. Would he really oppose her if she fought Grace's adoptive parents for custody? She'd believed she had his unflagging support and friendship. Which was stupid really. After all, hadn't her own father found it easy to cast her aside when she became an inconvenience? No relationship was unconditional.

And she'd be wise to remember that. Better that she reel

in the tender emotions toward him she toyed with tonight than in a few months find herself with another broken heart.

On Monday morning, Elise stared at the blinking cursor on her computer screen and replayed MysteryMom's warning not to do anything that could jeopardize the investigation her team had in progress. Surely that didn't include her photo essay and article on the circle of life at the small-town hospital. Her editor was waiting for her piece. This was her chance to prove herself valuable to the newspaper at a time when newspapers across the country were shrinking staffs.

"It doesn't work by telepathy."

Roused from her musing by the male voice, she turned and found Jack Calhoun, one of the newspaper's star reporters, sipping a mug of coffee behind her and grinning.

He aimed a finger at her keyboard. "See those buttons with letters on them? You have to push those to make the words appear."

She flashed him a lopsided grin. "Oh, is that how it works?"

He wiggled his eyebrows. "Amazing, huh?"

She rubbed the back of her neck. "Any tips on what order to push the keys? What words I should make appear?"

He snorted. "That's for you to figure out, greenhorn."

"You're so helpful," she called to him as he strolled away, then swiveled her chair toward her monitor. Flexing her fingers, she started pounding the keys, letting her creative juices flow. She wrote the article she'd envisioned, an eloquent depiction of a slice of life as witnessed by the small-town hospital. She kept her references to the labor-and-delivery and maternity wards as general as possible, focusing primarily on Dillon Thompson's birth and his parents' joy.

She was detailing the story of the boy with the broken arm in the emergency room when her cell phone chimed, alerting her that she had an email.

She fished the phone out of her purse and checked the screen.

I have new info. We need 2 talk. Can u log on msg board so we can IM? —MysteryMom

Elise's breath hung in her throat. Could MysteryMom have found Grace already? She replied, Logging on now, then quickly signed on to the newspaper internet connection.

MysteryMom was waiting for her at the Parents Without Children message board and sent an IM immediately. Elise leaned close to her monitor, her mouth dry with anticipation, and read.

My people have traced a few of the missing babies, including Grace, to an adoption agency called Second Chance. Not all of their adoptions are black market, which allows them to serve as a front for the illegal adoptions.

Tears stung her eyes. She was one monumental step closer to knowing what happened to her baby. With trembling hands she typed, Have you found Grace? Was she still at Second Chance?

No to both. We are trying to narrow down which family adopted her, but we aren't there yet. I'll keep you posted.

I don't know how to thank you. This means so much to me!

It's my pleasure. Remember, keep this close to the vest until the whole operation is complete and we bring these guys to justice.

I will.

Stay safe.

MysteryMom logged off, and Elise rocked back in her chair. A smile crept to her lips, and the warmth of hope spread through her.

Jared. She had to tell Jared the wonderful news. Snatching up her cell phone, she tapped the screen and called his number. She didn't stop to question why her natural impulse was to share her joy with him. He'd stood by her throughout the twists and turns of the past few weeks, and she wanted him beside her when she finally got Grace back. He'd believed in her and comforted her when she needed a friend, and that support meant the world to her.

Friend. The word stuck out as she listened to his phone ring. They'd been so much more than friends the last couple of nights. She'd slept in his arms, made love with him, whispered intimacies in the dark of night. Would she even want to go back to her own house when MysteryMom told her she was safe to return home? Had she already gotten in too deep with Jared? She prayed she hadn't set herself up for more heartache.

Jared hovered over a set of blueprints at a new construction site, consulting with one of his carpenters, when his cell phone buzzed.

He pulled it from the clip at his belt and thumbed the answer key without taking his eyes off the blueprint. "Jared Coleman."

"Hi, it's Elise. Sorry to bother you at work, but I have news."

He raised a finger to ask the carpenter to wait for a minute, then stepped away to talk in private. "Not a problem. In fact, I was going to call you later. Michelle wants us to eat dinner with them tonight. Are you game?"

"Tonight? I—"

"I know I told you it would be later in the week, but she's eager to get to know you. She figured out you stayed with me over the weekend, and she gave me the third degree."

"Really? What did you tell her?"

"Mostly to mind her own business. But I think my sappy grin gave me away." He smiled the way he had around his sister-in-law that morning. Smiling was easy when he recalled the incredible nights he'd spent with Elise and the lazy days they'd enjoyed, playing with Isabel and watching rented movies from his couch.

"I had a good time this weekend, too." He could hear the smile in her voice, and his chest filled with warmth.

"So I can tell her yes?"

"Sure. Sounds great."

He switched the phone to his other ear and leaned against a sawhorse. "You said you have news?"

"I do. I heard from MysteryMom this morning. She's tracked down the adoption agency that was selling the missing babies on the black market." Excitement filled her tone, and his own pulse picked up, catching her enthusiasm. "She said Grace is one of the babies that went to this agency."

Jared perked up, his grin widening. "That's great! Does that mean they know where Grace is now?"

"Not yet. Apparently the agency also handles legitimate adoptions as a cover so they can work the black-market ring on the side," she said. "The place is called Second Chance."

Jared jolted, nearly dropping the phone. Blood rushed past his ears in a deafening *whoosh,* and ice settled in his veins. Second Chance had sold black-market babies?

Acid pooled in his gut.

Isabel! Could Izzy be one of the stolen babies? Even the possibility left him cold and shaking to his core.

"I don't suppose you heard anything about Second Chance when you were looking into adopting Isabel, did you?"

"I—" Jared swallowed hard, panic swamping him. "No. I've…never heard of it." He winced as the lie tumbled off his tongue. Instantly he regretted the fib, but a gut-level protective instinct shouted down his conscience. Until he saw where this new information led, until he could reassure himself that Isabel's placement with him was safe, he had to proceed with caution.

"Oh, well. I just thought…whatever. Anyway, MysteryMom promised to let me know when she learned more, but…isn't it exciting? I'm so close to getting Grace back, Jared. I can feel it!"

He dragged in a rough breath and clenched his back teeth. *Cool it, Coleman. Don't overreact.* "Um, yeah. That's great. Listen, I have to go…"

"Of course. So I'll see you tonight? Dinner with Michelle and Peter?"

He wished he could get out of his promise to eat with his brother's family. He needed time to do his own investigating concerning Second Chance. Pinching the bridge of his nose, he said, "Yeah. See you tonight."

After disconnecting with Elise, Jared stared silently at

the dirt at his feet, stewing. He and Kelly had made inquiries about Second Chance before they adopted. They'd seen the agency's state license, had the recommendation from a friend who'd used them.

Apparently the agency also handles legitimate adoptions as a cover...

Nausea swamped him. Dear God, let Isabel's adoption be one of the legal ones! If MysteryMom's people exposed Second Chance in their operation to stop the black market baby-selling ring, Isabel's adoption could prove to have been illegal. Could charges be filed against him for his part in an illegal adoption? He'd operated in good faith, even if Second Chance might not have.

Or worst of all, a judge could demand he return Isabel. The courts could take his daughter away.

The sick swirl of acid in his gut surged up his throat, and he forced the bile back down by sheer force of will.

Don't get ahead of yourself. He had no evidence that Isabel's adoption wouldn't stand, and he'd not give his daughter up without a fight.

But he had no time to lose. MysteryMom's people were digging into the files at Second Chance at that moment. He had to gather his own facts and be ready to protect Isabel from whatever storm might be coming.

"This chicken is delicious, Michelle. I really appreciate your including me tonight," Elise said as she passed the basket of rolls to Peter.

"Well, we're happy to have the chance to get to know you better." Michelle smiled at her guest. "And it's a super easy recipe. I can print out a copy for you if you want."

"I'd love that," Elise returned.

Jared scooted his food around his plate, only half listening to the niceties being bantered about the dinner table.

His appetite had been squelched by the alarming information Elise had given him earlier about Second Chance.

In her high chair, Isabel squeezed a handful of peas and giggled as they oozed through her fingers.

"I know we kinda bumped this dinner up in the week," Michelle said, "but we have some good news to share, and I couldn't sit on it any longer!"

Curious, Jared raised his head, turning his attention to Michelle. His sister-in-law's happy tone reminded him of the excitement he'd heard in Elise's voice that morning. He prayed Michelle's news didn't have the dark side for him that Elise's had.

"Turns out I didn't have a stomach virus last week. It was morning sickness." She paused, sending Peter a wide smile when he wrapped his hand around hers. "We're having a baby. I'm due in June."

From the corner of his eye, he saw Elise cast him a side glance. His brother and sister-in-law watched him, as well, waiting for his reaction. A dozen thoughts filtered through his brain in rapid succession. Joy for his brother. Concern for how Elise would feel about the talk of babies. Bittersweet reminders of receiving the news that Isabel was waiting for him and Kelly.

He glanced quickly to Isabel's messy face, and his heart twisted. Knowing an appropriate reply to Michelle's announcement was needed, he shook off the momentary shock, pasted on a smile and quipped, "Well, it's good to know you were listening when we had our talk about the birds and the bees in seventh grade, Peter."

His brother laughed and rolled his eyes. "Yeah, never could have done it without you, bro."

"So Isabel will have a cousin to play with," Elise said. "How many months apart in age will they be?"

"Well, Isabel was one year old in early August so…" Michelle paused to count off fingers.

Elise blinked and flashed an intrigued smile at Jared. "Really? What day? Grace was born on August tenth."

August tenth? That was Isabel's...

Jared's chest seized. The apprehension that had haunted him since Elise's phone call that morning reared its head, nipping the nape of Jared's neck with a tingle of alarm.

"That's—" Michelle started.

"The *sixth,*" Jared said, cutting her off, his tone firm and unyielding.

"What?" Peter wrinkled his nose. "Jeez, man. Can't you even remember your daughter's birthday? It's the tenth, too."

Restless anxiety stirred in his gut. "No. That's…that's just when we had her party this year. Her, uh…birthday is the sixth, and we picked her up on the eighth. I'm sure of it."

Michelle and Peter exchanged glances.

"That's not how I remember—"

Jared forced a laugh, interrupting Michelle again. "Do you want me to get out her birth certificate to prove it?"

Peter scowled at him. "What's your problem?"

Elise raised both hands. "Whoa. I didn't mean to start a family squabble." She sent Jared a puzzled side glance, then beamed at her hosts. "Congratulations. I'm thrilled for you. I hope to have good news of my own to announce before long."

Michelle raised her eyebrows. "Oh? That sounds intriguing. Any hints?" She shot Jared a speculative glance. "Jared?"

Masking the frenzy of unease roiling inside him, Jared twitched a cheek. "Don't look at me."

Peter leaned close to his niece and asked in a stage whisper, "Izzy, do you know Elise's big secret?"

"Ba!" Isabel held up her pea-caked hand, showing it to her uncle.

He pulled back to avoid getting smeared with green. "No thanks, honey. I have my own."

"Let's just say I'm hopeful that a project I recently undertook may come to fruition soon." Elise reached over to wipe Isabel's hand, and the motherly gesture sent Jared's thoughts spiraling.

Isabel and Elise had a lot of physical similarities. Isabel and Grace were born on the same day. Grace was sent to Second Chance for black-market adoption.

Panic swelled in Jared's chest, pressing on his lungs until he couldn't breathe. He wished he could write those truths off as coincidence, ignore the facts that were screaming for his attention.

But Jared didn't believe in coincidence.

And he had precious little time to decide what he was going to do before Elise caught the scent of his suspicions.

Chapter 11

Throughout dinner and on the ride home from his brother's house, Jared seemed distracted, distant. Elise told herself it was just nerves over having his family meet her. Where a couple weeks ago she'd agreed to pretend to be his girlfriend, it was clear to both of them that something real and meaningful was blossoming between them. The changes in their relationship had her asking hard questions about what she wanted, where she saw their future, so she couldn't blame him for his reticence.

After he sighed and shifted restlessly in the driver's seat for the fifth time in ten minutes, she reached over and covered his hand on the steering wheel, giving him a comforting squeeze. "Want to talk about it?"

He jerked his gaze to hers. "About what?"

She lifted a shoulder. "Whatever has you so antsy tonight." She tipped her head in query. "Is it me?"

Perhaps it was a trick of shadows in the dim car, but Elise could have sworn he flinched at the suggestion.

"Why would you say that?" His voice didn't sound right to her. Was it nerves? She knew men hated talking about feelings, about relationships. Maybe pressing him for answers was putting him on the spot. She didn't want him to think she was looking for promises or commitments he wasn't ready to make. She wasn't sure she was at that stage yet, either.

Sure, she cared for him. Deeply. And she'd grown attached to Isabel, as well. But if events played out as she hoped, as MysteryMom indicated they might, Elise was about to have a baby in her life, a daughter with whom she needed quality time to bond and care for. Now might not be the best time to start a romantic relationship with Jared.

Perhaps Jared had even realized that himself and was uncertain how to broach the topic with her. After all, he'd started acting odd just after she'd called him about MysteryMom's progress in tracking Grace to the adoption agency called Second Chance.

"Well, tonight was a pretty big step," she said. "You know, formally introducing the new girlfriend to the family. And not even the fake new girlfriend. I mean, it's pretty obvious there's something between us, something more than the last few nights of sex."

He slanted another meaningful glance toward her, his jaw tight.

"Don't get me wrong. The sex has been great."

That earned her a quick, lopsided grin of agreement, but still he made no comment.

"The last couple nights have been…special to me," she continued, filling the silence. "And I've been giving our future together a lot of thought—where we are going with this, the timing—so I understand if you're having mixed feelings or asking yourself a lot of questions, too."

He pulled the car into his driveway and cut the engine. With a glance in the rearview mirror, he checked on Isabel, who'd fallen asleep in her car seat on the drive home. He turned his body to face her, resting his arm on the steering wheel. "I'm sorry if I've been acting weird today. I… have a lot on my mind. Not just about you, although I have been thinking about us, too. Wondering if I'm really ready for another relationship."

"Oh." Elise withdrew her hand and sat back in the seat. She felt her protective walls slam into place. A voice in her head shouted that retreat was her best defense, and she quickly steeled herself for what was coming.

Clearly he sensed her withdrawal, and he cupped her face. "Hey, that's not my way of breaking up with you. I would never have made love to you if I didn't have feelings for you. I just don't know what to do with those feelings yet."

Her resolve slipped a bit, and the tenderness of his touch chased some of the chill from her heart.

"No matter what happens in the next few days, I want you to know what you mean to me. You're a beautiful, strong, caring woman, and you've made me believe real love can happen twice in a lifetime." He stroked her chin with his thumb, and his dark gaze burrowed to her soul. "If things were different, I know I could fall in love with you. And maybe in time I will. But—"

"Wow," she cut in, catching his hand between hers and clasping it between her palms. "For someone who says he's not breaking up with me, that sure sounded like a goodbye."

"Uh, no… I just—" He lowered his eyes and sighed heavily. "Forget it. Like I said, I'm tired, and I have a lot on my mind. Ignore me. I—" He glanced to the backseat. "Let's get Sleeping Beauty inside and settled in. Okay?"

Without waiting for a response, Jared climbed from the front seat and opened the back door to unbuckle Isabel from her car seat. Puzzling over his odd mood, Elise gathered her purse while he carefully lifted the dozing baby onto his shoulder.

"I'll get her diaper bag. You go on in," she offered.

Once in the house, Elise fed the hungry cats that greeted them at the door while Jared put his daughter to bed. She bent to stroke Brooke's back while her kitty chowed down her dinner. "Are you getting along with your new friends, Brookie Wookie?"

Brooke leaned into Elise's hand as she scratched the cat's neck, and Elise took that as an affirmative. No hissing between the cats at dinnertime was progress.

Leaving the felines to their food, she sat down in the living room to wait for Jared. When he didn't come back out for several minutes, she wandered down the hall in search of him. She found him standing beside Isabel's crib, stroking her head and watching her sleep.

Tiptoeing up beside him, she whispered, "Is everything all right?"

He drew a deep breath that sounded choked with emotion. "Yeah."

Elise smiled, touched by the sweet innocence of the slumbering child. "She's precious."

"She's my world, Elise. I would never have survived losing Kelly if I hadn't had Isabel. I poured all of my grief into taking care of Izzy and giving her all the love I had." He raised a penetrating look to Elise. "I need her. She's a part of me. I couldn't bear to live without her."

Elise frowned. His boldly direct comments frightened her. "Jared, what's going on?"

"I just wanted you to know that."

She nodded. "I think most parents feel that way. I know I felt it for Grace. I *still* feel that way about Grace."

With a furrow in his brow, he jerked a nod and pivoted away from the crib. Elise followed him back to the living room where he flopped on the sofa and leaned his head back on the cushions. "You don't need to wait up for me if you're ready for bed. I'm going to stay up for a while and do some work, catch up on some bills."

A cool draft raised goose bumps on her skin, and she folded her arms over her chest to ward off the chill that burrowed to her heart. She was being dismissed. Jared clearly wasn't ready to share whatever was bothering him with her. After the intimacies they shared the last couple nights and the open book she'd made of her life, especially in regard to her grief over and search for Grace, Jared's unwillingness to open up to her felt like a snub. And the snub stung.

Elise turned without a word and left him alone and brooding. She changed out of her work clothes and slipped on an oversized T-shirt of Jared's she'd been sleeping in the last few nights—when she'd worn anything at all.

She lay on her side staring at the glowing numbers of the alarm clock on Jared's night stand for hours, waiting for him to join her in his big bed. A vast lonely ache filled her, and she longed to feel his arms around her. Amazing how quickly you could grow accustomed to having someone beside you, savoring his warmth and reassurance as you slept.

Eventually, despite her own restless thoughts about Jared, MysteryMom, Grace and Isabel, Elise drifted to sleep. The next thing she knew, her internal alarm woke her at 6:00 a.m., and she rolled over to find Jared's side of his bed empty. The pillow bore no dent indicating he'd ever slept there last night.

Pain slashed through her, along with worry over what was troubling Jared and a premonition of what it might mean to their future. She smoothed a hand over his pillow, burying her nose in the sheets to inhale his lingering sandalwood scent. The hollow ache that swelled in her chest forced her to admit her feelings for Jared were deeper than she'd wanted to believe.

She was in real trouble. Just as he was pulling away, she had figured out how much she cared for him. How much she'd come to rely on his support and companionship. She'd dared to trust in him.

She was falling in love with him.

Tossing back the covers, she swung her legs to the floor and made her way to the kitchen where the mellow aroma of fresh coffee brewing told her Jared was awake.

When she found him in the kitchen, he was staring out the window over the sink, a steaming mug clutched between his hands and a forlorn expression on his face. He still wore the same clothes from the night before, and the dark smudges under his eyes spoke of his lack of sleep.

Elise's concern for him spiked. "Jared?"

He jolted as if he hadn't heard her come in. She stepped up behind him, circling him with her arms and laying her cheek on his back. "Did you get any sleep at all?"

"I dozed a few minutes here and there." He covered her hand and gave her fingers a squeeze before pulling away. At the door to the living room, he paused. "I made coffee. Help yourself."

"Thanks." She poured herself a mug and strolled into the living room to join him.

Jared sat on the couch with a laundry basket at his feet and—Elise did a double take—a half-full suitcase lying open beside him. As he folded the laundry, he put the clothes, both his and Isabel's, in the suitcase.

A beat of apprehension made her pulse stumble. "Going somewhere?"

He looked up briefly, then returned his attention to his task. "Afraid so. Family emergency out of town. I don't know how long I'll be."

"Oh, no. I'm sorry to hear that." An odd combination of concern and relief tangled in her chest. Maybe Jared's odd behavior last night had to do with the family emergency and not her. Maybe his withdrawal was the way he dealt with stress, not an indication he was regretting the physical turn in their relationship. "What kind of emergency?"

He hesitated, a pair of Isabel's stretchy pants in his hand, but didn't look up. "A death. In Kelly's family."

"Oh, I'm sorry." She cradled her mug, a nervous uncertainty crawling through her. She wanted to do something to help or comfort him, but he still seemed so remote.

"You, uh…can stay here while I'm gone. It's safer for you here." He dumped a pile of socks on the couch and started sorting them.

Elise's stomach see-sawed. The prospect of being alone, whether in Jared's house or her own, unsettled her. Especially while the members of the black-market ring were being rounded up by MysteryMom's team. She'd lived alone for years, yet she'd never felt as vulnerable and isolated as she did now facing Jared's imminent departure. She was amazed how much she'd come to count on his reassuring presence, his strength and comfort, after just a few days with him.

She circled the sofa and sat beside him. "Why didn't you say anything last night?"

"I, uh…just got the call a couple hours ago."

She frowned. "I didn't hear the phone ring."

"I had my phone on vibrate." He shoved a few pairs of socks into the suitcase without looking at her.

"Oh." She sighed, the jittery sense that something wasn't right skittering through her veins. "Jared, are you sure—"

A cry filtered down the hall from Isabel's room. Jared jerked his head up, his body tensing. He started to rise from the couch, but she put a hand on his shoulder and pushed him back down. "Sit. I'll get her. It's the least I can do to help."

He cast her an uncertain look but finally nodded. "All right. Thanks."

Elise put her mug on the coffee table and headed down the hall to the nursery. Isabel stood in her crib whimpering groggily and rubbing her eyes. Elise smiled at the little girl's disheveled mop of blond curls and the faint impression of rumpled bedding still etched in her cheek. "Good morning, sunshine."

Isabel blinked at her, appearing a bit confused, then raised an arm to Elise, asking to be picked up.

Warmth tugged Elise's heart as she lifted Isabel into her arms and cuddled her close. But one sniff, one glance at Isabel's diaper confirmed that the baby needed a complete change before starting her day. Elise wrinkled her nose and made a silly face for Isabel. "Eew. Stinky-poo. Someone needs a clean diaper."

Isabel grabbed her nose and wrinkled her face, imitating Elise, then grinned broadly.

Elise chuckled and laid Isabel on the changing table. "You're a silly goose, Izzy."

After pulling off Isabel's pajama bottoms and diaper, Elise carefully cleaned and rediapered her, then took out a fresh set of clothes from the drawer beneath the changing table. "How about pink stripes today? This is a cute outfit."

Isabel squirmed, uninterested in the new clothes and clearly eager to be finished with the changing table.

"Okay, I'll hurry, wiggle bug." After removing the dirty pajama shirt, Elise fumbled one-handed with the new shirt while she steadied Isabel with the other hand. As she raised the pink top to pull over Isabel's head, she glimpsed something that made her heart stop.

Isabel had a birthmark on her right shoulder.

A red, pear-shaped birthmark.

Her mind stalled for a moment, too stunned to process what she was seeing. But as a shot of adrenaline sped through her blood, her brain worked overtime, piecing together a staggering truth. She stared at Isabel. The same age her daughter would be. Blond-haired. Adopted.

"Oh, God…" she rasped, shaking to her core.

Isabel was Grace.

A joy, sweet and pure, flooded her heart, and tears pricked her eyes as she drank in the sight of her daughter as if for the first time. "Grace…oh, Grace!"

She scooped her daughter into her arms and held her close, raining kisses on her mussed hair and laughing. "Oh, my God. Oh, Grace, it's you. I can't believe it!"

Spinning toward the door, she hurried down the hall to the living room, eager to share the wonderful news with Jared.

"Jared! Jared, she's Grace. Isabel is Grace! She has a birthmark on her shoulder just like Grace's." She laughed again, swiping happy tears from her eyes. "Isn't it crazy and wonderful? All along, Grace was Isabel! I—"

She stopped short, realizing Jared didn't look at all happy. He looked…stunned. No, worse. Terrified. Defensive even.

Frowning, she took a mental step back and tried to see the news through his eyes. Of course he was scared, confused, worried. He had to be wondering what this would mean for him and his family. It was a lot to process. A lot to—

Then, like a storm cloud rolling in to spoil a picnic, more realizations clicked into place, darkening her mood.

Jared's withdrawal after learning the name of the adoption agency.

The lies he'd told her about Isabel's mother, her birth date, her adoption.

She stared at Jared, taking in his combative stance, his guilty expression, the bleak desperation in his eyes.

Elise's stomach knotted, and fury flashed through her. "You knew."

His nostrils flared as he inhaled deeply and raised his chin. But he didn't deny it.

She clutched Grace closer to her chest. "You *knew,* and you lied to me to throw me off track!"

When he remained silent, she aimed a finger at him. "You used Second Chance to adopt Isabel, didn't you? Didn't you!"

Again his silence damned him, and her hurt and anger swelled. "You knew who Isabel really was as soon as I told you about Second Chance yesterday. That's why you were so distracted and upset last night."

His jaw tightened. "I suspected, but I—"

She gasped as her gaze darted to the suitcase and more truths snapped into focus. "There was no death in the family. Was there?"

He said nothing.

"You were going to run with her, go into hiding—"

"Elise, listen to me…" He took a step toward her, and she took a step back, protectively wrapping both arms around the child she now knew was her flesh and blood.

"You were going to kidnap her to keep me away from her, weren't you?" she asked, acid roiling in her gut.

"It wouldn't be kidnapping. She's my daughter. I have every right to—"

"You have *no* right!" Elise shouted, and Grace jerked, startled, then began crying. Elise stroked her daughter's head and swayed with her, trying to calm her baby. "Shh, sweetie. It's okay."

Keeping her voice pitched low, she grated, "You betrayed me. I trusted you with my deepest heartache, and you betrayed me!"

Jared shook his head. "No."

"What do you mean, no? You lied to me! You told me her birth mother was a teenager in Lake Charles!"

He spread his hands, his eyes fiery. "That was what Second Chance told us. I had no reason to doubt them."

"You lied last night about when she was born and again this morning about a family emergency..."

He gave a humorless laugh. "I'd call this an emergency."

She gaped at him, so hurt and angry and staggered by the turn of fate, that she didn't know where to begin making sense of it all. For his part, Jared only stared back at her, a myriad of emotions playing over his face.

"You know you can't leave town with her," she said finally.

"I know no such thing." His tone was flat and unyielding.

"Jared?" A fresh fear pushed in from the edges of her anger. She could still lose Grace. If Jared left the state with her...fled the country.

Protective instincts roared through her. New tears filled her eyes, and she hated the position Jared was forcing her to take. "I'll call the police if you so much as leave this house with her."

His hands fisted, and he took another step toward her. "We legally adopted Isabel."

"How can you say that when I never gave her away? She was stolen from me!"

"We signed papers and filed documents with the court. In the eyes of the law, Isabel is *my* daughter."

"You would try to keep her from me?" Elise asked, galled and sickened by the notion.

His jaw tightened, and he growled through clenched teeth, "I'll do whatever I damn well have to in order to keep my daughter—"

"She's my daughter!" Elise shouted, losing the battle to keep the writhing whirlwind of emotions bottled up.

Grace wiggled hard, still crying, and Elise loosened her hold, allowing her daughter to pull away from her embrace. Grace twisted at the waist, spotted Jared and lunged for him, arms extended. "Da-dee!"

He took a giant step forward to catch Grace, and Elise had no choice but to release her grasp on her daughter if she didn't want to start a tug-of-war over the baby. Seeing her daughter tuck her head against Jared's chest, whimpering and clinging to his shirt, wrenched Elise's heart.

Jared was the father Grace knew, loved and trusted. Would moving her to a new home with a new parent do irreversible harm to Grace? In time, Grace would love and trust her, too, Elise knew, but would there be a hole in her daughter's heart where Jared should have been?

I need her. She's a part of me. I couldn't bear to live without her.

Jared's comments from last night made sense to her now. He was pleading with her, laying the groundwork for what would be an emotional uphill battle between them over a baby they both loved.

Elise wrapped her arms around her middle, feeling as if

she had to physically hold herself together or she'd crumble any minute. How could she be so close to having Grace back and yet still have her biggest hurdles in front of her?

The open suitcase on the couch caught her eye, reminding her that Jared had been willing to play dirty, to leave town with Grace rather than surrender her. He'd lied to keep Elise from learning the truth. He'd realized who Isabel was and said nothing, despite knowing the depths of grief Elise had been through over losing her daughter and her desperation to get Grace back.

Gritting her teeth, she shoved down the tug of sympathy for Jared's dilemma and firmed her resolve. She met the hard and determined stare he sent her over the top of Grace's head. His stony expression told her he had already dug his heels in and was prepared to go the distance.

"I think you should leave now," he said in a monotone that brooked no resistance.

An icy disappointment and anguish pierced her soul, but she lifted her chin and blinked back her tears. If he wanted a fight, she'd give him one. "Not without my daughter."

"Isn't going to happen."

Acid pooled in Elise's stomach. This was *so* not how she wanted to handle their impasse. But as she looked into Jared's eyes, the compassion for her heartache that had drawn her to him in the past weeks was secondary to his steely resolve. The tenderness and affection for her that she'd experienced as they made love had been shoved aside for stubborn conviction, defensiveness…and fear. A fierce, gripping fear like that of a wounded, trapped animal who would fight his predators to the death. A fear she knew well, because it was rooted in parental love.

With a grieved sigh, she marched over to the kitchen chair where she'd left her purse. Slinging the purse strap over her shoulder, she returned to the living room and faced Jared with squared shoulders. "Leaving town with her will only hurt your case. You don't want criminal charges against you, so please don't force my hand on that issue."

He remained still and stoic, his hand gently patting Grace's back as she snuffled against his shoulder.

Elise stepped forward to stroke and kiss her daughter's head. "I love you, Grace."

Turning on her heel, she walked to the front door and paused with her hand on the knob. "You'll be hearing from my lawyer."

Chapter 12

The click of his front door closing behind Elise echoed hollowly through Jared's house…and his heart. He hadn't felt this empty and bereft since the highway patrol officer and chaplain left him sitting on his sofa, staring blankly into space on the night of Kelly's accident.

That day, he'd lost his wife. Today, he stood to lose even more. Not only could the courts side with Elise and take Isabel from him, but he feared he'd already lost a bright and vibrant woman with whom he'd fallen in love.

Elise's anger with him for the lies and deception he'd stooped to were understandable. He wasn't proud of his actions, but he'd felt cornered. His desperation to protect Isabel had skewed his judgment.

But even lies were forgivable, given time. Yet the hurt and betrayal he'd seen in her eyes bore witness to the deep wound he'd inflicted with his choices. He knew Elise's history, the value she placed on trust. He'd let her down, and he regretted to his marrow the pain he'd caused her. Regretted even more that in order to keep Isabel, he'd have to inflict more pain on Elise.

He hated the antagonistic and divisive tone of his confrontation with Elise. This wasn't the way he'd wanted to handle their stalemate. Hostility between them benefited no one. Least of all Isabel. Yet battle lines had been drawn, and he was afraid the damage to his rapport with Elise had been done.

He heaved a weary sigh, full of guilt and frustration for the way he'd hurt Elise and put her on the defensive.

Isabel raised her head from his chest and blinked at him with her bright blue eyes. Elise's eyes.

And Elise's golden hair. Elise's pert nose. Elise's perfect bowed lips.

His lungs felt leaden. For the rest of his life, he would look at Isabel and see Elise. The woman who'd wakened his heart from the slumber of grief and shown him the possibility of second chances.

Second Chance. Futile anger streaked through him when the adoption agency popped into his mind. He and Kelly had trusted Second Chance much the way Elise had trusted Dr. Arrimand. There was no shortage of betrayal in this scenario.

The butterfly touch of damp baby fingers on his face roused him from his dark deliberations.

"Da-dee?"

He gave Isabel a sad smile. "Hey, princess."

She turned toward the kitchen and wiggled a chubby hand. "Eat nana."

His daughter was nothing if not a creature of habit. She had no use for her father's crises. Routine dictated she eat breakfast as soon as she woke up. Banana and dry Cheerios with a sippy cup of milk. His smile brightened, but a bittersweet ache lanced his chest as he smoothed her rumpled curls back from her eyes. "Sure, let's go eat banana."

Jared headed into the kitchen, praying this wouldn't be the last chance he had to eat breakfast with Isabel.

And knowing his first task after they ate was to call his attorney.

Elise sent a desultory glance about her ransacked apartment as she entered, dropping her purse on the coffee table. She'd been in no mood to clean house four days ago after being run off the road, visiting the E.R. and finding a burglar in her home, so she hadn't touched the mess. Now, her fight with Jared and last night's lack of sleep left her drained and despondent.

She slumped onto her couch and kicked off her shoes. Pulling a throw from the back of the sofa and wrapping it around her shoulders, she gave in to the tears she'd held at bay while driving home. She released the knot of frustration and hurt, anger and dejection that crowded her chest and clogged her throat. She berated herself for having allowed Jared to slip past her defenses and into her heart. Years of experience had taught her to be more circumspect and more discerning with her love and faith, yet she'd repeated the same mistakes again.

She was alone once more, nursing a bruised ego and a battered soul without even Brooke to give her comfort and companionship. She'd been so devastated by Jared's deception and so stunned by the discovery of Isabel's birthmark that she'd even stormed out without her cat.

She had no doubt she'd be able to safely retrieve Brooke soon enough. Her real concern was how long it would take the wheels of justice to clear the way for Grace to be returned to her. If Jared fought her for custody—correction, *when* Jared fought her for custody, because he'd made clear he would move heaven and earth to keep his daughter—he could drag the legal battle on for years.

Her doorbell pealed, and she stiffened. Her heartbeat accelerated as she moved her feet to the floor. Who in the world would visit her at this hour of the morning? Had Jared had a change of heart? Unlikely.

She thought of the thugs who'd run her off the road and broken into her house, but she dismissed the idea. Why would a criminal, intending to harm her, bother ringing her doorbell? Still, she looked for something to use as a weapon as she made her way to the foyer. Hoisting a heavy vase with one hand, she cracked the door open, keeping the security chain in place.

Her brother stood on the front porch, a box of doughnuts in his hand.

"Michael?"

He peered through the crack at her and gave her chagrined smile. "Yeah, I know. Surprised to see me."

"Hang on a second." She closed the door long enough to remove the security chain, then let him in.

Michael's gaze landed on the vase in her grip, and he arched an eyebrow. "You weren't thinking of using that on me, were you?"

She set the vase aside and sighed. "No, I… Why are you here?"

"I've been a little worried about you after that call a couple weeks ago, so I—" He stopped when he saw the upheaval of her living room, and he frowned. "Damn, Elise, what happened here?"

"Someone broke in and ransacked the place, looking for records I had."

His scowl deepened. "What kind of records?"

"Ones that prove Grace was never at the Pine Mill Hospital morgue." Elise placed her hand on her brother's arm, curling her fingers into the sleeve of his jacket. "Michael, I was right. She's alive. And I've *found* her."

He shook his head as if to clear it. "Excuse me?"

"Long story. And right now I've got to find a good family-law attorney and clean this place up and…" She raked her hair back from her face with her fingers, then looked up at her brother again. "Wait, you came by because you were worried about me?"

He arched an eyebrow. "You sound surprised. I'm your brother. Why is it strange that I'd worry about you?"

Fresh tears pricked her eyes. "Because I…you—"

"Haven't been a very good brother in the past?" he finished for her. He twisted his lips. "I know. And I can't promise I'll be much better in the future. You know I'm not good with emotional stuff, but…" He shrugged and shoved the doughnuts toward her. "I'm here now, and I brought breakfast. So…if you want to talk…"

She took the doughnut box and set it aside. "What I want is a hug. I've missed you."

She put her arms around his back, and he returned an awkward squeeze. "Okay, tell me what's been going on."

Grateful for the sounding board to help her sort out the past several days, Elise led Michael to the couch and told him the whole incredible story, starting with meeting Jared at the grief-support group. She'd made it as far as describing how she and Jared had walked in on the burglar in her house when her phone chimed, indicating a new email.

She scurried from the couch to retrieve the phone from her purse, then returned to sit by her brother. Her pulse spiked when she saw who'd sent the email. "It's from MysteryMom."

Michael scooted closer to read the email over her shoulder. "You mean you still don't know who this woman is?"

She waved him off. "She has to protect her identity

because of the work she does. I trust her." Her chest clenched as soon as she spoke the words.

You trusted Jared, too, and look where that got you.

"So what does she say?" Michael wiggled his hand, hurrying her.

Steeling herself with a deep breath, Elise thumbed the key to open the email.

Progress! The federal agents working with me raided Second Chance and seized their records. I've narrowed down the list of possible adoptive parents to three names.

Elise didn't have to read the list to know Jared and Kelly would be one of the couples. But seeing the confirmation of her suspicions glowing on her phone sent a shiver to her core. MysteryMom had the paperwork to support her case to reclaim Grace.

With a heavy heart, she typed, Jared and Kelly Coleman adopted Grace. I know because Jared is the man I've been dating.

The man I love. The man who betrayed me.

As briefly as she could, Elise laid out the facts of how she met Jared, how she'd just found Isabel's birthmark and how he planned to oppose her in court. With a sad sigh, she hit the send key.

Michael repositioned himself to face her on the sofa. "So this guy you were seeing knew he had your daughter, and he slept with you without saying anything about what he knew? What a jerk!" He pulled a sympathetic grin. "Want me to beat him up for you?"

Elise frowned. "No. And I don't recall saying we slept together."

He tipped his head. "Really? You didn't?"

She rolled her eyes. "We did. But I don't think he realized what was going on until afterward. He said it was when I told him about Second Chance that he put it together."

"Jeez, Elise, what have you gotten yourself involved in?" Michael rocked back against the sofa cushions and buzzed his lips as he exhaled. "Federal agents? Black-market rings? Sounds like I was right to worry about you."

She hummed an acknowledgment, then tossed her phone on the coffee table and flopped back on the sofa pillows. A weight sat on her lungs, and thoughts of Jared made her throat thicken with tears. "What a mess."

"Yeah. Look, I know you didn't ask for my advice, but if I were you, I'd insist on DNA tests. You're gonna need every shred of proof you can get when you go to court."

Elise bit down on her bottom lip, knowing her brother was right. "I hate to think of them poking poor Grace for her blood."

Michael shook his head. "No blood. They can use a cheek swab nowadays. Completely painless."

She lifted an eyebrow. "And you know this because…?"

He chuckled. "Hey, not what you're thinking! I gave a DNA sample when I registered for the bone-marrow donors registry."

"You did?" She managed a warm smile. "That's great." Tipping her head, she asked, "I don't suppose you also know a good custody attorney?"

"I don't. But I have a friend who might."

"Let's give him a call." She sat forward, reaching for her phone when it chimed that a new email had arrived. She pulled the email up and opened it.

"MysteryMom?" Michael asked.

She nodded as she read aloud for Michael's benefit. "Unfortunately, your visit to Pine Mill Hospital and the raid last night at Second Chance have sent the rest of the people involved in the black-market ring scattering like roaches when the light is turned on. We have arrest warrants for all the scum involved, but we haven't rounded everyone up yet."

Michael grunted and scrubbed a hand over his face. "That doesn't sound good."

"No, it doesn't." The last two lines of the email caught Elise's attention, and her neck prickled.

Be careful and continue to lie low. You're still in very real danger.

"You really don't have to stay with me. I'll be fine," Elise insisted, though her brother's offer touched her deeply.

Michael pulled on his jacket and opened the front door. "No arguments. We don't know what these people are capable of, and I'm not taking any chances." He gave her a level look. "I'll be back as soon as I can pack up a few things for overnight. Lock the door behind me."

"Yes, Mother," she quipped, and he made a face that said "smart-aleck."

After her brother left, Elise straightened the living room a bit, mustering the nerve to phone the attorney Michael's friend had recommended. When she finally made the call, the attorney's secretary simply made an appointment for Elise to come in later that afternoon to go over the case details with the lawyer.

Elise sat on the couch, shaking with nervous energy for several minutes after she disconnected. Dread made her feel as if she had concrete in her veins. She wished she could find a way to convince Jared that as Grace's birth mother, Grace *belonged* with her. Having her mother was in Grace's best interests.

She knew at some point the issue of joint custody would come up, but she balked at the idea. Some selfish part of her rebelled against giving up even a little time with her daughter. She'd already missed fourteen months of Grace's life. And after he'd planned to run away with Grace today, how could she trust Jared not to violate a custody arrangement and take off with her in the future?

She imagined what it would be like to have Grace here at her house, using the nursery she'd set up over a year ago. Would she ever be able to look at Grace and not think of her as Isabel? Not think of Jared?

Her cell phone trilled, and the caller ID flashed Jared's name. Her heart rose to her throat as she lifted the phone to her ear. "Hello."

"It's me. I…think we should talk."

Just hearing his voice made her ache with longing and regret. "I know."

"Things got out of hand this morning, and…before you call a lawyer—"

"I just did. I have a meeting later today."

His sigh hissed through the line. "Elise, don't do this."

An edge of defensiveness crept back into his tone, and her temper rose to meet it. "Don't do what? Fight for my daughter?"

"Look, we don't even have proof she is your daughter. You can't—"

"Actually I do have proof." She explained to him everything MysteryMom had said in her last email about the raid at Second Chance and how he and Kelly were one of three possible adoptive couples to have gotten Grace.

Her revelation met only silence from Jared.

Elise drew a deep breath. "And just to be absolutely sure, I want her DNA tested."

"What!"

"My brother assures me they can do it with a simple cheek swab now. It's quick and painless, and we can know for sure whether or not she's Grace."

"Elise, be reasonable. If we sit down and talk this out—"

"I am being reasonable, Jared. What's not reasonable about a mother wanting her child returned to her!" When he didn't answer, she checked to make sure the call hadn't been dropped. "Jared?"

"I'm here." The hopelessness that permeated his tone speared her heart.

"If you think we can talk without arguing again…" she finger-combed the hair off her forehead "…I'll come by after my meeting with the lawyer. I have to pick up Brooke anyway."

"I'll be here. I've taken a personal day to handle this."

"Okay." Her pulse fluttered foolishly at the notion of seeing Jared again. Didn't her heart realize he was the same man trying to take Grace from her permanently? She squeezed her eyes shut waiting for him to say goodbye, to hang up on her…*something.* Instead a heavy silence hung between them, vibrating over the cell connection and saying more than words could.

I hate this. I miss you. I'm sorry. But she said none of it. As much as it hurt to be at odds with Jared, Grace was her priority, and she couldn't let her ill-conceived feelings for Jared stand in the way.

Finally, he heaved a sigh. "Where's Solomon when you need him, huh?"

Elise frowned. "Solomon?"

"You know, the king in the Old Testament. When two

women were fighting over a baby, he ordered the child cut in half."

She nodded even though she knew he couldn't see. "Oh, right. Him." She dragged herself off the sofa and crossed the floor to stare out a window where a gentle rain had begun to fall. "I should go. I still have to call my boss and explain why I'm not coming in today."

After hanging up with Jared, his comment echoed through her head.

Solomon. Two women.

In the Bible, the real mother had given up her claim on the baby to save her child's life, had sacrificed her right to the infant out of deep abiding love. And Solomon had known, by her sacrifice, who the real mother was.

Jared paced across his living room, jangling the change in his pocket, anxiety and doubt knotting his gut.

"What's going on?" Peter perched on the edge of the couch and shot him a troubled look. "You really scared Michelle on the phone. Is Isabel all right? Is she sick?"

He shook his head and fumbled for the right place to start. "It's about Elise."

"The lady you've been dating? Yeah, I like her. She's smart, pretty—"

"She's Isabel's mother."

Peter frowned and gave his head a little shake of confusion. "What? I thought you said Isabel's mother was a teenager in Lake Charles."

"That's what we were told. We were lied to. Scammed."

"And you know this how?"

"I've been helping Elise find out what happened to her baby ever since she got an email from this woman who calls herself MysteryMom, claiming that Elise's baby didn't die after birth like she'd been told."

Peter eased back on the sofa, his expression dark and wary. "Hell. I see where this is going."

Jared explained everything that had happened in the past few weeks, from Elise being run off the road and her home searched to the latest revelations about Second Chance.

"Not all of the children come through the black market, but MysteryMom found proof that Second Chance had an arrangement with Arrimand. When they find a desperate and gullible couple like us—" He didn't bother hiding his disgust and irritation "—They had an elaborate system in place for securing all the falsified documents to cover their tracks."

"And you've seen proof that Elise's baby was stolen? That Isabel was a black-market baby? Specifically *her* baby?"

Jared sighed and stopped in front of the window to stare at a bird chirping on an oak tree in the yard. His throat tightened with guilt over all he'd hidden from Elise. "I've had suspicions for days. Too many things matched up to be coincidence." He blew out a deep breath and raked both hands through his hair in frustration. "But I didn't say anything to Elise, because I wasn't sure, and… I didn't want to believe it was true."

He faced his brother, the same heartsick dread filling him that had guided his actions the past few days. "Then, this morning, Elise heard from MysteryMom that her agents working the case had narrowed down the number of families that could have gotten Grace to three. We were one of the couples on her list."

"But that's not—"

"This morning Elise was changing Isabel's clothes. She took Izzy's shirt off and saw the birthmark on Isabel's shoulder. She swears Grace, her daughter, had a birthmark just like Isabel's."

Peter shook his head and held up his hands. "Lots of babies have birthmarks. That's not—"

"She saw the birthmark *before* she heard from MysteryMom. She didn't know about Isabel's birthmark until today, but now Elise is convinced." Jared resumed pacing. "She's planning to see a lawyer to get Grace back even as we speak."

Peter cursed and scrubbed a hand over his face.

"And if the birthmark and the evidence MysteryMom found aren't enough to win her case, Elise wants a DNA test to prove she's Isabel's biological mother."

"Can she force you to comply?" his brother asked.

Jared stopped his restless wandering and slumped down in a recliner. "She doesn't have to. All you have to do is look at the two of them together and it's obvious. Isabel looks like Elise. She responds to Elise as if she instinctively knows there's a physical bond between them." A razor-like sorrow flayed his heart, and defeat settled on him, dark and heavy. "How do I let Isabel go? I don't think I can stand losing her on top of Kelly."

And Elise. The knife of despair already buried in his chest twisted, digging deeper.

He'd fallen in love with Elise, and now, because he'd tried to avoid the truth, tried to protect Isabel, he'd lost Elise's trust and respect. She'd filed him in the same category as the other monsters who'd conspired to steal her daughter. Not that he blamed her. If someone had tried to keep him from finding Isabel, he'd be livid, as well.

"You can't seriously be considering giving Isabel up. Hire your own lawyer! Fight her! You're Isabel's father, dammit!"

He faced Peter. “Maybe in my heart, but not biologically. She has the advantage.”

“But your adoption—”

“Was arranged through fraud and kidnapping and—”

“You had no knowledge of any of those crimes.” Peter aimed a finger at him to punctuate his point. “You adopted her in good faith.”

Jared scoffed. “Do you really think a judge is going to give a flip about my intentions or my good faith?”

Peter shoved to his feet. “But it’s been more than a year.”

“Elise never gave permission for the adoption! Her baby was *stolen* from her. She was lied to. She believed Grace was dead.” The agonizing truth landed in his chest like a wrecking ball. “She has every right to claim her daughter.”

Now Peter paced the floor. “There’s gotta be something you can do!” He pivoted on his heel and aimed a finger at Jared. “Run. Take Isabel and disappear. Go to another state.”

He gave his brother a weary glance. “I considered it. Was prepared to do just that this morning right before Elise figured out the truth.” Guilt gnawed his gut. “But kidnapping Isabel and becoming a fugitive isn’t the answer.”

Peter turned up a hand in concession. “I suppose you’re right.” He paced away then spun back toward Jared, his face brightening. “Oh, my God. It’s so obvious! You care about Elise, right? I mean, the night you were over here it was pretty clear you’d fallen for her.”

A bittersweet pang plucked his heart. “I love her.”

“Perfect! So marry her and Isabel comes, too, as part of the package.”

A fragile hope blossomed in Jared’s soul, warming him from the inside out. Before she’d discovered his cover-up, Elise had seemed happy with him. Though she’d never voiced her feelings, he believed she’d cared for him, that she'd loved him. But he'd broken her trust, the very thing that had scarred her in past relationships and kept her from opening her heart to him unconditionally. He'd betrayed their friendship. Hoping that she'd forgive him and accept his proposal was a long shot.

Unless…

Maybe she'd give marriage a chance if he convinced her it was what was best for Grace.

Grabbing his keys from his pocket, he hurried to the front door. "Can y'all watch Isabel for a couple hours?"

Peter tailed him to the door. "Sure, but…where are you going?"

"To buy an engagement ring and find Elise."

Chapter 13

Elise couldn't sit still. Nervous energy pulsed through her veins, and her mind jumped from one thought to another, dragging her emotions on a roller coaster.

She needed to get Grace's nursery ready. Could she even change her name to Grace after she'd learned the name Isabel?

How long would it take to get a hearing scheduled? How could Jared have hidden the truth from her?

How could she take Isabel from the only parent she'd ever known? How could she take Jared's daughter from him?

How did she survive the ache of knowing someone else she loved had betrayed her? Had Jared known the truth about Isabel when he'd made love to her? He'd said he only suspected after hearing about Second Chance, but how could she trust anything he'd told her in light of his deception?

Would she be compelled to testify at Dr. Arrimand's trial? How long would it take to round up everyone involved? How long would she be in danger?

When would MysteryMom know—

Her doorbell pealed, interrupting her latest round of turbulent thoughts. Elise started for the door, assuming it was Michael returning as he'd promised.

"Elise? Are you there?"

Jared. Her mouth dried, and bittersweet anguish twisted her heart. She wasn't prepared to face him. Her emotions were too raw and unsettled.

"Please, Elise," he called through the closed door. "I know you're home. Let me in. We have to talk."

She yanked open the door. "Why are you here? I told you I'd come by your place after I talked to my lawyer."

"I know, but I have an idea to propose. I think we can figure this out so that we both win." His face was bright with optimism, and her spirits stirred with hopeful anticipation.

The prospect of a mutually agreeable solution intrigued her even though his choice of words bothered her. "We both *win?* Jared, this isn't a competition. Grace is not some prize to be won or lost!"

He held up a hand in concession. "Agreed. Poor choice of words. I'm sorry."

Elise studied him, and another piece of her anger toward him melted. He looked a mess. His hair was thoroughly ruffled, evidence he'd plowed his fingers through it numerous times today in frustration. Despite the light of optimism in his eyes, his face was lined and haggard. She remembered seeing a similar face staring back at her from her mirror in the weeks following the news that Grace had died. Now, he faced losing his daughter, and he was in hell.

A prick of empathy for his agony compelled her to let

him inside, despite the hurt and anger she harbored for his lies and silence. After shutting the door, Elise folded her arms over her chest as she faced him, holding herself together with her last threads of control. What she wanted was to throw herself into his arms and soak up the strength and security she'd relished in his embrace as recently as yesterday.

Meeting his dark gaze, she felt her heart crack just a little more. "Go ahead," she said, hoping he didn't hear the quiver in her voice.

"First of all, I'm sorry I didn't tell you my suspicions sooner. When I realized Isabel could be yours, I…was selfish. I could only think of what it would mean to lose her. I panicked."

"You said you have an idea to solve this?" she prompted without acknowledging his apology. She wasn't ready to forgive him yet. Too much was at stake. Her pain went too deep, and the cut was too new.

He flashed her an uneasy grin. "The answer is obvious, really. I'm her father. You're her mother."

She stared at him blankly, even though her brain was already miles ahead of him.

"If we lived together, Isabel could have both of us. We could share custody."

"Share her?"

"It makes sense, doesn't it?"

"Isn't that a bit like cutting her in half? Am I supposed to cry foul now and give her up rather than start a tug-of-war over her?"

"No tug-of-war, Elise. I'm suggesting we marry."

A patter of wistful yearning fluttered in her chest, but she kept her face impassive. No matter how much she longed for the kind of domestic bliss and family he described, she refused to settle for a marriage of convenience.

Grace deserved to be raised in a home where her parents loved each other as much as they loved her.

And I deserve to be loved for who I am, not just a means to an end.

"We don't have to turn this into a bitter and expensive custody battle with lawyers and judges, Elise."

She stiffened. "Is that what this is about for you? Avoiding the costs and hardship of a lawsuit?"

He shifted his weight, his expression uneasy. "I'd be lying if I said it wasn't part of my reasoning."

"Oh, but you're so good at lying." Her tone dripped sarcasm. "Why stop now?" The words slipped out before she could stop them, some cruel part of her wanting to hurt him the way he'd hurt her.

Jared flinched, and his face reflected the pain she'd inflicted.

Elise was shaking so hard she could barely stand. Dragging in a ragged breath, she slid to the floor. Tears blurred her vision, and bile filled her throat. What was she doing? This horrible situation wasn't Jared's fault. What kind of man, what kind of father would he be if he didn't fight for his daughter? She clutched her stomach, swallowing hard to force down the sour taste of anguish.

Jared stalked several steps away before shoving both hands through his hair and growling his frustration. "I'm sorry, Elise. I should have never lied to you. I should have leveled with you from the beginning, just like we promised each other. Brutal honesty. No pulling punches."

Then with a harsh exhale, he dropped his hands to his sides and crossed the floor to her. He crouched in front of her, his face shadowed with sadness. He reached for her before apparently thinking better of it and withdrawing his hand. "I didn't come here to fight with you. I don't want us to be adversaries in this."

"Neither do I."

His cheek twitched in a rueful grin. "That's good. Can we start over? Pretend this morning never happened?"

She sighed and averted her gaze, unable to bear seeing the turbulent emotion in his eyes any longer. "Jared..."

"I came here for a reason. I'm trying to fix this mess." He fumbled in his jacket pocket, and said, "I brought you this."

She angled a cautious glance to see what he had.

He held out a ring box, and the weight in her chest sank harder against her lungs. Under other circumstances, she'd be weeping tears of joy, cherishing this moment as a dream come true. But the moisture that leaked from her eyes was born of regret, her mind rebelling at the sight of the velvet box.

"Marry me, Elise. Marry me and raise Isabel with me." He cracked it open to reveal the diamond solitaire inside. A lovely ring, but not the one she'd dreamed of when she imagined this moment as a girl. Everything about his proposal felt wrong. His ring, his motive, his reasoning.

A sinking realization settled over her, clarifying what her instincts were saying. The ring he was offering had nothing to do with love. Not for her, anyway.

The courts would give Grace back to her, she was almost certain. In time, she'd have her daughter again, even if he put up a fight. His marriage proposal was rooted in his desperation to keep the baby he thought of as his daughter. He didn't want a wife. He wanted Isabel.

Tears puddled in her eyes, blurring her vision as she stared at him, willing him to say he loved her. Praying he'd give her some reason to believe in his feelings for her.

But he didn't.

"No."

"Elise?" he said, a note of panic creeping into his tone.

"Getting married is the perfect solution. And having both of us around is what's best for Isabel."

She swiped angrily at the moisture on her cheek. "Her name is Grace."

He opened his mouth, made a noise as if to reply, then fell silent as he met her level gaze.

She flipped the lid of the ring box closed and pushed it back toward him. "And don't pretend you're proposing marriage for any reason other than because it's what's best for you."

Disappointment and frustration lined his face, and he shook his head in confusion.

"Elise, how can you say—?"

She shoved to her feet, pushing past him and scrubbing the tears from her cheeks with a sleeve. "Committing yourself to a relationship because it will spare you a custody fight may be enough reason for you to get married, but I can't do it. I need more from a marriage than convenience or simplified parenting."

"But Isa—*Grace*—" he lifted a hand in appeal as if his concession on her name would win him points "—needs both of us. I know I should have told you what I suspected sooner, but I was terrified of losing my daughter."

Elise shook her head, giving him a sorrowful look. "You're still scared. That's the only reason you're here. And that's why I have to say no."

"Elise, that's crazy. At least think about—"

She stiffened, insulted by his insinuation that she was acting irrationally. "I want you to go now. We have nothing left to discuss."

He didn't move, but his jaw tensed, and she could see him mentally scrambling for an argument that would change her mind. "Elise, don't—"

"No. Leave." She aimed a finger at her door. "Now."

He straightened to his full height, whether to intimidate her or not she wasn't sure.

"Elise, what else do you want me to say?"

Say you love me.

"I've apologized for not telling you—"

"Goodbye, Jared." She stalked to the door and yanked it open, hiding behind her anger so that she didn't crumble in front of him. "My lawyer will be in touch. Please don't make this any harder than it already is for either of us."

His hands fisted, and he tightened his mouth to a grim line. "Not a chance." He stormed to the door and stopped in the threshold to lean in close to her and growl, "If this is the way you want it, fine. I don't care how hard it gets. I will fight with everything I've got to keep Isabel."

Jared drove home with his hands clenching the steering wheel and his gut roiling with fear, disappointment and self-disgust. Why had he let Elise provoke him to say such argumentative things? He didn't want her as an adversary.

He wanted to marry her. He cared deeply for Elise. More than he thought he'd ever care for another woman after losing Kelly.

Elise's skepticism and anger were understandable considering the way he'd misled her and avoided telling her the truth as soon as he realized who Isabel was. Antagonizing her was not a good game plan.

Jared parked in his driveway and dropped his forehead to the steering wheel. Why had he issued that parting shot about fighting with all he had for Isabel? Defensiveness was hardly the best way to work out an amicable custody agreement. *Stupid, stupid!*

His fear of losing control of the situation, of losing time to change her mind—hell, his fear of losing *Isabel*—had colored his response to Elise.

You're still scared. That's the only reason you're here. And that's why I have to say no.

Elise had seen the truth, had known where his heart was. But why did she think his desperation to keep Isabel was grounds to reject his marriage proposal?

That's the only reason you're here.

Not so. Marriage made sense for them. It was the obvious solution.

I need more from a marriage than convenience or simplified parenting.

But…their marriage would be about more than shared custody. They had a good relationship, a growing friendship and sexual chemistry to spare. At least, he thought so. What had he done to make her think he wouldn't be a good husband?

Gritting his teeth, he shouldered open the car door and stalked inside. Isabel was playing on the living-room floor, and Michelle was folding laundry on the couch.

"Where's Peter?" Jared dropped his keys on the sofa table and peeled off his jacket.

"He's picking us up a pizza." Michelle's face lit with anticipation. "Well? What did she say? Can we reserve the church for a wedding?"

"No." He dropped heavily in an armchair and scrubbed a hand over his jaw.

Michelle frowned. "No…meaning no church, or—"

"No, meaning she said no. She turned me down flat." The disappointment that had gnawed at him in the car swelled into a sense of loss and defeat that left a hollow ache in his soul. He hadn't considered for a minute that she would refuse him, but her rejection stung more than his pride. If he didn't save his relationship with Elise, he stood to lose so much more than just his daughter. He'd lose the woman he'd come to love.

"How could she say no?" Michelle pressed, shock filling her expression and her tone. "It's such a simple and obvious solution. You love each other, and you both love Isabel…what's the problem?"

He shrugged. "Hell if I know. I knew she was mad at me about the way things played out, and I apologized but… she wouldn't hear of it." He leaned his head back and shut his eyes, weary to the bone and heartsick. "Maybe she doesn't love me. I thought we were on the same page, but we never talked about our relationship in those terms."

"But you did tell her how you felt when you proposed… right?" Michelle asked hesitantly.

Jared's pulse skipped a beat as he replayed the conversation in his head.

"Jared Coleman—" Michelle's tone was stern "—please say you told Elise you loved her when you asked her to marry you."

His breath lodged in his lungs. "I…guess…not. I—"

The doorbell rang, interrupting his train of thought. Michelle stood, and he waved her back to the sofa. "I'll get it."

He hurried to the door, praying it was Elise. Praying he still had a chance to convince her of his feelings for her.

His heart in his throat, he yanked open the door. But instead of Elise, a linebacker-size man he'd never seen before stood on his porch.

Jared tensed. "Can I help you?"

The man looked past him to the living-room floor where Isabel played. "Jared Coleman?"

Jared raised his chin. "Who wants to know?"

"You have something that's not yours."

Before Jared could reply, the man lifted his hand and touched Jared's chest with a small black device. *A Taser!*

Every muscle and nerve in his body screamed in pain. Convulsed.

Michelle shrieked in terror.

Jared's vision dimmed, and he slumped to the floor.

Chapter 14

Pain.

Jared fought the light that stirred him. The light meant pain. In the darkness, he'd known sweet oblivion. He dragged a sore arm over his eyes to block the intruding light.

But with the light came sounds. Muffled noises that made the hair on his neck stand up. Whimpers. Frightened tears.

Adrenaline shot through him, reviving him with a jolt. "Isabel!"

He sat up quickly. So quickly his head rebelled with a throb that made him think his skull would explode. When the spots quit dancing in his vision, he blinked Michelle into focus.

She sat on the sofa, tied and gagged, with tears streaming from her eyes. She tried to talk, and he recognized the muffled sob that had woken him. He scanned the room, fear grabbing him by the throat.

Isabel was gone.

Fumbling to his knees, he crawled to Michelle and eased the gag from her mouth. "Where's Isabel?" he rasped.

"He took her," she cried. "I tried to stop him, but he was too strong for me. He overpowered me and tied me up."

"Pizza delivery!" Peter called as he breezed into the house. "Isn't it a bit cold outside to leave the door op—" He stopped short and frowned at Michelle. "Honey, what the hell is—"

"Isabel's gone. She's been kidnapped." Jared clambered to his feet, though his legs still felt rubbery. "Call the police!"

Eyes wide with alarm, Peter tossed the pizza box on the coffee table and picked up the cordless phone. "Is Elise behind this?"

Jared shook his head, then grabbed his temples. "I wish I could say she was. At least then I'd know my daughter was safe."

"Then who—?"

The phone in Peter's hand rang, and he answered it. "No, this is his brother. Hold on." He held the phone out to Jared with a scowl. "It's Elise. She says it's an emergency."

Sitting on her bathroom floor beside the commode, Elise rocked forward, clutching her stomach. She fought another wave of nausea as she waited for Jared to come on the line. Dear God, she had to get herself under control if she was going to be of any use to Jared or herself…any use to Grace.

"Elise? Talk to me." Jared's voice sounded strained, hoarse. *Oh, God, it was true!*

"Jared." Her voice cracked as she sobbed. "I had a call. They said they had Grace. I heard a baby crying and…tell me it wasn't her. Tell me—"

"I can't. A man showed up here and used a stun gun to knock me out. He overpowered Michelle and took Grace."

With a strangled cry, she leaned over the toilet and dry heaved.

"Elise? Are you there? What did they say in your call?"

She swiped her mouth with the back of her hand. "They want money. A lot of it. To fund their escape."

"Money. Of course."

"He said w-we only have twelve hours. The feds are hot on their trail, and…and they've got a plan to l-leave the country. Tonight. But they need cash." Elise drew a shuddering breath. "Oh, God, Jared…he said if we called the cops o-or didn't get the money or interfered in their escape in any way—"

A sob choked Elise.

"Tell me," Jared said.

"We'd never see Grace again."

Elise tensed when the doorbell rang, and she gnawed her lip as Michael answered it.

"Are you Jared?" he asked, blocking her view of the person on her porch.

"Yeah. Who are *you?*"

The sound of Jared's voice had Elise on her feet and racing to the door. She pushed Michael aside and threw herself into Jared's arms, all bitterness between them shoved aside in light of her terror for Grace. She needed the strength and reassurance his embrace offered more than she needed her next breath. He clung to her with the same fierce intensity that she squeezed him, clearly as distraught as she was.

"Have you reached MysteryMom yet?" he rasped.

"No," she said, her voice muffled against his chest. She angled her head back to meet the stark expression in his eyes. "I replied to her email, but she hasn't answered. Michael and I have been watching the Parents Without Children message board. So far, she hasn't signed on."

"You would be Michael, I presume?" Jared said.

"Yeah, her brother." Michael's tone was cool, but he offered a hand in greeting.

Jared released Elise in order to shake hands with Michael, then stepped inside, one arm around her shoulders.

"So what's our next move?" Michael asked, closing the door behind them.

Jared guided Elise to the couch and drew her down beside him. They exchanged a look of mutual worry and impatience, and her stomach knotted. Knowing Jared was just as helpless to save Grace as she was left an icy apprehension in her soul.

"I hate to say it, but given the deadline, we'd better start gathering the money they asked for." Jared rubbed his hands on the legs of his jeans. "We don't have time to wait for MysteryMom."

Nausea swamped Elise. "Jared, they want a quarter of a million dollars. Even if I wanted to pay them off—and I would if it would bring Grace home safely—I don't have anywhere near that much. I spent most of my savings on the treatments to get pregnant and have Grace in the first place."

Jared sighed. "Yeah, the adoption fee we paid Second Chance stripped most of our savings, too."

"I have about ten thousand saved up that you can have, Elise." Michael sat down in a chair across from them. "It's not much but…"

Tears flooded her eyes. "Thank you. Every little bit helps."

The room fell silent, a pervasive sense of the terrifying conundrum they faced hovered over them like a looming storm cloud.

"Maybe it's time we call the police," Michael said.

"No!" Jared and Elise said in unison.

Elise's chest tightened, fear battling common sense. "He said no cops."

Michael scoffed. "They always say no cops."

"We can't risk having them hurt Grace in retribution." Her voice shook, and she lunged to her feet to pace, to burn off restless energy. "They have to think we're cooperating."

"Elise, think about it. The police have experts in handling cases like this. If we don't—"

"No." Jared drilled a determined stare at Michael. "Not with Grace's life on the line."

Grace. Despite the turmoil facing them, the disquiet in her soul, Elise noticed Jared's use of Elise's name for her daughter.

Michael spread his hands in a conciliatory gesture. "Look, I know you both are scared for Grace, but you need to bring the authorities in on this."

"Not yet." Jared's tone matched the unyielding set of his jaw.

A cold tremor shook Elise to her marrow. She knew her brother was right, but she couldn't break free from the grip of terror. She kept replaying the menacing warning in the kidnapper's voice, and she hugged herself as a fresh wave of agony washed through her. Legs shaking, she dropped on the edge of a chair and put her head between her knees. "Ohgodohgodohgod," she moaned, her grief and worry a living thing clawing inside her. "My baby. They can't hurt my baby!"

She felt a warm hand on her back and raised her head to find Jared crouched beside her. She reached for him, and he drew her against his chest again.

"Please, Jared…please, don't let them hurt Gracie. Oh, God…"

His arms squeezed her tighter, and he kissed her head. "We'll find her, honey. Whatever it takes. I promise."

She wanted to ask how he could make such a pledge when the situation was so far out of their control, but instead, she grabbed his reassurance with both hands and held tight to it, needing to believe he was right.

After indulging in a few tears, Elise scrabbled her composure back together and swiped her cheeks with her sleeve. "I'm sorry. I'm just so scared."

"I know. Me, too." Jared dug his cell phone from his pocket and waved a hand toward her computer. "Why don't you check to see if MysteryMom is online yet, and I'll call my broker and see how much money I can raise if I sell my portfolio and cash in my retirement funds."

Michael scowled and massaged the back of his neck, but he said nothing.

Elise moved numbly to the table where she'd set up her laptop and refreshed the web page for the message board. No MysteryMom.

She drummed her fingers impatiently and racked her brain for another way to reach her anonymous patron. They were down to ten hours and change before their deadline with the kidnappers. Every minute of inaction ate at Elise, sawing her frazzled nerves.

She moved her hands to the keyboard and typed a pleading message to MysteryMom.

MysteryMom, help! EMERGENCY!!

With a click of the mouse, she posted the appeal and sat back in her chair.

All she could do was wait.

"I don't care if it bankrupts me!" Jared shouted into his phone as he stalked her living room like a caged tiger. "I'd pay twice that amount if it will bring my daughter home safely. Hell, I'd give my *life* if it would save hers."

Elise's breath snagged in her lungs. She watched Jared pace with her heart in her throat and a tender ache swelling inside her.

"Just do it, Henry." Jared's tone was grim and final. "Transfer all of it to one account, so we can wire it to their account when I give the go-ahead." He closed his eyes and pinched the bridge of his nose. "I understand. Just get it ready."

He thumbed the keypad on his phone and slumped back down on the couch, his body language full of defeat. "If I liquidate all my accounts, I can cover most of the ransom." He raised a weary gaze to Elise. "But we still need fifteen thousand."

Elise could only stare, dumbfounded.

"You're emptying all of your accounts?" Michael asked, his tone as stunned as Elise felt.

Jared nodded mutely, his attention still locked on Elise. "It's just money." He drew a deep breath and released it, his eyes growing damp. "Of course, this means I won't have the money to hire a lawyer. I won't be able to fight your custody suit."

Elise absorbed his admission like a fist to her gut. The breath she'd been holding wheezed from her, leaving her lungs aching and starved.

"But I'd give you custody a hundred times over to save

her from these thugs," he said, emotion strangling his voice.

A sob hiccupped from her throat.

King Solomon. Cut the baby in half. The real mother's sacrifice.

The love behind Jared's gesture dug deep into Elise's soul. His was the love of a parent, a father. A *real* father in every way that mattered. The sacrifice of all his funds, and thereby his means to claim custody, could be the difference between getting Grace back or not. The difference between life and death for her daughter. *Their* daughter.

Hollow acceptance of his fate darkened Jared's penetrating gaze, burrowing deep into Elise's heart. She knew the heartache he was suffering, because she'd lived it herself when she'd thought Grace had died. She lived it now, fearing for Grace's safety with the kidnappers. Jared was in a living hell. In a pain too deep and personal for words.

And she knew she couldn't be responsible for inflicting that level of agony and suffering on someone she loved.

Her pulse quickened. She loved Jared.

Maybe she'd known that all along, but she was certain now. She loved him if for no other reason than the depth of character and the love for his daughter that his generosity showed. Something shifted inside her, bringing a certainty she couldn't ignore into sharp, if painful, focus. She couldn't take his daughter away from him. No matter how much she loved Grace—perhaps because of how much she loved Grace—she could no longer justify removing her from the only home she'd ever known, from a father who adored her.

Maybe, if they could redeem their relationship when this nightmare was over, she might convince him to give her visitation rights. But Grace—no, *Isabel*—belonged with Jared.

"Jared, I want you to—"

The chime of her laptop cut her off as an instant message screen popped up. She turned toward the screen and caught her breath.

Jared surged off the sofa, crossing the floor in three long strides. "Is it her? Is it MysteryMom?"

"Yes." Elise trembled as she read the short message.

Michael read over her shoulder, as well.

Elise, what's happened? What's your emergency?

Grace has been kidnapped. They've demanded money in the next 10 hours for her return.

She was shaking so hard with adrenaline and the swirl of emotions that she had to backspace and retype words a half dozen times.

"Here, let me." Jared nudged her aside, taking half the chair, and with fingers flying across the keyboard, he explained how he'd been knocked out and Grace stolen. He laid out the terms they'd been given and the warnings the kidnappers had issued about contacting the police.

Jared typed, We have most of the money ready to transfer to their account, but you have to pull your team back. Give us a chance to recover Grace before it is too late.

MysteryMom made no response for several nerve-racking seconds, then…

It's already too late.

Elise's heart stopped. With a gasp, she grabbed Jared's arm and dug her fingers into his wrist. "No…"

Another message popped up, and together they leaned close to the screen to read.

There are agents carrying out arrest warrants in three states even now. I can't pull anyone back without jeopardizing the whole mission. This case is bigger than just Grace. The people involved have side operations that include drug smuggling and human trafficking from Mexico, money laundering, bribery and intimidation of officials. They're accused of murder, kidnapping and child pornography. This is huge!

Jared rocked back, expelling a shaky breath. "Good God."

Elise typed, Dr. Arrimand is involved in all of this?

Heavens no. He was a pawn. His greed got him sucked into something bigger than he imagined and too dangerous to quit once he started. Same with his nurse.

Elise struggled for oxygen. What hope did they have for Grace against such odds, such a mammoth crime ring?

Jared stared at the floor, as still as a statue. His expression was pale, bleak.

Elise glanced at the framed ultrasound picture, the blurry white shape that was Grace at nine weeks' gestation. For so long, Elise had gazed at that picture and grieved for a child she'd believed dead. But a miracle had brought her baby back into her life, and she was far from ready to give up hope of finding Grace now.

Maternal love and protectiveness jabbed her, firing her determination, shaking her from her self-pity.

Elise typed to MysteryMom, I will NOT give up hope of getting Grace back.

I would never ask you to.

Jared cast a side glance at what she was typing.

So tell me what I can do. I won't just sit here while the clock ticks on the deadline the kidnappers gave us. I'll do whatever I must to get my daughter back!

Hang on. Let me consult with some of my team, and we'll come up with a plan. I'll message you within twenty minutes.

Eighteen excruciating minutes later, Elise hovered over her laptop, willing MysteryMom to return with a miracle solution. Across the room, Jared paced, his muscles tense and his mouth clamped in a grim line.

Little had been said since MysteryMom signed off to consult her colleagues, and Michael had disappeared into the kitchen to brew a pot of coffee no one wanted. Elise counted every tick of the clock, knowing each minute they waited was one less minute they had to find Grace before their deadline. Though she tried not to dwell on worst-case scenarios, her mother mind-set meant she couldn't help but fret over what would happen to Grace if the deadline passed. Would they kill her baby? Take her out of the country to be sold again? Use her in child porn and prostitution?

Her stomach rebelled at the thought, and bile rose in her throat. She squeezed her eyes shut, swallowing hard to force down the bitter taste and saying a silent prayer. *Please, oh, please, God, let Grace be all right!*

The chime of her laptop shattered the silence, and Elise

spun around on her chair to read the incoming message. Jared dashed over to sit beside her in a chair he'd pulled in from the kitchen. Their shoulders touched as they leaned in together to see the screen. Jared's familiar sandalwood scent filled her nose and managed to calm her to a degree. Knowing she wasn't facing this crisis alone mattered to her more than she could say.

What would it be like to always have someone beside her to face life's challenges and heartaches? To share her joys and the simple pleasures?

If they didn't rescue Grace in time, would she ever feel joy or savor any pleasures in life again?

Elise, are you there?

Jared and I are both here. What did you come up with?

We have an idea, but there are no guarantees it will work. It could prove costly to you.

Costly how?

We think, given our time constraints, that our best chance to track the men with Grace is to follow the money. Namely the ransom they've demanded. You said you could get most of it, right?

Elise glanced at Jared for confirmation, and he gave a quick, certain nod.

Between us, we can have all two hundred and fifty thousand dollars in a few hours.

Good. Before you authorize the money to be wired, we need the account numbers and bank information they gave you, so we can put a trace on the money and follow any subsequent transfers. We'll put a dozen agents, all computer experts and forensic accountants, to work tracking the names associated with the accounts and cross-referencing them with what we've already learned about the crime ring.

How will that help Grace?

We can use the information we get to pull up an address, a rap sheet, a vehicle registration or driver's license, a credit-card purchase...*anything* that can help us close in on where Grace might be. There is always the risk, however, that we'll lose the trail of the money, and we won't be able to recover it when this is over. We could wind up at a dead end with no useful information to help us rescue Grace.

Elise met Jared's gaze. "It sounds like a long shot, but we have nothing else."

"Are you all right with the idea of putting that much money on the line if it doesn't work?" he asked her, covering her hand with his.

She gave him a weak smile. "Like you said, it's just money, right? I'd do anything to get our little girl back."

Our little girl. Elise hadn't realized what she said until she saw the stunned and grateful warmth that lit Jared's eyes. She gave his fingers a return squeeze and drew a deep breath. "Let's do it."

Elise and Jared spent the next several minutes instant messaging with MysteryMom and her team, sharing the information the kidnappers had given them about how to make the payment and getting last-minute instructions on how and when to wire the money. Because she would be heavily involved in tracking the case herself, Mystery-Mom told them she might not be able to update them until everything had played out.

When she signed off, Elise and Jared looked at each other, the weight of the stress they shared unspoken but obvious.

"Well..." Jared said, lifting his cell phone to punch redial, "Here goes nothing. Or rather, here goes a quarter million."

Elise opened her mouth to thank him for his magnanimous gesture, but he turned his back as his broker answered.

"Yeah, Jared Coleman again. It's a go. Make the transfer to my savings account," he said into his cell phone as he strode across the room.

Elise felt the distance he put between them as a chill that sank into her bones. More than the loss of his physical presence beside her, she sensed a growing spiritual gap, as if he'd conceded defeat and was already withdrawing from her.

Could she blame him, after the heated words and bitterness they'd exchanged today? Had it all been today? It seemed eons ago she'd been dressing Isabel and found the birthmark on the girl's shoulder.

"I made lunch if anyone wants some," Michael said, coming back into the room with a plate of sandwiches.

Elise shook her head and lifted her cell phone to make her own call about transferring her savings to Jared's account, preparing for the payoff to the kidnappers. "If your offer of ten thousand is still good, Michael, we need it now."

Within minutes of the transfers reaching Jared's

account, MysteryMom's team had electronically wired the ransom payoff to the kidnappers. The hunt was on.

Within an hour, Michelle, Peter and Jared's parents had all arrived at Elise's house to join the vigil, waiting to hear from MysteryMom and lending their moral support to Elise and Jared.

Seeing the family's love and encouragement for Jared, Elise knew she'd made the right choice to let Jared retain custody of Grace. Her own brother tried to be supportive, but he was hit-and-miss at best. Grace deserved a big loving family, the family Elise couldn't give her.

She tried several times to speak to Jared about her decision, but with so many people in her tiny house, privacy was hard to come by. Finally, when he excused himself to retrieve a jacket from his car, Elise followed him outside, hoping for a couple minutes alone with him.

A light drizzle was falling, casting a gray pallor over the autumn afternoon, but Elise ignored the rain as she walked across her small lawn toward the curb where Jared had parked. He turned, his shoulders hunched against the rain, but straightened when he spotted her.

His face blanched, apparently mistaking her serious expression for an indication of bad news. "Elise, what is it? Did MysteryMom call?"

"No, I…just needed a chance to talk with you. Alone."

He held his hand out and tipped his face toward the sky. "And you chose here? In the rain?"

"There are too many people inside, and…" She licked the drops of rain from her lips and took a deep breath. "I wanted to thank you. For putting up so much money, all of your savings, to help bring Grace home."

He shook his head and lowered his gaze. "Don't thank me. It was no—"

She stepped close to him and covered his mouth with her hands. "Don't you dare say it was nothing! It was huge. And it showed me…" Her voice cracked, and she paused to clear her throat. "It brought home to me how very much you love Isabel."

He put a hand on each of her shoulders, and the gentle strength of his fingers sent ribbons of warmth through her. "Of course I love Isabel. Deeply. But that's not the only reason I did it."

Elise blinked as drizzle dripped from her hair into her eyes. "It wasn't?"

He shook his head and held her gaze. His dark eyes drilled to her core. "Beside knowing I couldn't live with myself if I didn't do everything in my power to save Izzy, I saw how much you were hurting, saw the depth of your agony and remembered everything you said about how Grace's death ripped out your heart. I couldn't let you suffer that again. I love you too much to see you hurt like that."

Elise caught her breath. "Wh—what?"

He stroked his hand along her cheek and captured her chin with his palm. "The other reason I gave all my money to save Isabel…to save *Grace*…is because I love *you*."

Elise tried to speak, but her voice was trapped behind the lump of emotions that clogged her throat.

"I know I should have said something before now." He lifted the corner of his mouth in a rueful smile. "Like when I proposed to you. I should have told you long ago how much you mean to me."

Tears joined the raindrops filling her eyes and tickling her cheeks. "But…I came out here to tell you I wasn't going to take Isabel away from you. I saw how much you loved her, and I could never hurt you that way." Her chest clenched. "Because… I love you."

He pulled his eyebrows into a dubious frown. "Wait, what? You're not going to fight me for custody?"

She wiped futilely at the moisture on her face. "No. Though…I'm hoping, praying, you'll be kind enough to allow me liberal visitation rights. I don't want to lose touch with her. Whether you tell her I'm her mother or not will be your choice."

He raked both hands through his wet hair and took a step back. He tipped his head back and shouted a laugh to the sky. "Elise, did you hear what I just told you? I love you." He seized her shoulders again, and the smile on his lips shone also from his eyes as he enunciated each word slowly. "I. Love. You."

Elise's pulse seemed to slow as realization dawned, and a bubble of hope expanded in her chest. "Jared, are you saying…"

"I still want to marry you. I want your courage and compassion and beauty and intelligence and loving heart in my life for always…" he paused, his face darkening "…even…even if we don't get Grace back."

Elise slammed her eyes shut and shook her head. "No! Don't even say that!" Now she pinned him with a hard, penetrating stare. "We can't think that way. We *can't!* MysteryMom's team *will* find her and bring her back. We have to stay positive."

He framed her face in his hands and brushed a kiss across her forehead. "Of course. You're right. My point is I would love you and want you for my wife, even if we didn't both love the same sweet baby girl with all our hearts."

Elise fought for a breath, joy filling her chest so completely there was no room for air. After a lifetime of rejection and betrayal, loss and disappointment, Jared was offering her an unconditional gift of love and acceptance. A future.

But what kind of future would they have if Mystery-Mom's agents couldn't find Grace in time?

Her fingers curled into the damp fabric of his shirt. "And if we don't get Grace back—"

"Shh!" He waved a hand, cutting her off. "We just said we weren't going to think that way."

Her grip on his shirt tightened. "I know, but…"

"Then I will stand by you and love you, and we will struggle through the loss together."

Together. No matter what life threw at her, she didn't have to be alone anymore. She nodded her head slowly, a tender ache flooding her heart, as tears of joy washed down her cheeks. "Yes."

He smiled and arched an eyebrow. "Yes…what?"

"Yes, I love you, and I will marry you."

An expression of bliss and relief crossed his face before a wide grin tugged his cheeks. Pulling her close and whispering her name, he captured her mouth with a deep, soulful kiss. As she wrapped her arms around his neck and leaned into the kiss, a sunbeam broke through the clouds and filled the sky with its buttery light.

The first purple shadows of evening had just begun to creep across Elise's yard when her phone trilled. Not a text-message beep, but a ring that meant someone was waiting to speak to her at the other end of the line.

The stir of conversations and idle activity in her living room ceased, and six pairs of eyes turned expectantly toward Elise as she lifted her cell phone from the coffee table to read the caller ID.

"Out of area," she reported, then cast an anxious glance to Jared. Fear crimped her gut, and her hand shook so hard, she nearly dropped the phone. "What if it's the kidnappers again?"

Jared moved to her side, circling her shoulders with his arm and giving her a reassuring squeeze. "Go on. Answer it."

She pulled in a cleansing breath and thumbed the answer button. "Hello?"

"Elise?"

The voice was a woman's. Elise's heart beat triple time.

"Y-yes?"

"This is MysteryMom."

The whooshing of blood filled her ears, and a wave of panic knocked the air from her lungs. She'd never spoken to MysteryMom before. What did it mean that she'd chosen to call this time instead of messaging her or texting?

She tried to speak, but all that escaped her throat was a choked-sounding whimper.

"First and foremost," MysteryMom said, "we found Grace. She is safe, and she is unharmed."

Relief crashed through Elise so hard and fast that her head spun and her knees buckled. She slumped against Jared with a sob of joy.

"I just wanted to tell you that up front," MysteryMom said, "because I know how worried you've been."

Elise felt the shudder that rolled through Jared, and when she raised her gaze to him, his devastated expression told her he'd misinterpreted her reaction. Swallowing hard to clear the emotion tightening her throat, she smiled broadly and laughed. "No, it's good news! They found her, and she's okay!"

A cheer went up in the room, and Jared hugged her so tightly she could barely breathe. Michael beamed at her and sent her a wink.

MysteryMom was telling her something, but the buzz of excitement in the room and rush of adrenaline in Elise's ears drowned her out. She waved a hand at the room, signaling for quiet. "I'm sorry, can you repeat that?"

MysteryMom chuckled. "I know it's a lot to take in. In a nutshell, because of the information we gleaned while tracking the money transfers today, we were able to issue a warning to airports, bus stations and border crossings."

Elise tilted the phone so Jared could put his head close to hers and listen with her.

"We had a fuzzy picture from a security camera at an ATM in Laredo, Texas, taken when our kidnappers accessed the account where the ransom had ended up after several transfers. That fuzzy photo, along with the picture of Grace you provided, was sent out far and wide, and an alert guard at the Mexican border spotted Grace in the backseat of a Ford Taurus that had been reported stolen earlier in the day."

"Oh, thank God!" Elise pressed a hand over her heart and shivered, realizing how close the kidnappers had come to getting Grace out of the country. Had they gotten her into Mexico, the odds of ever recovering her would have been drastically reduced.

Jared apparently reached the same conclusion, because a half-relieved sigh, half moan rumbled from his chest.

Happy tears dampened her cheeks, and Elise swiped at them with the back of her hand. "Where is she now? How do we get her back?"

"She's in protective custody at the Laredo police department. They have a child-services agent on the way to move her to a more child-friendly location until you can get there. They won't reveal that location until one of you proves a legal claim to her, so be sure you both take a photo ID with you, and any legal documents showing your relationship with her. Oh, and there will be a bit of red tape to handle with the police and the bank, but Jared should be able to recover the ransom money in a few weeks."

Jared stepped away from their huddle over the phone, plowed both hands through his hair as he laughed, then gave his mother a big hug. In hushed tones, he repeated what they'd learned to their family, and Elise moved to a quiet corner of the room to finish the call.

"I…I don't suppose you have any information about a baby girl born to Greg and Kim Harrison at Crestview Memorial about six months ago? They were told their baby died under the same sort of odd circumstances as I was and…well, I was hoping…"

"Oh. Let me check the records," MysteryMom said, and Elise held her breath as she heard papers ruffling in the background. "Yes, here they are and…their baby…hmm, is apparently still at a Second Chance foster home. The adoptive parents they'd lined up backed out when a health problem was discovered with the baby."

Elise frowned. "What kind of health problem?"

"Deafness in one ear."

She sighed her relief. "Nothing life-threatening then, thank God. Have they been notified about their baby?"

"Don't know. But if they haven't been, they'll soon be. We're going through the files and parent notifications slowly but surely."

Her smile returned along with a sense of peace and deep gratitude. "How can I ever thank you enough for everything you've done? I'll happily pay whatever fee you charge for your services or—"

"Oh, stop!" MysteryMom said. "There's no fee. I do this because I want to, because it's my calling. My reward is in the happiness and relief I hear in your voice. The best way to thank me is to cherish every day with your daughter and give her a safe, loving and happy home to grow up in."

Elise looked to the celebration in her living room and smiled. "I can promise that. She will be surrounded with love and family."

"As for you…" MysteryMom said, "don't be afraid to open your heart to Grace's adoptive father. Life is too short to hold grudges, and he clearly has a lot of love to give… and not just to Grace."

Elise's heart warmed, and she met Jared's gaze across the room. "That I can promise, too."

Jared stepped away from the clamor of his family and moved toward her, grinning from ear to ear.

"In that case, I'll say goodbye, good luck and live well, Elise."

"You, too, MysteryMom. And thank you again from the bottom of my heart." She disconnected the call and fell into Jared's waiting arms. She angled her head to receive a deep kiss that tasted sweet with triumph and new beginnings. When they finally came up for air, Jared rested his forehead against hers and murmured softly, "So what do you say? Shall we go pick up our daughter?"

Our daughter.

Elise smiled and nodded. "I thought you'd never ask."

Epilogue

In her home office, MysteryMom rocked back in her desk chair and gave a satisfied sigh. Helping reunite baby Grace with her mother had been immensely gratifying work, especially since her associates had been able to bust up such a large crime ring, as well.

She rolled her computer mouse, clicking a few links to surf over to a chat room where another Grace, this one the mother of triplets, was waiting to hear from her.

Triplets! MysteryMom smiled and shook her head. Yes, as a single mom to triplets, Grace Sinclair had her hands full. What Grace needed was someone to share the job of parenting. And MysteryMom knew just where to start…

* * * * *

COWBOY'S TRIPLET TROUBLE

BY

CARLA CASSIDY

Carla Cassidy is an award-winning author who has written over eighty books for Mills & Boon. In 1995, she won Best Silhouette Romance from *RT Book Reviews* for *Anything for Danny*. In 1998, she also won a Career Achievement Award for Best Innovative Series from *RT Book Reviews*.

Carla believes the only thing better than curling up with a good book to read is sitting down at the computer with a good story to write. She's looking forward to writing many more books and bringing hours of pleasure to readers.

To Gretchen Jones,
My personal computer genius, back deck sitter and shoe fetish friend. Thanks for your friendship and support.
I appreciate you!

Chapter 1

"I can't believe you're going to do something so risky," Natalie Sinclair exclaimed.

Grace leaned back in the kitchen chair and smiled at her younger sister. "This conversation is backward. Isn't it usually me saying stuff like that to you?"

The two were seated in Grace's kitchen where the late May afternoon breeze drifted through the open windows, bringing with it the sweet scents of early summer.

"That's because normally I'm the one doing the crazy, reckless things," Natalie replied. She picked up her lemonade and took a sip, eyeing Grace over the top of the glass as if suspecting her older sister had been replaced by a look-alike alien. "Maybe this is some sort of postpartum insanity," she said as she placed her glass back on the table.

Grace laughed. "It's been almost a year since I was pregnant. This definitely isn't postpartum anything." Her laughter faded as she leaned forward. "I have to do this, Natalie. I've made up my mind, and I'm leaving first thing in the morning."

Natalie shook her head. "At least give me the directions to where you'll be so I know where to send the police when you're in trouble."

Grace opened the manila folder next to her laptop and took out a piece of paper. "I already intended to give you the details, although I'm certainly not expecting any trouble." She handed Natalie the directions she'd printed off her computer earlier in the morning.

"You're leaving here to travel almost two hundred miles away to a place you've never been before because some person on the internet, who you've never met, told you to go there. Gee, sounds brilliant to me," Natalie said sarcastically.

Grace felt an uncharacteristic flush heat her cheeks. "It's not just anyone. It's MysteryMom."

"Yeah, and for all you know this MysteryMom is some fifty-year-old male pervert sitting around in his underwear and talking to you over the computer."

Once again Grace couldn't help but laugh. "I've been corresponding through email with MysteryMom for almost two years now. I'd think if that were the case I would have gotten a clue by now. Besides, I'm taking my gun with me."

Both Grace and Natalie had gotten handguns from their mother on their twenty-first birthdays, unusual gifts from a strong, nontraditional woman. She had endured a violent mugging and had sworn her daughters would never be helpless victims.

"At least that makes me feel a little better," Natalie conceded.

"It would make me feel a little better if you had a job. Are you putting in applications everywhere?" Grace asked, eager to get the conversation off her plans and on to something else. Certainly Natalie's lack of employment was a concern, especially since she wasn't going to school either. She was twenty-four years old and just seemed to be drifting through her life at the moment.

"Sure, I'm trying, but I can't find anyone who wants to hire me."

"Maybe if you'd take that ring out of your eyebrow somebody would be more interested in giving you a job," Grace replied gently. "Or you could go back to school and get some training. You have the money to do that and you could decide to go into whatever field you wanted to."

"Okay, that's my clue to get out of here," Natalie said, not hiding her irritation. She checked her watch. "Not only do I not want one of your loving lectures, but I'm meeting Jimmy in a few minutes for a late lunch."

"When do I get to meet this paragon of virtue that you've been dating?" Grace asked as they both rose from the table.

Natalie gave her a secretive little smile. "When I'm good and ready for you to meet him." Together the two walked to the front door. "You'll call me as soon as you get to where you're going tomorrow and let me know that you're okay?"

"Of course I will," Grace replied and pulled Natalie close for a quick hug. There was almost ten years' difference in their ages, and Grace had always mothered Natalie. Now that their mother was gone, she felt especially maternal toward her younger sister.

Natalie stepped out of the embrace and opened the front door. "You know the routine. You've said it often enough to me. Drive carefully and be aware of any potential trouble around you."

"I will. And when I get home I want to meet this Jimmy of yours," Grace replied.

Natalie waved her hand as she headed toward her expensive little sports car in the driveway.

Grace watched until Natalie's car zoomed out of sight and then shut the door and walked back into the living room.

For a moment she simply stood in the middle of the room and listened to the silence. It was rare for the house to be so quiet. Grace hoped it would stay that way for another thirty minutes or more so that she could finish packing for her road trip in the morning.

She scooted into her bedroom, determined t[illegible] advantage of what little time she had. As she bega[illegible] to pack the open suitcase on the bed, she tried not to think about what Natalie had said, but her words kept echoing in Grace's head.

Risky? Grace had only done one risky thing in her entire life and the consequence of that particular action had changed her life forever.

No, she didn't believe what she planned for the next day was particularly risky. As crazy as it sounded, she trusted the woman who had been her cyberfriend for almost two years. MysteryMom had been a source of support and comfort from the time Grace had found herself pregnant until now. She had never given Grace a reason not to trust her.

Grace put the last blouse in the suitcase and then closed and latched it. She left her bedroom and went to the doorway of the room next to hers.

The walls were a powder-pink and the furniture was white. There was a double dresser, a rocking chair and three cribs, each one holding a precious ten-month-old.

Grace leaned against the doorjamb as her thoughts drifted back in time, back to the night she'd attended her best friend's wedding.

The wedding had been glorious and the reception had been a wild party. The handsome cowboy from Oklahoma had danced and flirted with her as they'd downed glasses of champagne like water throughout the entire event.

When she'd awakened the next morning in her hotel room bed with him next to her, she'd been horrified. She'd stumbled out of the bed and into the bathroom. The hangover she'd suffered was nothing compared to the embarrassment that flooded through her as she realized what she had done…what they had done.

When she'd left the bathroom he was gone, and she'd shoved her first and only one-night stand to the back of her mind. She'd returned to her life as a third-grade schoolteacher and hadn't thought about him again. Until two months later when she'd discovered she was pregnant.

It was at that time that she'd tried to find him. But she only knew he was from someplace in Oklahoma and she thought his name had been Justin. She'd called her friend who had gotten married that night, but Sally had told her that the cowboy had been a friend of a friend and she had no idea what his last name was or exactly where he was from.

Two months after that, when the doctor told Grace she was expecting triplets, she'd stopped trying to find the father and instead had focused all her energy on preparing herself to be the mother of three babies.

It wasn't until a week ago that MysteryMom had sent her a message indicating that she thought she'd found the cowboy. His name was Justin Johnson and he operated a ranch with his brothers just outside of Tulsa, Oklahoma.

Grace had no idea how her cyberfriend had come

up with the information, but it felt right. She vaguely remembered Justin telling her he ranched with a couple of brothers.

She'd sat on the information for several days and then yesterday morning, after a slightly traumatic event the night before, had decided to pack up the girls and drive to his ranch outside the small town of Cameron Creek, Oklahoma.

She now smiled as Abby peeked over the crib railing. Her dark curls were tousled from her nap and a delighted smile curved her rosebud lips.

Grace hurried over and picked her up, hoping to sneak her out of the room before she awakened her sisters. But at that moment Bonnie and Casey also woke up, squealing to get down and breaking the silence that had momentarily gripped the house.

It was after nine the next morning when the girls were finally loaded in their car seats and Grace left her house, heading to a ranch just over the Kansas state line in Oklahoma.

Thankfully it was Saturday and the Wichita traffic was light, making getting out of town a breeze. But she wouldn't have needed to worry about traffic for a while. Summer vacation had begun a week earlier, and she had almost three months to do whatever she wanted and spend time with the daughters who were her heart.

She loved teaching, and it was wonderful to be working at a job that gave her summers off, especially now that she was a mommy of three.

The girls were contented passengers, especially since Grace had armed them with their favorite toys, oat cereal in plastic snack containers and sippy cups filled with apple juice. They chattered and giggled for the first hour of the trip and then eventually fell asleep, leaving Grace with only the softly playing radio music and her own thoughts.

MysteryMom. She'd met the woman in a chat room for single mothers when she'd first discovered she was pregnant, and the friendship had been instantaneous. It had been MysteryMom who had helped Grace cope with morning sickness and swollen feet, who had talked her through the fears of raising triplets all alone.

When Grace's mother had fallen down a staircase and died when the babies had been only a month old, it had been MysteryMom that Grace had turned to for comfort.

Even after MysteryMom had given her the information about Justin Johnson, Grace hadn't been sure she wanted to make contact. But then a near-fatal car accident had made up her mind. That night she'd realized that if something happened to her there was nobody to take care of the girls except Natalie—who shouldn't have care of a goldfish.

She now glanced at the directions MysteryMom had given her to the Rockin' J Ranch. She couldn't imagine that MysteryMom had any ulterior motive other than to help Grace find the man who had fathered her triplets.

Grace wanted nothing from the handsome cowboy who had shared her bed for a single night after too much alcohol. She certainly didn't expect any kind of a relationship with a man who had never tried to contact her again after that night.

But she did believe he had a right to know that he was a father, and she hoped that he would want to be a part of the girls' lives.

She wanted that. She wanted that more than anything for her daughters. She'd never had a father in her life, and the old saying that you can't miss what you never had simply wasn't true. The absence of a father had resonated deeply. Not only in Grace's soul, but, she suspected, in Natalie's heart and soul as well. Of course, she couldn't imagine any man taking a look at the sweet baby faces of her daughters and not wanting to be a part of their lives.

Thankfully, the small town of Cameron Creek, Oklahoma, had a motel, and she'd already booked a room for the night with the understanding that she might stay longer. If MysteryMom was right and Justin was at the address Grace had been given, then Grace was prepared to stay a couple of days in the motel so he could spend some time with the girls and they could decide how to handle things in the future.

She slowed the car as she realized she was near the turnoff that would lead to the Rockin' J Ranch. She was vaguely surprised the sleeping babies in the backseat couldn't hear the thump of her heartbeat.

Nerves. She was suddenly incredibly nervous.

Afraid that she'd been a fool to trust a woman she'd never met in person before. Afraid that this was all some crazy wild-goose chase.

Patting her purse, she felt herself calm somewhat. Her gun was inside, loaded and ready to use if necessary. She wouldn't hesitate to fire it if she sensed her own safety or, more importantly, her children's safety was in peril.

Her nerves eased a little more as she reached the entrance to the ranch. Massive stones with wooden plaques indicated it was the ranch she sought. In the distance a two-story house rose out of the lush pastures. The ranch looked huge and well-kept, definitely not the place you'd expect an old man to be sitting around in his underwear and pretending to be a woman named MysteryMom.

Still, as she pulled up in front of the house and parked the car, the first thing she did was pull her gun out of her purse and slip it into the pocket of her navy blazer.

"Better safe than sorry," she muttered beneath her breath. The girls were still soundly sleeping as she got out of the car. She'd left her car window cracked open a bit to allow in the sweet summer breeze, and she figured it would only take a minute to find out if she was at the right place or not.

Her nerves twisted in her stomach as she walked toward the front door. The worst that could happen was this would be the wrong place, the wrong man, and if that was the case then she and the girls would check into their motel room and make the trek back home in the morning.

It was just before noon, and she didn't see anyone around. A large barn stood not too far in the distance, along with several other outbuildings. Maybe everyone had knocked off work for the lunch hour or were out in the pasture where she couldn't see them.

As she reached the porch, she gave one last look at the car and reminded herself that she was doing this for the little girls asleep there. With one hand on the butt of the gun in her pocket, she used the other hand to knock on the door.

When the door opened, Grace's breath caught in the back of her throat. She stared at the man who was the father of her daughters.

She'd forgotten just how hot he was with his curly black hair and chiseled features. The last time she'd seen him he'd been wearing a dark suit and white dress shirt. He now wore a pair of tight, faded blue jeans that showcased his slim hips and a white T-shirt that stretched across his broad shoulders.

A coil of heat began to unfurl in the pit of her stomach. It stopped as she saw the utter blankness in his dark blue eyes. Instead of the heat, a cold wind of embarrassment blew through her. He didn't even remember her.

"Yes?" he asked with the pleasant smile of somebody greeting a stranger.

She was struck by a new attack of nerves. "Wait here," she said and turned and left the large porch.

She hurried toward the car, her heart pounding a million miles a minute.

She was a third-grade teacher. Maybe the best way to let him know what had happened since the last time she'd seen him was a little show-and-tell. She opened the trunk with the press of a button on her key chain and quickly withdrew the oversize stroller.

It took her only moments to unfold the stroller and fill the seats with sleeping little girls and a diaper bag. As she pushed the girls toward the house, she saw his expression transform from pleasant to utterly stunned.

"Let me jog your memory," she said when she reached the porch again. "Nineteen months ago, Sally and David's wedding? My name is Grace… Grace Sinclair. We were together at the wedding and the next morning you left me with a surprise. I'd like you to meet your daughters."

"Maybe you should come inside where we can talk," he said, his eyes dark and troubled. "I'm afraid you've made a mistake. I'm not the man you're looking for. I've never seen you before in my life."

Jake Johnson instantly knew he'd said the wrong thing. Her pretty cheeks filled with color as her green eyes narrowed dangerously. "The last thing I expected from you was a denial of even meeting me," she replied, her voice icy with an edge of contempt. "Surely you remember being at the wedding."

"Please, come inside where we can talk more

comfortably." Jake grabbed one end of the stroller to pull it up the stairs and into the house. As he gazed at the sleeping girls, there was no doubt in his mind that they were Johnsons. Their little heads were covered with dark curly hair and the shape of their faces reminded him of baby photos he'd seen of himself.

And there was no doubt in his mind of exactly who was responsible for this woman being on his porch with three babies. His stomach knotted with a touch of anger. This was one mess that wasn't going to just go away. Jake wouldn't be able to pay a ticket, take care of a fine or do some fast talking to make this one disappear.

Once they had the stroller inside the living room, he gestured her to the sofa. As she lowered herself down, he sat in the overstuffed chair opposite her.

He couldn't help but notice that Grace Sinclair was a gorgeous woman. Her long brown hair held shiny blond highlights, and her legs seemed to go on forever beneath the navy slacks she wore. At the moment her beautiful green eyes were filled with anger, and her lush lips were compressed tightly together as she glared at him.

"I didn't exactly think you'd jump for joy at the unexpected news that you were a father, especially a father of three," she said. "I know it was only one night, but we were together for a long time at the reception."

"I should explain that…." he began.

"Of course, maybe you make it a habit of sleeping

with lots of women and don't always remember them when you meet them again out of a bed," she continued, cutting him off midsentence. "Allow me to remind you again—Sally's wedding in Wichita?"

"I wasn't—"

"Look, if you're worried that I want something from you, that I might need anything from you, then don't. I just thought you had a right to know that you are a father."

"I'm not saying that—"

"I'll gladly have a DNA test done if that's what you want." She sat up straighter on the sofa and tucked a strand of her shiny hair behind her ear. "I know for sure that you're the father because I hadn't been with anyone for a long time before you and I wasn't with anyone after you. But I would understand if you have doubts considering the circumstances."

Once again her cheeks became a charming shade of red. "You don't really know me. You don't know what kind of a woman I am, and I can understand how the fact that I fell into bed with you so easily that night might make you think I do that all the time—which couldn't be further from the truth. I've never done anything like that before. My only excuse is that night for the first time in my life, I drank too much."

Jake didn't even try to say anything. He sensed she wasn't finished yet, and in any case wouldn't let him get a word in edgewise. The anger he'd felt moments before had passed, and instead a weary resignation had set in.

It was obvious what had happened—a wedding party, a night of too much booze and unprotected sex. Now somebody was going to have to step up and do the right thing. Jake knew for certain it wasn't going to be him.

Sometimes he felt as if he'd spent every day of his thirty-five years doing what was right for everyone else. Now it was his turn to do what was right for him, and there was no way he intended to get caught up in this drama.

Yet, even as he thought it, he knew there was no way he wouldn't be sucked into the mess. The precious little girls asleep in the stroller would ensure that he became a part of it in some way.

"I don't need any child support from you. I just thought you might want to be a dad to the girls. Girls need fathers in their lives."

There was a wealth of emotion in her voice, then she finally took a breath and stared at him expectantly. At that moment Jake's brother appeared in the doorway between the living room and the kitchen.

Grace's mouth formed a perfect O as she looked from one man to the other. Just then one of the little girls woke up with a cry, as if protesting the fact that her mother had no idea when it came to the question of who was the daddy.

Chapter 2

Grace looked from one man to the other, astonished as she realized they were obviously identical twins. No wonder the man seated across from her had insisted he didn't know her. He *didn't* know her.

She dug Abby's sippy cup out of the diaper bag and handed it to her, an action that immediately stopped Abby's tears and brought a happy smile to her face. Twins, for crying out loud. How was she supposed to know that the man she'd slept with had a twin?

At that moment a woman appeared behind the man in the doorway. She was a plump, pretty blonde. She placed a hand on his shoulder. "Honey, what's going on?" she asked. She took one look at the stroller and clapped her hands together. “Oh my goodness, aren’t they precious?”

Grace’s heart sank to the ground. If the man seated on the chair opposite her wasn’t the girls’ father, then the man in the doorway must be. A look at his hand showed her he was wearing a gold wedding ring that matched the one on the woman’s finger.

Married. Oh, God, had he been married on the night they’d slept together? Had he ditched his wedding band for a quick fling while out of town? The very idea horrified her. The last thing Grace would ever do was get involved in any way with a married man.

“I think maybe introductions are in order,” the man in the chair said. “I’m Jake Johnson, and that’s my brother Jeffrey and his wife, Kerri.”

“I’m so sorry. I’ve obviously made some sort of mistake,” Grace said as she rose to her feet. Jeffrey… Justin…maybe she’d gotten his name wrong at the wedding. Certainly coming here had been a terrible mistake.

She didn’t want to screw up a marriage. This had suddenly become an awful nightmare and all she wanted to do was escape from it all. “I’ll just take the girls and we’ll be on our way.”

“Grace—may I call you Grace?” Jake asked. She nodded and he motioned her back to the sofa. “Please sit down. Jeffrey isn’t the father of your daughters either.”

“Heavens, no!” Jeffrey replied. “I’d eventually like

to have children, but I definitely want to do that with my wife." He looped an arm around Kerri's shoulder and smiled at her lovingly.

"I think you're looking for our brother," Jake said.

"There's more of you?" Grace felt as if she'd entered either a comedy of errors or the Twilight Zone.

Jake gave her a tight smile. "One more. Justin. We're triplets."

Grace breathed a sigh of relief, although she was more than a little embarrassed that she'd just given Jake Johnson far more personal information than she'd ever want him to know. "Is Justin here?"

"He isn't," Jake replied.

"But he almost always shows up around dinnertime," Kerri said as she approached the stroller. "May I?" She gestured to Abby, who raised her hands to get out of her confinement.

Grace nodded and checked her wristwatch. It was just after noon. "Could you contact Justin and see if maybe he could come by earlier? Otherwise I'll just take the girls to the motel room where I'd planned to stay for the night and he can contact me there."

"Nonsense," Kerri said briskly. "I've got lunch ready and of course you and the girls will stay and eat with us." She laughed as Abby grabbed her nose with a giggle.

"I don't want to impose," Grace protested. The whole thing felt awkward. At that moment the other two girls woke up and suddenly chaos reigned.

"We definitely need introductions to these sweet

girls," Kerri said as her husband pulled Bonnie from the stroller and Grace got Casey.

"You have Abby, Jeffrey has Bonnie and I have Casey," Grace said. Each of the girls grinned as they heard their names. "And as you can see, they haven't met anyone they don't like yet. Although Casey here is definitely the most shy." She frowned. "Maybe it would be best if I just go to the motel and you can tell Justin to meet me there."

"You're here now," Jake said rather curtly. "You might as well stay for lunch and I'll see if I can get Justin on his cell phone." As he left the room Grace felt some of the tension that had coiled in her belly ease. At least Jeffrey hadn't been in the room when she'd told Jake that she'd been nothing more than a drunken one-night stand with Justin. Gosh, how utterly embarrassing.

"Jeffrey, why don't you go out to the shed and bring in the old high chairs," Kerri said, obviously a woman accustomed to being in command. "And while you do that, Grace and I will go into the kitchen and get to know each other a little better."

"Sounds like a plan," Jeffrey replied agreeably. He set Bonnie on her bottom at his feet and headed toward the door.

Grace felt as if everything was quickly spinning out of control and she didn't quite know how to get any control back. At that moment Jake returned to the room. "Justin didn't answer, but I left him a message to come here as soon as he can," he said.

"We were just about to take the girls into the kitchen," Kerri said. "But we seem to be short one pair of hands."

"The story of my life," Grace muttered beneath her breath.

Jake bent down and picked up Bonnie. He carried her away from his body, as if he'd never carried a baby before and wasn't sure he liked it. At that moment Grace decided she wasn't at all sure she liked him very much.

The kitchen was enormous, filled with sunshine from the floor-to-ceiling windows that created one wall. A heavy wooden table big enough to comfortably seat eight held place settings for three and a steaming casserole dish that smelled of chicken.

"Let's put the girls here on the floor," Kerri said. "I'll get them some plastic containers to occupy them while I finish getting lunch on the table and you and I can have a nice chat." She smiled at Grace, a friendly gesture that took some of the sharp edge off Grace's tension.

At least Natalie had been wrong about the person living here being a fifty-year-old pervert. "Where did Jeffrey go?" Jake asked as he gingerly set Bonnie on the red-and-white throw rug on the floor.

"I told him to see about the old high chairs in the shed," Kerri replied.

"I'll go see if he needs help." He escaped out the back door, taking with him much of the energy in the room.

Within minutes the girls were all on the rug with a variety of plastic spoons, bowls and lids to keep them happy. Grace sat at the table while Kerri bustled around the kitchen to finish preparing the meal and laid another place setting.

"How on earth do you tell them apart?" Kerri asked as she placed bread and butter on the table.

"Even though at first glance they look identical, there are subtle differences. Bonnie wrinkles her nose when she laughs and Casey's hair is just a shade lighter. To make it easier on everyone else, I just dress them in different colors. Abby is pink, Bonnie is blue and Casey is yellow."

"It's the same with Jake, Jeffrey and Justin," Kerri said. "Most people insist they can't tell them apart, but there are definite differences. Jake is definitely the alpha dog and his eyes are slightly darker than his brothers. My Jeffrey is thinner than the other two and sweeter tempered." Her voice held a wealth of love. "And you know Justin."

That was the whole problem. Grace didn't *know* Justin at all. She was ashamed to admit that she barely remembered being intimate with him. What she did remember from that night was how good the champagne had tasted and how Justin made sure her glass remained full and his flirting attention remained solely on her. "Do you all live here?" she asked.

Kerri placed a large salad on the table and then eased down in the chair next to Grace. "This was the family homestead but their parents died twelve years ago when they were all twenty-two. Jake took over running the ranch."

She laughed. "But that's not what you asked. To answer your question, Justin lives in an apartment in Cameron Creek and Jeffrey and I are only living here for another couple of weeks or so. We have a house being built on the property. And once we get moved in I want one of those." She pointed to the girls, who were gibbering and playing, perfectly content at the moment.

"Be careful what you wish for," Grace said with a smile. "I always wanted a son or a daughter. Apparently that triplet gene is strong, and despite how well they're doing now, they don't always stay all in the same place."

At that moment Jeffrey and Jake returned, carrying high chairs that looked as if they were from another era. "They're old," Jeffrey said, "but we cleaned them up and they will still serve their purpose. Thank goodness that old shed hasn't been cleaned out in years."

"Perfect timing," Kerri said as she jumped up from the table.

She helped Grace get the girls settled in the high chairs and then they all sat down to eat. The little girls had bowls with a bit of the casserole and green beans. Grace had retrieved their cups from the diaper bag and they dug into their meal with their usual enthusiasm.

"You didn't mention where you're from," Jake said as he passed her the bowl of green beans.

There was something about the directness of his gaze that she found more than a bit unsettling. Kerri was right. Now that Grace had spent a little time with him she couldn't imagine how she'd initially thought he was the man who had fathered her girls.

The cowboy she'd met at the wedding had been fun and flirty, with a bit of wildness in his blue eyes. Jake looked harder, his eyes a midnight-blue. He definitely looked as if he'd never lose control enough to drink too much, let alone wind up in a bed with a woman he barely knew.

"Wichita," she replied.

"Nice place," Jeffrey said as he buttered a slice of bread. "What do you do there?"

"I'm a third-grade teacher."

Grace was grateful when the conversation changed from her to the ranch and the work being completed on Jeffrey and Kerri's house. As the meal and talk progressed it became evident to Grace that Bonnie was flirting with Jake.

Her high chair was next to his chair at the table, and she fluttered her long, thick eyelashes as she cast him one toothy grin after another. He didn't pay attention until she managed to grab his arm, grin and offer him a slightly smooshed green bean.

Kerri laughed. "Looks as though you have a little admirer, Jake."

He eyed the green bean as if it was something

he'd never seen before in his life and was highly suspicious of where it might have come from. Bonnie gibbered to him and pressed the bean closer.

"Uh...thanks," he said as he finally took the bean from her and placed it gingerly on the edge of his plate.

Bonnie clapped her hands together in happiness, her button nose wrinkling as she smiled, then fluttered her eyes, making her long dark lashes dance.

Jake focused back on his plate and Grace was thankful he wasn't the father. He obviously had no interest in children and didn't appear to have any softness inside him. She definitely wanted more than somebody like him to be a part of her girls' lives.

She wanted a man who would be unable to resist the flutter of Bonnie's lashes, the sweetness of Casey's smiles and Abby's infectious giggles. She wanted a man who would be unable to resist loving them with all his heart.

The food was good and the conversation was light and easy with Kerri filling most of the awkward silences with friendly chatter. Still, Grace decided if Justin hadn't shown up by the time lunch was over and she helped with the cleanup, she'd go on to the motel and get settled in there for the night.

She'd intruded enough on these people. Granted they were Abby, Bonnie and Casey's aunt and uncles, but there was no way to know what part they'd play in each other's lives until she spoke to Justin.

In the best of worlds, no matter what happened

with Justin, these people would want to stay involved with the little girls. But Grace was realistic enough to know that life didn't always work that way. In fact, in her experience life rarely worked out the way it was supposed to.

The meal was just about finished when Grace's cell phone rang. It was in the opposite pocket from the gun in her blazer. She recognized the number of the caller and excused herself from the table.

"Natalie," she said as she answered. "I'm so sorry. I forgot to call when I got here."

"So, what's happening? Are you at the right place? Is he wearing a dirty undershirt and tighty whities?"

Grace laughed. "Yes and no. Yes, I'm at the right place, but I'm still waiting to meet with Justin." She quickly explained about the men being triplets and that she was waiting for the father of the girls to show up at the house. Promising to stay in touch, she ended the call and hurried back into the kitchen.

"I'm so sorry," she said to the others still seated at the table. "That was my younger sister. I'd promised to call her the minute I arrived here and then promptly forgot to do so. She was worried."

"You only have the one sister?" Kerri asked.

Grace sat back down in her chair. "Thankfully yes," she said with a touch of humor. "Natalie is twenty-four, almost ten years younger than me, and some days it feels like I have four children instead of three."

"What about your parents?" Jeffrey asked.

"We were raised by a single mother and she passed away nine months ago," Grace replied. She was acutely aware of Jake's gaze on her. Dark and unreadable, the intensity made her slightly uncomfortable.

"Jake, what's up?" A familiar deep male voice called from the living room.

Grace's stomach clenched tight as she realized Justin had arrived. Certainly the friendliness toward her and the children by the people around the table had given her hope, and that hope now surged up inside her.

She wasn't expecting instant happiness from Justin, but what she was hoping for was some sort of acceptance of the situation and the happiness would come later.

He came into the kitchen. In that first instant of seeing Justin again, Grace couldn't imagine how she'd mistaken Jake for him. Justin looked younger and his hair was longer and slightly wild with curls.

His blue eyes widened at the sight of her, and then he looked at the three girls in the high chairs. "Oh, hell no!" he exclaimed and then turned and ran out of the kitchen.

Jake watched Grace's lovely face pale as she jumped up from her chair. "Please excuse me," she said, her voice trembling as she left the kitchen, obviously in pursuit of Justin.

There was a long moment of silence around the table.

"Mama?" Bonnie said, but didn't seem upset by Grace's absence.

"She seems really nice," Kerri said.

"Yeah, she does," Jake agreed reluctantly. Grace Sinclair was lovely and seemed nice and she was probably in for a world of hurt thanks to Justin.

"Hopefully Justin will step up." Jeffrey looked at the little girls still in their high chairs happily finishing their meals. "What a mess," he muttered under his breath.

What a mess, indeed. Jake's stomach knotted as he thought of the moment of realization on his brother's face and his ensuing race out of the kitchen.

He shouldn't be surprised. That's what Justin did best…make trouble and then run from whatever the consequences. Even though there was only a seventeen-minute difference in their ages, sometimes Jake felt as if his brother was seventeen years younger.

Jake had cleaned up plenty of Justin's problems in the past, but he wasn't running to the rescue this time. He couldn't. Justin was just going to have to suck it up and deal with the fact that he was now the father of three little girls.

"Maybe I should go check on her," Kerri said and started to get out of her chair.

"No, I'll go check. You stay here with the kids." Wearily Jake pulled himself out of his chair.

"Bye-bye," Bonnie said as Jake started toward the kitchen door.

For a moment he paused and stared at the three consequences of two adults' carelessness. It had to be difficult for a third-grade teacher to be single-handedly raising three babies. Hell, it would be difficult for any woman alone, no matter what her profession.

Despite her words to the contrary, Jake had no idea if Grace needed financial help or not. Surely just buying diapers and essentials for three little ones would be a hardship on a teacher's salary.

Girls need fathers in their lives. That's what she'd said to him when she'd thought he was the daddy. Jake didn't know what little girls needed, but he'd always believed that he and his brothers would have been better off with far less father in their lives.

"Bye-bye," Bonnie said again, snapping him out of his momentary reverie.

He muttered a goodbye and then left the kitchen. Time would tell exactly what Grace needed from Justin and how his brother would step up to provide what she needed, what the little girls needed.

He was halfway to the front door when he heard Grace shriek from outside. With a burst of adrenaline he raced out the door. His heart nearly stopped when he saw her crumpled on the ground by the porch steps.

"Grace!" He rushed to her side as she sat up, her face unnaturally pale as she grabbed her left arm with her right. He glanced around but didn't see Justin, and his truck was gone.

"What happened?" he asked as he reached a hand out to help her up off the ground.

"It was stupid. I missed the step and fell." She winced as she got to her feet.

"What hurts?" he asked.

"I hit my shoulder." Her face was still bleached white even though she attempted a smile. "I'm sure it's fine." As she tried to drop it to her side she hissed in obvious pain and pulled it back up again.

"That doesn't look fine," Jake replied with a scowl.

"I'm sure I'll be okay. I just need to collect the girls and we'll all be on our way." They started up the stairs to the front door.

"I guess it didn't go so great with Justin?" he asked even though he knew the answer.

She shot him a glance and he was surprised to see tears brimming in her eyes. She quickly looked away, as if embarrassed. "He basically just screamed that I'd ruined his life and then got into his truck and peeled off down the road. Yes, I think it's safe to say that things didn't go so great."

"He doesn't handle surprises very well," Jake said as he opened the door for her. He cursed his natural impulse to make excuses for Justin. "I'm sure once he calms down he'll be more reasonable." At least that's what Jake hoped would happen. But he figured

Justin had probably done what he always did when he got upset—headed directly to Tony's Tavern.

Grace slid through the door in front of him. "Once he *calms down and is more reasonable* he can call me or find me in Wichita. As soon as I pack up the girls, we'll be on our way back home."

He didn't try to change her mind. Maybe the best thing would be for her to head home and give him an opportunity to talk some sense into his brother.

This wasn't a speeding ticket that could be taken care of with the writing of a check. This wasn't a drunk and disorderly charge where Jake could talk the sheriff into not locking Justin up in jail for the night.

"Everything all right?" Kerri asked worriedly as they reentered the kitchen.

"Fine," Grace replied. "I want to thank you all for your wonderful hospitality, but it's time the girls and I get back on the road. If I leave now I'll be able to get home to Wichita before dark."

"Are you sure you wouldn't rather spend the night here and get a fresh start in the morning?" Kerri asked as she got up from the table. "We certainly have plenty of room."

Jake watched Grace, who shook her head negatively. "Thanks for the offer, but I'd rather just get back home," she said.

Her cheeks hadn't regained any color. He didn't know if the paleness had to do with the situation or if it was the pain from her fall.

His question was answered the minute she tried to get Abby out of the high chair. Grace started to lift the child, but immediately cried out and grabbed her left shoulder instead.

"What happened?" Jeffrey asked as he jumped out of his chair and hurried to Grace's side.

"I took a little tumble in the yard." Her voice was filled with pain.

"Justin didn't push you, did he?" Kerri asked, a touch of outrage in her voice. Jake looked at Kerri in surprise. As far as he knew his brother had never laid a finger on any woman, but of course he'd never found out he was the father of triplets before either.

"No, nothing like that," Grace replied hurriedly. "I just missed a step, stumbled and went down."

"We need to get you to the hospital and have that shoulder looked at," Jake said, deciding somebody had to take control of the situation. There was no way he could let her leave knowing she couldn't lift the little girls. It wouldn't even be safe for her to drive her car.

He expected Grace to protest. Instead, after a moment of hesitation, she nodded, which let him know that it had to be hurting her quite a bit.

"Maybe you're right. It's really painful." Still she made no move. She gazed at her three daughters, who were happily smooshing and playing and eating what was left on their plates.

"Then let's go." Jake dug his truck keys out of his

pocket. "The girls will be fine here with Kerri and Jeffrey."

"Absolutely," Kerri replied with a reassuring smile. "It will be good practice for us."

"I promise you, they'll be fine," Jake said to Grace. She held his gaze, as if trying to peer inside him to see if she could trust him. "Come on," he said with a touch of impatience. "You can decide what you want to do about heading home after the doctor takes a look at you."

He could tell she was reluctant to go, but it was obvious she was in a fair amount of pain. She was going to the hospital if he had to throw her over his shoulder and carry her there.

They didn't speak as she followed him out of the house and they got into his truck.

A new surge of irritation filled him. He shouldn't be the one taking her to the hospital. It should have been Justin. His brother should be the one taking care of the mother of his children, no matter what the circumstances.

"I'm so sorry," she finally said as he pulled out of the drive and onto the main road that would take them to Cameron Creek.

"Don't apologize. You didn't fall on purpose," he replied. He could smell her, the scent of a bouquet of wildflowers that was far too appealing.

"True, but the last thing I wanted was to be any kind of a bother to anyone." She leaned back against the seat. For a moment she looked so achingly vulnerable Jake wanted to reach out and touch her, assure her somehow that everything was going to be fine.

Instead he clenched the steering wheel more tightly. "Look, I know Justin behaved badly. But I meant it when I said once he's had time to digest everything I'm sure the two of you will be able to work something out."

"All I really wanted was for him to know about them and maybe spend some time with the girls, be a positive role model in their lives." She shifted positions and hissed in a breath, as if any kind of upper body movement caused her pain.

"You must have hit the ground pretty hard."

"I did. I have a gun in my pocket, and even though the safety was on, as I was falling I was afraid I'd hit the ground so hard it would pop off and somehow I'd shoot myself, so I twisted to make sure my shoulder and not my side took the brunt of the fall."

"A gun?" He looked at her in stunned surprise. She definitely didn't look like the gun-toting type. "Why on earth would you have a gun in your pocket?"

"I didn't know what kind of people you were. I wasn't even sure I'd find Justin here. I wasn't about to drive into a place where I'd never been before without some sort of protection for me and my girls. Besides, I got your address from a cyberfriend and my sister was afraid I might wind up at the home of some pervert sitting around in his underwear and stalking women over the internet."

"I'm definitely not a pervert, but if Jeffrey and Kerri weren't living with me, there might be times I'd sit around in my underwear," he replied with a wry grin.

He felt himself relaxing a bit, some of his irritation passing. None of this was her fault, and he'd be a jerk to punish her for his brother's actions or inactions.

He was rewarded with her smile, and her beauty with that gesture warming her features struck him square in the gut. He quickly focused his attention back on the road.

Okay, he could admit it to himself, he felt a little burn of physical attraction for Grace Sinclair. He shouldn't be surprised. She was a beautiful woman, and it had been over a year since Jake and the woman he'd been seeing for almost six months had called it quits. Just because Grace attracted him didn't mean there was a chance in hell that he'd follow through on it.

She was Justin's issue, not his. And the very last thing Jake wanted in his life at this moment or at any time in the future was anyone who might need him. The last thing he needed was another issue to solve. He was totally burned out in that area.

He slowed his speed as they entered the city limits of Cameron Creek. Unlike a lot of the small towns in Oklahoma that were dying slow, painful deaths,

Cameron Creek was thriving and growing. There seemed to be no rhyme or reason for the anomaly other than the fact that the city council of Cameron Creek worked hard to make it a pleasant place to live. It also helped that on the south side of town was a large dog food factory that employed most of the people in the area.

"Hopefully I've just bruised it and it will be fine in an hour or two," she said as he parked in front of the attractive little hospital's emergency room entrance.

"You still have that gun in your pocket?" he asked as he shut off the engine. She nodded. She used her right hand to reach in her left pocket and pulled out the revolver. "It would probably be best if you didn't carry it into the emergency room. Do you mind if I lock it in the glove box?"

"You promise me you aren't a pervert?" she asked with a touch of teasing in her voice.

An unexpected burst of laughter escaped him. "I promise," he said as she offered him the gun. With it safely locked inside the glove box, they left the truck and headed through the emergency entrance.

Thankfully there was nobody in the waiting room and Grace was immediately whisked away to be seen by the doctor. Jake lowered himself into one of the waiting room chairs and tried to tamp down his aggravation with his brother.

There were times Jake dreamed of selling the ranch and leaving Oklahoma. There were days the thought of being on a deserted island all alone was infinitely appealing. But the vision was only appealing for a minute. He loved the ranch and would probably never leave.

Still, he'd thought that once he survived his childhood years life would get easier, but the death of his parents hadn't changed anything. His responsibilities had only gotten heavier.

He was tired, and the only thing he wanted now was for the doctor to fix up Grace so she could be on her way home. He'd encourage his brother to do the right thing and then Jake would wash his hands of the whole mess.

He wouldn't mind spending a little time with his nieces, eventually. But before that could happen Justin and Grace were going to have to figure things out. And that had nothing to do with him.

He'd spent most of his life shouldering responsibilities to make life easier on everyone else around him. Now what he wanted more than anything was just to be left alone.

It was almost an hour later that Dr. Wallington came out to greet him. Jake stood and shook the older man's hand. Dr. Wallington had been their family doctor for years.

"Grace wanted me to come out and let you know she's fine. X-rays showed no break, although her shoulder is severely sprained. I'm putting her in a sling to immobilize it for a couple of days and I've given her some pain medication. In the meantime she shouldn't do any driving or lifting and I've told her if it isn't better in three or four days she should come back in."

Jake smiled, nodded and thanked the doctor while inwardly cringing at the news. There was no way he could put Grace in her car with three babies to return home. She was going to need help, and plenty of it.

A weary resignation rose up inside him. All he'd wanted from life was a little peace and quiet, but any hope for that flew out the window. His life was about to be turned upside down with the invasion of three little girls and a woman who disturbed him in a way no woman ever had before.

Chapter 3

"Stupid, stupid, stupid," Grace muttered to herself as she waited for the nurse to return to the room to fit her with a sling. She'd been stupid to chase out of the house after Justin, and even more stupid to be so angry she'd managed to miss the first porch step and fall on her shoulder.

Now she was in a mess. The doctor had said she couldn't drive and she couldn't lift. How was she going to manage? The last thing she wanted to do was to ignore the doctor's advice and exacerbate the injury.

Tears suddenly burned at her eyes. This whole trip had been a nightmare. She'd been stupid to believe that there was a possibility of a happy ending for her babies, that she'd somehow walk away from here with a loving, caring man committed to being an integral part of their lives.

In her very first encounter with Justin she'd thought he was charming and hot, but now she realized he was just an immature hothead.

She wanted to give him the benefit of the doubt. She wanted to believe that once the initial shock of the whole situation wore off, he'd step up and be a man. Be the father she wanted for her girls. But her first impression of him had definitely been a bad one.

In the meantime, she was going to have to leave this examining room and ask Jake, with his dark blue eyes and that edge of aloofness about him, if she could stay at his place for a couple of days until her shoulder healed enough that she could make it back home.

There was no way she could take the chance of trying to drive home alone, no way once she got there that she could take care of the girls. She certainly couldn't depend on Natalie. Her sister might be good for an hour or two of help here and there, but not the kind of care it would take for the next couple of days.

She'd have to depend on the kindness of virtual strangers and she hated that. The tears threatened to fall and she wasn't sure if they were caused by her situation, by Justin's reaction or the pain that radiated down her arm from her injured shoulder. She quickly swallowed against the tears as the nurse reappeared in the room.

Within minutes her arm was immobilized, and

she'd called Natalie to let her know what was going on. Afterward she walked into the waiting room where Jake stood staring out the window. For a moment she didn't make a sound, just stared at his broad back.

He looked so solid. For a fleeting moment she wished he would have been the handsome cowboy at the wedding that night. It was a ridiculous thought. She knew no more about Jake than she did about his brother Justin. But what little she did know led her to believe that Jake would never find himself out of control, drunk in bed with a stranger. And he would have never torn out of a driveway after screaming to some woman that she'd ruined his life.

He whirled around as if he'd heard her thoughts, and he couldn't quite hide the scowl that had apparently ridden his features before he'd turned.

"Ah, there you are," he said smoothly as he approached her. "It looks as if you're going to be our houseguest for a few days. I've already called Jeff and Kerri to get things arranged at the house."

"I'm sure after a good night's rest I'll be fine to go home in the morning," she said as they left the hospital and walked outside.

"We'll see in the morning." He didn't sound too sure about her being capable of leaving that soon.

"I'm so sorry about this," she said when they were both back in his truck.

"You really have to stop apologizing." He smiled then and unexpected warmth fluttered in her chest.

He had such a nice smile. "Accidents happen, Grace. We're all just going to have to figure out how to make the best of things."

"That's what I was trying to do by coming here. I'd hoped to take a difficult situation and somehow make it work in the best interests of my daughters." She paused for a long moment, and then continued, "I was a fool to come here." A touch of bitterness laced her voice.

"I'm hoping by tomorrow you and Justin will be able to sit down together and work things through."

"If today was any indication of the way one works things through with Justin then I don't think my body can take it," she replied drily.

He shot her a quick glance. "We'll just have to make sure you stay on your feet tomorrow."

"Tell me about him," she said. "What does Justin do for a living?"

Jake hesitated a minute. "He works for me at the ranch part-time."

That didn't sound great. She wondered what he did with his other time. "I'm assuming he isn't married. Does he have a girlfriend?"

Jake shot her a tight smile. "Justin dates a lot, although he's been seeing Shirley Caldwell for the last couple of months. She works as a waitress at a café in Cameron Creek."

"I really don't want to make any trouble for him." Grace frowned and tried to focus on the conversation instead of the excruciating pain that racked her arm each time she moved. Surely by morning it would be okay and she could get home.

"Let's just get you back to the ranch and settled in and we'll sort the rest of it out later."

They both fell silent for the remainder of the ride. What she'd wanted to ask him about his brother was if Justin was trustworthy and kind. Was he a good man who would make a good role model for his daughters? She didn't want to judge him based on their initial interaction earlier that day. She hoped Jake was right, that Justin's actions upon seeing her and the girls weren't indicative of who he was as a man, and once the shock wore off things would be fine.

For now there was nothing she could do but rest her arm and hope that by the morning she could get back home. What she wanted more than anything was to get back to the Johnson ranch and make sure her girls were okay.

She shot a quick glance at Jake and once again couldn't imagine how she'd mistaken him for his brother. Although their features were basically the same, Jake's looked stronger, as if forged by a different metal than his brothers. Jake looked older and radiated a quiet confidence she found oddly sexy.

She moved her arm, welcoming the pain to banish any crazy thoughts about Jake that might enter her head. She released an exhausted sigh of relief as they pulled up in front of the house.

Kerri met them at the door. "You poor woman,"

she said to Grace. "Don't you worry about a thing. We're going to take good care of you and the babies until you're well enough to go home. I've got one of the guest rooms all ready for you, and Jeffrey got the old cribs out of the attic and has them set up in the room next to ours," Kerri continued as she led Grace into the kitchen.

"I hate being such an imposition," Grace said as she entered the kitchen to see the triplets once again playing on the floor with an array of plastic bowls and lids in front of them. The girls all smiled at the sight of their mother and continued playing as Grace sank down in one of the chairs at the table.

Thankfully the girls were used to being without Grace for hours in the day as she took them to day care while she worked. They were usually happy wherever they were as long as they were together.

Jeffrey and Jake came into the kitchen. Jeffrey sat at the table while Jake stood with his back against the counter, his gaze dark and enigmatic as he looked first at the children and then at Grace.

She could only imagine what was going on in his mind. He'd been invaded by unwanted children, by an unwanted woman. Was it any wonder he appeared rather grim?

"Don't look so worried," Kerri said to Grace. "We'll get them taken care of and all you need to be concerned with is getting that shoulder well."

Grace smiled at the woman gratefully. She certainly wouldn't be feeling as comfortable about things without Kerri here.

"Now, I'm going to make dinner," Kerri said.

"And you should take one of those pain pills the doctor gave you," Jake said to Grace.

She shook her head. "I'm fine. I really don't like to take pain pills. They make me groggy."

Jake pushed off the counter. "I'm heading out to the barn."

"Dinner in an hour," Kerri said.

He nodded and then left the kitchen. Once again Grace felt some of the tension ease out of her body. There was no question about it, something about Jake Johnson put her on edge. She felt a vague sense of disapproval wafting from him. Could she really blame him? For all he knew she was some kind of bimbo who made a habit of falling into bed with handsome cowboys.

He probably thought she was here for money despite her claims to the contrary. He had no reason to believe anything she'd told him.

They had a quiet dinner and then at about seven o'clock, with Jeffrey and Kerri's help, the girls were bathed, put into their pajamas and laid down in the cribs where they fell asleep almost immediately.

Jake had disappeared right after dinner, muttering that he was going into his office where he'd remained. With the girls asleep, Kerri showed Grace to the spare room and Jeffrey offered to bring in her suitcase and anything else she needed from her car.

The guest room was nice, decorated in shades of yellow and with a sliding glass door that led out to a small balcony. Grace stowed her things and by eight o'clock she, Kerri and Jeffrey sat in the living room. The television was on, but Grace's thoughts were far away from the drama unfolding on the screen.

In this single day her life had held enough drama to last her a lifetime. She was more than eager to get back to her home in Wichita, raise her daughters by herself and help her sister find her way through life.

Her shoulder throbbed with a pain that made any real depth of thought next to impossible. She'd already decided that before she went to sleep that night she'd take one of those pain pills the doctor had given her. Hopefully the girls would sleep through the night as they usually did and Grace would feel well enough to head home the next day.

They all turned as the front door opened. Grace's stomach clenched as Justin walked in. His eyes widened slightly as he saw the sling she wore. "What happened?"

"I fell and hurt my shoulder," she replied. She wasn't sure if she should be happy or angry to see him again.

He looked at Kerri and Jeffrey. "Do you mind? Can I talk to her alone?"

Kerri looked at Grace, who nodded slightly. "Come on, Jeffrey, let's go into the kitchen and have a piece of pie."

Grace looked back at Justin. He seemed calm and

contrite, although she thought she caught the scent of beer wafting from him.

"I'm sorry," he said once Kerri and Jeffrey had disappeared from the room. "About how I acted earlier. I was a real jerk and I truly do apologize."

She gave a curt nod, not exactly ready to accept his apology but at least willing to acknowledge it. He slid into the chair across from where she sat on the sofa.

"Man, what a freak-out." He released a sigh and raked a hand through his thick, dark hair. "So, how did you find me? I don't remember us exchanging too much personal information that night, although obviously we exchanged enough."

"Actually, I didn't find you. A friend of mine did." She quickly explained to him about MysteryMom.

"Wow, it just gets freakier," he exclaimed when she was finished. "So, I got three kids."

"Three daughters. Justin, I don't care about child support if that's what you're worried about. I just thought you should know about them. I thought maybe you'd want to be a part of their lives." Her heart hurt in her chest as she watched his expression, as she clung to the belief that somehow, some way this man would step up.

"Can I see them?"

Her hope found a bit of purchase at this request, although she shook her head negatively. "They're sleeping right now. I really don't want them disturbed tonight. Unfortunately, with my shoulder injury I won't be going home for a day or two."

"Then why don't I plan on being here at ten in the morning and spend a little time with them." He stood from his chair. "And we can talk then about where things go from here."

The tentative hope blossomed and she offered him a smile. "I'd like that."

"Then I'll see you at ten tomorrow." He disappeared out the front door and Grace breathed a sigh of relief. Maybe everything was going to be okay after all.

She turned to see Jake standing in one of the doorways nearby, apparently the door that led into his private study. "You were right," she said. "He just needed some time to process it all, I guess." She smiled.

"I'm just heading up to my room so I'll say goodnight," he said.

"Good night, Jake, and thank you for everything. Justin is going to be here around ten tomorrow to get to know the girls, so it looks as though things are going to be just fine."

"Let's hope so," he said, his eyes once again dark and unreadable. There was something in his tone and in the darkness of his gaze that made Grace realize maybe she shouldn't get her hopes up too high.

It was ten-thirty the next morning and there was still no sign of Justin. Jake wasn't surprised. What did surprise him was the ping of compassion in his heart as he watched Grace standing at the front window looking outside.

She'd been there for the last twenty minutes, her demeanor slowly shifting from eager anticipation to unmistakable discouragement.

The girls were playing on a blanket on the living room floor, surrounded by toys and any other item in the house that Kerri thought they might enjoy and wouldn't hurt them. Kerri had helped get them up and out of bed, fed and dressed in cute little outfits he suspected had been specifically chosen to meet their daddy.

"You want a cup of coffee or something?" he finally asked.

Grace whirled around, green eyes wide. "Oh, I didn't know you were there. No thanks, I'm fine." She turned back to face the window. "He's apparently running late."

"Justin is one of those people who would be late to his own funeral." Jake wasn't sure he believed his brother would show up at all. Thank goodness the babies were young enough not to know that already they'd been let down by the man who had fathered them. The one man in the world they should be able to depend on. Jake feared it wouldn't be the last time.

"How's the shoulder this morning?" he asked.

Once again she turned from the window and this time took several steps away and sat in a nearby chair. "I think it's a little better," she replied, but as she tried to move it to show him how much better it was a spasm of pain crossed her features.

"I think maybe you just told me a little fib," he noted.

She hesitated a moment and then flashed him a quick smile. "Maybe," she admitted. "Actually, I think it's worse this morning than it was last night."

"That doesn't surprise me. I've always heard the second day of an injury is the worst." He should be outside, riding the ranch, checking fencing, doing a thousand chores that awaited his hands. But he'd been unable to leave her alone standing at the window waiting for a man who might not show up until evening.

What he shouldn't be doing was standing there admiring the play of sunshine in her hair, enjoying how her yellow T-shirt, which made her green eyes even more vivid, clung to her breasts.

She got up from the chair and returned to the window. "Surely he'll be here any minute now," she said softly.

He heard the hope in her voice, the same hope that he'd heard the night before, and it disturbed him. He didn't want her depending on Justin for anything. Jake would like to believe that for once in his life, for something so important, Justin would step up. But Jake had been burned too many times. He knew about the hope Grace felt, and he knew the bitter taste left behind when it faded away.

He stepped up to the window next to her and was

engulfed by the clean, sweet scent of her, a scent that instantly created a faint pleasant fire in the pit of his stomach.

But he'd also noticed the tiny fatigue lines that radiated from her eyes, the slender lines of her body that indicated a woman who had little time to eat or sleep. She probably wasn't taking care of herself the way she should. How could she with a full-time job and triplets to raise all alone?

"He's here!" she exclaimed at the same time Jake saw his brother's truck pull into the driveway. "Oh, it looks as if he's brought somebody with him."

As the truck drew closer to the door Jake could see that Justin had Shirley with him. Jake swallowed a string of curses. Why on earth would Justin bring with him the woman he was dating, a hot-tempered, overly jealous drama queen with big hair and bigger breasts?

Justin and Shirley both got out of the truck. Shirley was dressed in a bright pink blouse, a pair of short shorts that exposed overly tanned legs and overly steep, sparkly high heels.

The two of them spoke for a moment and then Shirley got back into the truck and Justin headed for the front door. Jake was grateful his brother at least had the sense to leave Shirley cooling her heels outside. Although the odds of Justin spending any quality time with the triplets weren't good.

Grace met Justin at the door and the bright smile

she gave him ached inside Jake; just below the heady scent of her he smelled disappointment in the air.

"Hey," Justin greeted her, not quite meeting her eyes. "Uh, something's come up and I really don't have time to hang around here today. I was wondering if maybe we could set something up for tomorrow?" He glanced over his shoulder to the woman in the pickup who appeared to be glaring daggers at Grace.

"Justin, you know where I am. I'll be here probably through tomorrow, so let's just leave it loose and I'll see you when I see you," Grace replied, a faint weariness in her voice.

He gave her a grateful glance, never making eye contact with Jake. "Great, thanks. Then I guess I'll talk to you tomorrow." He turned and ran back toward the truck.

For a long moment Grace remained at the front door, and Jake dreaded seeing the depth of the disappointment in her lovely green eyes when she turned around. "So much for that," she said softly as she walked away from the door. She offered Jake a tentative smile. "I guess the good news is his girlfriend didn't get out of the truck and try to beat me up." She touched the sling on her arm. "I'm not exactly on top of my game right now."

The thought of the elegant Grace involved in a girl fight was so ludicrous a small burst of laughter escaped Jake's lips. It surprised him. He couldn't remember the last time he'd actually laughed out loud.

Unfortunately the laughter lasted only a moment and then they faced each other awkwardly. "I've got work outside to do," he said, realizing that he'd once again been admiring the shine of her hair in the sunlight, vaguely wondering if it would feel as silky as it looked.

"And I should check with Kerri to see if I can help with lunch." She stepped aside so he could go out the door.

As he headed for the barn he carried with him a vague irritation at Justin and a faint simmer of something quite different for Grace. Both emotions were equally unwanted.

Despite the fact that she'd obviously gone through the pregnancy and the first ten months of the triplets' lives pretty much on her own, there was a soft vulnerability about her that called to that old, familiar protective instinct in him, a protective instinct he'd been trying to banish for the past year.

He knew the ranch hands he employed would be out in the fields. But at least once a day Jake headed out on horseback to check the livestock and just enjoy the fresh air and alone time.

Alone time. Jake didn't feel as though he'd been truly alone since the moment of his conception. And it was what he longed for more than anything. As much as he loved Jeff and Kerri, he couldn't wait for their house to be finished and to have the house to himself. He just wanted the time to come when nobody needed anything from him ever again.

Still, as he saddled his horse his thoughts returned to Grace. Maybe things would have been easier if she was more like Justin's usual women. Justin's normal types were tough, life-weary women who knew the score where he was concerned. They knew how to fight for what they wanted and they didn't always fight fair. They also knew to expect nothing from Justin and that's usually what they ended up with where he was concerned.

Grace had a quiet elegance about her. She worked as a schoolteacher, and he'd believed her when she'd told him she wasn't the type to fall into bed easily with any man.

Minutes later he was racing across the pasture, shoving thoughts of the beautiful brown-haired woman out of his head. When his parents had died and left this large ranch to the three young men, Jake knew it would never work with three cooks and no chef.

He knew that Jeffrey had never wanted to be a rancher. He preferred working with numbers, loved being an accountant and had no desire to have anything to do with the ranch except help keep the books.

Justin didn't have the work ethic necessary to keep it a successful, functioning business and so Jake had offered to buy them both out. They'd banged out the details, worked with the bank and a lawyer and now the land was his, except for the plot where Jeffrey and Kerri were building their place.

Both Justin and Jeffrey got a payment each month from the profits the ranch made and would do so until their part of the inheritance was paid off.

He rode until just after noon and then headed back to the house for lunch. The three little girls were already in their high chairs, chattering and taking turns laughing as if enjoying each other's conversation.

"Are they always so happy?" he asked as he walked over to the sink to wash up.

"Pretty much all the time," Grace said. She was already seated at the table while Kerri stood at the stove stirring a big pot of vegetable soup. "The only time they're at all fussy is if they get overly tired."

"That's the only time I get fussy," Kerri said with a laugh. She began to ladle the soup into a large tureen.

Lunch was a quiet meal. Grace seemed pulled into herself, her gaze lingering often on her three daughters as they ate their finger food.

Jake tried not to notice the sadness that wafted from Grace, a sadness he knew his brother was responsible for. *Not my problem,* he reminded himself over and over again. But when lunch was finished and the girls were down for their naps, the sight of Grace sitting alone on the sofa in the living room made it impossible for him to just leave her there and disappear into his study.

"How about a walk outside for a little fresh air?" he said to her. "I'll show you around the place."

She glanced toward the stairs and then looked at

her watch. “Okay, that sounds good. The girls usually nap for about an hour and a half and they just went down.”

“I’ll let Kerri know we’re going out. She can keep an ear open for any of the girls waking up,” he said. It took him only a moment to alert Kerri of their intention, and then he and Grace stepped out on the porch into the midafternoon spring sunshine.

“Ever been on a ranch?” he asked.

“No, I’ve always been an urban girl,” she replied. “Although I sometimes take my class to a petting farm in Wichita for a field trip. Looks as though you have a lot of land.”

He nodded. “It’s almost six hundred acres. I use some of it for crops, but most of it is for cattle.”

“You run it all alone?”

They walked in the direction of the barn in the distance, the sun warm and the air spiced with the scents of flowers and pasture. “No, I’ve got several men who help out.”

“I haven’t seen anyone around.”

“They’re usually out in the fields by this time of the day. I’m sure if you’re here long enough you’ll eventually see them.”

“No offense, but I hope I’m not here that long,” she replied.

“Already tired of our company?” he said, half teasing.

“You all have been wonderful, but I came here with a specific purpose in mind and now that I’ve accomplished what I set out to do, I'm eager to get home."

And he wanted her gone, he reminded himself, although it was difficult to maintain that feeling when she looked so beautiful and smelled so good. "You didn't exactly accomplish what you wanted," he said.

A tiny frown danced in the center of her forehead. "Your brother is obviously not cut out to be much of a family man." She looked up at him. "What about you? You have a girlfriend with plans to marry and fill this big place with lots of children?"

"No," he replied firmly. "Never. I know it sounds crazy, but with my brothers I feel as if I've been parenting most of my life. Once Kerri and Jeffrey move out, I am looking forward to being alone. The last thing I want is the responsibility of a wife or kids." He realized he sounded harsh and he tempered his words with a smile. "But that doesn't mean I'm not ready to step up as an uncle."

"I appreciate that. I'd just hoped…" She allowed her voice to trail off.

Jake didn't know how to reply. He couldn't make his brother into the man she wanted him to be, although heaven knew he'd tried over the years to make him into some kind of a responsible man.

At that moment his cell phone rang. He pulled it from his pocket and realized it was a call he had to take and he needed to be in his study in order to refer to some documents. "I'll call you right back," he said to the man on the other end of the line.

"I'm sorry, I've got to get back inside," he said to Grace. "That was a business call I need to return. Shall we head back?"

"If you don't mind, I think I'll walk around a little bit longer. It feels good to be out here in the fresh air and sunshine."

Once again that protectiveness surged up inside him. She looked lost, and he knew the disappointment of the morning with Justin weighed heavily in her heart. He steeled his own heart against her. "Okay, then I'll just see you inside in a few minutes."

As he walked back toward the house, he fought the impulse to turn and get one more look at her. He told himself again he wasn't going to get sucked into this drama, that Justin and Grace were going to have to figure it all out on their own.

That protective streak Jake had in him had resulted in many a beating throughout his youth from their father, who had handed out corporal punishment for any infringement, slight or imagined. Jake had taken more than one beating for Justin, and he was determined to never take another on behalf of either of his brothers.

It took him nearly twenty minutes to take care of the business that needed attending. He was just leaving his study when he heard the unmistakable sound of a gunshot.

What the hell?

He raced to the front window and looked out, stunned to see Grace with her back pressed against the side of the barn. Another shot split the air and it was immediately obvious to him that somebody was shooting at her. The shots were coming from a thickly wooded area on the right of the property.

Jake's heart leapt in his throat as he raced back into his study and grabbed his gun from his desk drawer. Somebody was shooting at Grace. It didn't make sense. His mind couldn't wrap around it. As another shot exploded he only hoped he could get outside before whoever it was managed to kill her.

Chapter 4

Grace pressed against the rough wood of the side of the barn, terror clawing up her throat as another bullet splintered the wood precariously close to where she stood.

Her brain had stopped functioning when the first bullet had whizzed by her. If she hadn't heard the explosion of the gun she would have assumed the loud buzz was an annoying insect too close to her ear.

When she'd realized what was happening she'd slammed herself against the barn in an effort to make herself a more difficult target. If she could, she'd push herself right through the wood and into the barn itself.

Who was shooting at her and why? None of this made any sense. But there was nobody else around, no way to mistake that those bullets were intended for her.

She cursed her bright yellow T-shirt that made her an easy target as her eyes darted around frantically seeking some sort of a safe escape.

Her heart pounded so loudly in her ears she couldn't hear anything else. Why was this happening? What was going on? The sight of Jake barreling out of the front door with a gun in his hand forced a sob of relief to escape her lips.

He fired several shots into the woods where the original bullets had come from as he ran toward her. Jeffrey appeared on the porch with a rifle and he began to fire into the woods as well, providing cover for Jake as he approached where she stood.

Jake slammed against the barn next to her. "You all right?" he asked, his voice a terse snap of tension.

She gave a curt nod, unable to find her voice. Her terror had stolen it clean away from her.

"We're going to get you back into the house," he said, his eyes narrowed to dangerous-looking slits. There had been no more gunfire coming from the woods since he'd appeared.

"I'm afraid to move," she finally managed to reply.

"We need to move," he replied. "Did you see anyone?" he asked, not taking his gaze from the woods.

"No, I just felt the first bullet buzz by my head and I ran, but I didn't know where to run to." A tremble tried to take hold of her body but she fought against it, knowing she couldn't give in to her fear until she was safe and sound.

She certainly felt safer with Jake by her side and with Jeffrey on the front porch, but someplace out there was somebody who had apparently just tried to kill her not once, not twice, but three times.

There could be no other explanation for what had happened. Any one of those bullets could have hit her…killed her…and she wasn't safe yet. They still had to get from the barn back to the house.

Several men appeared on horseback, rifles pulled and faces grim. "The cavalry," Jake muttered beneath his breath.

One of the men pulled up in front of Grace and Jake, providing an effective barrier. "We heard gunfire," he said. He was a big man, with shoulders as wide as a mountain and a paunch belly to match, but his eyes were dark and dangerous as he gazed first at Grace then at Jake.

"It came from the woods over there. Maybe you and the boys can go check it out while I get Grace safely back into the house," Jake said.

The cowboy gave a nod of his head and then he and the other two took off riding toward the woods.

"Can you run?" Jake asked her.

"Not as fast as usual with my arm in this sling, but I'll do the best I can," she replied. She'd do whatever she could to get away from this barn and into the house.

Her babies. She needed to be with her babies. She

needed to kiss their plump cheeks, smell their baby sweetness and hug them tight.

"I'm going to wrap my arm around you," he said. "And then we're going to go as fast as we can to the house. Ready?"

He put his arm around her. For a moment she wanted to bury herself against him, to meld into the hard safety of his arms, to lose herself in his scent of sunshine and woodsy cologne.

"Ready," she murmured.

They took off and it was the most terrifying run Grace had ever experienced. With each step she expected a bullet to pierce through her back, to hit her body and slam her into the ground. And with each step her shoulder jarred, shooting pain through her and making her wonder if they'd ever reach the safety of the house.

All she could think about were her babies. If she died who would take care of them? Natalie certainly wasn't at a place in her life where she would be a fit parent. Justin definitely wasn't an option. Grace had to get back to the house safe and sound.

Jake used his bigger body as a shield. When they reached the porch and stumbled past Jeffrey and into the house, Grace wrapped her good arm around Jake's neck and clung to him as tears of fear and relief mingled together and finally erupted.

He remained stiff and unyielding for a long moment and then his arms went around her waist and he held her as tight as her slinged arm would allow.

"It's all right. You're okay now." His deep voice reached inside her and soothed some of the jagged fear that still spiked through her as one of his hands slid up and down her back in a soft caress.

She buried her face in the front of his T-shirt as the tears fell freely. Someplace in the very back of her mind she recognized she liked the way he smelled, she liked the feel of his strong body so close to hers.

She didn't cry for long, but after the tears had stopped she was reluctant to leave his embrace. He felt so solid, so capable, and she hadn't realized until this moment how desperately she'd hungered for a man's embrace. For just a moment to be able to lean on somebody, anybody other than herself.

As Jeffrey came through the front door, she reluctantly released her hold on Jake and stepped away from him. Kerri grabbed her by the arm and led her to the sofa. Grace sank down and allowed the shudder that had threatened earlier to work through her.

"What on earth is going on around here?" Kerri asked, obviously distraught as she moved from Grace to her husband's side.

Everyone looked at Grace. Her shoulder ached, her heart raced and she still couldn't wrap her mind around what had just happened. "I don't know. I was just walking, enjoying the fresh air and sunshine. I heard the gunshot at almost the same time I felt the whiz of a bullet go by my head."

She began to tremble, the motion causing her shoulder to ache more and bringing with it a headache that screamed across the back of her skull. "At first I didn't realize what was happening, but when I did, I didn't know what to do. So I pressed against the side of the barn and then it was as if I was pinned there. Whoever it was kept firing. I thought I was going to be killed." She was rambling, her mouth working almost faster than her brain.

"Call the sheriff," Jake said to Kerri, who immediately went into the kitchen to use the phone in there.

A knock at the door whirled Jake around, his gun still drawn. Grace felt her breath catch painfully in her chest in frightening anticipation of more trouble. She relaxed as the cowboy Jake had sent to the woods came through the door.

"Somebody was out there," he said in a deep, booming voice. "Looks like whoever it was had been there for a while. The grass was tamped down and a blanket of some sort had been spread out."

"A blanket?" Grace stared at him in horror. That implied somebody had been sitting out there just waiting for her to make an appearance, just waiting to put a bullet through her.

"The sheriff is on his way," Kerri said as she came back into the living room.

"By the way, Grace, this is Jimbo Watkins, my

ranch manager. Jimbo, this is Grace Sinclair, a visitor here on the ranch," Jake said.

Jimbo tipped his black cowboy hat. "You brought some nasty critters with you when you arrived here from wherever you came from?"

"Wichita. And, no, I don't even know any nasty critters," Grace said, aware of the slight edge of hysteria in her voice. She was a schoolteacher, for crying out loud. She didn't know people who laid in wait to shoot a helpless woman. She knew eight-year-olds who had trouble with math and talked out of turn.

"Me and the boys will check out the rest of the property, but I'd say whoever was there is probably long gone by now," Jimbo said.

"You find anything else you come let me know," Jake said.

With another tip of his hat to Grace and Kerri, Jimbo left the house.

"Could this have been some sort of a mistake?" Grace finally ventured. "You know, a hunter taking some wild shots?"

"Honey, you *are* from the city," Kerri said drily.

"This was no mistake," Jake replied. His dark blue eyes lingered on Grace. "This isn't hunting season and there's no way anyone could confuse you with a wild turkey or a deer."

"So somebody just tried to kill me." The words fell from Grace's mouth and hung in the air as she stared at the people around her, hoping somebody would negate her words or at least somehow make it all make sense.

Instead, she heard a cry from upstairs and knew that the triplets were awake from their naps. "Go on, I'll let you know when the sheriff arrives," Jake said to Grace and Kerri.

As the two women climbed the stairs, Kerri grabbed hold of Grace's hand. "I can't imagine how frightened you must have been," she said as she squeezed Grace's fingers. "Nothing like this has ever happened before."

"I feel like it's all a horrible dream," Grace replied.

"It has to have been some sort of terrible mistake," Kerri replied as she dropped Grace's hand.

Only the sight of Abby's, Bonnie's and Casey's sweet little faces grinning at her over the tops of the cribs could finally calm some of the fear that had iced Grace's heart for what seemed like forever. "Hey, girls," she greeted them with a forced bright smile.

It took several minutes to change diapers, and with Abby and Casey on Kerri's hips and Bonnie riding Grace's good side, they went back down the stairs.

By the time they had the girls happily settled on the floor with toys surrounding them, the sheriff had arrived.

Sheriff Greg Hicks was a tall, gray-haired man with kind brown eyes and a deep cleft in his chin. "Would you get a load of these little beauties," he said with a look at the girls after Jake had made the introductions. "They're like peas in a pod and cute as buttons."

"Thank you," Grace said, noticing that Bonnie was grinning and batting her eyelashes at Jake, obviously flirting as usual.

"Now, what's this I hear about a shooting taking place out here?" Sheriff Hicks asked as he looked at everyone standing around in the room.

Jake gestured them all to chairs. Grace found herself on the sofa next to him, and the memory of being in his strong arms played in her head. She had never felt so safe in her entire life as she had in those moments with his arms wrapped around her and his heart beating next to her own. For a wistful moment she wanted that again, that feeling of safety while standing in his strong arms.

"Grace and I were taking a walk outside when I got a phone call I needed to attend to in my study," Jake began. "It was a supplier and I needed to order some things. I had the list on my desk."

Grace picked up the story. "Jake asked me to head inside with him, but I told him I wanted to walk a little bit more and enjoy the sunshine and fresh air."

As she told the sheriff about the gunshots her heart began to beat faster and her throat went achingly dry as she thought of those moments when she was so certain she was about to be killed. "I've never been so scared in my entire life."

"I had some of my men check out the area in the woods where the gunfire came from. Jimbo told me it looks as if somebody had a blanket out there and was hanging around, maybe camping or something."

"You haven't seen anyone unusual around the place?" Hicks asked Jake.

He shook his head. "Nobody."

"Anybody around here have a beef with you?" Sheriff Hicks asked Grace.

"I don't know anyone around here," she replied. "I live in Wichita. This is my first time to the area, and I only just arrived yesterday." She paused a moment and averted her gaze from Jake. "Of course, it could have been Justin. He wasn't real happy to see me when I arrived here with his daughters."

Sheriff Hicks looked at her in surprise at the same time she heard Kerri gasp and felt Jake tense next to her in obvious protest.

"I can't imagine Justin doing anything like this," Sheriff Hicks said dubiously, "but I'll check it out. It's probably more likely a drifter who thought you were getting too close to where he'd been camped."

Grace had a crazy image in her head of the Johnson family circling the wagons to protect one of their own against an intruder. And there was no question in her mind that she and her daughters were the intruders. No matter how nice these people had been to her, she was really on her own.

"Justin wouldn't do something like this," Jake exclaimed as he leapt to his feet the moment Sheriff Hicks walked out the front door. "I know my brother, and he might be a lot of things, but he's definitely not a cold-blooded killer." He glared at Grace as his stomach churned with anxiety.

"Well, I don't know him," she replied with strain in her voice. "Although I've certainly been trying to get to know him." She raised her chin as she returned his glare. "I'd be a fool not to mention his name to the sheriff given what's happened with him since I arrived here."

Bonnie crawled over to Jake and grabbed hold of his pants leg. She wobbled to her feet and raised her arms, obviously wanting to be picked up. Grace jumped off the sofa and hurried to the little girl, trying to wrangle her up in her arms one-handed. It was obvious from the awkwardness of her effort and the pain that spasmed across her face that her bad shoulder made it impossible.

Jake bent down, picked the child up and drew a deep breath to steady himself. "Look, I know Justin has behaved badly, but there's no way anyone can make me believe that he was out there in the woods trying to shoot you." Bonnie grabbed his nose with one hand and patted his face with the other.

He realized at that moment it was impossible to sustain any kind of anger with a ten-month-old giggling in your arms and squeezing your nose in delight. Besides, he wasn't really angry at Grace, he was angry with Justin for putting himself in the position to even be a suspect in a shooting. He was livid that a guest at his home had been nearly killed by an unknown assailant.

"Maybe you weren't the specific target," he finally said.

She frowned. "What does that mean?"

"Maybe it's just as Sheriff Hicks suggested. If it was a drifter or somebody who had set up some kind of makeshift camp, he might have shot at anyone he thought threatened his space." It was a stretch and Jake knew it, but none of it made any sense as far as he was concerned. No matter how he stretched his imagination he couldn't put this on his brother. Justin just couldn't be responsible for this.

"So what now?" Grace asked. There was something in her expression that told him she was taking a secret delight in the fact that Bonnie was now pulling the hairs in one of his eyebrows.

"We wait and see what Sheriff Hicks can find out," he replied. And personally he hoped to hell his brother had a good alibi for the time of the shooting.

At that moment Grace's cell phone rang. She pulled it from her pocket and answered. "How did that happen?" she asked after a minute. The frown that had already ridden her forehead deepened. "Okay, whatever. There's a credit card in the top drawer of my dresser underneath my camisoles. Take it and use it, but just for what you need and then put it back where you got it. Okay, yes, I love you, too."

Jake set Bonnie back on the floor, trying to dispel the thought of Grace in a camisole from his mind.

The visual image that had instantly sprung into his head was as sexy as it was unwanted.

"Everything okay?" he asked.

She sighed. "Everything is as usual. My sister, Natalie, has a small trust fund and gets a monthly allowance, but somehow there's always more month than there is money for her. Anyway, it's taken care of for now."

"You didn't tell her what happened."

"There's no point in worrying her about all this. It's not as if she can do anything about it from Wichita." She released a sigh of obvious frustration. "Look, I didn't mean to throw your brother under the bus, but, under the circumstances, it would have been foolish of me not to mention him."

Kerri and Jeffrey had drifted out of the room, as if not wanting to be caught in the middle of any argument that might be brewing between Jake and Grace.

Jake didn't want to argue. He sat in the chair across from her and released a weary sigh. The adrenaline that had pumped through him when he'd seen Grace pinned against the barn had disappeared, leaving him confused and upset about everything that had happened.

"I know," he replied. "And it was the right thing to do."

There was a moment of awkward silence between them. Once again his head filled with a vision of her in a sexy, silky red camisole. He was grateful when she broke the silence.

"You know, it was a near-death experience that made me decide it was the right thing to do to find Justin in the first place," she said.

Jake looked at her in surprise. "What do you mean?"

Her cheeks flushed a delicate pink. "It probably doesn't sound like much now, but two days before I left Wichita to come here, I was on my way home from the grocery store. It was after dark, and Natalie was watching the girls while they slept so I could make a fast run to get some milk and a few other items. Anyway, I was on the way home and a car forced me off the road. I went down an embankment and it was only by the grace of God that the car didn't flip over and kill me."

"That's terrible," he said, surprised that the thought of her getting hurt created a tight band of pressure across his chest. He glanced at the triplets playing on the blanket. "And thank God they weren't with you."

She nodded. "Thank God is right."

"What did you do?"

"I was shaken up badly, but thankfully not hurt. The car had no real damage and the only result was groceries had spilled all over the backseat."

"Did you call the police?"

"No. There was really no point. I didn't get a good look at the car that forced me off the road and it was long gone by the time I finally pulled myself together. I managed to get back on the road and drive home and that was that. But that night I decided life was too short and too unpredictable and it was time I make contact with Justin."

Jake leaned back in his chair. "It doesn't make any sense—the shooting, I mean. First and foremost, I don't believe my brother is capable of trying to shoot you or anyone else. But, aside from that, it wouldn't make sense for him to do that. You being dead doesn't change the fact that he's their father. In fact, your death would only put more responsibility on him."

She raised a hand to the back of her neck and rubbed, as if trying to ease a tension headache. "That's true. I just need to get home. I need to take the girls and get back to Wichita," she murmured, more to herself than to him.

"But we both know that's not an option right now," he reminded her with a pointed glance at her shoulder. He stared out the window, unable to look at her and not remember how she'd felt in his arms.

Soft and yielding, she'd filled him with a heat that had him instantly responding to her. Her hair had smelled slightly fruity, mingling with the floral scent of her, and when she'd stopped crying he'd been almost reluctant to let her go.

He definitely didn't want a woman in his life permanently, but that didn't mean he wouldn't mind one occasionally.

Just not Grace.

Definitely not Grace.

"Look, what I'm really hoping is that this is all some sort of weird mistake, that it was some delusional drifter on the property or a drunk cowboy just popping off his weapon," he said, forcefully pulling his thoughts away from their brief physical contact.

"Do those kinds of things happen a lot around here?" she asked, one of her perfectly arched pale eyebrows raised dubiously.

"No, they don't," he admitted. "But that doesn't mean it can't happen." He got up from the chair, feeling the need to distance himself from her.

"I'm going to go out and talk to my men. Maybe one of them indiscriminately shot off a couple of rounds and now is too embarrassed to admit to it."

What he really wanted to do was get hold of Justin and find out where he'd been when this whole thing had gone down, he thought as he walked to the porch. Although he couldn't imagine his brother having anything to do with what had happened, there was a tiny part of him that knew when Justin had a few beers in him almost anything was possible. But surely not this, his heart rebelled.

Finally, what he needed was some distance from Grace and the little girls. The triplets filled the house with a joyous noise he wasn't accustomed to, and Grace filled his head with thoughts—very dangerous thoughts.

Never in all his years had he been attracted to any

woman Justin had brought around, and yet he was intensely attracted to Grace.

A couple of days, he told himself. A couple more days and they'd all be gone, back to where they'd come from, back to a life that had very little to do with his.

Things would be much easier when she went back to Wichita. He was far too conscious of her on a physical level, drawn to her in a way that was completely undesirable.

He pulled his cell phone from his pocket and punched in Justin's phone number, unsurprised when the call went directly to Justin's voice mail.

He turned at the sound of the door opening and gave a tight smile to Jeffrey, who stepped out on the porch next to him. "Did you get in touch with him?" Jeffrey gestured to the cell phone Jake still held in his hand.

"No, it went straight to voice mail." Jake pocketed the phone and stared at the barn in the distance. No matter how many times he worked the events of the last couple of hours through his brain he couldn't make sense of it.

"He wouldn't do something like this. It doesn't make any sense," Jake said in frustration.

"When has anything Justin done made any sense?" Jeffrey countered drily.

"Yeah, but this is different than borrowing money or getting drunk or running up a bunch of traffic tickets. Grace could have been seriously hurt. She could have been killed." Jake's stomach muscles tightened. "If I find out he was behind this, then I'll wash my hands of him. I mean it," he said at Jeffrey's dubious look.

"You've carried him for a long time, Jake. Sooner or later he's got to stand on his own." Jeffrey clapped Jake on the shoulder. "And now to something else that's not going to make your day. You do remember that Kerri and I are leaving tomorrow for Topeka for a couple of days?"

Jake stared at his brother in horror as the full impact of his words struck. He knew better than to ask his brother to postpone the trip. It had been planned for months, an anniversary celebration at a bed-and-breakfast that was almost impossible to get reservations at.

With Kerri and Jeffrey gone, that meant Jake would be alone in the house with Grace. He'd be alone with a woman with three little girls, an arm in a sling and, worst-case scenario, a murderer after her who had missed once, but might not be done trying.

Chapter 5

Grace sat on the edge of the bed in the guest room and stared out the sliding glass door that led to a small balcony. They had finished a quiet, tense dinner and then she and Kerri had gotten the girls into bed. She'd excused herself for an early night, just wanting to go to sleep and put all the troubling thoughts away for a while. But sleep had proved elusive.

Her shoulder hurt more tonight than it had since she'd fallen, and she knew there was no way she could make the drive home the next day. But it was the ache in her heart that made her feel half-sick.

Was it possible that the man who had fathered her daughters had tried to kill her? Jake certainly didn't believe so. He'd been adamant in his defense of Justin. There had been no word from the sheriff since he'd left the house and no sign or contact from Justin himself.

What she'd like to do was open the sliding door and step outside, get a breath of the fresh scent of night air in hopes it would settle her thoughts. But she was afraid. What if the shooter was still out there, just waiting for another opportunity to get to her? She'd make herself a perfect target out on the balcony.

Grace's mother had been a strong woman who had no tolerance for weakness of any kind, and Grace had tried to live up to that, but at the moment she felt weak and vulnerable and utterly alone.

She decided to call Natalie, who rarely went to bed before dawn, even though she knew there would be little comfort there. Natalie was always in the midst of her own drama. It was Grace who was usually fixing Natalie's life, not the other way around. In any case, the call went to Natalie's voice mail.

Although she didn't leave a message about the shooting, she did say that it had been a mistake to come here, that it was obvious being a father was the last thing in the world Justin wanted and that he'd probably never want to be part of the girls' lives. She explained that it would be another couple of days before she got home but that the trip had certainly been a waste of time where Justin was concerned.

Enough self-pity, she thought when she hung up. Maybe if she went downstairs and got a glass of milk or something it would help her sleep. She'd taken the sling off when she'd gotten into bed, finding it cumbersome. With difficulty she pulled on the red-and-black silk robe that matched her nightgown.

The house was dark and quiet as she left the bedroom. She slid into the room next door where a night-light gave off enough illumination for her to check each crib and see that the girls were all sleeping peacefully.

She stood for a long moment by each crib, her heart swelling in her chest with love. All she'd really wanted was for the girls to know their father and him to know them. She'd hoped that Justin would be the kind of man who would embrace the girls, a man she could be confident would take her babies and care for them if anything ever happened to her. Now she certainly wasn't going to leave here with that confidence. He didn't seem to have any real interest in even getting to know the girls. She just had to make sure she stayed alive and well until the triplets were adults.

Leaving the room as quietly as she'd entered, she made her way down the darkened hall to the stairway. From the living room she saw the glow of a small lamp on.

She followed the glow and found Jake seated in a chair. "Oh, I didn't know anyone else was still awake," she said as she self-consciously held the robe closer around her neck with her good hand.

"I couldn't sleep. Looks as though you're suffering

from the same affliction." He gestured her toward the sofa. She noticed he had a glass of amber liquid in his hand. "Scotch," he said. "Would you like one?"

"No thanks. Contrary to what happened the night of Sally's wedding with a bottle of champagne, I'm really not much of a drinker." She sat on the sofa.

"Neither am I," he admitted and set the glass on the end table next to him. "I just occasionally like the taste of a little good Scotch. Sheriff Hicks called earlier."

Grace sat up straighter, trying to staunch the pain the motion created in her shoulder. "And?"

"And apparently there has been a drifter in the area. He stole some clothing from Rebecca Castor's clothesline and she chased him off with her broom. He was also apparently sleeping in Burt Kent's barn off and on. Several people around the area have seen him and told the sheriff he appears to be mentally unstable."

"So, it could have been him who took those shots at me." She wanted to believe it. She desperately wanted to believe that it had been anyone but Justin.

"It's possible. At least that's what Sheriff Hicks believes happened, although nobody who has caught sight of him has seen him with a weapon. Hicks and his men are trying to hunt him down, and once he does maybe we'll have more answers."

"And Justin? Have you heard from him?"

He shook his head, his rich, dark hair gleaming in the artificial light. "Not a word."

"Doesn't that worry you?"

A small, humorless smile lifted the corners of his mouth. "Everything Justin has done since the age of about ten has made me worried."

"Sounds like me and my sister."

"She a handful?" he asked.

"Definitely." Grace frowned as she thought of her younger sister.

"How did your parents deal with her?" He picked up his drink and took a sip, then returned the glass to the end table.

"They didn't. I mean, Natalie and I never knew our fathers. My mother was an unusual woman. She never wanted a man in her life on a permanent basis." Grace felt herself begin to relax, grateful to talk about anything except what had happened earlier that day.

"I'm not sure why she had Natalie. I'm not even sure why she had me. She certainly wasn't mother material. She was wealthy and beautiful. She was also cold and distant and loved to travel. By the age of six I pretty well knew I was on my own. When Natalie came along I was the one who raised her, and I think sometimes I was way too indulgent with her."

"Welcome to my club," he replied drily. "Only in our case it wasn't a problem of a cold and distant mother, it was an issue of a tough, tyrannical father who thought a beating a day made a better kid. It didn't take long when we were kids to realize that most of his rage for some unknown reason seemed to be directed at Justin. Of course, Justin was good at stirring up trouble."

"What about Jeffrey?"

Jake flashed her a smile that warmed every cold spot her body might have held. "The middle child. He was good at being invisible, especially when Dad was in one of his rages."

"And what about you?" she asked. She told herself that her interest was only in learning more about the family where her children's father came from and nothing personal as far as Jake was concerned.

"What about me? I got through it just like Jeffrey and Justin did. I was tougher than them, tried to protect them when I could. My mother died a year before my father. She got sick, and I think she just died to get away from him. But we all survived and here we are."

Grace had a feeling there were plenty of scars beneath the surface in all of the Johnson men. She couldn't help remembering Kerri saying that Jake was the alpha dog. She wondered how many beatings he'd taken on behalf of his brothers.

She'd certainly had more than her share of sleepless nights where Natalie was concerned. There were times Grace wondered if Natalie was doing drugs and hanging out with the wrong kind of people. Grace tried to be a good sister, a good mentor, but there was no question that since their mother's death the relationship between the two sisters had gotten worse instead of better.

"So, what do you do in your spare time, Grace?" He smiled ruefully. "I mean, before the babies came when you had spare time."

"Nothing very exciting," she replied, grateful for the change in subject. "I enjoy cooking and food. I used to really enjoy going out to dinner, trying new restaurants and food experiences. I like to read and go to the movies. My life was fairly quiet before the girls came along. What about you? What do you like to do?"

"Enjoying good food is right up there at the top." He seemed to be relaxing also. Some of the tension that had been in his body language disappeared and the stern lines along the sides of his handsome face relaxed. "But I'm definitely happiest on the back of a horse riding the pastures and dealing with the ranch. You ride?"

"I took riding lessons when I was younger. It was one of those wild hairs my mother got. She decided her daughter should know how to ride. The lessons lasted about four weeks and then she had me quit and take tennis classes. But I enjoyed riding for the brief time I got to try it."

"I guess having the triplets changed your life considerably."

She laughed. "That's the understatement of the year. I've definitely had to sacrifice some things, but any sacrifice has been worth it. I've never known the kind of joy and love they've each brought into my life."

She sobered and met his gaze seriously. The conversation had been going too light and easy. She almost hated to mention his brother's name again, but she wanted Jake to understand exactly where she was coming from.

"I'll be fine without Justin. We'll all be fine without him. When my mother died she left both me and my sister a bit of an inheritance and then left the bulk of her estate to the triplets, so I'll never have to worry about college funds or buying cars or any kind of financial burden where they're concerned. I just didn't want them to grow up without a father like I had to. Little girls need daddies."

The tension lines were back in Jake's face as he reached for his drink once again. "I can't make him be what you need him to be." There was genuine pain in his voice.

"I know. I just want you to know that whatever happens I appreciate the hospitality you and Kerri and Jeffrey have given us here."

"You're welcome. And you should have your sling on," he said with a touch of censure in his voice.

But it wasn't the tone of his voice that made her feel the absence of the cumbersome sling, rather it was the quick slide of his dark gaze down the length of her body that suddenly made her feel half-naked.

Tension crackled in her head, in the very air between them, and Grace recognized it for what it was—a sexual awareness, a heady whisper of desire she hadn't felt for any man in a very long time.

Just that quickly it felt more than a bit dangerous to her, to sit here in the middle of the night with him, to be exchanging bits and pieces of their personal lives with each other. She was all too aware of her lack of clothing, and her body felt fevered despite the lightweight nightgown and robe that she wore.

She wondered what it would be like to kiss him. His mouth would taste of the Scotch he'd been drinking, and she knew the kiss would be heady and hot. She had a feeling he'd kiss with the same intensity he did everything else, that it would be an experience difficult for a woman to ever forget.

His cell phone rang, shattering the uncomfortable silence that had sprung up between them and the risky direction of her thoughts.

He pulled his cell phone from his pocket and answered. A deep frown slashed across his forehead as he listened to whoever was on the other end of the line. "Yeah, okay. I'll be right there." He closed the phone and dropped it back in his pocket with a weary sigh.

"My brother has finally put in an appearance. He and a couple of his no-account friends showed up at Tony's Tavern, a bar in town. They were all drunk and disorderly and Sheriff Hicks is holding them at the jail." He got up from his chair and she rose from the sofa. "You should probably get some sleep. I'm sure I'll have some news about Justin first thing in the morning."

She walked with him to the bottom of the stairs.

She felt the need to say something, anything to ease the worry lines on his face, to rid him of some of the tension that held his shoulders so rigid. But what could she say?

It was possible Justin and his friends were the ones who had gotten drunk and shot at her. It was also possible Justin had spent the afternoon getting drunk with his friends and had been nowhere around when the shooting had occurred.

In either case it was obvious Jake had his hands full with the brother he obviously loved, and Grace could relate to that because of her often difficult relationship and worries about Natalie.

"I'll see you in the morning," he said. Once again his gaze slid down, lingering briefly on the exposed skin of her collarbone, the curve of her breasts beneath the silk material. "Good night, Grace."

"Good night, Jake."

As he went out the front door she began to climb the stairs, the heat of his gaze still warming her stomach.

How was this even possible? How could she be so attracted to Jake? The answer wasn't so complex—because he was hot and stable, because he'd been kind to her and seemed to be everything opposite of the man who'd already let her down. More important, because when his gaze had slid over her she'd sensed with a woman's instinct that he definitely felt something for her, too.

Once her shoulder was well enough she would

leave here and probably never see any of the Johnson triplets again. One of them had already let her down and might have been responsible for trying to shoot her, and she'd be a fool to allow another of the hot, handsome triplets to get close to her in any way.

Jake gripped the steering wheel tightly as he headed toward Cameron Creek and the sheriff's office, which had become far too familiar in the past couple of years.

What he didn't want to think about was Grace in that sexy robe that had wrapped around her slender body just tight enough to display all the curves she possessed—and she possessed plenty.

He liked her. It wasn't just the way she looked in her sexy black-and-red robe with her hair slightly tousled. He liked the warmth of her smile, the way she loved her children. He liked the strength she obviously possessed, a strength that had seen her through a rough childhood and had buoyed her up as she'd become caretaker for a younger, obviously troubled sister.

She'd have to be strong to get through what had probably been a difficult pregnancy and the first ten months of raising those girls all alone.

If that wasn't enough, the smoky green of her eyes drew him in, the whisper of her perfume muddied his senses, and yet the very last thing he wanted in his own life was a woman and three children. Justin's problem, he reminded himself.

He just needed to get Justin home and sobered up and find out if he had anything to do with the attack on Grace that afternoon. There was nothing that would make him believe that Justin had been a part of the shooting unless he heard those words from his brother's own mouth.

Justin was thoughtless, irresponsible and showed poor judgment most of the time, but he wasn't a mean man. He didn't have the cruel streak that their father had exhibited over the years.

If any of them had that capacity it was Jake at this moment, who would like nothing better than to wrap his hands around his brother's throat and squeeze a little bit of sense into him.

Grace and the babies might go back to Wichita, but that didn't mean they just went away. Somehow, someday, Justin was going to have to face his daughters. He could do it now with love and support or he would do it later met with bitterness and recriminations from three young women who would have hard questions about where he'd been all their lives.

Jake desperately wanted his brother to make the right choice now and save those little girls a lot of heartache and tears down the road.

The sheriff's station was located on Main Street. It was a small, unassuming brick building with a couple of jail cells that were rarely used in the basement.

For a moment Jake remained in his car, staring at the building where he'd spent far too much of his time lately. Justin liked to drink, and when he drank he got stupid.

Jake had bailed him out of jail or talked Sheriff Hicks into just letting Justin go more times than he could count, and here he was again, riding to the rescue. Wearily he got out of the car and headed for the front door.

Lindsay Sanders sat at the front desk and gave him a rueful smile as he walked in. "We've got to stop meeting like this," she said, a slightly flirtatious glint in her dark eyes.

Jake didn't bite. He never did. "Hicks in his office?" he asked.

She nodded, as usual a hint of disappointment in her eyes as he refused to flirt with her. "He's waiting for you."

As Jake walked down the hallway to the sheriff's inner office, he thought of Lindsay. She was an attractive single woman who more than once had let him know she was available.

Maybe he should bite, he thought. Then he realized the only reason the idea had crossed his mind was because he thought it might get the scent of Grace out of his head, the memory of how she'd felt in his arms out of his brain.

He gave one short rap on Sheriff Hicks's door and then opened it, catching the older man with his feet up on his desk, his chair reclined and his hat over his eyes.

"I should be home in bed with my wife," he said

without moving. "I should be dreaming about a native woman named Lola feeding me fresh mango on an exotic island." He pulled his feet off the desk, shoved his hat to the top of his head and sat up. "You know I'm only still here because it's you."

"I know, and I appreciate it," Jake said. He sank down in the chair opposite the desk. "Did he tell you where he was at the time of the shooting out at my place?"

Hicks snorted. "He told me that, along with intimate details of his relationship with Shirley and every other woman he's dated, and some crude jokes that made his two friends laugh like the drunken hyenas they are. He told me that he and Shirley had fought earlier this morning and he'd dropped her off at her place, then he hightailed it over to Elliot Spencer's house, they called J. D. Richards to join them there and they proceeded to get trashed. Elliot's wife confirmed that the three were there all day until they left late this evening."

"So he couldn't have been at my place firing shots at Grace." Jake hadn't realized how tight the knot had been in his chest until this moment when it eased somewhat.

"If you're to believe the two drunks that are with him and Elliot's wife—and I've got no reason not to believe Darla. She never lies to cover for her husband. According to them, they were all at Elliot's place until about an hour ago when they thought it was a good idea to show up at Tony's. The bartender called me, said they were out of their minds drunk and he was afraid there might be trouble. So I rounded them up and brought them here more for their own safekeeping than anything else."

Greg reared back in his chair. "It appears J.D. and Elliot will be my guests and sleep it off for the duration of the night. J.D. has nobody who is willing to come and get him and Darla told me to keep Elliot until he's sober. I'm assuming you're here to take Justin home."

"Unless there's some charges pending?"

Greg shook his head. "Fortunately for them I can't charge for stupidity, otherwise none of them would ever get out of here."

"Anything new on the drifter?" Jake asked.

"Nothing, but I've got my men still looking for him. I'll keep you posted." He got out of his chair and Jake stood as well. He knew the routine. Together he and Greg would take the stairs down to the bottom floor where Greg would unlock the cell door and Justin would stagger out.

It had been a long time since Jake had felt any kind of embarrassment over this situation. Weary resignation was what sat heavily on his shoulders as he followed Greg down the stairs that led to the cells.

And if the current situation wasn't tough enough, he had to face the fact that tomorrow Jeffrey and Kerri were leaving and that meant he'd be responsible for helping Grace with the three girls.

Not going to happen, he determined. One way or the other he was going to sober up his brother and force him to take some responsibility, at least until Jeffrey and Kerri got back into town or Grace healed up enough to take her girls and head home.

The cell area smelled like a brewery. J.D. was on his back, snoring loud enough to wake the dead, and Elliot sat on the edge of the bunk, staring off into space in an obvious drunken stupor. Only Justin was animated, staggering back and forth in front of the bars and muttering beneath his breath.

"Hey!" His face lit at the sight of Jake. "There's my brother. He's the man. I knew he'd show up to get me out of here." He stepped back from the bars so Sheriff Hicks could unlock the door.

Justin stumbled out of the cell and threw an arm around Jake's shoulder, the smell of booze seeming to seep out of his very pores. "You know I love you, man."

"I know. Let's just get you home," Jake replied.

He got Justin loaded into his car and then headed to his brother's apartment. There were a million things Jake wanted to say to Justin, but he'd learned a long time ago not to argue or try to have a rational discussion with a drunk.

Within minutes Justin had fallen sound asleep. By the time Jake arrived at the apartment building he had to help his brother out of the car and into his place.

Justin went directly to the bedroom and fell onto

the bed, passed out cold. Jake remained standing just inside the door of the one-bedroom apartment looking around in dismay.

Pizza boxes and food wrappers littered the floor, along with beer bottles and other trash items. The place looked like a room after a frat party had taken place, but Justin was no college kid. He was a thirty-five-year-old father of three and somehow, some way, Jake had to figure out how to make him step up to be a man.

Jake cleared a space on the sofa and sank down. He'd wait for Justin to sleep it off and then he and his brother were going to have a man-to-man talk that would get Jake out of the middle of this mess and away from the woman and the little girls he feared had the potential to make him rethink his desire to spend his life alone. And that would be the biggest mistake he'd ever make in his life.

Chapter 6

"You and Jeffrey are leaving today?" Grace stared at Kerri in stunned surprise.

"We'll only be gone for three nights," Kerri said as she refilled Grace's cup of coffee. "It's kind of our honeymoon/anniversary trip. When we got married we never took a honeymoon. We both agreed that for our first anniversary we'd stay at The Bouquet Bed and Breakfast in Topeka. But it's a really popular place and we had to book almost a year in advance."

Kerri rejoined Grace at the table. "If you're worried how you'll do without us, you shouldn't. Jake will take good care of you and the girls. He's perfectly capable of changing diapers and doing whatever else is necessary for you to get along just fine."

"It seems as though Jake takes care of everything

and everyone," Grace replied. There had been no sign of Jake since he'd left the night before to retrieve Justin from the sheriff's office. "I imagine the last thing he'll want to do is spend the next couple of days taking care of me and the girls." Worry worked through her, along with a sense of dread at the thought of it just being her and Jake alone.

She told herself she was worried about how the two of them would deal with the responsibilities of the girls, but it was more than that. Some of her worry had to do with that slow slide of his gaze down her body and the responding heat she'd felt whenever he looked at her.

"Jake always steps up to do the right thing. Don't you worry. Now, if you don't mind I'm going to excuse myself and tend to some packing."

As Kerri disappeared from the kitchen, Grace fought back a wild sense of panic. If she could heal her shoulder through sheer willpower alone, she would have done it at that very moment sitting at his kitchen table. She looked at the girls playing on the floor and frowned. Her shoulder was still sore enough that she couldn't even pick up one of her daughters.

She'd tried to call Natalie twice that morning to see if perhaps she could somehow get a ride here and take Grace home and then stay with her or help her find a nurse to hire until Grace's shoulder was healed enough for her to be on her own.

Unfortunately, Natalie hadn't answered her phone,

and knowing her sister she was probably still in bed despite the fact that it was after ten.

Maybe by tomorrow she'd be well enough to go home, she thought. She experimentally moved her shoulder and gasped at the pain that sliced through her. Okay, maybe not tomorrow, but perhaps the next day she told herself. As soon as possible, that's all she could promise.

She finished her coffee and carried the cup to the sink. Once she'd rinsed it and placed it in the dishwasher, she decided she'd rather sit in the living room than in the kitchen, which required her moving the girls. She was trying to figure out how to make the transition when Jake and Justin walked in.

Jake looked grim and determined and Justin looked hungover and contrite. "Hey, Grace," Justin said, but it was the sight of Jake that made Grace's heart beat a little faster.

"I think it's time we all sit down and have some sort of a rational talk," Jake said.

"I was just going to move into the living room," she replied and looked pointedly at the girls. "If somebody will hand me one of them, I can manage one if you can get the other two."

Jake picked up Casey and landed her on Grace's hip on her good side. Then he picked up Bonnie, who snuggled into him with a contented grunt. Justin looked at the last triplet. "Who is that one?" he asked.

"That's Abby, and she doesn't have enough teeth to bite hard," Grace said drily.

Justin paused a moment as if unsure what to do, then he finally picked her up and Abby immediately began to fuss. "Why don't we go ahead and take them upstairs," Grace said as she changed her mind. "They're probably ready for a nap and it will be much easier for all of us to talk if it's just the adults." Although in Justin's case, she thought, she used the term "adult" very loosely.

Minutes later with the girls in their cribs, the three adults returned to the living room. Jake sat next to Grace on the sofa and Justin sat in the chair facing them, still looking slightly green around the gills.

"Look, the first thing I want to do is get something straight. I had nothing to do with the shooting that happened here," Justin said. "I swear I left here and took Shirley home and then went directly to Elliot's where I spent the whole day." He leaned forward, his features pale but earnest as he looked at her. "Grace, I'd never do anything like that. I'd never want to hurt you. Heck, I'd never try to hurt anyone."

Grace wanted to believe him. No matter what their relationship, no matter what she thought of him personally, he was the father of her children.

Justin shot a glance at his brother and then looked back at Grace. "I don't know what happened or who took those shots at you, but I had absolutely nothing to do with any of it." He leaned back in his chair and ran a hand across his forehead, as if he had a hangover headache. "So, where do we go from here?"

"I'd say that's pretty much up to you," she replied,

not feeling a bit sorry for him. There was a little wicked part of her that hoped his hangover lasted for at least another twenty-four hours. "I mean, right now I'm here, the girls are here, but I've been trying to get in touch with my sister to see if maybe she can come and take me back to Wichita."

"You aren't in any condition to go home," Jake protested.

"I figured I could hire a nurse to help me for a couple of days," she explained. "With Jeffrey and Kerri leaving town, perhaps that would be best for everyone."

"That's not necessary," Jake replied smoothly. "You should be fine in a couple of days, and I'm sure between the three of us we can manage to take care of things here until you're healed up enough to go back home."

Grace thought Justin's face blanched slightly at the prospect of being part of the team for the next few days; but there was such a ring of certainty in Jake's voice she almost believed that it would be okay.

Besides, no matter how much Grace told herself that Natalie would step up if necessary, she knew from experience her sister was nobody to count on. In that respect she and Jake shared a lot in common.

"I know I've acted badly so far," Justin said to her. "And I want to do the right thing, I really do. I'm just not sure what you expect from me. I mean, I've never been in this position before."

Just love my babies, love your daughters, she

thought. It was that easy as far as she was concerned. It was all she really wanted or needed from him. "The first thing I'd like is just for you to get to know the girls while I'm here," she said aloud.

"I can do that," he agreed readily. "I still can't believe there's three of them, but I guess I shouldn't be surprised. I mean, with me being a triplet and all."

"I was definitely surprised when the doctor told me," Grace said drily. "I had no idea you were a triplet."

"Yeah, I guess I didn't mention that the night of the wedding."

Grace felt her cheeks warm. She didn't even want to think about that crazy night. There was plenty they hadn't talked about. "And then before I leave here maybe we could work out some sort of visitation for once I go back to Wichita," she said.

She wanted so much more than that. She wanted him not just to be a father who occasionally saw his girls on a weekend here and there, but rather she wanted him to be a dad in every loving sense of the word.

"That sounds good," Justin said agreeably and flashed another quick look at Jake. "So, maybe I should go home and pack a suitcase and plan on moving in here while Kerri and Jeffrey are gone." He looked at his watch. "I should be able to pack up and be back by the time the girls wake up from their naps."

"I think that sounds like a perfect idea," Jake said.

Grace was sure he was more than a little bit eager to get out of the middle of this whole mess.

He'd been thrust into this drama through no fault of his own. He'd already told her he had no interest in having a wife or a family, and yet she was sure he'd felt saddled with the weight of her and the triplets for the last couple of days. And unless Justin stepped up, nothing was going to change in the immediate future.

Justin shot out of his chair. "Then I'll be back here in about an hour or so." He flashed them both a boyish smile as he flew out the front door.

"Do you really think we'll see him again today?" Grace asked Jake after Justin had disappeared.

"Who knows? I can only hope he'll do the right thing."

She offered him a tentative smile. "That's the way I feel about my sister. I've given up trying to force her to make the right choices and just spend a lot of time hoping she'll eventually grow up."

"In any case, we'll figure things out, and you don't need to worry about Kerri and Jeffrey leaving. Surely if it comes to that, between the two of us we can easily handle three little girls."

Three hours later she had a feeling Jake was eating those very words. Kerri and Jeffrey had left for their trip an hour earlier, Justin had never returned and at the moment Jake was on the floor covered with babies.

Bonnie bounced up and down on his chest, Abby

had him by the hair and Casey crawled back and forth over his legs as if they were the most fascinating obstacle course she'd ever encountered.

The whole thing had begun with a diaper change that had quickly spiraled out of control as the triplets saw Jake on the floor as a brand-new fun toy.

For the first time in days Grace's laughter bubbled out of her as Jake wrestled with the girls, and his laughter and their giggles combined to make sweet music to her ears.

He seemed surprisingly at ease with them considering how he'd acted the first time he'd been around them. He tweaked Bonnie's nose and tickled Abby's belly and then reached to tousle Casey's hair as they all laughed.

"Do they always have this much energy?" he asked as he finally managed to extricate himself and get to his feet.

"Mostly in the afternoons right after their naps," she replied. She thought he'd never looked as sexy as he did now with his dark rich hair mussed, a stain that looked suspiciously like drool on the front of his shirt and a genuine smile of amusement lifting the corners of his mouth.

This was a side of Jake she hadn't seen before, and it was breathtakingly appealing. Fun-loving and with laughter lighting his eyes, he made a wistful want rise up inside of her. There was a little part of her that warned her not to get caught up in him, not to allow herself to like him so much.

It was at that moment she recognized that she'd arrived here with a little fantasy running in the back of her head—the fantasy that she'd come here, reunite with Justin and they would fall in love and get married and parent their children together and live happily ever after.

From the moment MysteryMom had given her this address, the image of a happily-ever-after had begun to form in her head. She hadn't consciously built it, but it had been there all the same.

That fantasy had been smashed into pieces the moment she'd had her first encounter with Justin. She warned herself now that no good would come from her falling in love with Jake. It would just be plain stupid and too weird for them to get involved in any way. He was the wrong brother. It would only complicate what was already a complicated situation.

"How about dinner out tonight?" Jake asked an hour later. He felt the need to get them all out of the house that for the last hour had rung with Grace's laughter, with the giggles of the delightful little girls and with his own.

The girls had been all wiggling warmth as they'd crawled all over him. They'd smelled of baby fresh powder and everything innocent in the world.

God, he couldn't remember the last time he'd laughed with such abandon. It had felt so good, so right. It had been frightening. He'd had a momentary glimpse of what life might have been in this big house if he allowed himself a future that included others, if he allowed himself a future that included Grace and the girls.

"Oh, Jake, I'm not sure that's such a great idea. It's quite a job to get everyone ready and into a restaurant." Even as she said the words there was a faint wistfulness in her pretty eyes. "I haven't attempted to go out to eat since they were born."

"Then I'd say it's high time you did. Surely between the two of us we can manage it. There's a pretty good Italian restaurant in Cameron Creek. Actually, it's the only real restaurant in town, and I have a sudden hankering for some lasagna."

She ran a hand through her blond-streaked brown hair and looked down at her jeans and T-shirt. Although he thought she looked lovely just the way she was, it was fairly easy to read her mind. "Why don't I keep an eye on the girls while you go do whatever it is women do before they go out to dinner?"

"Are you sure you really want to attempt this?" she asked hesitantly.

"Positive."

She smiled at him gratefully. The warmth of her smile coiled a ball of heat in the pit of his stomach. As she raced up the stairs, leaving him in the living room with the girls, he tried to control not just the physical desire she created inside him, but also a nebulous desire for something more.

Dinner out with the triplets would surely staunch any crazy feelings that were brewing inside him.

There was no doubt in his mind that the evening would be utter chaos, just what he needed to remind himself of how much he didn't want this kind of chaos in his life.

When Grace came back down the stairs to go to dinner, all thoughts flew out of his head. She'd changed into a royal-blue dress that clung to her every curve and enhanced the lighter highlights of her hair. Her long legs looked silken and her feet were dainty in dark blue high-heel sandals whose open toes displayed pretty pink polish.

She looked elegant and sexy and nearly stole his breath away. "Wow, you clean up real nice," he finally managed to say.

Her cheeks grew pink and she ran a hand down the skirt. "Too much? I threw this into my suitcase last minute in case..." She allowed her voice to trail off as her blush darkened.

He knew what she'd been about to say—she'd packed the dress in case Justin decided to take her and the girls out someplace.

He shook his head. "Not at all. Very all right. I'll just go do a quick change myself and then we'll get this show on the road." He hurried upstairs to his own bedroom, trying to still the crazy beat of his heart.

Within a couple of weeks Jeffrey and Kerri would be moved out, Justin would still be living in his pigpen of an apartment and this big house would be all Jake's. It would resonate with the silence he'd longed for most of his life, and he'd be responsible for nothing more than his own happiness.

All he had to do was be patient, and in a short period of time Grace and the girls would be back to their lives and his brothers would be living theirs elsewhere. Then it would finally be his turn to truly be alone. He had to hang on to that thought, had to remember that it was his dream for himself.

He changed into a pair of dress slacks and a clean shirt, slapped a little cologne on the underside of his jaw and went back downstairs.

"Do you ever dress them all alike?" he asked when he rejoined her in the living room.

"Never. I figure when they're older if they want to dress alike that will be their choice, but I thought it was important at the very beginning that they each have their own identities. Did your parents dress you all alike?"

"Blue jeans and white T-shirts were our uniform for most of our childhood," he replied. "Mom and Dad never had any trouble telling us apart. Now, let's get on the road."

It took nearly thirty minutes to load up all the car seats and diaper bags and get the girls buckled in safely in the backseat of Jake's car. It would have been easier to take her car, but Jake insisted they take his. He hadn't forgotten that somebody had shot at her. He thought it safer to be in his vehicle.

"And that's why I don't go out," Grace said once

they were finally settled in the car and headed down the road.

"It is a big job, isn't it?"

"Especially for one person. Usually by the time I get them all loaded up and ready to go, I've forgotten where I intended to go in the first place," she said with a smile.

"And your sister isn't a lot of help?"

"My sister helps when it's convenient for her, which is very rare. Lately she's been far too busy with a new boyfriend to have much time for me."

"Nice guy?" He tried not to notice that scent of her, the fragrance that seemed to reach inside him and stir up all kinds of crazy desires.

"She says so, but I haven't met him yet, which worries me a little bit. If past behavior dictates future behavior, then he's probably a loser and a user. She doesn't have a terrific track record when it comes to men." Grace released a self-deprecating laugh. "Of course, I should talk." She frowned suddenly. "Sorry, I shouldn't have said that."

"Let's make a deal that we won't talk about Justin for the rest of the night. To be honest, I've had about all the drama I can take where my brother is concerned right now."

"It's a deal," she replied easily.

In the backseat, the little girls gibbered to each other, creating a pleasant white noise that filled the silence that suddenly grew between him and Grace.

"Do you think they know what they're saying to each other?" he asked.

"Who knows? They say twins sometimes develop a language of their own. They certainly spend a lot of time gabbing to one another."

"Probably discussing how foolish adults can be," he said drily, and was rewarded with one of her warm, beautiful laughs.

"They do laugh a lot," she replied.

It didn't take long for them to arrive at Maria's, the only Italian restaurant the small town of Cameron Creek boasted. In fact, it was the only official restaurant in town, although there was a fast-food place, a pizza parlor and a small café, as well.

It took much longer for them to finally get settled at a table with three high chairs the waitstaff had hurried to round up and provide. The triplets garnered plenty of attention from the other diners, but just as quickly the novelty wore off and people got back to focusing on their own meals.

Once the girls were happily settled with sippy cups and crackers and Jake and Grace had ordered their dinners and both had a glass of wine in front of them, Jake leaned back in his chair and began to relax for the first time in days.

"Tell me more about your mother," he asked, wanting to talk about anything but his own family. He also wanted to focus on something other than how the blue of Grace's dress contrasted with the beautiful green of her eyes, how the scoop neckline gave him just a glimpse of the top of her creamy breasts.

"She was a very successful interior designer. She owned her own company and had famous clients on both coasts. She went on buying trips all the time to Paris and Italy, and I think I was probably one of the few things she acquired that was disappointing."

"What makes you say that?" he asked in surprise.

"Mother wanted a mini-me and I was absolutely nothing like her. I didn't care about what a chair cost or where it came from. I didn't appreciate expensive clothes or shoes or any of the finer things in life. I loved animals and children and knew I wanted to be a teacher when I was still in grade school."

"An admirable profession," he commented. Her hair looked like spun silk in the candlelight that flickered in the center of their table. More than anything he wanted to reach his hand out and touch it, wrap one of the loose curls around his fingers and draw her closer to him.

At that moment Bonnie banged her sippy cup on her high chair tray. "More," she said and pointed to the box of crackers visible in the diaper bag.

Without missing a beat Grace gave each of the girls another cracker. "Natalie was much more like my mother. She loves nice things and she was desperate for my mother's attention. Sometimes she got it and sometimes she didn't." She paused to take a sip of her wine. "Sometimes I think I've indulged her too much to try to make up for the attention she didn't get from our mother. And without any father present in her life, I think it was really difficult for her."

"Family dynamics can definitely be difficult," he replied. "Even though my brothers are the same age as me, I feel as if I've been taking care of them all my life. That's why I've decided never to marry or have kids of my own. Once Kerri and Jeffrey move out I'm looking forward to being alone for the rest of my life with nobody to take care of ever again."

She smiled ruefully. "And here I am with a busted-up shoulder and three babies depending on you for the time being."

"But it's not permanent," he countered. "Although, no matter what happens with you and Justin, I'll always consider you and the girls a part of the family." He could tell his words touched her.

"That's nice, but we both know how this is going to work. I'm going to leave here and probably never see or hear from Justin again. I'll get on with my life and you all will get on with yours. The odds of us staying in touch are pretty minimal." There was no self-pity or recrimination in her voice, just a calm stating of the facts of reality.

At that moment the waitress arrived with their orders. "They may need to get out the garden hose after we're finished here," Grace said with a touch of humor as she scooped up a small serving of spaghetti on three little plates for the triplets.

Jake had expected chaos, and there was, but there

was also a lot of laughter as they ate the meal. Casey picked at her spaghetti with dainty fingers and ate one noodle at a time. Abby seemed more interested in the people around them than in the food in front of her. But Bonnie ate with gusto, smooshing the spaghetti into her mouth until sauce decorated her face from ear to ear.

As the kids ate, Grace and Jake enjoyed their meals, but even more, Jake enjoyed the conversation. He liked the way her eyes sparkled as she talked about teaching, sharing funny stories of the children who had passed through her classes. It was obvious that she was well suited to be a teacher, not only from her love of children, but also by the steady patience he sensed in her.

All the qualities that made her a good teacher made her a great mother. Her patience throughout the meal with the girls never wavered, not with spilled drinks, sloppy faces and an occasional cry for attention.

She was beautiful and quick-witted, and every minute he spent with her fed a well of desire that he knew was dangerous. He wanted her. He wanted her in his bed, but the last thing she needed was another Johnson man to take advantage of her and let her down.

And he would let her down. Just like his brother, Jake had no interest in being a husband or a parent for her or any other woman. Still, that didn't mean he didn't enjoy the here and now with her and the girls. And it didn't mean he wouldn't enjoy having her in his bed for just a single night.

When he'd offered dinner out he'd expected a frantic chaos that would turn him off, but instead what he'd found was three well-behaved little girls and a delightful dinner companion who stirred all the senses he possessed.

When they were finished eating, Grace cleaned off the girls' faces and hands with wet wipes and then looked at him. "Do you mind holding down the fort for a few minutes while I make a fast trip to the ladies' room?"

"We'll be fine," he agreed with a smile to the shiny clean faces of the triplets. "While you're gone I'll settle up the bill." He raised a hand as she started to protest. "My idea, my treat."

"Thank you," she said graciously.

He watched as she made her way to the back of the restaurant where the restrooms were located. Her hips held a subtle sway as she walked that enticed him more than a stripper's strut.

There was no cheap flash to Grace, just an understated sexuality coupled with a quiet elegance that made him wonder why Justin had pursued her in the first place.

Justin liked flash and Grace wasn't flashy. She was much more Jake's type. He clenched his jaw tight at this thought. Of course she wasn't his type. He didn't have a type. Hell, he didn't *want* a type.

At that moment, as if conjured up by his very thoughts alone, his brother entered the restaurant. Shirley was at his side, clinging to his arm like a tick to a big-haired dog.

Justin waved and wove through the tables toward Jake, who felt a rise of his blood pressure as they drew closer. This could not be good.

"Hey, what a coincidence seeing you here," Justin said with a bit of a sheepish grin.

"The way I remember our last conversation, I was supposed to see you back at the house," Jake replied with a curt nod to Shirley.

"Yeah, but he forgot he had promised me dinner out tonight," Shirley exclaimed as she looked at the three little girls. "So, this is Moe, Larry and Curly?" she said.

Justin's laugh was cut short by Jake's glare.

"We were just getting ready to leave," Jake said. This had disaster written all over it, and he suddenly wanted to bundle up the girls and get them out of here and away from Shirley and Justin as quickly as possible.

Shirley glanced around and then smiled at Justin. "I'll be right back. I think I need to use the little girls' room."

Before Jake could stop her she took off in the direction Grace had just headed.

Chapter 7

It had been a wonderful night, and Grace couldn't remember the last time she'd enjoyed a man's company as much as she enjoyed Jake's. He scared her just a little bit—because she did like him so much, and because she knew there was nothing there for her or her daughters where he was concerned.

Still, it was far too easy to imagine herself and the girls living with Jake in that big house, sharing days filled with laughter and then going to sleep each night in the safety of his strong arms.

She shook her head to dispel the inappropriate visions. She'd be crazy to even entertain those kinds of dreams. That was definitely the stuff of heartbreak.

She was at the sink in the ladies' room washing her hands when the door opened and a tall blonde woman walked in. She instantly recognized her as the woman who had been with Justin.

"Grace, we haven't officially met yet," the woman said. "My name is Shirley Caldwell. I'm Justin's fiancée, and I just wanted to let you know that you can't have him." She raised her chin in obvious defiance.

Grace fought the impulse to laugh. "That's fine, because I don't want him." She dried her hands and tossed the paper towel into the trash. "And I hope the two of you will be very happy together."

Shirley frowned, as if she was spoiling for a fight that she now recognized probably wasn't going to happen. "I'm going to give him lots of babies, and he'll never love yours like he'll love mine."

Grace saw the desperation in Shirley's eyes, heard it vibrating in her voice. This woman was obviously in love with Justin and saw Grace and the triplets as a threat to that love.

"Shirley, I'm not your enemy," she said as kindly as possible. "I don't want to take anything away from you and whatever life you build with Justin." She edged toward the door, just wanting to escape the awkward situation.

"We weren't together, you know, when you got pregnant. We weren't dating then so he didn't cheat on me to be with you." Shirley raised her chin proudly. "We've been together for six months and he loves me like he's never loved any woman before."

"Then I wish you both the best of luck." Grace left the bathroom with Shirley at her heels. She felt sorry for the woman, had a feeling there was plenty of heartache in her future if she was planning on hitching her star to Justin. She didn't even want to think about the fact that if Justin married Shirley, then Shirley would be the triplets' stepmother. That was the stuff of nightmares.

She was conscious of Shirley following right at her heels as she headed back to the table where Jake stood, a look of strain on his face, quickly followed by an expression of relief at the sight of her.

He stepped toward her and grabbed her good arm. "You okay?" he asked with a quick glance at Shirley.

"I'm fine," she assured him, surprised by how much she liked the feel of his arm on hers. She felt protected by his nearness even though she didn't need any protection.

"Hi, Grace," Justin said. "Guess you and Shirley already met."

"We did," she replied, vaguely disappointed when Jake dropped his hand and stepped away from her.

"Good, then you can help me carry the girls out to the car," he said to his brother. He plucked Casey from her high chair and handed her to the surprised Justin. "As you can see, it's difficult for Grace to carry the kids with her arm in the sling. Shirley, if you can grab that diaper bag, then we can all get the girls settled into my car."

There was a ring of authority in Jake's voice that Grace was surprised both Justin and Shirley responded to. Jake picked up Abby and Bonnie, and

Grace followed them all, slightly bemused by the procession that had her empty-handed and lagging behind.

"That has to be the most bizarre thing that has ever happened to me," she said moments later as Jake was driving her and the girls back to the ranch. "Starting with being confronted in the bathroom by my baby daddy's latest girlfriend."

Jake shot her a quick smile. "I was afraid I might have to storm in there to protect you from her pulling out all your hair or something."

"And what makes you think I couldn't have kicked the stuffing out of her if I'd needed to?" she countered with a grin.

"You look more like a lover than a fighter," he replied. He snapped his gaze from her to the street ahead and just that quickly it was there between them again, that simmering tension that curled heat in her stomach and made her want…something…something she shouldn't, something she couldn't have.

"It was a surprise to turn around from the sink in the bathroom and see Shirley standing there," she said in an effort to ease some of that tension. "She's in love with Justin. She just wanted to stake her claim."

"He'll only break her heart, too. That's what he does, breaks hearts."

Grace smiled. "He didn't break my heart. Oh, he might have destroyed a little fantasy I'd entertained."

Jake cast her a quick glance. “What kind of fantasy?”

“You know, the kind where I meet the man who fathered my children after a long time apart and sparks fly and we suddenly realize we belong together and live happily ever after.”

“Did you really expect that to happen?”

“No, but as I was driving here I kind of hoped it might. Of course, it took about two seconds with Justin to realize that wasn’t going to happen.” She shifted her gaze and stared out the window into the darkness of the night. “But eventually I’ll find my happily-ever-after, not just for my girls, but also for myself. I don’t want to live alone like my mother did for all her life. I want somebody to share both the good times and the bad times with me. I want a soul mate.”

“It’s not going to be easy, finding a man who will not only want to be with you but will also want to be an instant father to three little girls.”

“I know I’m a package deal. Nobody ever told me life would be easy,” she replied. “It doesn’t have to happen today or next week or even next year, but eventually I’ll find a man who wants to be a part of my life and my children’s lives.”

“At this point I think we can both agree that it isn’t going to be Justin,” he said drily.

“We definitely can agree on that,” she replied with a small laugh.

By this time they had reached the ranch, and all

three of the girls had fallen sound asleep in their car seats.

Jake managed to place Casey over Grace's good shoulder and then he carried both Bonnie and Abby in his arms. He looked so right with a sleeping little girl in each arm as they climbed the stairs. He laid each of them in the crib with a gentleness that touched her heart.

He stepped to the back to the doorway as she covered each child and touched each sleeping face with love. Then, together, she and Jake went back down the stairs.

"How about some coffee?" he asked.

"Sounds good," she agreed. As she followed behind him toward the kitchen, she tried to tamp down the emotions that pressed tight in her chest where he was concerned.

Jake Johnson was getting to her, inching his way into her heart in a way that could only lead to heartbreak. She moved her shoulder beneath the sling, unsurprised by the sharp pain that was her reply.

Not yet. She wasn't ready to take off from here tomorrow, but maybe by the next day she could load up her daughters and head back home. In the meantime she just needed to guard her heart the best she could from Jake.

They lingered over coffee in the living room, continuing their conversation about everything and nothing. They talked about favorite foods and books read, about the antics of the girls and the fact that Bonnie would probably be the first of the three to walk.

"Abby is too content wherever she sits to walk too quickly. Casey is too shy to be the first one to explore the world of being upright. Bonnie is definitely my adventurous little soul," she said.

"She's a corker," he agreed with an easy smile.

"She definitely likes you."

"They all seem to like people," he replied.

"I think it's because from the time they were two months old they've been in day care. They're used to seeing new people all the time."

Jake drained the last of the coffee from his cup. "We should probably go to bed. I imagine the girls are early risers."

"They are," she agreed, reluctant to call an end to what had been a wonderful evening. She stood and together she and Jake carried their coffee cups to the kitchen.

She wasn't sure exactly how it happened, but as they both reached to set their cups in the sink, her face was suddenly too close to his. His breath felt warm on her cheek and his eyes flared dark with a desire that was unmistakable.

They both straightened, and somewhere in the back of her mind she knew she should step away from him, gain some needed distance, but her feet refused to obey her mental command.

He was going to kiss her. She saw his intent shimmering in his eyes, and as sure as she knew he was going to kiss her she also knew she wasn't going to stop him.

She'd never wanted a kiss as much as she wanted his at this very moment. When he dipped his head she met him halfway, rising up on her tiptoes.

His mouth touched hers softly…tentatively at first, as if unsure of his own intent or his welcome. She opened her mouth and he took the welcome, deepening the kiss with a searing intensity that shot thrilling sensations through her body.

It lasted only a minute and then he stumbled back from her, his midnight-blue eyes still blazing with desire. "That was a mistake." His voice was deep, almost gravelly as his gaze lingered on her mouth.

"I agree." The words whispered from her with a sigh of longing.

"I want to do it again." The words sounded as if they'd been pulled from the very depths of him.

"Oh, Jake, I want you to."

The words were barely out of her mouth before his lips silenced her once again. Hot and greedy, his lips plied hers and she melted against him as well as her sling would allow.

His arms wound around her gently, as if he remembered her shoulder and didn't want to hurt her, yet needed her as close to him as possible. And she wanted to be that close.

His tongue swirled with hers, demanding a response that she gave eagerly. Somewhere in the back of her mind she knew this was wrong, so very wrong.

This wasn't a man she should be kissing, this wasn't a man she should be wanting. But that didn't stop her from doing either.

His mouth finally left hers and trailed a blaze of hunger down the side of her throat. She dropped her head back with her eyes closed, dizzied by his scent and by his very touch.

He kissed her just behind one of her ears. "Stop," he murmured against the sensitive skin. "We have to stop this." He slowly dropped his arms from around her and once again stepped back, this time his eyes dark and unreadable. "I'm sorry. That shouldn't have happened."

"I know, but I wanted it as much as you did," she admitted, her voice slightly shaky with the emotions still raging through her. She still wanted him, she thought.

"You know by now that there's no future here with Justin. There's also no future for you here with me." He jammed his hands in his pockets, as if afraid of where they might wander if left somehow untethered.

"To be honest, I wasn't looking for any kind of a future. I was just in the moment and looking forward to the next. I'm a big girl, Jake, and you've made it very clear to me what your desire is about being alone for the rest of your life. I just thought maybe you didn't want to be alone tonight." She felt the burn of a blush fill her cheeks. She had never said anything so forward to a man before, but she'd also never felt this way about a man before.

The blaze was back in his eyes and she wanted to fall into that dark fire and just for one night feel like a sexy woman, not like a schoolteacher with triplets. It was a foolish desire, but at the moment she wouldn't mind a little bit of foolishness with him.

"There's no question that there's something between us, Grace, some crazy physical attraction that has been there since the minute I laid eyes on you. But because we're adults we aren't going to follow through on it. It would only complicate what's already a pretty good mess."

She knew he was right. Now that the heat of the moment was passing, rational thought was returning. "I know you're right. You and I together would just be plain stupid. I just got carried away in the moment."

He offered her a small smile. "We both did. And now I think it's definitely time we say good-night." He didn't wait for her response but turned on his heels and left the kitchen.

Grace wasn't sure whether to be disappointed or glad at the way things had turned out. On the one hand, she knew that Jake would never be more than a one-night stand—the second in her life and another one with unwanted consequences. Although she wouldn't have wound up pregnant, she had a feeling it would have been impossible to keep her heart uninvolved.

On the other hand, she knew it would have been a night to remember when she was back home by herself and with that whisper of loneliness that sometimes struck her.

She turned off the kitchen light and then climbed the stairs and went directly into the room where the triplets were sleeping. She wanted to be the best possible mother she could be for them, but that didn't stop her needs and wants as a woman.

She'd told him the truth when she'd said she wanted somebody to share her life, a soul mate who would grow old with her and watch their grandchildren grow.

As she left the triplets' bedroom she glanced down the long hallway to the very end where she knew the master suite was located. Was Jake in bed now thinking about what might have happened? What could have happened if he hadn't stopped it?

Was he in bed still feeling the burn that filled her stomach, that ached deep inside her? She knew with a woman's certainty that if she walked down that hallway and opened the door to his bedroom they'd wind up in his bed making love.

Her feet actually took three steps in that direction before she stopped herself and instead turned and went into her own guest room.

At least this room didn't smell of his scent—that of a wonderfully clean male combined with a woodsy undertone. She'd cracked open the sliding door that led to the balcony earlier in the day and the slight breeze blowing through brought with it the scent of fresh grass, evening dew and country flowers.

She undressed and changed into her nightgown, then put the sling back on. She was going to try to sleep in it, although usually when she woke up in the mornings she discovered she'd taken it off at some point in the night.

As she placed her cell phone on the dresser, she realized she hadn't heard anything from Natalie that day. She wasn't sure if that was a good thing or bad.

Grace got into bed, feeling as if it had been a lifetime ago that she had loaded the girls into her car to leave Wichita. She'd had such hope in her heart that she'd come away from here with a father for the girls, a father who would love and emotionally support them as they flourished and grew.

She knew now that wasn't going to happen. If Justin wasn't the kind of stable, mature man he needed to be by the age of thirty-five, she didn't see it happening ever. She suspected Justin had a drinking problem, and that only added to the many reasons she knew he'd never be the man she wanted in her daughters' lives.

Maybe someday she would find somebody to love her, to love them, and he would take on the role of a good and loving stepfather. Grace hoped if that ever happened it might be enough for the girls.

There was no way of knowing for sure, but her gut instinct told her that Justin hadn't had anything to do with whoever had shot at her. She was willing to believe the sheriff's speculation that a drifter had set up camp in the woods and in some deluded thinking had seen her walking around as a threat to his little temporary home.

Justin had been a mistake, and she was more than a little half-crazy for his brother. She squeezed her eyes closed, seeking sleep rather than thoughts of Jake.

Although her shoulder was still sore, it was less so than it had been. She was hoping that by the day after tomorrow at the very latest she could head home. She just needed to get back to her ordinary life, raising her children and enjoying the summer before fall came and she had to return to work.

With a deep sigh she closed her eyes, knowing she needed to get some sleep in order to have the energy to deal with her daughters and anything else that might come up the next day.

She wasn't sure what awakened her…a noise… a whisper of breath on the side of her face? For a sleepy, half-conscious moment she thought it was Jake who had come to her room to finish what they'd started earlier in the night.

She came fully awake and immediately a cloth was shoved in her mouth, preventing her from releasing the scream that instantly leapt to her lips.

Somebody jumped on top of her, although in the dark it was impossible to tell who it was. What was going on? She couldn't make sense of it. She only knew pure unadulterated terror as gloved hands wrapped around her neck and began to squeeze.

With one arm in her sling and her legs trapped

beneath the sheets, she was nearly helpless in any effort to fight back. She flailed her good arm, trying to make contact with the face of the attacker.

Air.

She needed air.

Her lungs were slowly being depleted of precious oxygen as it was being squeezed from her. She bucked her hips, kicked wildly at the sheets and twisted her head back and forth, trying to break the grip on her throat.

Help! Somebody please help me!

The words screamed in her head but had no way around whatever had been stuffed in her mouth as a gag. She was going to die!

Her babies. Who was going to take care of her babies? As she felt the edges of unconsciousness creeping in, she made one last desperate attempt to help herself. She flung her free arm out and it connected with the bedside lamp. The Tiffany-style light crashed to the floor with a shattering of glass and an answering cry came from one of the triplets.

Don't hurt my babies, she thought wildly.

The intruder jumped off Grace and ran for the balcony. As the person disappeared over the balcony edge, Grace pulled the gag from her mouth and released a scream.

Chapter 8

The crash awakened Jake from a wild, sexy dream about Grace. In the dream she'd been in his bed and they had been making love. The cry of one of the girls galvanized him to leave the dream behind, get out of bed and pull on his jeans. But the sound of Grace's scream shot him out of the room and down the hallway toward hers.

As he ran his heart pounded with adrenaline. What on earth would make her scream like that? He entered her room and flipped on the light to see her sitting up, her hand at her throat and utter terror shining wildly from her eyes.

By now all three girls were crying, but Jake's complete attention was focused on the woman in the bed. "What happened?" he asked, feeling as if his heart was about to pound out of his chest.

"Somebody came in…attacked me…he went over the balcony." The words rasped from her as she half stumbled from the bed. "I've got to get to the girls."

"Don't move," Jake replied. She looked as if she was in shock, her legs barely able to hold her up. Her throat was red and angry looking, and as Jake ran to the balcony there was nothing more he wanted to do than rip somebody's head off.

Unfortunately, as he stepped outside on the balcony and looked around, there was nobody to see. The night was complete with darkness and barely a sliver of moonlight to faintly illuminate the landscape.

It was easy to tell how the intruder had gotten inside. The balcony could have been accessed by the sturdy wooden trellis that climbed up the house next to it, a trellis that would no longer exist after he got done with it.

He went back into the bedroom, closed and locked the sliding glass door, unsurprised to find Grace not there. Even crazy with fear and with her throat burning and raw, her first thought would be to soothe her crying daughters. He spied her cell phone on the dresser and used it to call Sheriff Hicks, then went to where he knew Grace would be.

Sure enough she was in the girls' bedroom, moving from crib to crib in an effort to put the girls back to sleep, and it was working. As she rubbed a back, spoke softly and gave kisses, the girls eventually all settled back to sleep.

It was only when the room was quiet again that she met him in the hallway. He gestured for her to follow him back into the bedroom. There, under the overhead light, he could once again see the angry red ring that decorated her neck.

As he stared at it, she began to shiver, as if the initial shock was wearing off and now that she felt like her daughters didn't need her anymore she was about to fall to pieces.

He opened his arms and she collapsed against him, deep sobs ripping up from someplace deep inside her. He didn't ask any questions. Those would come later. For now he just held her as she trembled almost violently in his arms.

He would kill the person responsible for this. Anger roared through him as he held her tight, her heartbeat frantic against his own.

"Come on, let's go downstairs to wait for Greg," he finally said when some of the trembling had eased. He wanted to get her out of the bedroom where the attack had taken place in case there might be some evidence that could be collected.

"You called him?" she asked as she grabbed her robe. She pulled it around her and they left the bedroom.

"I did. He's on his way." He kept one arm around her as they went down the stairs and then he sat next to her on the sofa, still with an arm around her as she continued to shiver off and on.

"I had the sliding glass door open a little bit," she said, her voice filled with self-recrimination. "I didn't imagine that anyone could get inside. I didn't think that anyone would want to get inside, to get to me…to try to kill me." Her voice rose slightly with each word. "Why is this happening? Who's doing this to me?"

"Shh, it's all right now," Jake said, but his mind raced. This attack tonight put the shooting incident in a whole new light.

There was no mistaking the fact that somebody had breached the sanctity of his home in the middle of the night for the sole intent of hurting Grace. They'd climbed up that trellis, crept into her room and wrapped their hands around her throat.

That meant in all probability those shots had been intended specifically for Grace and not the result of some drifter trying to protect a temporary homestead.

Somebody had tried to kill Grace not once, but twice, and Jake had never felt so helpless or so damned angry in his entire life. Thankfully, at that moment Greg Hicks and a couple of his deputies showed up at the door.

Jake and Grace took the lawmen upstairs to the bedroom to explain what had happened. Two deputies stayed behind to begin collecting evidence and processing the scene while Greg, Jake and Grace returned to the living room so Greg could ask Grace some questions.

"Now, tell me exactly what happened," Greg said.

Jake was impressed by the way Grace had pulled herself together. The robe was belted tightly around her slender waist and she'd not only stopped trembling, but even had a steely strength radiating from her eyes.

"I woke up knowing somebody was in my room. Before I could do anything, he was on top of me and had shoved a gag into my mouth. Then he tried to strangle me."

She raised her hand to her neck. Some of the redness had faded, but the idea of anyone wrapping their hands around her neck, the throat he'd kissed with such desire earlier, filled Jake with new rage.

"I thought he was going to kill me. I tried to fight but with my sling on I only had one hand. I finally managed to knock over the lamp next to the bed, which woke up one of my girls, which apparently woke up Jake." She cast him a grateful look. "I pulled the gag out of my mouth and screamed."

"By the time I got to the bedroom, whoever had been inside was gone. I went out on the balcony but didn't see anyone. Unfortunately, there's no light out there so he could have been anywhere in the yard and I probably wouldn't have seen him."

"Do we know for sure it was a him?" Greg asked.

Grace looked at him in stunned surprise, as if the idea that her attacker might have been a woman hadn't occurred to her. It certainly hadn't occurred to Jake.

"I don't know," she said slowly. "I just assumed…" Once again her hand went to her throat. "The grip was awfully strong to be a woman. And the person felt heavy…big." She dropped her hand and released a deep sigh. "But I was also terrified out of my mind, and my perceptions of those moments could be way off."

"Hopefully Deputy Bartell and Deputy Lathrop will find something…a fingerprint or a hair," Greg replied.

Grace shook her head. "There won't be any fingerprints. Whoever it was, he or she was wearing gloves." She winced, as if able to feel those gloves still around her neck.

"Greg, you've got to do something about this," Jake snapped angrily, and then caught himself and offered a tight smile of apology. "Sorry, I didn't mean to yell at you. I'm just frustrated."

"Don't worry," Greg replied easily. "No offense taken."

"Does Shirley know how to fire a gun?" Grace asked. Both Greg and Jake looked at her in surprise. "Well, it's obvious she resents my connection to Justin. I was just wondering."

"I don't know if Shirley knows how to shoot or not. Certainly most of the women around these parts aren't unfamiliar with guns," Greg replied. "I believe her daddy is a hunter."

Jake tried to wrap his mind around the idea of Shirley as some crazed, jealous killer. Crazed jealous girlfriend, yes, that was easy to imagine, but a killer? He'd known Shirley for most of his life and wouldn't have thought it of her, but wasn't this the kind of real-life stuff television movies were made of?

He listened as Grace explained to Greg about the earlier confrontation with Shirley in the ladies' room at the restaurant. "It wasn't really ugly," she said. "I assured her I had no grand design on Justin, and when Jake and I left them at the restaurant I assumed everything was fine between me and Shirley."

"So right now I've got a list with a grand total of two suspects on it—Justin and Shirley." Greg shook his head. "Justin's alibi for the time of the shooting was fairly solid. Maybe I need to have a little chat with Shirley about where she was when those shots were fired and where she was tonight. At least that's a place to start."

He looked at Grace for a long moment. "You sure there isn't somebody else in your life that might have a grudge against you?"

"A grudge deep enough to want me dead?" She gave a half-hysterical laugh. "Nobody that I can think of. I can't even imagine what Justin or Shirley would hope to gain by my death. None of this makes sense, none of it!"

Jake once again placed an arm around her shoulder

as he heard the rising emotion in her voice. She was scared and bewildered and he felt the same way.

"I need to go home," she said, more to herself than to anyone in the room.

"I understand your desire, Ms. Sinclair, but I'd really like it if you'd stick around another couple of days while I do a little investigating," Greg said.

"I'll keep you safe, Grace," Jake exclaimed. "I'll turn this place into a damned fortress if necessary to make sure that nothing else happens to you while you and the girls are here."

She looked at Greg. "I'll stay through tomorrow, but first thing the next day I'm going back home."

Jake wanted to protest but realized he had no right to ask her to stay any longer. Justin had certainly given her no reason to hang around. Somebody had tried to kill her twice. Could he really blame her for wanting to get out of town as soon as possible?

He had a feeling if not for her shoulder injury she'd already be packed up and in her car headed back to Wichita. He knew with certainty that come hell or high water, she'd force her shoulder to be okay to get her out of here the day after tomorrow.

He should be glad to see her go. After all, that's what he'd wanted from the moment she'd shown up here with those adorable little girls and a gun in her pocket.

Thoughts of the gun sat him up straighter on the sofa. He hadn't thought about it since they'd locked it in his glove box at the hospital the day that Grace had fallen. If she'd had that gun tonight maybe she would have been able to stop the attack, wound the attacker. Or the gun could have been taken away from her and used on her instead.

A headache blossomed across his forehead, along with a tight vise across his chest as he realized what might have happened tonight. If she hadn't managed to hit the lamp, if one of the girls hadn't started to cry, he might not have gotten out of bed and the intruder might have been successful in killing her.

Chapter 9

Grace awoke the next morning in Jake's king-size bed between the navy sheets that held his familiar scent. For a long moment she didn't move, just remained still and breathed in the essence of him.

After Greg and the deputies had finally left, Jake had insisted she sleep in here for what was left of the night while he bunked in Kerri and Jeffrey's room next door.

She'd expected to be awake all night. She'd expected to be scared senseless until dawn lit the morning skies. But almost the minute she'd wrapped herself in the sheets that smelled of Jake, she'd fallen into a deep, dreamless sleep.

She suddenly shot up, aware that the sun was drifting in through the window at an angle that let her know it was late. The girls! Why hadn't they awakened her with their morning cries? They never slept this late.

She jumped out of the bed and grabbed her robe and her cell phone from the nearby chair. She pulled on the robe as she raced out of the room and held the cell phone ready to call for help if necessary. She realized at some point in the night she must have taken her sling off in her sleep, but that didn't matter now. All that mattered was that she check on her daughters and make sure they were okay.

One glance in the girls' room showed three empty cribs. Panic soared through Grace as she half ran, half stumbled down the stairs.

The normal scents of fresh-brewed coffee, crispy bacon and eggs calmed her as she entered the kitchen and saw her three girls all happily seated at their high chairs and enjoying a mess of scrambled eggs on their trays.

Jake stood at the stove with his back to her. He wore only a pair of jeans and was singing a rap-style rendition of "Rock-a-Bye Baby."

It was at that moment that Grace knew without a doubt that she was in love with him. She was head over heels in love with Jake Johnson.

She'd seen his tenderness with her daughters, tasted the passion in his kiss. She was in love with him and there was nothing she could do about it, no way to change it.

She must have made some sort of noise, for he

whirled around, spatula in hand, and gave her a smile that warmed her from her head to her toes.

"There she is, girls. Your mommy, our own sleeping beauty, has finally decided to get out of bed." He pointed her to a seat at the table. "Sit and relax. Bacon and eggs in about three minutes. I hope you like your eggs over however. Sometimes they're sunny and soft and sometimes they break."

"Over however is my very favorite," she said as she gave each girl a kiss on their foreheads, then sat at the table. Abby's T-shirt was on inside out and Bonnie was wearing Casey's shorts, but it was obvious Jake had done his best to get the girls up and dressed for the day.

She was grateful when he turned back to face the stove so she could have a moment to get her newly recognized emotion under control. She'd known she was getting too close to Jake, feeling wildly sexually attracted to him, but it wasn't until now that the full force of her love for him crashed inside her heart.

"Where's your sling?" he asked as he placed a plate of bacon, eggs and toast in front of her.

"Probably on the floor next to your bed. I take it off in my sleep. Aren't you eating?" she asked as she took the fork and napkin he offered her.

"Already ate. I wasn't sure what all the girls should have for breakfast so I smooshed up some banana for them before I gave them the eggs. Was that okay?"

"Perfect." His bare chest made it difficult for her

to concentrate on anything he was saying. That muscled chest should be outlawed for its effect on helpless women trying to eat their breakfast.

He grabbed a cup of coffee and joined her at the table. "How did you sleep?"

"Surprisingly well, considering."

His eyes narrowed slightly and lingered on her throat. "How's your neck?"

"A little sore, but I'm going to be fine." She watched as he used a napkin and wiped egg from Casey's chin as if it was the most natural thing in the world for him to do.

"You'd make an awesome father, Jake." The words slipped from her unbidden.

He frowned and tossed the napkin aside. "I've spent most of my life fathering my brother. I don't have the desire or the energy to father anyone else."

"Why don't you stop?"

"Stop what?"

She broke off a piece of her toast, but instead of popping it into her mouth she set it on the side of her plate and kept her gaze focused on his eyes. "Why don't you stop fathering Justin?"

She could tell her question irritated him, and maybe that's what she'd intended. Maybe she wanted to see him a little bit angry with her to somehow diminish what was in her heart for him.

"It's complicated." He took a sip of his coffee and eyed her over the rim of the cup. When he lowered it he gave her a tight smile. "I could ask you the same question. Why are you still mothering your sister?"

She hadn't expected him to turn the tables on her. "Okay, you're right. It's complicated. There are some nights I go to bed and swear to myself that the next time she gets herself in a fix I'm going to force her to get herself out of it."

"I've had plenty of those same kinds of nights," he replied. "I know Justin drinks too much and he's irresponsible. I know he makes bad choices, and most of the time I clean them up for him. But just about the time I decide to wash my hands of him, I get a vision in my head of my old man beating the crap out of him when he was about six, and I remember I made myself a promise that I'd always take care of Justin."

She heard the tension in his voice and realized he'd gone to a dark place in his mind with his memories of his father. "It was a tough childhood," he continued. "Every morning I'd wake up and wonder if that was the day my dad was going to kill either me or one of my brothers."

"What a terrible way to live," she replied softly.

"It was, and the worst part was we never saw it coming. Dad was mercurial with his moods. I remember one night at dinner we were all sitting at the table. It had been a relatively pleasant day and Dad seemed to be in a pretty good mood. Then Justin reached for the bowl of mashed potatoes. Dad backhanded him so hard his chair tipped over backward and Justin crashed to the floor. He got up, got settled back in his chair, and Dad asked him if he wanted more of what he'd just gotten. Justin said no, but he'd still like to have some more mashed potatoes."

Jake shook his head and released a small laugh. "Justin never did know when to stop playing the fool."

Grace's heart hurt for the little boys they had been. She couldn't imagine a childhood like what they had endured. "What happened?"

Jake shrugged. "Dad passed him the potatoes and the meal went on as if nothing had happened." He leaned back in his chair and drew a deep breath, then released it on a weary wind of resignation. "I know I cut him too much slack, run to his rescue way too often. There are times I just can't get the vision of him as a kid out of my head."

"But he's not a kid anymore," Grace said gently. "He's a man. It was different for me and Natalie," she said, trying to ease some of the darkness in his eyes. "I recognized fairly early that my mother wasn't capable of giving me the emotional support and love that I needed. I also realized fairly young that it was not a problem with me, but rather a problem with her."

"That's a pretty astute thing for a kid to figure out." He got up to pour himself more coffee.

"Mom was different with Natalie, more involved with her but not in the ways Natalie needed most. Mom would buy things for Natalie, spoil her with expensive items and toys, but she never gave Natalie what she needed most, which was her time and love."

"And so you have tried to make up for that with your sister." He returned to the table and offered her a rueful smile. "We're quite a pair, you know. Both of us trying to heal the damage our parents inflicted on our siblings." His smile faded as he looked at the girls in their high chairs. "He's never going to be what they need in their lives. I just don't think he's capable."

She nodded. "I know that now, and that's okay. I can't force him to be something he isn't." She raised a hand to her throat. "Now I just want to know if Shirley was the one who tried to kill me. It would be nice if I left in the morning with some kind of closure about what really happened here."

"I'm hoping Greg will have some news for us sometime today. Are you sure you'll be well enough to head home in the morning?"

Experimentally she moved her shoulder and winced slightly. "It's still sore, but much better than it's been. I think I'll be fine. If I need help when I get home I'll arrange for some." She stared at him for a long moment and once again her love for him buoyed up inside her, pressing tight against her chest. "It's time for me to go home, Jake." She had to leave, because she so desperately didn't want to leave him.

He opened his mouth as if he wanted to say something, and then closed it again and nodded. By that time the girls were finished with their breakfast. "Da-da," Bonnie said to Jake and held out her arms.

"Don't worry, she doesn't mean it," Grace said as she carried her plate to the sink, rinsed it and placed it in the dishwasher. "Most babies say 'da-da' pretty regularly. It's an easy sound for them to make. We'll just get them settled in the living room for some playtime and you can take care of whatever chores you need to do."

"I'm not doing any chores today. I'm not leaving your side, Grace. I told you last night that I'd make sure nothing else happened to you while you were here and I meant it. My ranch hands can take care of anything that needs attention outside. Today it's just you and me and the girls."

He grabbed Bonnie from the high chair and then filled his other arm with Abby. There was nothing more appealing that a man dressed in babies, Grace thought as she carefully picked up Casey, using her good arm to do most of the work.

They got the girls settled in the living room. At that moment Grace's cell phone rang. She dug it out of her robe pocket, pleased to see on the caller ID that it was Natalie.

"Hey, sis," she said, trying to ignore how cute Jake looked seated on the floor with the girls. "I'm glad to finally hear from you."

"I was busy all day yesterday. I got a job," Natalie said.

"Natalie, that's wonderful! Where? Doing what?"

"It's just a waitressing job, but it's at a nice restaurant and the tips are decent and I kind of like it."

"But that's great," Grace exclaimed. "There's nothing wrong with waitressing, and at least it will give you a reason to get up in the mornings." *And hopefully a sense of responsibility,* Grace thought.

"So, what's up with you? When are you coming home? I miss you."

Grace smiled at her sister's words. "I miss you, too. And I'm planning on heading home first thing in the morning, so I should be there by noon at the latest."

"I'm working until five or so. I'll stop by your place as soon as I get off. Nothing has changed between you and Justin?"

"I've never met a man less likely to step up to be a father, so no, nothing has changed."

"Sorry about that. Kiss the girls for me and I'll see you tomorrow."

"I will," Grace agreed. She hung up and smiled at Jake. "She got a job."

"Congratulations," he replied. "That's got to be a relief."

"It is. She started yesterday, waitressing someplace. Let's just hope she can keep it for more than a week. Natalie has always been fairly good at getting jobs, it's been keeping them that's been the issue."

"Maybe this time will be different."

"Famous last words," she said and flashed him a rueful smile.

"Now, why don't you run upstairs and get dressed for the day while I watch the munchkins," he suggested. "Because I've got to tell you the truth, seeing you in that silky robe through breakfast has made my mind wander to places it definitely shouldn't."

"Oh." Grace's cheeks filled with heat. "And maybe while I do that you should pull on a shirt so I don't have the same problem," she replied and then turned and hurried up the stairs.

Desire for Jake nipped at her heels as she raced into her bedroom, a healthy desire coupled with the quieter, wondrous feeling of love.

She had somebody who wanted to kill her and she was in love with the brother of the man who had fathered her children, a man who had made it clear in every way possible that she would never have a place in his life. Grace knew with a painful certainty that one way or another she wasn't going to leave here unscathed.

"The sheriff told me and Shirley to stay away," Justin exclaimed, his voice slightly slurred as if he'd already had too much to drink. "He said Grace was attacked last night and he thinks maybe me or Shirley had something to do with it. Jake, what in the hell is going on?"

Jake pressed the cell phone closer to his ear. "Where were you both last night?"

"I was home in bed, and I assume Shirley was home in her bed. I left her place around eleven, tired of all the drama. She kept going on and on about how much baggage the kids were going to be and when were we going to get married and have our own kids and stuff like that. Jake, I'll be the first to admit that Shirley wasn't exactly happy to learn about Grace and the kids, but she wouldn't try to kill Grace. You know me, Jake, and you've known Shirley most of her life. How could you believe such a thing of either one of us?"

Jake had already heard from Greg earlier in the day that Justin and Shirley's alibis for the night before were shaky at best.

He glanced in the kitchen where the girls were once again in their high chairs and Grace was finishing up the dinner preparations. "I don't know what to believe, Justin," he finally said. "The only thing I know for sure is that twice somebody has tried to harm Grace, and I intend to make sure she stays safe until she leaves here to go home. If I were you and Shirley I'd make sure until Grace leaves town you're in the company of other people so you have a solid alibi if anything else happens."

Jake knew his words were harsh, but he wanted his brother to understand the reality of the situation. Greg was looking for an attempted murderer, and at the moment the only two suspects on his list were Justin and Shirley. Jake simply couldn't believe his brother had anything to do with this, but he wasn't so sure about Shirley.

"Where are you now, Justin?"

"Me and Shirley are at Tony's having a few brews."

"You really think that's a good idea? Maybe it's time you do a little less drinking, Justin. Maybe a stint in rehab wouldn't hurt."

"Whoa, buddy," Justin said with a forced laugh. "You're in a foul mood."

Jake released a tired sigh. "No, I'm not in a foul mood, Justin. I just want what's best for you and everyone else concerned. Sooner or later you're going to have to figure out how you're going to handle all this. But, for now, Greg is right. You and Shirley need to stay away from here."

"Problems?" Grace asked when he'd said goodbye to his brother and entered the kitchen.

"No, everything is fine," he assured her. The only real problem he'd had all day was his nearness to her. Watching her interact with the girls, enjoying the warmth of her smiles, the very fragrance of her, and remembering the fire of their kiss had set him on slow burn throughout the entire day. "Something in here smells good."

"Meat loaf, homemade mac and cheese, and peas," she replied as she stirred the peas simmering in a pot on the stove.

"Anything I can do to help?"

"Just sit and relax. I've got it all ready to put on the table."

He sat, but it was almost impossible to relax as he watched her bustling about. *She'll be gone tomorrow.*

The words jumped into his head unbidden, as they had off and on throughout the afternoon.

It's what you want, he reminded himself. All he'd ever wanted since the moment she'd arrived was to be out of her drama and left alone. Tomorrow morning he would get his wish, and he couldn't understand why he didn't feel completely happy at the prospect.

Maybe it was just because he didn't like mysteries, and the gunshots and the attack in the bedroom were certainly mysteries that hadn't been solved. And it didn't look as if they were going to be solved before she left town.

"You're very quiet," she said once she had everything on the table and had joined him there.

"I was just thinking that it's going to be pretty quiet around here once you and the girls leave." As if to punctuate his sentence, Bonnie squealed in delight as Grace set her plate of mac and cheese, and peas in front of her. The other two reacted in much the same way then grew silent as they began to eat.

"I'll bet you can't wait to get your house back to the peace and quiet it was before we arrived," Grace said.

"Yeah, right," he replied, not meeting her gaze as he began to fill his plate. Peace and quiet, that's what he wanted. No babies crawling on him, drooling kisses or giggling with glee. No hair or ear pulling, no batting eyelashes, nothing that would bring a smile to his lips or any warmth of connection to his heart.

No Grace scent muddying his mind, twisting him inside out with feelings he'd never had before. It would just be plain stupid to allow anything to develop with Grace and the girls. It would be counterproductive to everything he'd decided he wanted in his life.

"It's too bad Greg didn't have a definitive answer for you about the attacks before you left," he said when the silence between them had stretched for too long.

She paused with a forkful of macaroni and cheese halfway to her mouth. "He could call with an answer before I go in the morning. I don't believe your brother was behind the attacks, Jake. However, my verdict is still out on Shirley. There was no question that she thought I was somehow a threat to her relationship with Justin." Her green eyes darkened. "I guess that kind of jealousy and desperation can make an unstable woman capable of almost anything. Besides, it's the only thing that makes any kind of sense. I'm fairly certain that once I leave here tomorrow I won't hear from Justin again and Shirley will have no reason to feel threatened anymore."

Jake wished he could protest her words, tell her that he was sure his brother would not only get in contact with her but would be a supportive presence in his daughters' lives. But at this point he knew they would just be empty words.

The only thing they knew for sure about the attack was that a red bandana had been used as the gag in Grace's mouth, and they were sold at every store in the area.

And tomorrow she would be gone.

Jake felt as if there was an invisible presence in the room that made itself known in a sizzling burn in the pit of his gut.

Desire. It had chased him through the house all day, ached deep inside him as they finished the meal. It whispered want to him as they cleaned up the kitchen, and it grew noisier in his head two hours later when they put the girls down to sleep for the night.

There was a part of him that believed that if he had her, if he made love with her just one time, then she'd be out of his system for good and it would be easier for him to tell her goodbye the next morning.

But there was another part of him that feared it would never be enough, that if he made love to her once then he would want to repeat it again and again. And she represented everything he didn't want in his life.

With the girls in their cribs for the night, they went back down to the living room where she sat on the sofa and he sat in the chair opposite her. He wanted to maintain as much physical distance from her as possible and yet be in the same room.

"I'm sorry things worked out the way they did for

you here," he said. "You know you could take Justin to court, force him to at least pay child support."

"I would if it meant my babies having something or nothing," she replied. "I absolutely believe every child has a right to have the financial support of both parents. But in this case, the girls are well taken care of. And, to be honest, I'm ready to walk away from Justin and not look back."

A flash of pain crossed her features. "He's obviously not ready to be a father, and making him pay child support isn't going to change that. Someday he'll have to answer to the girls, but he doesn't have to answer to me."

"You're a strong woman."

She smiled and nodded. "Yes, I am. And you're a strong man, and I hope the day comes when you can stop carrying the sins of your father on your back."

He sat up straighter and looked at her in surprise. "I'm not doing that," he protested.

"Of course you are," she countered. "I think we've both been doing more than our share of that," she replied. "Trying to make up to Natalie and Justin for things they didn't get in their childhoods, things we didn't get in our childhoods. Personally, I plan on making some changes when I get home where Natalie is concerned. She's going to have to learn to stand on her own. It's past time I cut the cord. I have three baby girls to focus my energy on."

"And what happens in the fall when you go back to work?"

"They go to a terrific day care." She gazed off into space thoughtfully. "I have to admit there's a part of me that would love to be a stay-at-home mom until they got to be school-age. I have my contract for working next fall sitting at home on my desk. I haven't signed it yet. I love teaching, but I'm also aware that I can't get back the girls' toddler years. I'm lucky in that if I don't live lavishly and am smart, I can afford to make a decision rather than the decision being forced on me."

"Whatever choice you make, I'm sure it will be a good one. You strike me as a woman who only makes good choices."

She smiled with a touch of humor. "Don't forget there were two of us in that bed when the triplets were conceived. I acted as stupid and reckless as Justin did that night. I'm ashamed to admit I hardly have any memories at all after a certain point in the evening, but there's no question that I decided to throw caution to the wind and let the booze and Justin sweep me away."

"Tell me more about this MysteryMom who brought you here." He knew she was probably eager to go to bed so she could get an early start in the morning, but he wasn't ready to tell her good-night. There was a part of him that wasn't ready to tell her goodbye.

"I don't know a lot about her personal life. I connected with her in a chat room for pregnant and single women. I just lurked for about a week and I noticed that she gave good advice, seemed knowledgeable about pregnancy and single parenting. She even gave one of the women in the chat room enough information to help her find the father of her baby who had disappeared when he'd found out she was pregnant. I finally started posting and told a little bit about my situation. Then MysteryMom and I started emailing each other outside of the chat room."

"And you became friends," he replied.

She nodded. "Cyberfriends. Good friends. Especially when I found out I was having triplets. I was more than a little freaked out, and she saw me through some of my rough moments."

He wished he would have been there for her, when she needed somebody to rub her tired back, when she just wanted somebody to talk to, to fix her a cup of tea or whatever. "I'm sorry you had to go through it all alone except for the support of a cyberfriend."

"I have a feeling even if I'd found Justin the day I discovered I was pregnant I would have still gone through it all alone," she returned.

"What about other friends?" he asked.

"I have acquaintances, but true friendships have been a little difficult to maintain. First there was my involvement in Natalie's life, then the triplets' arrival pretty much chased away any of my other single women friends."

"That stinks," he replied.

She smiled. "Not really. It was mostly my fault. I was just too busy to be a friend." She raised a hand

and yawned. "And now I should probably call it a night. I'd like to get an early start in the morning."

She got up from the sofa and a wild panic shot through Jake. These were the last moments they would have together alone. He knew she was right, that once she returned to Wichita the odds of them maintaining any kind of relationship were minimal. He'd send birthday presents to the girls, call to check in on them every once in a while, but for all intents and purposes his connection with Grace would be severed.

And that's what you want, he reminded himself as he got out of his chair. He'd said goodbye to dozens of women in his lifetime, and she should be no different than any of them.

And yet she was different, a little voice whispered in the very depths of his soul. The other women who had drifted in and out of his life hadn't made his heartache for something undefined, something he felt he needed and yet found that very need frightening.

"Go ahead and sleep in my bed again tonight," he said as they walked toward the stairs. "I'll bunk in Jeffrey and Kerri's room again." He didn't want her anywhere near the room with the sliding glass door, and he would sleep with one eye open throughout the night.

He'd taken necessary precautions to make sure that nobody got close to the house again. Jimbo was camping out on the front porch for the night, and

Rick Carson, another ranch hand, was bunking down on the back porch. *Bunking down* wasn't really the right term. Both men had promised to keep their eyes and ears open throughout the dark hours of the night, and Jake trusted those men as much as he trusted anyone in his life.

Jake would stick to his promise; he'd keep her safe and sound until she left here to go home. As they climbed the stairs, he tried not to inhale the familiar scent of her that called to every raging male hormone in his body. He tried not to imagine that he could feel the heat of her calling to him, wanting to share with him.

As always she stopped in the girls' room and checked each little child. He thought of Bonnie's flirting with him, of how Casey tucked her head down when feeling particularly shy, of Abby laughing with delight as he played peekaboo with her. Grace wasn't the only female here who had found her way into his heart. Each and every one of the triplets had also crawled into tiny places that would make them hard to forget when they were gone.

How had this happened? How had he allowed them all to get so close? They weren't his…they were never meant to be his.

"Then I guess this is good night," he said when they finally reached the door to his room.

"It doesn't have to be good night," she replied. The green of her eyes shone overly bright in the hallway light.

"What do you mean?" His pulse stepped up its rhythm.

"You could sleep in here with me."

Her words, so unexpected and so enticing, caused his heart to momentarily skip a beat. His head filled with a vision of her between his sheets, her lips swollen from his kisses and her naked body pressed against his.

"Grace..." He wasn't sure what he intended to say, but his voice came out as a hoarse whisper. He needed strength, but he wanted to be weak.

"Tonight we make love and we sleep in each other's arms, but you don't have to worry about anything changing, Jake." Her eyes shone with both desire and a promise. "I still leave here in the morning. You still get your life of being alone."

Wrong. It was all wrong, his conscience suggested. *You're strong enough to resist this temptation. You need to be strong enough to resist.* But he wasn't. He was weak where Grace was concerned, and at the moment he couldn't think of anything he'd rather do than make love to her.

Big mistake, he thought as he followed her into the familiar bedroom that suddenly felt like a strange and wondrous place.

Chapter 10

As Jake turned on the lamp next to the bed, Grace took off her sling and placed it on the nearby chair. Her hands trembled slightly as she thought about what she was about to do.

There was absolutely no doubt in her mind that they were going to make love. She wanted this, she wanted him, and even ultimately knowing that it was going to be just another one-night stand with a Johnson man couldn't change her mind.

She was doing this for herself, making a memory that would bring a smile to her lips, a warmth to her heart when she needed it in the weeks and months ahead.

Somebody had tried to kill her, and just for a little

while, just for tonight, she wanted to pretend that somebody loved her.

Jake stood inches from her, frozen except for the burning hunger in his eyes, a hunger that filled her up with a heat she'd never known before.

"You don't have to worry. I'm on birth control," she said, wanting to get that issue settled right up front. There would be no set of triplets or even a single baby made tonight.

He took a step toward her, her breasts making contact with his broad chest. "This isn't right," he said, his voice low and filled with deep longing.

"But it isn't wrong, either," she countered. "We're both single. Our hearts belong to nobody. I want you, Jake. I want this before I leave here tomorrow."

His mouth crashed to hers at the same time he wound his arms around her and pulled her against him, and just that easily she was lost in him.

There was no thought of going home, or of taking care of babies. There was no worry about her sister or who might have tried to hurt her. There was only Jake. Sweet, strong Jake.

His scent smelled like home, like sweet comfort, and his kiss tasted of hot, wild desire. Everything seemed to be happening in a dream, a wonderful dream that she wanted to last forever.

She didn't remember taking off her clothes, but found herself naked in his bed. She didn't remember seeing him undress, but he was also naked with her beneath the sheet, his body all hot muscle beside her.

As he drew her into his arms for another searing kiss, her hands caressed the width of his back, loving the feel of muscle and hot flesh beneath her fingertips.

He kissed just as she'd imagined he would, with intensity, with command and yet with a gentleness that melted her senses even more.

A small moan escaped her as his lips left hers and began to blaze an exploratory trail down the side of her throat, along the line of her collarbone. When his tongue lightly flicked across one of her taut nipples, a flash fire of sensation shot through her.

His hands cupped her breasts as his tongue loved first one nipple then the other. Tangling her fingers in his thick hair, she was lost to everything except the man and his caresses.

One of his hands left her breast and began to stroke slowly, languidly down her stomach. Every muscle in her body tensed with the anticipation of his intimate touch.

Teasingly, he slid his fingers down the outside of her thigh, then moved to the inside of her thigh and stopped just short of where she wanted him most, where she needed him most.

She mewled in frustration and was rewarded by his husky chuckle. "This is a one-shot deal, Grace. I don't want to be in a hurry. I want us to take our time. I want this to last all night long."

His words caused a shiver of delight to race up her spine. Yes, she wanted to be in his arms, with his hands and lips touching her all night long.

When he gazed at her with those dark, intense eyes, when he stroked her skin with his slightly work roughened hands, she felt like the most beautiful woman on the face of the earth. No man had ever looked at her the way he did. No man made her feel like she did at this time.

There was a moment as his lips drank of hers that thoughts of leaving intruded, that her heart folded into itself in anticipation of the pain it would feel the next morning when she bid him a final goodbye and drove away from here.

Still, she shoved the thought away, not wanting to think, just wanting to feel, to be in this moment with this man.

He was fully aroused, his hardness pressed against her thigh, and she reached down and wrapped her fingers around his velvet soft skin, eliciting a low, deep moan from him.

She felt him throbbing in her grasp and loved that she was doing that to him, that she had him so aroused and ready to take her.

And she wanted him to take her. A sweet urgency of need sizzled through her as they continued to touch and taste each other.

She cried out in pleasure as his fingers finally found the center of her, moving against the sensitive skin and calling forth a tidal wave of pleasure. As the wave rushed over her his name escaped her lips as her body shuddered with the force.

His eyes shone with satisfaction as the shudders

finally stopped and she released a sigh of sated pleasure. But he wasn't finished yet.

He rolled on top of her and she opened her thighs to welcome him, her need rising once again as his mouth found hers in a kiss that seared her soul.

Still kissing, he eased into her and released a sigh of utter bliss. "I think I've wanted this since the moment I first saw you," he whispered.

She closed her eyes, not wanting to see the depth of emotion his contained, knowing that it was the emotion of the moment, one that would be gone when their lovemaking was over.

He moved inside her and her breath caught in her chest at the sensual assault. Then there was no more thought as their hips moved together, friction firing up a wildness that consumed her.

Her second orgasm washed over her as she clung to his shoulders. While she was still trembling with the force of it she felt him reach his own.

As sweet as her joy was, the sudden depth of her despair at the knowledge that it was over whispered through her made tears burn at her eyes.

"Hey, you okay?"

She opened her eyes to see him gazing down at her, a look of concern on his face. She swallowed against the threat of tears and offered him a smile. "After that how could I not be okay?"

For several long seconds they held each other's gazes. She wondered if he could see the love shining in her eyes. Unfortunately, she couldn't read his; they remained dark and enigmatic.

He kissed her then, a deep kiss that tasted of love and yet also held more than a whisper of goodbye. When the kiss ended she rolled out from under him and went into the bathroom.

Minutes later she stood in front of the bathroom mirror and stared at her reflection. If it wasn't insane, she would pack up the girls at that moment and leave with the scent of him still clinging to her skin, with the taste of him still sweet in her mouth. She would leave before she spent the rest of the night in his arms, letting him dig deeper into her heart.

But she wasn't going to drag her girls out in the middle of the night. And she wasn't going to deprive herself of the rest of this night, even though she knew each moment she spent with Jake would only make the pain of leaving in the morning worse.

It was crazy, wasn't it? To even want a future with him—to see him as the soul mate she'd always dreamed of. It was stupid and weird to believe that there could ever be a future with the brother of the father of her children.

When she left the bathroom and got back into bed, Jake immediately pulled her into his arms. She smelled the soapy scent of him and realized he'd washed up as well.

He turned out the bedside lamp and she fit neatly into the spoon of his body. Once again she found herself giving in to him, settling into his arms as if it was where she belonged.

"Did I hurt your shoulder?" he asked, the words a soft whisper just behind her ear.

"No, it's fine."

"Are you sure you don't need to hang around here another day or two to let it heal a little more before you head back?" he asked.

What she wanted was to hang around here another ten, twenty, fifty years. She wanted to be with Jake for the rest of her life. She wanted him to be the father of the triplets. But that was fantasy thinking, foolish wistfulness.

"I should be able to handle going home tomorrow with no problem," she replied.

"I have to confess there's a part of me that's going to miss you and the girls." His arms tightened around her.

She held her breath, waiting for, desperately wanting something more from him. *Just ask me to stay,* she inwardly begged. *Just tell me you want me and the girls in your life forever.*

A long silence grew, and then she realized he'd fallen asleep.

Squeezing her eyes closed, she realized with a heart-sickening finality what she'd known the first time she'd met Justin—that there was nothing for her here.

Jake awoke early, before dawn had even begun to streak tentative light across the sky. Grace was no longer in his arms, but rather sleeping soundly, curled up in a fetal position on the opposite side of the bed. He wished there was enough light so he could watch her sleeping. To fill his heart with the sight of her, her hair sleep-tousled and all the worry gone from her face.

He crept out of the bed without waking her, grabbed his clothes for the day and then walked quietly down the hallway to the other bathroom in order to shower and dress without bothering her.

She was leaving today. She was taking her children and leaving his house. Things would go back to the way they had been before she'd arrived.

He should be happy, but as he stepped beneath the hot spray of the shower, happiness wasn't the emotion that resonated through him.

As he washed away the scent of her, all he could think of was what a mess this had all become. He hoped that if Shirley was responsible for the attacks on Grace then Greg would get evidence of it and Shirley would face the consequences.

In the very depths of his soul he thought she was the likely culprit. He just didn't want to believe that Justin had played a role in the attacks in any way.

But if nothing else had come out of this time with Grace, Jake now realized he needed to let go of his brother. It was time for Justin to stand or fall on his own.

Grace had been right when she'd told him he'd been carrying the sins of his father for too long.

Nothing he could do would fix the childhood the three men had endured, a childhood they had all endured together. It was time to let go of the responsibility and let Justin be a man.

After he'd showered and dressed and left the bathroom, he thought he heard a sound from the girls' room. One peek into the room and he saw Bonnie peering over the top of her crib, her wide smile sliding straight into his heart as she raised her arms to him.

Seeing that the other two were still sleeping, he hurried to her crib and picked her up. He didn't speak to her until he'd left the room.

"You're a little early bird this morning," he said as he carried her down the stairs.

She bounced on his hip and wrapped her arms around his neck, as if delighted to have him all to herself. He was going to miss them. He'd never thought it possible, but he was going to miss seeing the triplets' smiling faces first thing in the morning, hearing their babble and giggles filling the house.

As he placed Bonnie in one of the high chairs in the kitchen, he didn't even want to think about how much he was going to miss Grace.

Always before the thought of silence in the house had filled him with a sense of pleasure. But when he thought about how quiet the house would be with the triplets and Grace gone, his heart pressed painful and tight in his chest.

They weren't his issue. They'd never been his

issue, he reminded himself. Justin and circumstances out of his control had put him in the middle of this, and he should be grateful that within hours he'd be out of the middle of it all.

He gave Bonnie a handful of the round oat cereal he'd seen Grace give her before, then set about making a pot of coffee. As he waited for the brew to drip through, he stood at the window and watched dawn break across the sky, aware that the minutes of Grace and the girls being here in the house were ticking away.

He knew she cared about him. It was obvious in the way she looked at him, in the very fact that she'd made love with him the night before. She cared about him a lot, might even fancy herself in love with him.

But he couldn't help but wonder if most of her attraction to him was because he looked like Justin, because she could fantasize just by looking at him that he was her daughters' father.

When he'd held her in his arms last night and she'd closed her eyes, had she imagined that he was his brother? Had she pretended that it was Justin kissing her, Justin loving her? After all, Jake was the version of Justin she'd probably like to have.

He shook his head to dislodge the thought. At this point what did it matter? Justin wasn't going to suddenly become the man she needed in her life. Jake wasn't going to abandon his own dreams. She was leaving. Within weeks Jeffrey and Kerri would be moved out, and he'd decided moments before that from now on Justin would truly be on his own.

The future he'd always dreamed for himself was a mere stone's throw away. All he had to do was get through the goodbyes of this morning and the rest of his life would fall into place.

He heard the water start running someplace upstairs and knew that Grace was up. *Another early riser probably eager to get back to her real life,* he thought as a hard knot formed in the pit of his stomach.

She'd been fine before she'd come here, and there was no reason for him to believe that she wouldn't be fine when she left. She was a strong woman, had apparently had to be strong all her life. He didn't need to worry about her.

Minutes later she came into the kitchen. "Looks as if I'm not the only early riser," she said as she dropped a kiss on Bonnie's forehead and then moved to the coffeemaker on the countertop.

"Did you sleep well?" he asked, trying not to notice how pretty she looked in a pair of jeans and a jewel-green blouse that electrified the green of her eyes.

"Very well," she replied. As she turned to pour herself a cup of coffee, he fought the impulse to step up behind her and press his lips against the nape of her neck.

He wondered if it was just an effort to somehow continue the intimacy they'd shared the night before.

When she turned to face him he was glad he hadn't, for there was a distance in her eyes that let him know she was already gone. Mentally and emotionally she was already back on the road headed home.

"You want some breakfast?" he asked.

She shook her head and carried her cup to the table. "No, when Abby and Casey wake up I'll feed them before we take off, but I'm really not hungry."

He remained standing at the window. "Going to be a beautiful day for your drive home."

"I'm just looking forward to getting home and back into my own routine."

"How's the shoulder?"

She moved it experimentally. "Still a little stiff and sore, but manageable. We'll be fine, Jake."

"I know," he replied. "I'm just sorry it has to be this way. I'm sorry you didn't get what you came here for where Justin is concerned."

She offered him a small smile. "I told you before, you don't owe me any apologies on his behalf. Besides, nothing ventured, nothing gained, right?" She took a sip of her coffee and then placed the mug on the table. "The good thing is I know where to come if any health issues should arise with the girls and I need answers. They will know where they come from. I won't have to have the embarrassment of telling them I don't know who or where their father is. Eventually Justin will probably have to deal with them one way or another, but there's nothing more

I can do here." She released a deep sigh. "I'm ready to go home."

At that moment one of the other girls upstairs cried out and officially the day began. It was just after nine when the triplets had been fed, the car had been loaded and there was nothing left to do except tell her goodbye.

He stood at her driver's side door and watched as she slid behind the wheel. There was a part of him that wanted to stop her, to tell her that somehow, someway, she'd gotten under his skin, delved into his heart in a way he hadn't expected.

He wanted to pull her out from behind the steering wheel and grab her, feel the warmth of her against him once again and tell her that he didn't want her to leave. But his body refused to follow through on the thought.

"Bye-bye," Bonnie said, and the other two little girls echoed the sentiment.

"And I think that's my cue," Grace said as she started the engine. "I left my address and phone numbers on a piece of paper on the kitchen table for Justin. If he ever decides he wants to discuss the girls or come and see them, then all he needs to do is call me and we'll set something up."

"Grace?" He wasn't sure what he wanted to say, but he was fairly sure it wasn't goodbye.

"Yes?" For a moment in the depths of her eyes he saw something shiny and bright, something that made him feel if she drove out of his driveway it would be the worst thing that ever happened to him. Yet he wasn't willing to change anything.

"Drive safely," he finally said.

The light in her eyes dimmed slightly, and she put the car into gear. "I will." She drew a deep breath. "Jake, you're a man who is meant to be a husband and a father. This big house was meant to be filled with family. You've spent the first half of your life fixing everybody else's. Don't spend the last half of your life running away from your own."

She didn't wait for him to reply but stepped on the gas and shot down the driveway as if chased by the devil himself. He watched until the car disappeared from his vision and only then turned and headed back inside.

The utter silence of the house should have embraced him with welcoming arms. He walked through the living room and heard only the sound of his own beating heart.

It's what he'd always wanted. It's what he'd dreamed of. Tomorrow Kerri and Jeffrey would be home, and he doubted that he'd hear from Justin anytime soon. He'd have the house and the silence to himself for the remainder of the day.

The sight of the three high chairs in the kitchen speared a surprising feeling of loss through his heart. For the last couple of days they'd felt like his children.

And Grace had felt like his woman.

But I don't want a woman, he told himself as he

sank down at the table. And he didn't want children. He didn't want the mess, the fuss and the noise. He didn't want the dramas or the responsibilities that came with relationships and parenthood. He'd done enough where that was concerned.

Peace and quiet. What more could a man ask for? He picked up the sheet of paper where Grace had written her address and phone numbers.

By all rights she should have run as fast and as far as she could after her first meeting with Justin, but she hadn't. She'd stuck around to give him a second chance. She'd desperately wanted a father for her daughters. She told him she knew what it was like to grow up without one, and that wasn't what she wanted for her babies.

Of all the men in the world she could have fallen into bed with at a wedding, why did it have to be Justin, who would probably never find it within himself to be what Grace and the girls needed?

He leaned back in the chair and closed his eyes, playing and replaying each and every moment he'd spent with her and the triplets.

He made himself a mental note to call Greg later in the day to see if he had any news about the attacks. Even though Grace was gone, Jake still wanted the guilty party found. And if it had been Shirley, then Justin would be crazy to stick with a woman capable of that kind of thing.

Grace had told him that it had been a near-death experience that had made her decide to come here to the ranch in the first place, and then she'd gone from the frying pan into the fire by being attacked here.

He opened his eyes and sat up straighter with a frown. She'd told him she'd been forced off the road a couple of days before coming here. It had only been by the grace of God that her car hadn't flipped over and killed her. It had been a close call.

His brain suddenly fired with all kinds of suppositions. Was it possible that the shooting had been the second attempt on Grace's life? That the first attempt had been that night in Wichita before she'd ever left to come here?

If that was the case, then it changed everything. That had happened before Justin even knew about the triplets, before Shirley had known anything about Grace and Justin's night together.

His heart began beating an unnatural rhythm of stress. If that was the case, then it meant somebody had tried to kill her in Wichita and then had followed her here to try again.

And if that was true, then that meant she wasn't driving back to safety but rather was driving back into danger.

Chapter 11

Alone.

Grace had been alone most of her life. When she'd been young she'd learned to give herself the comfort and love she didn't get from her mother. She certainly got little true companionship or caring from her sister.

The triplets filled her heart and soul like nobody and nothing ever had before, but they weren't meant to fill the loneliness that had been a part of Grace's life for as long as she could remember.

Jake had filled that space, that loneliness, and more than that there had been several times when he'd given her a touch of crazy hope that there might be something there with him for her and her girls.

Until the moment she'd put her car into gear, that

little touch of hope had shimmered in her heart. He'd spoken her name with such wanting, and her heart had nearly stopped in anticipation of him pulling her out of the car and telling her he loved her and the girls. But he'd let her drive away, and by the time she'd reached the end of the ranch's driveway, tears raced down her cheeks.

It had been crazy for her to even think for one minute that he'd want to take on her and the triplets, that somehow he'd fallen in love with her and that love was deep enough for him to throw his own wants, his own needs, away.

Alone. She was going to be alone for a long time to come. It would take a very special man to want to take on not just her, but her three daughters as well. She was a woman who came with baggage, three little suitcases who babbled and drooled, who would grow up to walk and get into things and create chaos.

For just a stupid, crazy moment she'd thought that special man was Jake. She raised a hand from the steering wheel to swipe at an errant tear.

She felt half-sick to her stomach with the pain that pierced through her center. She never knew heartache could be such a physical pain.

It was her own fault that she was leaving here with a broken heart. She'd allowed him to get too close, had opened her heart to him as she'd never opened her heart to a man before.

She had the two-and-a-half-hour drive to pull herself together, to shove thoughts of Jake out of her mind and focus on her real life.

At least Natalie had a job. Maybe it was time Grace took some of the advice she had given Jake. It was time for her to stop rescuing Natalie, stop trying to make up for the lack of a father and the less-than-perfect relationship with her mother.

Natalie had her monthly income from her inheritance, and with even a part-time job she should do fine as long as she learned to stop partying and live within her means.

Grace could only hope the Jimmy she was dating was a good and decent young man, but it was time Grace took her own advice and stopped rescuing her sister.

She frowned, wondering what damage Natalie had managed to do to the credit card she'd let her use. Supposedly Natalie had just needed gas money and groceries, but there was no telling what Grace might find charged on the card when she finally got the bill.

It didn't take long for the lull of the wheels on the pavement to put the girls to sleep, leaving Grace alone with her thoughts. And they were all of Jake.

He had been everything she'd ever dreamed of in a man for herself, everything she'd ever dreamed of as a father for her children. It was as if Bonnie had identified Jake as somebody important in their lives the first time she'd batted her eyelashes at him.

Watching him with them had filled Grace's soul with a sense of rightness.

He'd loved the girls like Grace had hoped their father would. When he'd played with them, wiped their mouths, laughed at their antics, there had been a feeling of family, a warmth that had filled Grace's soul.

Grace blinked away a new flurry of tears. What she didn't understand was how she could feel such loss when she'd never really had him to begin with. They had played house for a couple of days due to circumstances beyond their control.

Everything he had done for her while she'd been at the ranch had probably been part of him doing what he always did—taking care of Justin's messes.

She jumped as her cell phone rang. With one hand she dug it out of her purse and looked at the caller ID. Jake. The very last person in the world she wanted to talk to at the moment.

Why would he be calling? To tell her she left something behind? She was fairly sure she'd gotten out of there with all her belongings. Her heart was a different story.

She didn't even want to hear his voice right now. She knew the sound would merely pull forth the tears she'd been desperately trying to hold back. She turned the phone off and dropped it back into her purse. She'd return his call later, when she was back home in her own environment and not feeling quite so vulnerable to him.

The girls' nap didn't last long. Within half an hour they were awake and chattering like magpies, filling the silence that had been in the car but incapable of soothing the hollow emptiness that resided in Grace's heart—the space where Jake had been.

By the time she pulled into her driveway she was grateful the drive was over. The girls had started to get cranky, needing lunch and a longer nap, and Grace's shoulder ached from the driving.

It took another hour to get everything unloaded from the car, feed the girls and get them down for their naps, and then she took one of the pain pills the doctor in Cameron Creek had given her and stretched out on her sofa.

There were a million things she should be doing, like throwing in a load of laundry, figuring out what she was going to have for supper or contacting MysteryMom to let her know that Justin had been found but was ultimately lost.

What she wouldn't confess to MysteryMom was that she'd been fool enough to fall in love with one of Justin's brothers. That she'd been fool enough to get pregnant by a man incapable of being a father and had fallen in love with a man incapable of loving her back.

Jake, her heart cried out as she closed her eyes and sought the oblivion of sleep. If nothing else she hoped that someday he would get over his own baggage and find love with somebody, build a family that would make him see that chaos and noise when filled with love was so much better than silence and being all alone.

She finally fell asleep with her heart aching, wondering how long it would take before she could forget all about Jake Johnson. She dreamed of him, of being held in his arms as they made love. The dream transitioned to him holding her babies and all of them laughing. Then she went from dreamland to sudden awakeness, her heart beating a frantic rhythm that had nothing to do with the visions that had filled her sleep.

Sitting up, she looked around and listened. No crying babies, nothing to indicate what had pulled her from sleep or had made her heart race so fast. A glance at her wristwatch let her know she'd only been asleep for about fifteen minutes.

It must have been a dream, she thought as she placed a hand over her pounding heart and drew a deep breath. She must have been having a dream that created the sense of panic that had awakened her.

At that moment Natalie appeared in the doorway between the kitchen and the living room.

Grace released a startled gasp and realized it must have been the sound of the back door opening and closing that had awakened her. "Jeez, Natalie, you scared me to half to death," she exclaimed. "I thought you told me you had to work today."

"I really don't like working," Natalie replied. "Life is too short to work, especially when I shouldn't have to." There was a tough edge to Natalie's voice and a wildness in her eyes.

"What are you doing sneaking in the back door?" Grace asked, her heart sinking as she realized it was possible her sister was on something. Grace's heart suddenly resumed its rapid beat. "Natalie, have you been doing drugs?"

"Maybe so, maybe not." Natalie grinned as a tall, lanky, dark-haired young man appeared just behind her. "You've been wanting to meet Jimmy, so here he is."

He stepped up next to Natalie. "Hey, Grace."

He didn't look like the decent kind of young man Grace had hoped for. He had a rough edge, made more rough by the tattoo that nearly covered one side of his neck and his general unkempt appearance. His jeans hung low and his hair was long and greasy.

"It's nice to finally meet you," Grace forced herself to say.

"You've been quite a problem," he said. His dark eyes looked as wild as Natalie's.

Grace frowned at him, wondering if the pain pill she'd taken earlier had somehow scrambled her brains or if she'd misunderstood him. "Excuse me?"

"He said you've become quite a problem," Natalie repeated with a touch of impatience. "Actually, you became a problem the minute you had those babies and Mother changed her will."

Grace watched in horror as Jimmy pulled a gun

from the back of his waistband and pointed it at her. "Your sister and I want to be together. We love each other, but she's been very unhappy with her inheritance and I can't stand to see her so miserable."

Grace felt as if she was still asleep, in the middle of a terrible nightmare as her gaze went from Jimmy to her sister. "I don't understand. Natalie, you and I both got the same amount of an inheritance when Mom died." Grace struggled to make sense of what was happening.

"They got it all," Natalie said, her features showing the first signs of anger. Her green eyes narrowed and her chin thrust forward. "Those babies got everything, and that means *you've* got it all."

"That's not true," Grace exclaimed, a panic welling up to press tight against her chest. "It's for them, not for me. It's for their college."

"But you can get to it whenever you want," Natalie screamed. "You can just write a check and buy whatever you want with it. It's not fair. It was never fair."

Horrible thoughts suddenly tumbled around in Grace's head. She'd always known deep in her heart that Natalie was selfish and more than a bit narcissistic, but now she recognized the depth of Natalie's rage, a rage that had apparently been building since the reading of their mother's will.

Natalie drew a deep breath as if to calm herself, but her eyes remained wild and filled with anger. "She promised me. Mother promised me when I was growing up that I'd have everything I wanted, that when she was gone I'd never want for anything. She promised and I believed her and you screwed it up by having those damned kids."

Grace searched her sister's features, looking for something soft, something vulnerable, something of the sister she thought she knew, but there was nothing there. The full realization of what lengths Natalie had gone to sank in. "*You* followed me to Cameron Creek? *You* tried to shoot me?" her voice was a mere whisper.

"If those stupid cowboys hadn't shown up when they did we wouldn't be having this conversation now," Natalie said.

"So far you've been like a cat with nine lives." Jimmy stepped closer to her, the gun pointed at her head. "I tried to run you off the road, I tried to shoot you, and then I tried to strangle you. Each time you've managed to get away. Unfortunately, the cat has now run out of lives."

"Jimmy and I can take care of the girls," Natalie said as if she were talking about taking care of a couple of goldfish. "As their guardian I'll make sure they have what they need, but I can also live the life I want to live, the one I deserve to live."

"Natalie and I are going to live a great life. Unfortunately, you're in the way of that." Jimmy smiled, but there was no humor in the gesture. "Face it, sis. You have to go."

Grace looked at her sister, hoping this was all

some kind of a terrible joke, but Natalie's eyes held a hard glaze she didn't recognize.

"I won't have to hear you bitch at me anymore. I won't have to listen to your stupid advice." Natalie's hands balled into fists at her side. "All the times I wanted Mother and she wasn't there for me, I always remembered that she told me it would be worth it in the end, that if anything happened to her I'd have a life most people dreamed about. I'm not going to let those brats take that away from me."

"While you were gone somebody cased your house," Jimmy said. "They broke in and didn't realize you were back home. As they started to rob the place, you confronted them and sadly you didn't survive the attack."

Horror rose up inside Grace's throat. "Natalie, you can't be serious about this. I'm your sister, for God's sake."

"I don't care about you," Natalie replied. "I just want the money."

"Even if you kill me, the girls have a father who would get custody," Grace said, trying to reason her way out of danger.

"He doesn't want custody," she scoffed. "You told me he isn't fit material to be a guardian. You told me the last thing he wants is to be a father. Trust me, from what you said about him he won't fight me. He'll be glad that somebody else is ready to step in to take care of them. I'm their aunt, your only living relative. I'll get custody and I'll get their money. The only thing that stands in my way is you."

As Grace looked into the very soullessness of her sister's eyes, she realized she'd vastly underestimated Natalie's mental problems and as a consequence she was in terrible danger.

Jake tried to call Grace several times, but each of his calls went directly to her voice mail. Since he couldn't imagine her risking driving while talking on the cell phone, he could only assume that she had the phone off.

Still, with each passing minute that took her closer to her home, an urgency banged in his heart. It was crazy for him to think she might be in imminent danger, and yet was it really so far-fetched?

Somebody had tried to kill her, and he'd begun to think it wasn't somebody from here but rather somebody close to her back in Wichita.

Even though he knew it was probably illogical, he felt as if he needed to get to her as soon as possible, and without being able to call her, he did the next best thing. He grabbed the sheet of paper with her address on it, got into his truck and took off after her.

He was a good thirty or forty minutes behind her. It was possible if he pushed the speed limit he could catch her on the road. If not, he'd use the address she'd left and get to her house.

And tell her what? That a car accident might

not have been an accident at all? That he thought somebody was chasing her all over the country in an effort to kill her? That somehow this made more sense than Shirley being responsible for the two attacks on her?

His foot eased off the gas pedal as doubts filled his head. Was he chasing after her with these crazy ideas because deep in his heart he didn't want to let her go?

Was his heart telling him something his brain refused to acknowledge? This time was it him creating drama instead of his brother? Chasing after a woman with some conspiracy plot just because he wanted to see her one more time?

No, this wasn't about some imagined drama. He pressed his foot back on the gas, once again filled with a sense of urgency. This had nothing to do with what he wanted or didn't want with Grace and the children. This had to do with their safety, and despite all rational thought, he felt that she was heading right into trouble.

As he passed each roadside café and gas station along the way, he slowed to look for her car but didn't see it parked anywhere. He could only press the speed limit so much. The last thing he wanted was to get reckless and be in an accident of his own or cause a problem for other drivers.

He consciously didn't want to think about his feelings for Grace and the girls. He still had no intention of offering her anything that looked like a future. He just wanted to get to her now, to let her know what he suspected.

The drive to Wichita seemed to take forever. He tried to call her several more times with the same results, but the calls went directly to her voice mail.

Why wasn't she answering the phone? Surely she'd know that so many calls from him would mean he was trying to get in touch with her for an important reason. If she worried about driving and talking, she could always pull to the side of the road to find out what he wanted.

Maybe she doesn't want to talk to you, a little voice whispered in his head. They'd had a beautiful time together; but ultimately he'd never been the brother she'd come for, the one she'd wanted, needed in her life.

When she'd driven away from the ranch, maybe the last thing she'd wanted was to think about or talk to any of the Johnson men again. He couldn't really blame her for that.

But he had to talk to her whether she wanted to hear from him or not. She needed to know his suspicions. The more he thought about it, the more it made sense. He'd be a fool not to consider that the person who stood to gain the most if anything happened to her was her sister.

Grace had told him that the children had gotten the bulk of whatever estate her mother had possessed. If anything happened to Grace, the triplets would go to Justin, who could easily be talked out of taking guardianship by a loving, caring aunt. It was what made the most sense and yet what he didn't want to believe.

How on earth was he supposed to talk to Grace about the fact that her sister might not have her best interests at heart when his own brother had been the one who had broken her heart?

As he entered the city limits of Wichita, he figured he'd cross that bridge when he came to it. Right now all he really wanted was to see her and the girls safe and sound and warn her that the danger might be closer than she thought.

Jake had been to Wichita several times in the past, but he didn't really know the city well. He had to stop at a convenience store and ask for directions to Grace's area of town.

When he found her street, some of the adrenaline that had been with him since he'd jumped into his truck finally began to ease somewhat. Within minutes he'd see that she and the girls were fine and the worst that would happen was that he'd feel like more than a bit of a fool for making the race instead of just waiting to contact her by phone.

At least he'd know he'd forewarned her that the danger to her might not be over just because she'd returned to Wichita. She needed to be aware that there could still be trouble here.

He found her address and parked along the curb. It was a neat ranch house painted a soft beige and with darker brown trim. A large oak tree stood in the center of the yard and would provide welcome shade in the summer.

It was obviously a working-class neighborhood, and he imagined that most of the houses were empty at this time of the day, parents working and kids at babysitters or enjoying summer camp.

It was a good place to raise three children, he told himself. The house appeared solid; the neighborhood looked nice. There was no reason why she and the girls couldn't live a happy life right here.

She'd probably been telling the truth when she said she didn't need anything financially from Justin. She'd just wanted a father for her girls.

He got out of the truck and stretched, mentally preparing himself for seeing her again, for guarding his heart against the tug it felt in her direction.

He was here to give her information and nothing more. Nothing had changed as far as he was concerned, and in any case he'd never be the man she truly wanted in her life.

He walked up to the front door and glanced at his watch. It was nap time for the girls, so he decided not to ring the bell or knock on the door.

The front door was glass, and hopefully he could catch her attention by looking through without having to knock and possibly wake the girls.

He peered into the window and for a moment didn't see anyone. Again he wondered if this whole frantic drive to Wichita and his own crazy thoughts about danger everywhere were just long-term moments of total insanity.

Grace insanity. That's what he should call it, the insane desire to see her just one last time, to assure himself that she was really in the right kind of physical condition to take care of herself, of the girls. Or just because he hadn't been ready to tell her goodbye.

He had just about talked himself into turning around and leaving without saying anything to her when he saw the shadow of somebody too tall to be her, tall like a man, inside the house. Whoever it was stood in the hallway to the living room and obviously wasn't aware of Jake's presence at the door.

Who was he? And what was he doing in Grace's house? He mentally shook himself. It was really none of his business. He had no right to know.

As Jake watched, the man turned halfway and Jake saw that he had a gun in his hand. Instantly Jake slammed himself against the side of the house, where he couldn't be seen if the man looked out the front door.

Jake's heart banged hard against his ribs. He had no idea who the man was in Grace's living room. He definitely had no idea why the man had a gun, but he knew with a certainty that it didn't bode well for Grace. He'd been right. She was in trouble and he knew that if he didn't do something fast and drastic, then disaster was about to strike.

"For God's sake, Natalie, think about what you're doing," Grace pled with her sister. Grace was seated in a chair they'd dragged from the kitchen into the living room, her arms tied to the rungs of the chair back behind her.

Jimmy still held the gun trained on Grace while Natalie began unplugging the flat-screen television and the computer. "Don't forget the jewelry," he said to Natalie. "Thieves would take everything like that they could fence or pawn."

"Got it," Natalie replied.

"Natalie, don't listen to him. Look at me—I'm your sister." Grace had worried about what kind of a man her sister had hooked up with and now she knew—Natalie had hooked up with a dopehead criminal, one who had apparently filled her head with all kinds of bad things.

"You're the reason she didn't get what she deserved," Jimmy replied.

"Shut up," Grace exclaimed. "I wasn't talking to you, I was talking to my sister."

Natalie closed the laptop and whirled to glare at Grace. "That's all you do, Grace. Talk, talk, talk! I'm sick of it. I'm sick of you. Half of the money that went to the triplets was supposed to be mine."

"I'll give you the money," Grace replied hysterically. "Take me to the bank right now and I'll take it out and put it in your hands. You can have all of it. I don't care about it."

"Yeah, right, and then you call the cops and have us arrested," Jimmy said with a sneer. "It's too late for that, Grace. You're a liability."

"Yeah, a liability," Natalie parroted. "Okay," she said to Jimmy. "You can start carrying this stuff out the back door and loading it in the truck."

He walked over to Natalie and gave her a rough kiss on the lips. Grace wanted to gag as she saw the way her sister responded to him, with eager desperation.

But when Jimmy handed Natalie the gun and then picked up the flat-screen television, the first stir of hope filled Grace. If Jimmy walked out with the television, then that would leave her alone with Natalie. Surely if the two sisters were all alone Grace could talk Natalie away from the edge.

"Remember, baby, we're doing this for us, for our future," Jimmy said, and then he walked through the living room and into the kitchen.

Grace waited until she heard the back door open and close and then she gazed at her sister. "Natalie, untie me and let me go." She kept her voice soft and soothing. Natalie's gaze shot all around the room, everywhere but at Grace's eyes.

"Natalie, honey. Untie me and give me the gun," Grace continued. "We'll make this all right. Nothing bad will happen to you, but you have to stop and think. You don't want to do anything now that can't be made right."

"We're making it right. Jimmy and me, we're making it the way it was supposed to be," Natalie replied. "For me. I deserve this." When she finally met Grace's gaze her eyes were still wild and crazy looking. "You made a stupid mistake and Mom gave you almost all the money. I make stupid mistakes and all I get are lectures from you."

"I won't lecture you anymore. I'll let you live your life however you want. Natalie, I love you. I'm your sister. I know you really don't want to hurt me. It's the drugs and Jimmy making you do all this."

Natalie's eyes narrowed and she laughed. "Do you really think this was all Jimmy's idea? He's too stupid to come up with this. This is what *I* want, Grace. I want you gone from my life forever. Don't worry, I'll see that your brats are fed and clothed, but from here on out I call the shots. I'll have the money to do whatever I please and won't have to answer to anyone, especially you!"

It was at that moment that any hope Grace might have had died and one of her "brats" woke up and began to cry.

Chapter 12

The first thing Jake did was call 911 on his cell phone and give them Grace's address. He had no idea if the dispatcher took him seriously, had no idea how long it might take for the cops to arrive. He only knew he couldn't cool his heels and do nothing.

But what could he do? He was unarmed and unaware of Grace's or the babies' whereabouts in the house. He couldn't ride to the rescue when he wasn't sure exactly what was taking place inside. The last thing he wanted to do was bust inside and cause more danger.

The only thing he knew for sure was that a man brandishing a gun shouldn't be inside Grace's house. The only thing he knew for certain was that he had a sick, urgent feeling inside his very soul.

It was at that moment he remembered the gun in his glove box, the gun he'd placed there for safekeeping on the night he'd taken Grace to the hospital. He'd forgotten about it and apparently so had she when she'd packed up and left Cameron Creek earlier that day.

Jake made his way back to his truck and breathed a sigh of relief as he plucked the gun from inside the glove box. It was a nine-millimeter and fit comfortably in his hand. It took him only a moment to check to make sure it was loaded and ready to go.

Now that he was armed, he intended to get a better look inside to see if he could discern exactly where Grace and the children were located and get an idea of exactly what in the hell was going on.

He walked stealthily around to the side of the house and peered into the first window he came to. It was obviously the triplets' bedroom, all pink and white and frills.

If he hadn't known anything was wrong in the house by then, he would know it now. All three of the girls were awake and crying to get out of their beds. From where he stood he could see the tears trickling down their cheeks, letting him know they had been crying for several minutes. He could hear their plaintive wails through the glass, piercing straight through his heart.

Grace would have never allowed that to happen. She was usually there the minute the first of the three woke up from a nap. The knot that was in his chest twisted harder, tighter.

He was about to slide around to the back of the house when he heard the back door open. He peeked around the corner and watched as the tall, thin man he'd seen earlier carried out a computer.

Confusion battled with fear inside Jake. Was there a robbery taking place? An armed robbery or some sort of home invasion? Was Grace unconscious?

Already dead?

The thought nearly crashed him to his knees in agony. He could scarcely breathe as he imagined her hurt or worse. The girls. He had to get inside and save the girls even if it might be too late for Grace.

He couldn't go in through the front door, not knowing exactly what was happening, and it was obvious he couldn't go through the back. But there was no way he intended to stand around and wait for the authorities to arrive.

There was really only one way inside and that was the window to the triplets' room. He used his car key to tear the screen and easily removed it, then used the butt of the gun to break the window just above the lock, hoping the cries of the girls would mask the sound of the breaking glass.

He was aware that at any minute somebody could come into the room to tend to the crying babies, that he could be shot half in and half out of the window itself. But it was obvious the kids had been crying for a little while now and nobody had come to their aid. That fact only made Jake's heart tighten more in his chest.

He eased in through the window and hit the floor on the balls of his feet. "Da-da?" Bonnie sniffled and held out her arms to him and then the other two did the same.

Their outstretched arms and smiles of relief at the sight of him were nearly his undoing. He wanted nothing more than to pick them all up in his arms and hold them tight, soothe their tears and let them know they were safe. But he couldn't do that until he knew where Grace was and exactly what was going on.

His heart felt as if it bled as he walked past the three cribs and tried to ignore the cries of the little girls. With his heart pounding loudly in his ears, he held the gun tight in his hand and peered out of the room and down the hallway.

Nobody was in sight but he heard Grace's voice coming from the living room. "Natalie, please, let me go. Can't you hear the girls? They're frightened and they're crying. They need me."

"They don't need you. Nobody needs you!" a female voice cried, a voice Jake assumed was Natalie's.

He slid his way down the hallway, checking each room as he went to make sure he didn't run into the man he'd seen earlier. All he knew was the sweet relief that at least for now Grace was well enough to talk, well enough to plead with her sister.

He didn't try to make sense of what was happening, he only knew he wanted it to stop. He didn't want to confront Natalie without knowing where the man he assumed was her boyfriend was…the boyfriend with the gun.

And where were the cops? It felt as if it had been hours since Jake had made that 911 call, although in reality he knew it had only been minutes.

"All done," a deep male voice said. "Everything is loaded up in the truck and we're ready to rock and roll."

Every muscle in Jake's body tightened. He now knew they were all there in the living room. If he was going to make a move it needed to be now, before anyone "rock and rolled."

He just prayed that he was about to do the right thing and that it wouldn't get anyone hurt or killed, especially Grace. He slid a glance around the corner into the living room and what he saw made his heart skip a beat.

Grace was tied to a chair in the middle of the room. Thankfully, she didn't look hurt; but Natalie and her boyfriend stood in front of Grace and the boyfriend once again had the gun in his hand.

"So, what happens now?" Grace asked. "Do you shoot me right here? Is that what you want him to do, Natalie?"

"I didn't want any of this," Natalie replied. "This

is all Mother's fault. If she'd just left her money to me instead of to the triplets then none of this would be happening. It's her fault, and it's your fault for having those kids in the first place."

"If you allow this to happen, then it's nobody's fault but your own, Natalie," Grace replied, and Jake heard the weary resignation in her voice.

"Let's get this done," Jimmy exclaimed. "We've been here too long as it is."

Jake knew he could wait no longer. He whirled into the living room, his gun pointed directly at Jimmy's chest. Thankfully Jimmy's hand with the gun was at his side. He'd obviously not expected anyone else in the house.

"Either one of you twitch and you're dead," Jake said, his gaze focused on the biggest threat—Jimmy and the gun.

"What the hell?" Jimmy exclaimed, but he didn't move. He must have believed the cold resolve Jake knew was in his own eyes. He'd shoot the kid without his heart skipping a beat to save Grace.

Natalie fell to her knees and began to sob, and at that moment there was a sharp knock on the front door. "Wichita Police Department," a deep voice yelled.

"In here," Jake cried out.

Two uniformed policemen entered the room and immediately took control of the situation. Jake was disarmed and handcuffed along with Jimmy and Natalie, and then Grace was untied from the chair.

To everyone's surprise except Jake's, she ran out of the room and down the hallway. One of the officers ran after her while the other kept his gun trained on the three adults left cuffed and standing in the living room.

Jake knew she'd go to her girls, all of whom had been crying since Jake had entered the house. He couldn't imagine what it had been like for her, to be tied to a chair not knowing if she was going to live or die while her babies cried for her from another room.

Although Jake was handcuffed, he wasn't worried. He knew the officers had cuffed him for their own protection, because they'd walked into a situation they didn't understand and because Jake had been one of the men with a gun. He knew that once Grace had a minute to talk to the officers he'd be freed and everything would be sorted out.

Natalie hadn't stopped crying since he'd appeared on the scene and she'd realized the scheme had been foiled and they'd been caught. Jimmy looked sullen and scared. He should be scared. He and Natalie would be looking at attempted murder charges.

Grace came back into the room carrying Casey, and the officer followed behind her with Bonnie and Abby in his arms. "He's a good guy," Grace said and pointed a finger at Jake.

"I'm the one who called you guys," Jake said.

"If you'll release him then he can help me put up

a playpen for the girls," she said. Jake noticed she didn't spare a glance for her sister or Jimmy.

The officer released Jake from his cuffs and together he and Grace set up a playpen that had been folded up and hidden behind the sofa.

Within minutes the three girls were in the playpen and the officers were asking for answers. "They were going to kill me," Grace said to the man who'd identified himself as Officer Jacobs, and who appeared to be in charge. "They were going to make it look as if I disturbed a robbery and then they were going to shoot me." Only the faint tremble in her voice gave away how distraught she was as she sank down on the sofa.

"He made me do it," Natalie exclaimed, tears cascading down her cheeks. "It was all Jimmy's idea and he beats on me all the time and I was so afraid not to do what he told me to do." She tried to step closer to Grace, but the other officer, Officer James, jerked her back. "Grace, tell them…tell them I'm not really a part of this, that it's not what it looks like. Tell them to let me go, that I'm innocent."

Jake felt Grace's pain as she looked at her sister. He knew exactly what she was thinking, what she was feeling; but he was afraid of what she might say, what she might do.

Would she save her sister, as he'd saved his brother so many times in the past? Would she be in a sense of denial about what had happened here today? About what part Natalie might have played in it?

"I love you, Natalie." The words caused pain to cross Grace's features. "But I can't save you. What you tried to do here is beyond belief. You need help and you need to stay as far away from me and my girls as possible."

"We need to get everyone down to the police station and sort all this out," Officer Jacobs said. By this time three more patrol cars had arrived. Jimmy was loaded in one and Natalie in a second. Grace and the girls went into the third car and Jake found himself alone in the back of Officer Jacobs and Officer James's car.

He'd seen the questions in Grace's eyes as she'd gotten into the police car and knew she was wondering what had brought him back here. He'd also seen her gratitude and knew she was wondering how he'd managed to be here in time to save her life.

He'd seen something else in the depths of her eyes when her gaze had lingered on him—a hint of hope. And that scared him almost as much as whirling around the corner of the living room to confront Jimmy and Natalie.

Was she entertaining some kind of hope that he'd come back here for her and the girls? Hope that he'd shown up here to offer her a future with him? Could she believe that he was here to give her the happily-ever-after she wanted?

She'd just had the biggest betrayal of her life by

her sister, coming on the heels of the biggest disappointment in her life from Justin. He hated that it was possible he was going to be the third blow to her world that would send it all completely crashing apart.

Afternoon turned into evening as the questions continued. The triplets had eaten a dinner brought in by a female cop around five. They'd sat on a blanket on the floor in one of the conference rooms and had eaten French fries and grapes, a few chunks of apple and crackers. Not exactly the best meal, but adequate enough to fill their bellies while the adults worked on the details of the crime.

Grace felt as if her heart would never truly heal from Natalie's actions. No matter what happiness she found in her future, there would always be a tiny scar left behind by Natalie.

Still, as she told the police what had happened, what Natalie and Jimmy had planned and why, there was also a part of her heart that hardened where her sister was concerned.

Natalie had crossed a line Grace had never even seen coming. Grace had made excuses for Natalie's selfishness in the past, she'd overlooked a meanness of spirit that her sister possessed, but now she recognized the depth of malevolence Natalie had. Grace knew her sister belonged in prison along with her boyfriend, Jimmy.

Throughout the questioning process Grace tried

to keep thoughts of Jake out of her mind, but it was impossible not to wonder why he'd shown up when he had. What had brought him to her when she had needed him most?

If it hadn't been for him she might have been killed. She wanted to believe that when it actually came time for Jimmy to pull the trigger and kill her Natalie would have intervened to stop him, but in her heart of hearts she just didn't believe that.

Jake had saved her life. He'd allowed her to live to continue to raise her daughters. But what had brought him to Wichita in the first place?

She wanted to believe it was love. Love for her and her daughters, his need to be with them forever and always.

She wanted that. She wanted it so much it ached inside her as much as her shoulder ached from the renewed insult of having her arm jerked up behind her and tied to a chair.

But she was afraid to embrace that hope. With everything that had gone so crazy since she'd arrived back home, she was afraid to even wish for a little bit of happiness and love.

It was after nine by the time she finished up with the police. The girls had fallen asleep on the blanket and Grace felt as if she'd been in the midst of a tornado that had finally stopped blowing destructive winds.

"I'll have Officer James take you home," Sergeant Walker said when the questioning was finally over. "We'll hold your sister and Jimmy overnight and they'll be arraigned first thing in the morning on attempted murder charges."

"What about Jake Johnson? Is he still here?" she asked.

Sergeant Walker shook his head. "We let him go about an hour ago. You were lucky he realized you might be in trouble from somebody close to you here in town and followed you back here."

So that's what had brought him here, she thought. It hadn't been the need to tell her he wanted her forever and always. He'd somehow figured out that the danger to her was here rather than from some source in Cameron Creek and he'd come to warn her. He'd tried to get her on the phone and when she hadn't answered he'd jumped in his truck and had driven here.

There was no question in her mind that he'd come to care deeply about her and the girls, but he was probably halfway back to his ranch by now, back to living the life he wanted—a life alone.

If was Officers James and Jacobs who helped carry the sleeping babies to the patrol car that had been equipped with three child seats in the back.

As she watched the officers carefully buckling her daughters into the seats, tears sprang to her eyes as she realized how very close she had come to being lost to them.

She wished she had six arms so she could wrap each of them in a set and hold them close for at least the next twenty-four hours.

On the drive back to her house she thought of how

easily she'd been able to give Jake advice about Justin, never seeing the depth of her own issues with Natalie. She owed Jake an apology. Heck, she even owed Justin and Shirley one for believing that they might have been behind the attacks on her.

"You okay?" Officer James asked softly.

She flashed him a forced smile. "As well as I can be considering my sister and her boyfriend had plans to kill me."

"Is there anyone you'd like me to call for you? Maybe somebody to come over and stay for the rest of the night with you?"

"No, thanks. I'll be fine." She appreciated the man's concern, but the danger was over now and she would be fine alone. She had spent most of her life being fine alone. She was just tired, more of an emotional weariness than a physical one.

She'd scarcely had time to process leaving Jake before she'd been thrust into a life-or-death situation. She was truly alone now. No father for her babies, no sister to deal with and no Jake to love.

She even lacked in the friend department. The few single women she'd run around with before she'd gotten pregnant had drifted away after the triplets were born. Grace understood. They were at a place in their lives that didn't include diapers and drooling multiplied by three, and Grace didn't have the time or energy to feed a friendship the way it should be fed.

"I'll help you unload the kids," Officer James said as he pulled up in her driveway.

"Thanks, I appreciate it." She opened the passenger door and stepped out into the darkness of the night. As she opened one back door, Officer James opened the other.

"I can take it from here," a familiar deep voice said.

Grace straightened and looked across the top of the car to see Jake. She couldn't help the way her heart leapt in response. She reached into the backseat and unbuckled Bonnie, then pulled the little one into her arms.

By the time she reached the other side of the car Jake had both Abby and Casey in his arms. The girls were all asleep and remained so as she and Jake walked inside and put them down in their cribs.

Grace had a million questions for him. Why was he still here? What had made him realize the danger was here? And why was he still here? If he'd only come back to warn her, to save her, then why hadn't he just driven back home after he'd left the police station?

She started out of the room, but paused and watched as he moved a tall dresser over in front of the window. She frowned at him in curiosity as they left the room together.

"I broke that window to get inside earlier," he explained. "The dresser will have to stay there until it's fixed."

"I'll have it fixed tomorrow," she replied. They entered the living room and she motioned him to the sofa, trying not to feel anything when she looked at him, wishing she had the numbness of shock to insulate her against her love for him.

"It seems as though I'm always thanking you for something. Tonight I'm thanking you for my life. How did you know?"

"I didn't know for sure. I just started wondering if maybe that car accident you'd been in before coming to Cameron Creek had been intentional, and that meant whoever was trying to hurt you was from here." As always, his eyes were dark and unreadable. "It suddenly seemed important to me that I tell you, and when I couldn't get you on your phone I jumped in the truck and drove here."

"Thank God you did." She leaned back against the sofa cushion and shook her head. "I had no idea the depths of Natalie's hatred for me. I always just wanted what was best for her. I wanted her to be happy."

"I have a feeling all the money in the world won't make Natalie happy. She has issues that even wealth can't solve," he said softly.

"I know. And I'm sorry I suspected your brother and Shirley."

He gave her a wry grin. "Hell, I suspected them for a little while. No apology necessary."

"So, I guess that's it. Mystery solved and life goes on." She told herself the burn at her eyes had nothing to do with telling him goodbye yet again, but rather because of a culmination of everything that had happened since she'd arrived home. Her heart felt too big for her chest as she looked at him. "You should probably head home. You have a long drive ahead of you."

It would be an appropriate thing to do for her to offer him her guest room and suggest he make the drive first thing in the morning. But she didn't think she could stand having him beneath her roof for a single night, and she didn't think she could survive yet another goodbye in the morning.

"You know, I was going to head home straight from your place once an officer took me back to my truck. I even got on the highway to head home and then turned around and came back."

"You wanted to explain to me why you thought I might be in trouble. I appreciate you stopping by." The words tasted tragic on her lips.

"That wasn't what made me come back. Right after you left earlier this morning, I walked back into the house and there was blessed silence." He got up from the sofa and paced across the floor in front of her, as if too agitated to sit still.

"It was the kind of silence I'd dreamed about, the kind I'd sworn I wanted for the rest of my life." He stopped and stared at her. "And I hated it. You were right, you know. I've spent most of my time taking care of Justin and had decided to spend the rest of my life running away from my own."

A tiny ray of hope sparked in her heart, but she was afraid to fan it in any way, afraid to allow it to burst into full flame. For all she knew he was just telling her he was grateful for her and the girls bringing him to life, a life he intended to live with somebody else.

"When I got here and realized you were in trouble, I looked for a way to get inside and saw the girls crying. I felt their cries deep in my heart, in my soul. And when I broke through that window and stepped into the bedroom, Bonnie smiled through her tears, called me da-da and raised her hands to me."

Grace was riveted to the sofa, afraid she was somehow misunderstanding what he was telling her. She didn't want to be wrong. Despite her need to keep control of her hope, it had grown so big in her heart she felt as if she might suffocate.

"So you've decided you want children," she finally managed to say.

He smiled then, that warm, wonderful smile that shot heat through her. "No, Grace, what I'm saying is that I want your children. I want you and your children. I love you and I love those girls as if they were my own." His smile faltered and failed. "But I'm also aware that I'm not Justin and maybe whatever feelings you have for me are because I look like the man you came for, because I look like the man you want to father your children, their real father."

"Are you crazy? You don't look like Justin at all. You look like Jake, the man I fell in love with, the man I wished was the real father of my babies. I love you, Jake, and I'm not a bit confused between you and Justin."

"If that's true then why are you still sitting on the

sofa?" he asked, the smile once again lighting his features. "Why aren't you in my arms?"

She flew off the sofa and into his waiting arms, her heart beating a million miles a minute as he wrapped her in a tight embrace and they shared a kiss that held all her longing, all her dreams, all her love for him.

When the kiss ended he gazed down at her. In the depths of his beautiful midnight-blue eyes she saw her future. "I want to marry you, Grace. I want to be a stepfather to the girls. I want that big ranch house to be filled with love and happiness like it has never known before."

Grace's heart expanded. Justin would always be the triplets' father, but she knew that Jake would be the man they could depend on, the man they would run to, the man they would call dad.

"MysteryMom got it right after all," she murmured. "She reunited me with the father of my children and gave me the love of my life. Does it get any better than this?"

Jake's eyes shimmered with promise. "Trust me, it gets so much better than this." He kissed her again and Grace knew she'd found her happily-ever-after in Jake's arms.

Epilogue

"Bonnie, don't pull Daddy Jake's hair like that. He'll be bald before he's forty," Grace said.

"Bald." Bonnie nodded and yanked on Jake's hair again. He laughed, kissed her on the cheek and set her on the grass where her sisters were enjoying cookies.

Grace handed Bonnie her cookie and then she and Jake sat in the nearby lawn chairs. It was early September and a perfect evening to enjoy being outside.

It had been a summer of change. Kerri and Jeffrey had moved out of the ranch house and Grace and the girls had moved in. She and Jake had married in a simple ceremony at City Hall in Cameron Creek. Kerri and Jeffrey had been their witnesses, and Justin had been MIA.

Grace had sold her home in Wichita and torn up her teaching contract. For the next couple of years she would be a stay-at-home mom/rancher's wife, and when the girls were old enough to start school she would perhaps return to teaching.

Natalie and Jimmy were still in jail awaiting trial on the attempted murder charges, and although there was still some residual pain in Grace's heart where Natalie was concerned, she spent little time or energy thinking about the sister who had betrayed her.

After the wedding Justin had moved to Texas to work and try to get his life together. He spoke to Jake occasionally, but still showed little interest in being any kind of a presence in the lives of his daughters.

Grace knew there would come a time when she and Jake had a lot of explaining to do to the triplets. But at the moment that time seemed far away, and Grace's life was filled with too much happiness to worry about it.

As Abby got to her feet and started running away from the blanket, Jake turned to Grace. "Your turn," he said with a grin.

Grace got up from her chair and ran after Abby. When she reached the child, she scooped her up in her arms and kissed her cheek. "We're all sitting right now," she said as she plopped Abby back down next to her sisters.

She returned to her chair and Jake reached for her hand. She smiled at him as she saw the heat in his gaze. "You're having naughty thoughts, Daddy Jake."

He grinned. "I am. I'm thinking that after the girls go to bed I'm going to ravish you."

His words created a pool of heat in her very center. "And it will be your last time ravishing me as the girls' stepfather."

"I know." His gaze went from her to the girls and Grace saw his love for them on his face. "It's the first and best unselfish thing Justin has ever done in his life."

Grace squeezed his hand. Justin had signed his parental rights over to Jake, and tomorrow they would go to court for Jake's official adoption of the girls. "Having second thoughts?"

He looked back at her. "No, I can't wait to make it official. They're already the daughters of my heart. After tomorrow they'll be my daughters by law."

"Have I told you lately how much I love you?" Grace asked.

"Yes, but I never get tired of hearing it," he replied.

"I love you…and it's your turn." She pointed to Casey, who was up and running.

As Jake jumped up and ran after her, his laughter filling the evening air, Grace's heart was at peace. When she'd arrived here at the ranch for the first time she hadn't been sure exactly what she was looking for, but as she watched Jake drop down in the middle of the triplets, she knew she had found it. She had found her soul mate.

* * * * *

MILLS & BOON®

The Italians Collection!

2 BOOKS FREE!

Irresistibly Hot Italians

You'll soon be dreaming of Italy with this scorching six-book collection. Each book is filled with three seductive stories full of sexy Italian men! Plus, if you order the collection today, you'll receive two books free!

This offer is just too good to miss!

Order your complete collection today at
www.millsandboon.co.uk/italians

0815_ST17

MILLS & BOON®

It Started With...Collection!

Be seduced with this passionate four-book collection from top author Miranda Lee. Each book contains 3-in-1 stories brimming with passion and intensely sexy heroes. Plus, if you order today, you'll get one book free!

Order yours at
www.millsandboon.co.uk/startedwith

715_ST15

MILLS & BOON®

The Rising Stars Collection!

This fabulous four-book collection features 3-in-1 stories from some of our talented writers who are the stars of the future! Feel the temperature rise this summer with our ultra-sexy and powerful heroes. Don't miss this great offer—buy the collection today to get one book free!

Order yours at
www.millsandboon.co.uk/risingstars

0715_ST16

MILLS & BOON®

It's Got to be Perfect

* cover in development

When Ellie Rigby throws her three-carat engagement ring into the gutter, she is certain of only one thing. She has yet to know true love!

Fed up with disastrous internet dates and conflicting advice from her friends, Ellie decides to take matters into her own hands. Starting a dating agency, Ellie becomes an expert in love. Well, that is until a match with one of her clients, charming, infuriating Nick, has her questioning everything she's ever thought about love...

Order yours today at
www.millsandboon.co.uk

515_ST_12

MILLS & BOON®

By Request

RELIVE THE ROMANCE WITH THE BEST OF THE BEST

A sneak peek at next month's titles...

In stores from 21st August 2015:

- **His Virgin Bride** – Melanie Milburne, Maggie Cox & Margaret Mayo
- **In Bed With the Enemy** – Natalie Anderson, Aimee Carson & Tawny Weber

In stores from 4th September 2015:

- **The Jarrods: Inheritance** – Maxine Sullivan, Emilie Rose & Heidi Betts
- **Undressed by the Rebel** – Alison Roberts

Available at WHSmith, Tesco, Asda, Eason, Amazon and Apple

Just can't wait?

Buy our books online a month before they hit the shops!

visit www.millsandboon.co.uk

These books are also available in eBook format!

0815/05